FRICTION

Friction

Edited by:

Jae Ashley

Mildred Jordan,

Sandra Shipman, Cover art by Lori Jackson

Photo by Michelle Lancaster

Cover content is for illustrative purposes only. Any person depicted in the content is a model.

ISBN ebook: 978-1-941450-73-4

Trademark Acknowledgements

Dedication

Kindle, you are forever in our hearts.
Perry, you're missed every day.

Note From The Author

Friction has been fully edited by a team of trained editors, but no manuscript is perfect.
Please email me with any mistakes you find at.
Creative license was taken with this story. Places and situations reimagined. It's a work of fiction.

Table of Contents

PART 1

1: The Dog River
Beau

Late Spring, 2000
Mobile, Alabama

The fresh morning air and bright sun drew me from my second-floor window out onto the rooftop. I followed a well-worn path that I'd trekked hundreds of times before. When I reached the point just beyond the downstairs living room windows, I leaped to a grassy patch below, easily landing on my feet. From there, I followed the fence line to my favorite place, our property's edge along Dog River.

Small ripples lapped gently against the shallow shoreline. I took a seat on my butt, just shy of the river's edge. Life's troubles stayed at a distance here, which was why I spent most of my time in this spot.

But the river didn't work its usual magic. Probably due to this being my last time here.

My heart seriously hurt.

Absently, I picked up a rock and tested its weight by sifting it through my fingers. My grandfather, my pop-pop, came to mind, causing the pain in my heart to ramp up a notch, thinking about the care he used to teach me how to skip a rock properly. Because of him, I could throw a stone better than most. It might even be my superpower.

The last time I saw him, he called me to his side for a final bit of advice. It echoed through my head as if he were sitting right next to me. He explained that experiencing pain was essential in the process of love. Pain showed us how deeply we cared, and how lucky we were to have loved in the first place. Pop-pop knew he was at the end of his life, even if I had refused to believe it.

At fourteen years old, a week shy of my fifteenth birthday, I knew way too much about pain and not near enough about love.

"Beau. Are you awake, son?" The muffled sound of my mom's voice called from inside the house. If I guessed correctly, she was probably near the kitchen. She'd then call me again at the base of the stairs before trotting up to see I wasn't in my bedroom. It gave me a few more precious minutes of privacy before she found me outside.

She... Me too, I guessed, but for the sake of my current pity party, this was all on her. She planned to exile me from my childhood home in Alabama to live in Sea Springs, Texas, where she grew up and where my other set of grandparents still lived.

I had until the long-haul movers loaded everything we owned into the back of their truck then moved us across the country to my grandparents' bed-and-breakfast. Maybe the distance wasn't quite that far, but for the sadness clogging my world, I needed the dramatic flair.

"Beau! Quit pouting and come downstairs. It's time," my mom called louder.

I glanced at the empty covered boat dock built fifty feet into the river. Only a ghost of its former self. Empty and void of all the personality that once hung on the walls. Pieces of décor and memorabilia my father had collected over the last fifteen years.

The rock in my hand hummed, drawing my attention there. I got to my feet, readying the toss. After all, as the two-year reigning champion of stone skipping, awarded by the governing body of the Dog River Festival, I knew how to make the rock bounce across the ripples.

With my arm reared back, I threw the stone forward, sending it flying low across the river. My eyes locked on its descent, ready to count the skips. A throw that should have garnered at least twelve jumps.

It didn't. Not even one. The rock sank underwater before it ever had a chance to get started.

If a moment represented a life, this was mine.

"Beau, come on, babe! The movers are almost here." Her heavy clomps up the stairs rang of her irritation.

"You there?" Scott Lee, my lifelong best friend, called from behind the privacy fence. We'd been neighbors for as long as I can remember. We did everything together. Spent some part of every day with the other, and had each other's back no matter what the situation.

We also had a healthy competitive streak between us. Well, if healthy meant we approached every task with a battle-to-the-death attitude. Each determined to win, no matter the cost. We fished, exercised, and did all our schoolwork together in a race to see who was the strongest, fastest, or smartest.

But, if I were being honest, the invisible connections that bound us together had begun to show signs of unraveling. Scott had grown stupidly girl-crazy, like his brain cells had gone haywire. He wanted and was determined to find a girlfriend who put out. It was all he talked about anymore, and I wasn't there with him.

Seconds later, Scott poked his head over the high fence. A couple of colorful balloons sprang up behind him, bouncing in the air as he fluidly jumped over the tall slats, landing easily on his feet. The balloons stayed on the other side, unattached to my friend.

"Who's with you?" I hissed quietly, moving quickly toward Scott to keep him from my mom's line of vision.

"Come over, I got you," Scott spoke louder than necessary, sure to have drawn my mom's attention. "Don't worry," he added, looking over at me as he lifted his arms in the air. Mine followed his up. "I put a ladder up. We just gotta help 'em down. They wanted to surprise you."

"I'm scared," Lauren said. The very worst possible voice for me to hear right now. My arms dropped to my sides. She'd ruin my last few moments alone.

I'd known Lauren for as long as I'd known Scott. We all lived in the same cul-de-sac. She'd gone from being a good friend to a stalker in training about six months ago when her sights set on me with laser point accuracy. Nothing I did ever dissuaded her. She was determined to make me her boyfriend. With the way she planned our lives together, maybe she thought I already was.

We were to be married straight out of college, and have four children, three boys and one girl for me to spoil. We'd have a lot of money due to my lucrative career with the National Football League. She referred to herself as my beautiful, arm-candy wife. She planned to be a stay-at-home mother, and shop with all the money I made.

Lauren was a pretty girl. Her dark hair and tanned complexion made her unique in a town where freckles and sunburns were the most common.

Her scared face poked over the cap board. The balloons jostled frantically under her death grip. Her dark gaze sought mine then riveted there, staring for several long seconds as tears welled.

My brows dropped in response. "Who's she with?"

"Katie," Scott whispered excitedly. He tapped his elbow against my arm in a weird conspiratorial gesture. His brows waggled suggestively with excitement.

"Come on. We got you," Scott reassured.

Lauren hiked a leg over the top of the fence. Scott nodded at me to join in helping her down.

I hesitated, knowing that any time I touched Lauren, she took it as a sign of encouragement. My hands fisted at my sides. I didn't want to help.

My strict adherence to manners instilled in me since birth fought my bad attitude, and I forced myself forward. Lauren wiggled around until she dropped down against me, chest to chest, wrapping her arms tightly around my neck. I heard the balloons knock against one another behind my back.

She clung to me. I hit a growth spurt last year. Nine inches in twelve months with no sign of slowing. My current height of six feet, two inches tall towered over most of my friends. I was also strong due to ten years of playing football. My father was the varsity head coach of the local high school. Since he had won more than he lost, he held local celebrity status. Of course, I was given no choice but to play ball.

Lauren, on the other hand, had peaked at around five feet tall, and weighed maybe ninety pounds. She hung on to me until I bent to put her feet on the ground. Her viselike hold remained. We stood eye to eye, me looking down, her looking up, in an awkward stance as tears trickled down her cheeks.

"When're you comin' back to see your dad?" she asked. The waterworks made her voice raw, and she sniffled an awful sound right in my face.

I tried to straighten to my full height, but she held on tight. It took my hands gripping her forearms, giving a quick push to break her hold.

The balloons jostled free, floating into the sky above my house.

"Darn it," Lauren said, using her fingertips to wipe at the tears and eyeliner under her eyes. "I made you the chocolate chip cookies you like. Katie's got 'em."

As if on some sort of cosmic cue, Katie hiked a leg over the fence, immediately losing her balance. The cookie tin dropped to the ground. It landed in such a way that the lid popped open. The cookies tumbled onto the grass.

"*No*," Lauren yelped. "I made these for your ride." She scurried for the cookies, making her best effort to salvage them.

"Beau. They're here to load the truck. They could use you and Scott's help to speed things along," my mom said firmly from the kitchen door. She had finally found me. "Come on. It'll put us on the road sooner and they'll pay each of you twenty-five dollars."

I acted as if I didn't hear her.

At least until the right verses wrong code that I'd been born with reared its dumb head. I sucked. My mom had fought with my father, arguing to allow me the freedom to make my own decisions. It was the beginning of the end of my parents' marriage.

My father had earned a reputation for being meaner than a diamondback rattlesnake. Seriously angry most of the time, but my choice to quit football took his wrath to an all-time high. Where my father refused to look at or speak to me, not a single word since the night I broke the news months ago, he directed the brunt of his anger out on my mom.

I finally cast a look at her. The pretense of not hearing her was lost anyway when all three of my friends turned her way.

"Hi, Mrs. Brooks," Lauren said, still bent over the cookies. "I made you guys something special to eat for the drive. They dropped, but some survived."

"Hi, girls." My mom lifted a hand in a wave. "You're sweet. Beau will have them eaten before we ever reach the interstate."

Lauren beamed at me, clearly loving the idea.

Scott whacked me with force on the chest. "Get your ass movin', Brooks. We got money to make."

What was left of my mood sank.

Scott and I started toward the house in unison, step for step. My mother waited at the door as we walked across the yard. She didn't trust me to actually follow through and come inside. Only stepping aside to hold the door open for Scott and stopping me with a hand on my forearm.

"Please try to be happy for us. This is the fresh start that we need." Her words ran on a loop, like a broken record, over and over again. I got it. And she wasn't wrong.

I finally gave a single nod, my gaze focused on the man with a clipboard, assessing the many boxes and furniture in the living room.

Scott came into my line of vision and took on a fighter's stance in front of me. His fists drawn, executing the perfect playful one-two punch at my shoulder. "Burnin' daylight, son. I'm stronger than you, no matter what you think. I got two to your one today."

"You're a douche," I muttered, rubbing a hand at my shoulder. He'd used way more strength than necessary. My mom released her hold on my arm, allowing me to follow Scott inside.

"Don't worry. I'll console the girls when you're gone," Scott tossed out, winking at me from over his shoulder.

I added cluelessness to Scott's irritating traits.

"Still a douche," I said.

With a quick glance over my shoulder, I saw the worry on my mother's face. We shared a brief stare, which meant something, but I wasn't sure what. I didn't like her being worried about me. I did enough of that for both of us.

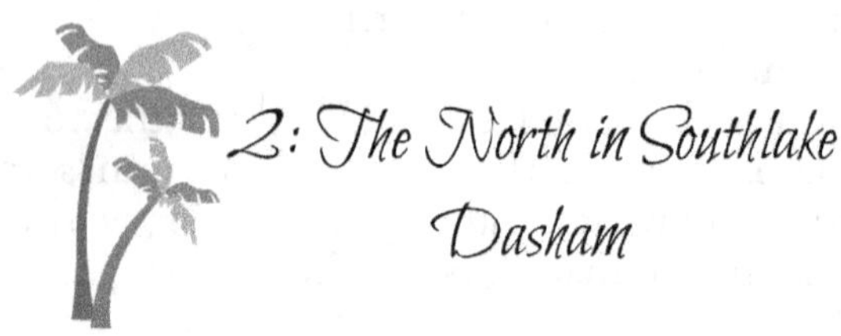

2: The North in Southlake
Dasham

Southlake, Texas

"Dasham Richmond, you do understand that you're only fifteen years old?" Amelia asked, but it wasn't the question it seemed, since she regularly said I didn't act my age. As my nanny, I suppose she'd know.

I didn't respond from my seat on the edge of the bed. My feet rested on the side rail, my elbows on my knees. Amelia stood in my closet, pulling out hanger after hanger, showing me various articles of clothing.

Amelia had been with me since birth. She knew me better than anyone. Right now, we played the staring game, and I was winning. I always did. Eventually, she rolled her eyes. Her shoulders followed the same pattern as she turned to the rack of clothes and placed the oversized short-sleeve shirt on the rod.

"If you don't stop rejecting these clothes, you're not gonna have anything to take out of town with you."

She wasn't wrong, but I also had an appearance to keep up. "Where did this stuff come from? Who makes the trends? Why would anyone wear slouchy, baggy clothes?"

Amelia presented another shirt. A short-sleeved, front button, slim fit that had me taking a closer look. She read me like a book, easily seeing my interest, and was ready to answer my next questions.

"It's from the GAP so no one will think you're pretentious. But it'll fit your frame so no one will think you dress poorly."

I raised my brows. Hers shot up too while trying to hide a grin. I stuck out a foot, lifting from the bed to take the hanger.

"So, is it safe to pull this style shirt? They'll also go with the khakis and plaid shorts you're taking."

"Nothing blue," I reminded her. "It's not my color, and absolutely no cargo shorts or shorts that go past my knees. And no blue jean shorts."

She gave me a knowing look that I interpreted to mean this wasn't her first time dealing with me. Now it was me trying my best to hide a grin.

"Dasham." I glanced over my shoulder at the intercom system installed close to my bedroom door. The sound of my mother's voice was too faint. After all the years of living in this prodigious home, how had she not learned to work the communication system properly?

I went for the banister outside my bedroom door and yelled downstairs. "Wrong room, Mom. Push button number nine, not eight."

"You know your mother doesn't like for you to holler downstairs," Amelia hissed. She wasn't correcting me as much as trying to stave off my mother's frustration. "Tell her on the intercom."

My head shook at the absurdity of the situation as I came back inside the room. "She doesn't remember to lift her finger off the talk button. She can't hear me if I use the intercom."

"Dasham-darling, we've scheduled your birthday party for September third at the club. We'll be home from Sea Springs by then. I believe school starts the Monday after. They'll keep the swimming pool open for us. How does that sound?"

I stared at the box on the wall. My mouth opened, but no words came. I dropped my hands to my sides, my chin hitting my chest. *Noo*. She'd plan a huge affair, pretending it was perfectly normal to have a birthday party months after my actual birthday.

What did I say? I expected very little in terms of a celebration since my parents had only remembered my birthday a couple of days ago. And that only happened while sitting together at breakfast when I brought up the new car I wanted.

"Did you hear me?" my mom asked again. "I've scheduled a birthday party for you in the beginning of September. I have the club's party planner sending save the dates this week. She'll keep us updated on the plans while we're away. Would you like to look over the list of invitees?"

No, I did not want to see the list. Only members who paid an exclusive fee were allowed on the property. My friends without a membership wouldn't be able to attend.

I lifted my finger to the button and pressed. "No, I'm sure it's fine."

"Dasham, are you teasing me in some way that you think is funny and I don't understand?"

I cocked my head toward Amelia and whispered, "See? I guarantee her finger's pressing the talk button. She can't hear me."

There were five decent sized steps from where I stood to the banister. I made it in four. My frustration with everything—my birthday, our summer plans, my clothing options—got the best of me. "Mom! Take your finger off the talk button."

"All right, son," she said through the speaker.

I took a deep breath and centered myself as I went back to the intercom and lifted my finger to the button again. I felt like a loser for not standing up for myself, but the argument didn't matter. She wasn't a nurturing kind of mother. Especially since I was a late-late-in-life baby. "I'm sure whatever you decide is fine. We don't even need to have a party."

"Oh no, of course we do. Especially since your father's under such scrutiny. We need to have our best foot forward for the foreseeable future. Did you see the new swim trunks I had Amelia put on your bed?"

Honestly, I had no idea if I had seen them or not and twisted around toward my bed. Two large open suitcases took up the majority of the space on my mattress. Two cases seemed ambitious with as picky as I was about how I looked. Outside of those, assorted clothing littered the rest of the space.

Amelia quickly shifted through the mess to lift a pair of solid baby blue swim trunks. I scrunched my nose. They were certain to be expensive, but not my taste in swimwear.

"I do see them," I said.

"Good. I also had Amelia pack a white T-shirt. We're doing a family photo at the entrance of the pool. We're all wearing some variation of matching blue swimsuits and coordinating wraps."

Omigod. That sounded truly dreadful. My brows wrinkled in distaste as I glanced over at Amelia, who shrugged. "We're taking a family picture at the resort, in swimsuits? All of us?"

"I feel like you're attempting to tease me again, and I don't understand, and I don't have time to try to make sense of your humor. You're getting too old for this silliness. Our itinerary for tomorrow is to be ready to leave at nine a.m. sharp. The plane's scheduled to take off around ten. Don't dawdle, Dasham," she said firmly. "Have Amelia put your luggage by your door tonight. I'll have someone gather it to take to the plane in the morning."

My finger pressed the button. "Is there any way I can come home before my birthday? Celebrate here with a few of my friends. Chandler's coming home," I added as an incentive. My parents loved both Chandler and his parents. They thought he was a great role model, as if. "I can stay here with Amelia. It won't be the first time."

I released my hold to cross my fingers for good luck.

"You sure know how to push my buttons," my mother started. Her voice turned sterner with each syllable spoken. "This trip is to support your father. He's been too good to us all and this is big for him. The national press is covering the resort's opening. We need you on your best behavior, and absolutely no sneaking off to come home. Invite Chandler to join us for your birthday. But there will be no shenanigans between you two. Best behavior all the time."

My father, Jackson Richmond, was one of the most successful businessmen in Texas. He took pride in being a dedicated family man. All of my brothers and sisters worked for his company and all had a stake in the success of the brand new four hundred room resort and playground, Richmond Resorts, along the Gulf of Mexico coastline.

The hitch in the plan? The local Sea Springs business community wasn't pleased with big business coming in and stealing their customers.

They started a war against my father, trying every possible means to close the project down. Lawsuit after lawsuit had delayed the resort's opening by about a year. When their legal recourses failed to get their desired result, they waged a smear campaign against my family. A long picket line formed in front of the resort where they pushed the idea of small, hometown business values.

Here came the Richmond family. This was a working holiday. We had a reputation for being a pretty family. An all-American success story. If you can judge a book by its cover, we pulled off a wholesome family appearance better than most. The plan was to use our togetherness against our enemies. There were thirty plus of us descending on Sea Springs for the next three months.

"Did you hear me?" Her tone was sharp this time. "I wasn't pressing the talk button so don't even try."

His gaze skidded toward Amelia as he answered, "Yes, ma'am, I heard."

"Good. I'm going for drinks at the club. I'll expect you downstairs in the morning at eight forty-five."

I sighed and silently nodded, wondering how our conversation had gone from happy to angry in the few minutes we'd spoken. My finger pressed the button to respond quickly, trying to diffuse the trouble I caused. "I'll be downstairs on time."

"Hmm..." I said aloud, and stood there for a few seconds longer, waiting to see if she responded with anything more.

"Let it go, Dasham. You never win," Amelia whispered.

She wasn't wrong.

3: The Birthday Beau

One week later
Sea Springs, Texas

The smell of birthday pancakes quickened my steps as I trotted down from my third-floor bedroom to the kitchen on the first floor. Even in the early morning hours and dimly lit spiral stairwell, I deftly managed the steps two at a time, my stomach leading the way.

I could hear my grandmother grumbling quietly. She didn't sound happy. She never did anymore. The small group of local business owners fighting to stop the new resort's expansion were running out of time and money to keep the fight alive. It was all everyone talked about these days.

My hunger had me jumping the final three steps to land on the peeling tile of the kitchen floor. My booted feet lithely pivoted toward the stovetop where the delicious scent guided me. My mom was there, making her special pancake recipe that only came out two times a year. On my birthday and on Christmas morning. Both times presents were included. As far as I was concerned, especially this morning, the pancakes mattered the most.

"Happy Birthday," my nana said from her regular spot at the old oak table, pausing with the coffee cup at her lips. The happy tone and relaxed brow conflicted with the permanent frown etched on her face since we first arrived.

I gave a small smile and nodded to acknowledge her greeting. Glad to see her life's drink heading to her lips. Both my grandparents loved coffee, kept a pot hot all day long.

"Happy birthday," my mom said cheerfully, expertly flipping a pancake in the pan. Based on the solid stack plated just to the side of the stovetop, she'd been at it for a while. She had skill. Each pancake was the same size, perfectly round, and looked like an advertisement for IHOP. So good in fact, I swiped one off the top.

"Hey," my mom teased and swatted the spatula at my hand. I was quicker, even with the heat making it hard to handle. I tossed it from hand to hand, looking for the bottle of honey—my preferred choice in toppings.

I'd missed the plate, silverware, and glass of chocolate milk sitting on the table, directly across from my grandmother. The honey was right there waiting with the rest.

It didn't take long for me to roll the pancake and squirt a generous portion of honey over the top before eating it like a burrito.

"Mmm, Mom..." I said with my mouth still full. "Really good."

"You look more like you're goin' on twenty rather than fifteen," my nana teased.

"I'm too skinny," I said before stuffing the last of the pancake into my mouth and reaching for the chocolate milk. My mom placed the rest in front of me. Probably not all for me, but I felt like I could make a strong play at finishing the plate off by myself.

"It's not due to how much you eat," my paw said, coming in through the kitchen entrance door, making a beeline to the coffeepot. "Your mom's gonna go broke feedin' you."

I didn't pay them any attention as I scooted my seat over to make room for my mom to sit beside me. This was the working hub for the B&B. Two meals a day, seven days a week, prepared for the guests in this small, outdated galley-style kitchen.

My mom didn't sit. Instead, she laid her hand on my shoulder, gently squeezing before sliding her fingers into my hair. "You need a haircut."

Yeah, I'd needed a haircut months ago, but I liked the growing-out look. Not short, but not long. I didn't worry about the style. With the slight wave in my hair, I only had to swipe the strands off my face and they stayed away.

"Not 'til school starts," I said with a knife for the butter in one hand and the bottle of honey in the other.

My devious mom was on her game, showing her ninja skills. She occupied me with food to then surprise me with a small, newspaper-wrapped gift over the shoulder. I was torn but ultimately decided to take a good hearty bite before taking the gift. I could chew as I opened the wrapping.

"Beau, you can barely keep the bite in your mouth," my mom chided. But based on her own rules, she couldn't get mad at me today. It was my birthday. I gave in and nodded because she wasn't wrong and picked up the milk to wash it down.

My gaze stayed fixed on the present. Money was tight for us. My father was stalling on paying child support and giving my mom her portion of the sale of the house. He hadn't helped pay for anything since she filed for divorce months ago.

"Are you sure about this?" I asked, my actions in complete contradiction. I rubbed my hands with a cloth napkin and reached for the gift.

"Of course. It's your birthday," my mom said cheerfully. She took the seat next to me, watching as I opened the present. It only took a good tug to rip the paper free to see a Nokia telephone box inside.

A cell phone. My gaze shot up at my mom. This had always been a hard no in the past. All my friends had phones, but I was never allowed.

"No way," I said, not wasting any more time with the gift wrap as I tore into the box.

"Calm down," my mom teased. She was happy, grinning broadly at my surprise.

"Can we afford this?" I asked, pulling out the blue phone, making easy work of the plastic case that kept it safe. The instruction manual fell onto the table beside my plate.

"Your plan has six hundred talking minutes and a hundred text messages a month for forty dollars," she started to explain, but I interrupted her.

"I'll pay for it." I immediately saw the holes in my suggestion. Since we were staying at my grandparents' bed-and-breakfast close to the bay, there were no jobs to be had within walking distance. The big business resort was apparently booming, giving a lot of locals the employment they needed. If I even considered getting a job there, my grandparents might never speak to me again. "I mean when I find a job."

"It's fine," my mom said and moved a pancake off the stack to her plate. "Just make an effort to stay under your minutes." Her gaze came back to me. She reached over to pat my thigh, smiling. "You deserve it. You've been through a lot."

I reached for the charger, lifting from my seat to plug it into an outlet.

"Paw and I got you somethin' too," my grandmother said, getting to her feet before edging around the table.

"It's all right, Nana," I said. "I get what's goin' on around here."

She smiled again at me, which was weirder than the first time. Two smiles in one day after a week of pure scowling. Maybe I needed to have birthdays more often.

"It's not what I wish we could give you..." Paw said, pushing open the back door. The humidity hit first, then the warmth. From my angle, I couldn't see what they tried to share.

I stood and craned my neck to see a ten-speed bicycle with a small red bow on the handlebars.

"No way," I said and stood frozen for several long seconds before I darted forward. All I'd heard for months was how hard things were for us financially, so I never expected any of this.

Now I had a way to get places. I started past my grandmother.

"Hey there, mister. Just because you're as tall as my house doesn't mean the rules have changed." I'd spent many summers right here in this house over my life. The only rule I had to adhere to was every time I passed my grandmother, I was required to hug her. It was something special we shared. Her small, short frame was becoming more difficult to give a proper side hug to, but we managed.

Paw stood close to the door with his fist sticking out. I gave him a bump as I darted outside.

"Happy birthday, Beau." Chae, who lived next door and helped with breakfast and house cleaning services, chimed from the bottom step. Due to Chae's proximity, we'd been friends for as long as I could remember, but times had changed the closeness. Chae was seventeen, starting her senior year at the new high school where my mom was now vice principal.

This particular age gap meant she could do things I couldn't. It made a real friendship difficult.

"Are these your new wheels?" she asked, coming up the steps as I went down.

"Yeah, Nana and Paw just gave it to me," I said, hiking a leg over the seat. My mind went straight to the mechanics. I needed to adjust the seat, and the pedals needed to be replaced, the chain might have some rust...

"He's not listenin' to us anymore, is he?" Chae asked, grinning down at me.

My mom was standing on the small porch, my grandparents behind them. No, I hadn't been paying attention. I was thinking about where the best junkyards were in town until I made my first paycheck.

"I'm leaving for work," Mom said, taking each step down toward me. "What're you doing today?"

"I gotta mow for Paw—"

Nana interrupted me. "We'll put that off until tomorrow."

Since all my work was free labor, that sounded pretty good.

"Then meet me at The Pizza Box tonight at five thirty," my mom said. "We'll all have dinner."

"Sounds good. Thank you for this mornin'," I said again. This was already shaping into a great birthday.

"It's not over yet. Have a good day," she said, and bent to kiss me on the cheek.

4: The Saving of Lives
Dasham

I lifted the whistle to my lips and blew, catching every eye in the vicinity. "Stay in your inner tube," I yelled at a set of tween-aged boys that I'd had to discipline several times today.

I was tasked with keeping a bunch of unruly children from drowning, which was much harder than it seemed.

"Last warning," I said, flexing my power.

"Sorry." One of the kids shouted in my direction and scurried back to his tube.

Lifeguarding at my family's resort didn't require any real training. I had no idea how to save a life. I barely knew how to swim properly. I was in the wrong place at the wrong time and somehow managed to be roped into the job four days a week. And honestly, as much money as my dad made off this resort, he should be paying me more than minimum wage.

My frown had me lifting my employee issued visor and scratching the itch at my sweaty hairline. It enabled the whistle to fall until the chain around my neck kept it from dropping to the ground.

My father's normal roll-with-it personality had been stretched thin. He was angry and out to destroy every local business in his firing range. The atomic bomb had nothing on my father's intentions. I'd never seen this side of him. Ruthless all the time, he never gave a single inch.

I'd always liked my dad so this shade of him was hard to reconcile. Over the years, we'd spent time together whenever we could. We had breakfast together every morning when we were in the same place. My older brothers and sisters considered me his favorite. They also said he had mellowed with age. I didn't know about that, but he did take an interest in me. We shared hobbies, discussed in depth the current events happening in the world, and he taught me about finance. When he learned of a sudden employment vacancy in the swimming area, he signed me up for the job without asking, but it was fine.

A positive thing I learned from the experience was that I looked pretty good in blue. I generally shied away from the color, being sandy, blond-haired and blue-eyed, I thought wearing blues washed me out. They didn't at all.

A downside was that the media had figured that out before I did. The press was covering the relentless picket line in front of the resort and happened to capture me at work. Me and my short, tight lifeguard uniform made the local news, wondering who I was.

Then the national news got wind that I was a Richmond. AOL's AIM and Yahoo chat groups filled with details about me. Without realizing it, I gained a following. So much so the local news let up on us, congratulating my parents on raising me in such a grounded, responsible way. Inadvertently saying something positive about the resort.

My dad was very proud and happy with me.

I, in return, was forced into a summer job, regardless of my qualifications.

Think positively. My tan was coming along nicely. After the first few hours on the first day, I'd taken my tank top off. The shorts weren't speedos, but I wouldn't have called them shorts either. They didn't hide much.

Also, the sun added natural sun-blond highlights to my hair.

Another downside, the chicks—not really a word I used to describe females, but they referred to themselves that way. The ones who lay on the loungers and walkways all around me made me self-conscious and nervous. I felt like prey, and they were predators. When I relocated to the next guarding point, they followed, stretching out there too.

My father kept saying I should take it as flattery.

Maybe, but I couldn't get there.

"Dasham," Tamara, another lifeguard, said, drawing my attention to her as she came up behind me. I went for my shirt, towel, and water bottle, preparing for the next cycle. "They're calling you up front."

"Why?" I asked, shoving a hand through my tank top to pull it over my head.

"Don't know. Go up front and find out. They're taking you out of rotation," she said, dismissing me. She dropped her towel on the concrete walkway and squirted a large amount of sunscreen on her forearm.

"Why?" I asked again.

Tamara had the standard lifeguard vibe. She was older than me and had real training. All she did was look at me as if I were dumb and shook her head. Where the public loved me, the other lifeguards considered me privileged and unworthy of the job. They weren't wrong.

"I still don't know why," she quipped.

As I walked across the pool area, I made a quick detour to drop my towel and company-issued water bottle into the recycle bin. I removed my visor, running my fingers through my hair. I'd stop in the locker room on my way. Everything I wore, down to the water shoes, was designed to fit well and not hinder me in the water. I didn't normally believe in baggy clothes and certainly didn't wear any, but I felt barely dressed as I pushed through the resort's swimming pool entrance.

I was surprised to be met by my brother, Collin, the sibling closest to my age. "You're a douche," he greeted in his standard way. His entire life's focus this summer was to give me shit. Collin believed he should have been the baby of the family. I messed it all up on my arrival, and never heard the end of it.

"Why am I now?" I asked, glancing past him to see the rest of my family standing in the main foyer of the resort, directly down the hall from us.

"I don't know why you're a douche, but you can't seem to shake it, can ya?"

"What're they all doing down there?" I asked, barely paying him any attention as I stepped past him and started toward the employee locker room to change.

Even being in the resort at the same time, the family was rarely ever together. Something big must be going on.

"Waiting on your douchey ass." Collin walked the few steps to the long windows showcasing the swimming pool. "You've got all that tail running after you. Why haven't you tapped any of them?"

"Why're they waiting for me?" I asked again. Whatever drew his focus, released him. A mischievous grin tugged at the corners of his lips.

"Why do you look so scared? What did you do?" Collin asked, laughing at me as his gaze did a full-body scan. "You should fix your hair."

"Let me go change real quick," I said, letting the visor hang on my arm as I ran my fingers through my hair again.

"There's no time." Collin grabbed my forearm tightly and started to drag me down the hall toward my parents.

"Tell me what's happening," Panic rose, knowing Collin loved the worry in my voice.

Joy, my niece who was sixteen, met us about halfway to the foyer. With a practiced WWE move, I yanked my arm free of my brother. The three of us came together, walking stride for stride. Joy never missed a beat. The opulence of the main part of the resort made me woefully underdressed. The dress code didn't allow anyone in swimming attire to be outside of the pool area.

The thing about Joy was that she might possibly be my best friend in the family, but she liked to give me shit as much as Collin did. "You know, you're officially a douche after what happens next." She gave me a side wink, letting me know she was teasing.

The other glaring difference between me and the rest of my family was my high IQ. Theirs weren't. I doubted they knew any other insults to give. "If one of you will fill me in before we reach the rest of the family, I'll give you my first paycheck."

"Some incentive," my brother barked. Joy followed in his laughter. "I spent more on breakfast than you'll make all week."

"But, Uncle Collin, he's working for a living," Joy teased, grinning like a Cheshire cat. "And saving the family's reputation and business with all his prettiness."

"Shut up!" I countered, knowing they wouldn't, but it helped my heart to say the words aloud.

"Shut up," Collin squeaked, mimicking me.

"Leave him alone," Joy said, her hand flipping out to playfully hit Collin in the chest. "He can't help what's going on."

I cast a quick glance at my niece as she reaffirmed my decision to call her my best friend.

Time didn't allow me to process anything more. We stepped into the main greeting foyer of the resort where my mother and father stood waiting. They both had giant grins on their faces, directed at me.

Even at my parents age, my mom was just shy of her sixty-third birthday and my father close to sixty-six years old, they appeared an impressive force. My mom looked boardroom ready all the time. Sculpted hair, freshly applied makeup, and a business suit—a jacket and matching skirt. Barbie had nothing on the permanent arch in my mother's feet. I'd never seen her without high heels on.

My father wore his usual bespoke suit, silk tie, and Italian loafers. As for the rest of my family, all but Collin were married with children. There were thirty-two of them in total. All miniature versions of my parents, looking at home in the most ornately decorated lobby I'd ever seen.

"What's going on?" I asked.

"Dasham," my father started toward me, wrapping a strong arm around my shoulders.

My mother came up beside me, smiling tenderly. My brows lowered in disbelief. The smile felt so real... I was truly unnerved.

"Happy birthday, son. You've made us proud," my father said both loudly and boldly. My parents caged me in with their love. I reared back, giving an unsure glance past my parents to

Collin. Probably not the best call. He stuck a finger down his throat in a gagging motion.

None of this made sense. I still had weeks to go before my birthday.

With my dad on one side and my mother on the other, they walked me across the marble tile entry and through the main doors of the resort. The valets stood on either side of the impressively large portico with the ocean churning its waves in the distance. The drive leading to the valet stand was blocked off. A shiny red Ferreri with a giant white bow on the windshield was parked between me and the ocean.

With a glance in either direction, I searched for who drove such a beauty even as my brain gave a blip in understanding.

No. My parents believed the first car needed to be a safe, yet expensive sedan. Usually in the BMW or Mercedes class. I, of course, had asked for something sporty and quick, but I never expected to receive it. I had only said it to get underneath my mother's skin.

Under the arm of my father's hand gripping my shoulder, we walked toward the car. The sun was bright, the sky clear, a gorgeous day that I barely recognized in my current state of stunned silence.

"You don't have anything to say?" my father asked teasingly and dangled a key fob with two keys in front of me. My mother gave a cultured singsong laugh then a side hug as I took the offering.

"Go see," she said happily.

My father kept me in his hold as he and I walked the distance to the driver's side door. "I thought we were waiting until September," I said lamely as he let go of me and opened the door. It was then I saw the photographer in the distance, snapping pictures.

"Don't look over there," my father guided quietly. "It's staged. We're pretending we don't know they're here."

The excitement I did my best to rein in deflated. This was a setup. Some play to show strength, or wealth, or family first. Maybe all of the above. Most definitely a mighty flex of financial power, showing his strength to continue the legal battle for the expansion of the resort.

I looked over the top of the car to where my entire family stood watching. Joy's brother, Jon, came jogging toward us.

"He's twenty-one and going to ride with you to keep it legal," my father said proudly, and whacked me on the back, packing in a solid punch. "Go."

Whatever he saw on my face had laughter booming. He grabbed the bow while taking several steps backward, waving his hand in a motion to get me moving.

"Thanks, Dad," I mumbled and tried to drop the blinders I'd been wearing for several days back in place. My opinions on the dishonesty and manipulation I'd watched happening for days had to stay at a distance. I had no control over any of this.

"Get in," Jon called and opened the passenger side door.

Back in the moment, I decided if they let me keep the car, I was going to have a badass ride.

Where the outside was designed to be seen, the sleek interior, with butter soft Italian leather, spoke to the innermost primal guy inside me. My dream car. Everyone's dream car. I dropped into the bucket seat as if it were crafted for my body.

The new car smell mixed with the fine scent of rich leather and ocean breeze, became my new favorite scent. My fingers reached for the dash as the prancing horse logo on the steering wheel had me making a promise to myself: To do whatever it took to always own a car like this.

"You're damned lucky. This is badass," Jon murmured in my same awe.

"I know. I'm not sure what I did to deserve it." My hands roamed as far as I could reach on the dashboard.

"I do. Reservations have doubled. The reviews of the resort are changing. People are finally willing to risk the wrath of the picketers to stay here. The female teenage demographic that drives their parents' spending, and decision making, don't have a care about the hometown businesses. People magazine wants to interview you..."

I wrinkled my face at the horror of such an idea.

Jon's tone rang with humor. "Everybody's talking about you. Dasham's so polite. Dasham's such a hard worker. Dasham's such a good-looking guy."

I tuned him out, pushing the key into the ignition. With the twist of the wrist, the engine roared to life. My father gave me a double thumbs-up. I waved and shut the door.

"Where are we going?" I asked, buckling my seatbelt.

"Anywhere as long as you do a U-turn and drive past the photographer," Jon instructed, his thumb hooking over his shoulder. "Grandad said you could drive a stick."

"I can." And I did for the best ride of my life.

5: The Little Red Ferrari

Beau

As far as miles went, I'd put far too many on my new-to-me bike today. I'd been everywhere, all over the older part of Sea Springs, having the best day reconnecting with the area.

I liked it here. Sea Springs was full of hard-working people, largely middle class. They cared for one another and the community they lived in. No one had much money these days which was the reason for my good day. Just about everyone had a mini junkyard in their backyard. Whether I knew them or not, once I introduced myself, they let me dig through their piles and take whatever I needed to help make my bike run a little smoother.

Now I had different goals for the day. I peddled harder down the main strip, determined to make it to The Pizza Box before my mom arrived. If I was able to get the extra time, I wanted to call Scott and tell him about my new cell phone then hit the small arcade inside the restaurant. *Ninja Assault* was my jam. I held the top score in our main burger place in Alabama. I needed to leave my mark here as well.

Honestly, I missed Scott, and the way we pushed each other. The competitive side of my personality came from my father, but his came with a mean edge.

Why was I thinking about him right now? Ruining my perfect day.

I reaffirmed my commitment to never be like him. A goal I intended to keep.

What kind of father doesn't call their kid on their birthday? The same one who refused to pay child support, regardless of the judge's order.

Stop thinking about him.

Before my thoughts dropped my mood any lower, I scoped out the intersection across from The Pizza Box. I quickly popped the curb on the yellow light that turned red before I ever got the back wheel on the street. I pedaled faster when one of the cars gave a loud, long honk. My fingers lifted from the handlebars in apology when I spotted the red Ferrari in the next lane. They'd begun to drive forward before coming to a sudden halt a few feet from the crosswalk.

There was no way to explain what happened next. The world slowed to an almost standstill, sending my senses into a frenzy. The neurons in my brain suddenly hyper-focused. The beat of my heart thumped slowly yet thunderously inside my head.

My body turned to a mass of tingles as if a million butterflies prepared for flight from inside me. I felt everything. The warm breeze, the faint squawk of seagulls in the distance, the smell of fresh dough baking in the pizzeria. My whole being fixated on one of the two people sitting inside the car.

In my peripherals, I caught the passenger flipping me off, but the driver held my attention. I felt his concentration as strongly as my own.

The darkness and fear in my life faded.

My entire body cinched tight, my muscles tensed and strained. A warm heat spread through me like lava from an erupting volcano.

The few seconds felt like an hour as I stared at him. Whoever he was, he was stunningly beautiful, like a sculpture crafted by Michelangelo. Maybe the best-looking guy I'd ever seen. Male model material. I'd never experienced anything like my reaction to him before.

I rolled past the Ferrari, lost to his world.

The sports car took off. Not with the peel out that I might've tried to execute if driving that car, instead at a normal speed. All I could do was turn my head to watch the car drive away.

The sudden stop of my bicycle shocked me. I lurched forward, catapulting me over the handlebars. Unfortunately, the back wheel followed me when my legs tangled in the bike's frame.

The world sling-shotted back in place as my years of being tackled had me instinctively preparing for the fall. I ducked and rolled, landing in a skid on the concrete sidewalk. My stop came by way of the small bushes lining the path in front of The Pizza Box.

With that strange standstill-in-time moment extinguished, I opened my eyes and assessed my body for injury. When it appeared I might not have broken any bones, the pain of the road rash lit the left side of my body on fire.

I shouldn't be embarrassed, but I was. In a hopefully fluid motion, I rolled to my feet. From the way I fell, my bike had landed on a grassy patch on the other side of the bushes.

"You good?" I glanced over my shoulder to see Josh Bigly in a parking spot in front of the restaurant with his truck window rolled down.

I gave a thumbs-up and bent to pick up my ball cap that had fallen off. "I think so," I yelled.

In a practiced move, I scooped my hair off my forehead and pulled the cap down backward over my head. Then I swiped at the dirt and debris on my shirt and shorts. The crunch of the grass made me look in the direction of my bike to see Josh walking toward me.

"You got scraped up pretty good there," Josh said, nodding toward my arm then reaching for my bike. He brought it up. Remarkably, it appeared okay. The front tire was flat, but I could fix that.

"Yeah." A drop of blood landed on the concrete.

I lifted my arm and knocked the small rocks and dirt from the skin. The distinct sound of my mom's high heel shoes clicking quickly across the parking lot had me groaning inwardly. If she lay witness to my accident, I might not ever be allowed to ride again.

"I'm Josh. Don't know if you remember me. My father owns this restaurant," Josh explained, pressing his thumb in the front tire, confirming it was flat.

"I remember you." The blood picked up speed and dripped again, another drop followed. I didn't know what to do so I placed my hand tightly over the scrapes, trying to stop the bleeding. I hiked a leg over the bushes to be on the same side as Josh and my bike.

Josh and I had spent quite a bit of time fishing, but the same thing happened with him that happened to Chae. He was older than me, doing what older kids do. Last time I remembered seeing him, he was a shortish, overweight, and stocky kid. He'd changed. Tall and broad with a face that looked made to smile as he did right now.

"You've grown."

"That's everybody's reaction. I heard you were back in town. For good this time," Josh said and started toward the front door of the pizzeria, my bike in hand. "We have a first-aid kit inside."

"Honey, what happened?" my mother asked, her arms crossing over her chest, her signature sign of worry. I could tell she wanted to reach out to me and take care of my injuries, but I'd broken her of that habit years ago. The embarrassment of the fall didn't need my mom's overprotective brand of care mixed in. That needed to be done in private where I'd gladly let her cuddle me.

"The curb came out of nowhere and tripped him up," Josh said good-naturedly. "Probably that shiny red Ferrari's fault. That thing was badass." My mom gave Josh a hard stare at the use of profanity. Josh grinned bigger. He looked like a big ole teddy bear. "Sorry, Mrs. Brooks."

"Mom, remember Josh Bigly? That's him."

Maybe the only thing that could have taken her worry off my fall was her astonishment when she took a closer look at Josh. Her expressions ranged from uncertainty to shock in a matter of a few seconds.

Josh laughed again and gripped my handlebars tighter, starting toward the restaurant. "Come inside. We'll get you cleaned up."

When I followed, my mom did too. Her palm came to the center of my back, lightly caressing. I loved that move. She was such a good mom.

"Are you all right?" she asked quietly. "Did you get hurt?"

"Probably only scratches and a bruised ego," Josh teased from over his shoulder. "The bike seems good. The tire's shot. Not sure I've seen such a perfectly executed tuck and roll before, except maybe in the movies."

My mom kept the worry on her face as she gave me a critical up and down assessment. Since everything had gone wrong with my family, she poured herself into mothering me. And I let it happen, sometimes.

"I'm fine. I promise. Just hungry."

Speaking of food had her tense features softening.

"You're always hungry," she said and gave me a small smile that didn't quite reach her eyes.

"My parents can barely keep me fed and they own a restaurant," Josh said, leaving my bike in the small foyer between the parking lot and the dining room. "I'll get the first-aid kit and meet you in the restroom. I'll also tell my dad to go heavy on the buffet to feed us both in a timely manner."

Great. I was into both ideas and started for the arrow sign pointing me to the bathroom.

"I'll get a table," my mom said. "Call me if you need me."

We were on the same page. If my injuries took a bad turn, she was the first person to know.

My birthday dinner had gone from two people to three with Josh choosing to stick with me and Mom, instead of doing his own thing. I was having a pretty decent time, especially since I was on a winning streak in *Ninja Assault*, jumping up the leaderboard to third place.

"The town hall crowd's gonna release soon. They always come here after a meetin'. It's never good anymore," Josh said quietly at the vintage pinball machine beside me.

"Yeah," I said, distracted. "Sounds like it's goin' bad for them. All they have left is the picket—"

"No, dude," Josh, making it hard to hear over all the death and destruction I was executing. "You're not pickin' up what I'm layin' down."

Those words bounced around my head as my fingers moved deftly over the game's buttons.

Josh's big hand clamped down hard on my shoulder, causing my hand to slip. My fiery death exploded on the screen. I reared back, looking at my score as the end game graphic flashed my fate. What the hell? Josh broke a top guy code rule. Don't mess with each other while playing a video game. My disappointment barely stayed behind my lips as my stare slid to Josh.

"What?" I bit out, not able to keep all my frustration hidden. If Scott had done something like that to me, I might've actually tackled him to the ground. He'd never hear the end of it.

"There's a party at the acres. You in?"

"The acres?" I asked. Josh said it like I should know the place. And parties? I really wasn't that guy.

Did I have a curfew? Did my mom allow me to go to parties like that?

The excuses began to tumble from my lips. "I have to get my bike home then fix the tire."

Josh laughed in my face and brought his hand back to my shoulder. This time with a little less force. "I got you covered. Come on."

"Not tonight. I gotta change my clothes, clean some of this dirt off me. Maybe another time..."

Josh was already at least ten steps in front of me, heading to my mom sitting in one of the booths.

"Hey, Mrs. Brooks. We're havin' an end-of-year party tonight. Can Beau go with me?" Josh asked. If there was any way for me to catch my mother's eye and shake my head no or even mouth the word, I would, but Josh's booming voice and large frame blocked my mom from me. Josh's mom sat across from her, the deep conversation they shared consumed her. She looked startled at the interruption.

"Ask me again," my mom said. "I don't think I heard that right. Beau going to a party?"

"Yeah, it's supervised," Josh added. Where my mom looked happy for me, Josh's mom appeared more skeptical.

"It's supervised, huh?" his mom asked.

"Yeah," Josh answered as if a party could happen any other way. "I'll have him home by eleven forty-five. I'll be home by my midnight curfew." He then dropped the bomb that took me by complete surprise. "You know, I gotta show our guy a good time so we can recruit him onto the team next season."

Oh no. Not that. My shoulders dropped at the suggestion.

"Well, that sounds wonderful," my mom said happily, sitting back in the booth seat, clearly relieved.

Josh's mom frowned, having the exact opposite reaction. "You were supposed to build up to that, young man." She crossed her arms over her chest, giving him a critical stare, as she leaned back in the booth.

"Ah...Mom, you know I'm not very good at followin' directions." By then I was beside Josh with both our parents waiting for my response. Josh gave me no time to think of a better excuse as his arm draped around my shoulders, landing on the aching one. I tried to move out from underneath him at the same time Josh reached out, patting—no, hitting—at my chest. "Everybody's gonna help him make the right decision. Trust me."

"Keep your phone on," my mom said as if it was perfectly normal for me to go do anything without Scott by my side. "He's just gone through so much." Oh God. I felt the walls closing in on me. "He's such a good boy, but he's withdrawn, and I don't know why..."

All the customers in the restaurant had to have heard too. I pivoted around, and started for the door, needing to get the heck out of there since everyone was going to think I was a charity case. I pushed through the entry door with Josh on my heels.

"My dad said you could bus tables. He heard you've been all around lookin' for a job today. My advice is to find somethin' else. He's shorthanded and we all gotta do way more than the jobs we're assigned with no extra money." I grabbed my bike, and Josh opened the exterior door, letting me through first.

"I can meet you there." As far as I was concerned, I'd rather walk home pushing my bike. "I need to change. Probably shower. I've been digging through junkyards today. Let's call it done."

"Put your bike in the back of my truck," Josh said. "It's not a problem. I gotta pick up Chae anyway. We've been goin' out for about a year. She's never ready on time. You'll probably have to wait for her."

If Josh had to go to my house anyway, I'd be saved from a four-mile walk. Then greatness popped into my head and I spurted the idea before thinking it over. "I don't wanna play football anymore. I'm not goin' to. It's a hard no for me. My dad wasn't acceptin' of my decision. That's why we moved here."

"I'm not gonna say I'm not sorry to hear that," Josh said, stopping at the other side of the truck's bed. "The team could use the help. You're nationally ranked as a freshman. You're badass. I've watched some of your footage. And I get Sea Springs isn't even on the map. I also heard your dad's a massive douche bag, and he's been real hard on you, so I get why you don't wanna play. But I'm not the only one assigned to talk to you. Stick with me and I'll steer 'em clear."

Emotion welled, clogging my throat for finally having someone understand even if it was only a small portion of my reasons why.

"Come on, Brooks. Whatever's got that look on your face ain't worth the effort. You'll meet lots of people at the party. You can just chill then I'll take you home."

Maybe he was right. The imaginary neon sign flashing above my head, telling people I'm gay wasn't a real thing. Nobody had figured it out yet. With more time under my belt, would it even matter?

I didn't know the answers. Chilling seemed cool. It'd be fine. I guessed.

Maybe.

6: The Country Folk
Dasham

"What're we doing here?" I asked my niece, Joy. She drove, I sat in the passenger side seat taking in the entire frightening scene.

For as far as my eye could see—which wasn't that far since it was late and dark outside, was a piece of carved-out land that Joy kept calling a pasture, surrounded by a thick bunch of forestry. More a u-shape if the sides of the u were abnormally long.

Parked pickup trucks circled a grassy patch, their headlights illuminating a decent size crowd in the middle. No one was distinguishable, they all looked the same. A sea of vintage blue jeans, old T-shirts, and assorted baseball caps. Nowhere close to the mid-thigh plaid shorts, flipped-up collar of my polo, and deck shoes I wore.

I quickly lowered my collar and tugged my shirt free of the waistband. It's all I had to help blend in. On second thought, I lowered the visor and ran my fingers through my styled hair in hopes of appearing more rumpled.

Joy pulled in next to the other cars haphazardly parked with no discernible organizational patterns. It was like a crazy free-for-all out here. What happened if someone parked up front had to leave early? Did every vehicle have to move?

"I feel like this is a really bad idea," I added, mentally retracing my steps on how I got wrangled into this in the first place. A locals party? I wasn't "local." Neither was Joy. More importantly, nobody here liked us.

Joy pushed the gear shift into park completely unbothered by my concern. Her newish Mercedes C-Class also didn't fit here. She cut the engine and physically turned the headlights off, not waiting for the automatic dim.

We stared quietly at the large party happening maybe fifty feet away. I was living a scene from every teenage movie ever aired. Who had any idea these gatherings were real and actually took place?

The girls sat to the side in short skirts and halter tops. I couldn't tell from this angle, but I bet there were lots of flip-flops on their feet. Didn't they know the dangers of wearing flimsy sandals out in the middle of nowhere like this?

"Stop fretting," Joy finally said, releasing an unsteady sigh as she dropped the visor. The small mirror lights flashed bright as she checked her lipstick. "It's fine. We're invited."

"I don't believe a casual afterthought from a local guy, inviting you to the party, was an actual invite. These people hate us," I reasoned, digging into my unwillingness to leave the car.

"Stop, Dasham. Granddaddy's handling all that. I promise you, these people don't care. They want to hang out, drink beer, smoke, and hook up. They live by the code of the teenage handbook. We need to get you a copy so you can learn to have a little bit of fun," she said flippantly and reached for the key which I ninja'd out of her hand.

Since I doubted the handbook existed, making the code nonexistent, I decided to keep the key with me, then all I had to do was outrun Joy to the car.

She'd deserve to be left behind for agreeing to come here in the first place.

As if Joy read my thoughts, she laughed at me and pushed the button to open the trunk. She bounded from her seat as if she didn't have a care in the world.

Country music blared from the various trucks. I left the car at a much slower pace than Joy. Once I got to my feet, I took everything in from my new angle.

At least the music had a decent beat.

Still cowboys and gay city dwellers didn't usually mesh well together before factoring in the local animosity toward my family and the resort. I scrubbed my hands down my face as the anxiety of the moment got the best of me.

I wasn't overt. My sexuality didn't define me. I came out to my father when I was twelve years old. He explained that certain people would rather do me harm than allow me to be myself...

"Let's go, Dasham. Or stay in the car. I'm going to the party," Joy said with a six-pack of Heineken in hand. Who knew where she got those from?

Joy walked away, leaving me alone in the middle of nowhere, all the darkness turning eerie fast. "Wait. I'll go."

The walking path was barely recognizable with the ruts and grooves made naturally rather than by vehicles. I bookmarked the information in my mind just in case I did have to run for it.

Screw television teen dramas, how many horror flicks had I seen where this kind of party was the moment everything went south for all the people there? Chainsaws and hockey masks picking off drunk and rowdy kids who always made very bad decisions in their fear.

My thoughts shifted again.

How many babies would be born nine months from now?

Stop.

"I thought you said there was a keg," I said, pretending to be comfortable while heading into hell.

"Have you forgotten how disgusting the keg hose is?" Great response. She knew me too well. My thoughts diverted again. No, I hadn't remembered. I don't think I even knew.

Joy's hand came to my shoulder, a beer bottle followed. "Here. Hold it so you fit in and probably best to get that freaked-out look off your face. We're in Sea Springs for three months. We're gonna need something to do."

Okay, another great response. She wasn't wrong.

"Remember, you're the DD tonight."

I stopped in my tracks. "I can't be the DD, I don't have a driver's license yet, and you're not twenty-one. I have to have someone twenty-one years old or older in the car with me."

"Then you better be extra careful driving home," she teased and flipped her long blonde hair over her shoulder, leaving me in her dust. She was on the prowl.

Wait. Did I really know I'd been invited? Joy had a thing for a server at the resort. If she took me with her to the party, her parents wouldn't ask too many questions.

Dang, I'd been played. Why had it taken me so long to figure it out?

I scrubbed a palm down my face then dropped my chin to my chest as I started forward again. Maybe if I hung out in the periphery, I wouldn't stick out. Joy owed me big for this one.

An hour in and I had to admit I'd misjudged the situation. Outside of all the camo and cargo, these kids weren't all that different from my friends at home. Well, except we'd never have a party in the woods. Alcohol was poured freely at most of our homes. But here, people really presented the personification of being good ole country folk—at least how it was explained to me by my new friends, Ginny and Jessica. They were welcoming girls who spoke with a charming southern twang.

On the flip side, the music and humidity sucked. No matter what happiness filled my heart watching Joy try and fail to learn the two-step, the hot, moist air did its best to give me pit stains and the insects were crazy big.

I sat on top of an old tree log positioned at the edge of the party. The party hadn't gotten far enough in to have couples pairing off yet, but we were close. The guys stood about ten feet away talking about local guy interests—football and fishing. I didn't do either.

But these girls were grounded and down to earth. Completely different from the ones I'd encountered at the resort. Everything was casual, nobody even seemed to know who I was. They relaxed me and I somehow let it happen.

Remaining true to my DD obligations, I passed on the pot and the pills circulating. It wasn't a hardship. Besides, the same concerns about the spout on the keg applied. I didn't know these people or where their lips had been.

A set of headlights rounded the corner separating the party from the road. A truck barreled forward at full speed, grabbing everyone's attention. I honestly had no idea what was happening until a cheer rang out as the single cab pickup truck came to a screeching halt, dust flying every which way.

A giant stepped out of the driver's side, throwing his hands in the air, shouting, "I'm here. Let the party begin."

Another much louder cheer came from the majority of the guys headed in his direction. On the other side of the truck, the door opened. I couldn't see who it was but heard an audible intake of breath from beside me.

"It's Beau," Jessica said. She leaned forward, craning her neck. "I can't believe he's here. How did Josh get him here?"

"I don't know, but he's smokin' hot just like we knew he'd be," Ginny said, getting to her feet to crane her neck to see better. "I don't care that he's fifteen. I'd go out with him anytime, anywhere."

"Absolutely," Jessica seconded. "Coach wants Josh to talk Beau into playin' this year. He's supposed to be really good with a national ranking, or somethin' like that. That's what Chae said."

"What did I say?" said a girl that must have been Chae. She was tall, looked more mature than the rest of the group, but not necessarily older. Pretty in a natural way.

"About Beau and football," Ginny answered when Jessica didn't readily reply. Instead, she stood on top of the log to better see the circle of guys slowly moving back to the center.

She was funny. This Beau had to be something. I got to my feet to see the newcomer. My brain blipped as I stepped two feet forward. It all happened again. My heart hiccupped. My breath slowed to shallow puffs. Beau? The guy who crossed the road in front of me on his bike. The very one who slowed time, who lit my body on fire for the first time in my life. All the same primal urges bowled me over again.

An all-consuming, foreign sensation ricocheted over me. A chain reaction of sorts in its most fundamental form, making me unsteady and unsure.

I saw his face so clearly in my mind. I quickly forged an ambitious plan to spend the next few minutes persuading him to get to know me then making him mine. We'd have a long future together. My breath caught as I watched Beau follow the guys, but he appeared in no hurry to catch up. He glanced down at his feet and absently tucked at his T-shirt, making sure it lay right in the waistband of his jeans. He was tall, lean, and moved like a jaguar, owning the space around him.

Owning my heart was more like it.

Beau. The name played like a symphony through my mind.

No, that wasn't right. It slammed through me like a loud Slipknot concert, sledgehammering his way into my heart.

From the backward baseball cap on his head, which I'd never seen anyone do before, all the way to a strong jaw and nice full lips, my heart imprinted his image across its surface to never be forgotten. I'd guess he was an athlete without knowing about the football.

From my rearview mirror, I'd seen the tumble he'd taken on the road. Now, I saw a large bandage on the underside of his left arm.

My heart might not ever beat properly again.

The idea of Beau being unhappy overwhelmed me. He walked chin to chest, tucking his fingers into the front jeans pockets. What did that mean? What was he hiding?

"So you're the guy everyone's talkin' about?" I glanced over at Chae. She only held my attention for a fraction of a second before I shifted my gaze back to Beau.

My entire body tensed. A slow exhale escaped. Everything in my life changed in a moment.

I was physically overwhelmed by him. How hadn't I noticed before? My nipples tightened, the fabric of my polo brushed lightly against them, sending tingles racing along my body. My cock strained against my shorts.

The world ran in slow motion. Although time had stopped for me, it hadn't for anyone else. Somewhere in my peripheral vision, I saw Chae looking at me, then over at Beau again.

"I see," Chae said, knowingly.

"See what?" Ginny asked, standing on the log with Jessica to ogle Beau.

I continued to stare as he walked to the crowd of guys. Clearly, he'd known them for a long time with the dap slaps and knuckle bumps he gave as he passed by.

To give my crazy body's reaction a break, I forced my attention to the beer bottle in my hand that I wasn't drinking and placed it on the ground at my feet. With Beau not consuming my vision, I could think easier.

"What's your deal, Dasham?" Chae asked. Her tone gave away her dawning speculation.

Of course, I knew what Chae implied, but I had a lot to consider before I spoke my truth.

"My name means the number ten. I'm my parents' tenth child. I'm also smart," I answered absently and grinned down at my Sperry shoes. "I skipped a grade in elementary school and I'm on track to graduate high school a semester early with my associate degree." I lifted my head enough to wink at Chae, trying to hide my smile. "I'm also sporty. I played Lacrosse for my school's team but stopped because I'm graduating early."

I shifted my gaze to stare at the silhouette of Beau. My breath shuttered again at the nice-looking view.

"You know I work for his grandmother?" Chae asked, garnering all my attention. My head whipped her direction. Screw hiding because my dad's resort rested on my shoulders. Chae had the answers I needed.

"Tell me?" I whispered.

"His name is Beau Brooks. He's hot, obviously. Maybe he'd be interested in you because he's not interested in any of us," Chae teased, flipping her long dark hair over her shoulder and glancing back to the small circle I'd been sitting with.

"Not for a lack of tryin'," Jessica added.

Hope built fast.

"His grandparents live here. He comes here every June and July but had to go back home in August for football practice. His dad's a football coach and a massive jerk. He's really mean. Nobody likes him."

"Yeah, but he and his mom moved here permanently about a week ago," Jessica said.

"You know exactly how long ago they moved here," Ginny teased, calling Jessica out. "I bet you're hidin' in his bushes at night."

"He quit football. Somethin' happened. I don't know what," Chae explained.

"Everybody here hopes Josh can talk him into playin' again. He's supposed to be really, really good. I believe he's a tight end or maybe a receiver. He makes lots of touchdowns but also blocks, so whatever position that is," Ginny said, and glanced over at me for verification.

I only shrugged. How did I know?

"Josh is my brother. I overheard him and my dad talking about it. They live for football. I don't," Ginny said.

My gaze turned laser beam focused, willing Beau to look at me.

I understood my overwhelming attraction was my limbic system bolting like a speeding bullet causing my body's extreme physical response. But when he did finally look my way, breath slowly left my lungs. After a moment's stare, I decided there was no question that he was looking at me. Words like fate and destiny shouted from every fiber of my being.

This was the most significant moment of my life.

If souls were real, mine did loops around Beau's, trying to rope us together.

7: The Guy

Beau

"My old man caught a twenty-inch speckled trout at Tabbs Bay yesterday. We need to go check it out," Hunter Jenkins said, knocking me in the arm. Hunter was a year older than me, and along with Josh, we spent a lot of time fishing together over the years.

I nodded, trying my best to listen to Hunter as my body's nerve endings took flight. I fought the inner call insisting I turn to where the girls sat. If I did, I'd draw unwelcome attention.

I anchored my hands on my hips for balance and gave a shake of my head to clear the low-level buzzing in my ears.

"I'll go with y'all to Tabbs Bay. I haven't been there in a while," Josh piped in and whacked me hard on the back, causing me to step forward or fall down. Irritated, I glanced up ready to tell the guy to kiss my ass, only to see Josh winking at Hunter. "Our guy here's gonna think about joinin' the team."

Oh hell, here we go again. The annoyance building inside me amped up about fifty percent. My brows snapped together as I stood to my full height, ready to fight Josh to the death. Probably mine, but I didn't care.

"He's gonna take my MVP spot," Josh added good-naturedly.

"Yeah. I'm guessin' that wouldn't be too hard to do," I shot back without thinking of the implications of my burn. "My national ranking's about your age. You wouldn't be able to catch me if I gave you a twenty-yard head start."

I got a round of whoops and hollers, mostly laughing as I threw the gauntlet. Josh didn't care, he joined in with the others, impressed with the way I came back at him.

"It's all good. You can have it because we'll be goin' to state for sure," Josh added loudly and lifted a hand for a round of high fives from the other guys.

The hum in my ears grew louder, drowning out all the other sounds around me. The pull I'd experienced overrode everything else, giving me no choice but to turn toward the girls. When the object of my subconscious attention came into my vision, it was as if I'd been struck from out of nowhere by a heat-seeking missile. I was stunned I stayed on my feet.

My heart drummed frantically against my rib cage. My body tingled all over. For the first time in my life, the self-disgust I lived with vanished. Replaced with a radiant, beautiful, stunning guy.

A heavy weight lifted off my shoulders, but the feelings didn't last. The urge to hide was too much a part of my psyche. My heart became a battlefield, fighting against my core.

Luckily, the choice in the decision was taken from me with a hard knock against my aching shoulder. When I turned, at least four sets of eyes stared at me. I forcibly resisted the connection until I understood better what was going on.

"Which one are you interested in? Remember, Ginny's my sister." Josh swelled his chest in an effort to look intimidating. I gave a half-hearted smile. No, Ginny held no appeal to me.

"Who else's over there?" I asked.

"Chae, Jessica, and Ginny. Mandy and Tracy are over there too. You gotta remember them. I guess. Maybe they've changed," Josh said. "I don't know."

"Who's the guy? I don't remember him." I prayed my voice sounded casually interested.

"You wouldn't know him. He's here with his sister I guess, who's here with Donny. Their dad owns the resort everybody hates. That's why nobody's talkin' to him. We all had to promise not to give 'em shit. Donny's got a thing for whatever her name is." Josh gestured toward a couple swaying as close as they could get to one another. I didn't remember Donny.

"Go for Mandy. She's easy," Hunter said.

"Hey, that's my girlfriend," J.J., another guy in the circle, said, using both hands to shove Hunter backward several feet. All the attention was taken off me, landing on Hunter. J.J. leaped forward, tackling Hunter to the ground.

It was like a wild wrestling match that somehow felt expected with the way their friends circled the guys to get a better view. Sides were instantly taken. The cheers rang, urging on the fight.

"J.J." Mandy screeched at the top of her lungs. The high pitch pierced an octave above the boisterous crowd. I was impressed as she bolted into the fight, Jessica on her heels. "*Stop*!"

My heart raced like a Kentucky Derby winner as I took several steps backward. I needed a way out of the situation and all the bad decisions this guy was likely to stoke within me.

I made a beeline along the outskirts of the party. Hopefully, once I hit the road, I could hitch a ride back to my grandparents' house. If not, the walk wasn't more than four or five miles. My escape turned into reality as I neared the closest cluster of trees, allowing me to slip away.

"Beau, where you goin'," Chae called. My shoulders tensed. I could pretend not to hear her but she might follow. But maybe she wouldn't...

"I'll be back. I gotta go..." My words trailed off, letting the implication handle itself.

"Hang on," she said closer to me. "There's someone I want you to meet."

No matter who she was with, I wasn't in the right frame of mind for small talk. I took another step toward the trees, but my damn ingrained manners got the best of me, reluctantly forcing me around.

My injured knee buckled into a funky stumble as I saw the blond guy walking stride for stride beside Chae. Jesus. He was as pretty up close as he was at a distance. Actually, prettier. Honestly, too beautiful to be real.

I put my fists on my hips, but I wasn't sure why, so I lifted a hand and nudged my ball cap from my forehead, scratching the hairline that wasn't in the least bit itchy. "Hey."

"Hey," he chimed back, mimicking me. Something confident and knowing crossed his face. What did that mean? "I'm Dasham."

I nodded. Dash-am. More like Dash-ing. Dash.

Maybe I pulled off casual as I pushed at my hair to place the cap back on. It was probably in my best interest not to look directly into his eyes, making my stare land on his chin. "I'm Beau. Or I guess you know that because she used my name…"

My normally steady tone cracked like it had when I entered puberty. Jesus, I wasn't fit for company. Best to stick to my plan and hightail it out of there ASAP. "Sorry. The airs got me…allergies…" As I fumbled over my lie, I clamped my mouth shut and cocked a brow at my own stupidity. I fisted my hands again and put them on my hips.

"You go by Dash?" I asked. What the hell was happening to me? I never put my hands on my hips, causing me to drop them to my sides.

"I do now." He grinned a genuine smile, making my heart ache. Chae laughed at me—not with me—like she'd been doing for most of my life. They weren't wrong. I wasn't fit for company. I pivoted around to continue with my escape plan. Screw my worry about being rude.

"Dasham!" The voice drew all of our attention, thankfully off me. His sister. The resemblance was uncanny. Maybe even his twin. "Donny and I are taking off. Drive my car home?" Donny strolled up behind her with all the swagger in the world, effortlessly giving off that cool guy edge.

"What? Joy. No," he countered, outraged, instantly squaring off with Joy. His pretty exterior didn't change, but the hard edge to his voice and the way one eyebrow arched, changed the casual guy into a force. "Of course, I can't. I don't have a driver's license."

"You can handle it. You drive better than me. Besides, you're the most responsible person in our family," she reasoned while Donny came up behind her, wrapping his arms under hers, tugging her backward into an embrace. The smile on both their faces spoke of lots of things, none that could be done there.

"You got it, man?" Donny asked. "I'll make sure to get Joy home—"

"No, I don't got it," he said, interrupting Donny. "I'm not driving by myself. End of story." He dismissed the idea. His answer was given. "And you have a curfew. And you barely know him. Why would you go off alone? You're absurd."

Joy tossed his words away without a care. "I've never been home when I say I will be. My parents go to bed at like nine o'clock every night. Yours do too."

"So?" he snapped back. "What about your word? And what about your promise to me? Nobody here likes me. I only came for you. If you're gone, there's no reason for me to stick around?"

"Oh, you're ridiculous, Dasham," Joy singsonged, rejecting his argument. "Go home now then."

"Drive me home," he shot back. "Then you can go wherever you want. We'll see if I tell your parents."

The exchange happened relatively quickly, but it allowed me the time to calm my body and regroup my thoughts. I did my best to rein in my over-the-top physical response while managing all this emotion I'd never experienced before.

"Maybe if you drive home, you can give Beau a lift," Chae added reasonably, which sounded like the worst idea I'd ever heard. "I should've told you that Josh never gets home on time. I don't have a curfew. I was gonna drive you home myself. I bet your mom's the kind of mom who waits up. None of our parents do."

The rush of uncertainty was back in full force. My gaze collided with Dash's. My insides trembled.

His absolute refusal to go against the rules showed cracks. He appeared to consider the idea. "I get my license in a few weeks," he said to me. "It's late so probably no one will see me."

"Our little celebrity," Joy chimed with humor. I didn't understand.

Joy and Dash had both won the genetic lottery. They had those pretty sun-kissed features and unique crystal blue eyes. They were both tall, thin, and wore preppy clothes, different from anyone else at the party.

"So we're gonna go," Donny said, his arms tightening around Joy, cuddling her against his chest as he took a step backward.

Dash appeared less than impressed and reached for his cell phone in his back pocket. It was a far fancier model than mine with a small keyboard attached.

"Tell me this guy's information," he said, briefly lifting his stare to Joy, his thumbs working the phone.

"Stop," Joy said with a put-upon groan, then she turned to wrap her arms around Donny's neck. He lifted her and started walking toward one of the trucks. We watched them go.

"She's always been so irresponsible," he mumbled, tucking his phone back inside his pocket. Chae burst out with laughter as the guys' fight began to encroach on us. Josh was trying to stop the brawl by lifting Hunter off J.J. and carelessly tossing him to the side. He landed with a thump, rolling close to us. Hunter was up and on his feet within seconds, doing a free dive back into the center of the guys. His resolve to fight to the death, earned an even louder cheer.

"I'll let y'all handle this. I'm gonna go get a beer and see what's goin' down," Chae said. "I don't imagine either of you drinks too much. Especially not him," she added and patted a palm on Dash's chest before walking away backward. "If you need a ride, Beau, tell me quick. Otherwise, I refuse to be the DD again tonight."

Here I was, staring at Dash the dashing, who stared right back at me.

Instinctually, I knew this moment was pivotal to my life. My senses warned that he was into guys, and he knew I was too. Since I'd never told another living person about this chaos inside me, I didn't understand.

The corners of his lips quirked up, the smile taking my heart.

I guessed I was riding home with him.

"I saw you on the road today."

Surprisingly, with Chae gone, I became less defensive, lifting my arm to see the sloppily applied bandage. "Not my finest moment. It wasn't too bad though. I survived the antiseptic."

"Good," he said, grinning broadly. "Did we stop you from using nature's bathroom?" Dash swept a hand out to the patch of trees in a quick, graceful move. My gaze followed the sweep, taking in the muscular bicep and defined forearm. His hand didn't appear to have calluses. When understanding replaced concentration, I chuckled.

"Honest answer?"

"Absolutely," he chimed back.

"No. I was in a turn-and-burn escape." My hand went to my head again, dislodging my ball cap. I was still nervous. "This isn't really my thing. I'm more of an introvert. There's too much happenin' here. I usually stick to myself."

"I'm the same. Joy forced me here. Our family was having dinner together..." Dash stopped, shaking his head. Frustration laced his next words. "I didn't want to come, but it was decided for me. It seems a lot is decided for me these days."

Of course, I didn't understand but I didn't need to.

Our gazes locked. Not awkwardly. I never wanted to look away. Slowly, his smile tilted up. "I take it all back. I'm glad I followed along. It's nice to meet you."

8: The Ride
Dasham

A couple of quick assessments to this point.

For whatever reason, Beau gave off a skittish vibe. Did that only have to do with me? Or maybe a personality trait? Either way it complicated my desire to have a quick commitment for a long-lasting relationship. It also made it hard to throw down right here, right now, and make out with the guy.

Even under all this intense physical attraction, I instinctively knew he mattered more than sex. He needed me. Which was weird for me to consider. I was inherently a self-centered guy.

I couldn't look away as I fisted my hands, itching to reach out and touch him. I needed to take my time. Go slow.

Clearly, confidence came easy to me, but as the stars aligned, I saw my future as more than just the baby son of the wealthy Jackson Richmond. Beau gave me a sense of purpose I didn't understand. In what? Who knew? I'd figure it out as we went.

"Do you live around here?" I asked.

He shook his head and stuffed his fingers inside his front jeans pockets, stretching the material. I fixed my gaze on his eyes, instead of where they wanted to look. It didn't come easy. "No. Well, yes, a few miles away. Maybe three, probably four, could be five."

"You don't drive?" I asked.

"I'm not old enough. Next year."

"So you're fifteen?" Which had to be the obvious answer. "I'll be sixteen on July fourth."

"Today's my birthday so I have exactly a year to go before I drive." Whatever held Beau at a distance, lightened in his grin. My heart stuttered, fluttering frantically around my chest. After having such a powerful reaction to a smile, I wasn't sure I heard the rest of his explanation. "I guess this is my birthday party."

I said the only thing that came to mind. "Happy Birthday. Good party, but it's not as amazing as the party our country club puts on for me..."

His smile turned into a quiet chuckle, and I was utterly captivated.

"I don't really want to be here. I can take you home now if you wanna go."

Beau's face read like an open book. The uncertainty was back. He glanced over his shoulder at the party, leaving me to stare shamelessly at his profile.

"Look, I've been getting a lot of attention lately. I think I should drive the back roads to your house. It'll take us longer to get you home. If I get caught and give my dad any more bad press, I think he'll disown me," I said, trying for humor.

"I don't wanna get you in trouble..."

I wasn't going to allow him the out. "I'm kidding. My dad's a good guy. My whole family's pretty good. Like Joy, they play hard..." I stopped before anything negative tumbled from my lips.

Chae and I had cut him off from his escape in the darkened shadows of the trucks' headlights. Since I'd noticed everything about him, my concentration zeroed in on the way his jewel-toned amber gaze flickered. The small gold flecks gave a natural depth. He was truly beautiful to me and clearly physically fit. He had to play a lot of sports, all the time.

"They play hard?" he asked.

"Yeah," I finally said and let that be enough. I ducked my head then nodded toward the car. "I don't think anyone's paying attention to us. We could take off now." I pivoted to walk toward Joy's car. The panic my decision created wanted me to look over my shoulder to ensure Beau followed. I fought the urge as my head and my heart battled to the death inside me. What I should have done was to get behind him and push him to the car.

The forty or so feet I walked might have been the longest of my life. But if I dug deep, the connection between us held strong. Somehow, I knew he was following. Only at a much slower pace.

Surely, he fell somewhere under the LGBT umbrella.

My step stumbled.

I had zero indication that assumption was true. What if he was straight or even homophobic and offended by my attraction?

No, the world wasn't that mean.

As I got closer to the car, I reached for the key fob, pushing the button as I pulled it from my pocket. The unlocking mechanism snicked on the driver's side door, and I hit it again to unlatch all the locks. Once I'd opened my side, while on the verge of sitting, I finally ventured a look in Beau's direction.

He was still a good distance away, maybe twenty steps or so behind me, but I counted it as a win that he was still walking toward the car. I dropped down in the seat and reached to turn off the interior overhead lights then pushed the headlights button off before I started the car. I kept watch on him with every step he took.

I read about the intensity of love at first sight. When you see someone from across a space and every instinct connected you to them. I didn't doubt such a thing happened but never considered I'd be on the receiving end.

Suddenly, I experienced a deep sense of vulnerability. At the same time, a comforting warmth spread through me. I brought my other leg inside the car and shut the door. I needed the minute alone to try to gain perspective.

The worry of driving without a license no longer mattered. Let the consequences fall where they may. I'd drive anywhere as long as Beau was in the seat next to me.

So much for taking it slow.

The passenger door opened, and he took a seat, shutting him inside. My head swam with his scent, all guy mixed with a spicy, clean cologne. I held my tongue that wanted to confess how much I dug the way he smelled and started the engine, putting the gear shift in reverse. I needed to put distance between us and the party.

"Where do you live, and how familiar are you with the back roads?" I asked. "Can you get us there?"

"Probably," he said. "I've spent summers here for most of my life, but that isn't sayin' a whole lot."

In the silence, my body soaked up the rich tenor of his voice. Beau felt like home. A place I needed to be... *Stop.*

"This is my first time in Sea Springs," I said. "Joy has a GPS in the glove box if we need it."

Beau didn't reply as the car bounced down the trail, hitting each deep rut and oversized rock in the way. After we took the first of two turns that hid the field from the road, I flipped on the headlights. "The only rule given to us about the party was to turn the headlights off and not draw any unwanted attention. Think we accomplished it or will I have some angry cowboys after me?"

The trail came to an end, having me drive the last leg through a field. The night was much darker out here than I was used to. I couldn't see too far in front of me, requiring the lights to guide my way.

Beau gave a huff and reached for his seatbelt. "If you're really the son of the owner of Richmond Resorts, turning your headlights on is the least of your problems."

The reply held warmth and humor.

"I figured my problem might be more the plaid walking shorts I'm wearing in a sea of Wranglers and cowboy boots. I know it sounds crazy, but I do blend in well in many parts of the world." As I said the last few words, I turned to waggle my brows.

The stare we did so well held again. My glance shifted between him and the field as I navigated the car onto the frontage road. It sure appeared that he blushed. I'd never known anyone to be shy about anything.

"So you live around here now?" I asked.

"I guess so."

I waited but nothing more was said. He now stared out the passenger side window, seemingly ignoring me.

"What does I guess mean?" I finally asked.

It took a few seconds more before Beau answered. "I'm from Mobile, Alabama, but my mom's from here. My grandparents have a B&B in Sea Springs where my mom grew up. My great grandparents bought the house. But times aren't good. I don't know if we'll stick around here for longer than a couple of years."

"I think I heard you played football?" I asked as I came to a four-way stop close to the entrance of Highway 146. I let the car idle, unsure which way to go, and took the opportunity to openly ogle Beau. He continued to stare out the passenger window. That didn't stop me from the slow perusal of his body. He was hot. Lean and muscular. A trim waist and strong thighs. The tingles were back with a vengeance.

"Football," he said dryly. My gaze shifted up. He'd caught me staring. I wasn't even embarrassed in the least. He pointed a finger out the front windshield. "Take the highway."

Got it. I was to drive, so I did, taking the ramp to merge onto the highway.

"Sorry." But I wasn't at all. "So you play football?"

"Not anymore."

Clearly, this Beau wasn't a man of many words. "You're from Alabama but you live here now. How did that happen?"

"My parents split up a few months back. Me and my mom moved here after the divorce. She's gonna be the new vice principal at the high school I'm supposed to attend. And no, I'm not playin' football anymore. It's pretty much the reason we had to move."

I scowled at the explanation as I tried to understand. "Does that mean your father wants you to play and you don't want to?"

Beau gave a quiet huff. This time I felt his eyes on me as he answered, "My father's the most winnin' coach in Mobile County's history. He's a varsity coach. I've been playin' football since I was three years old. I've done rec teams, select teams, and school teams. It's been a year-round deal for me."

The puzzle pieces slipped into place. "I bet your father wasn't happy that you decided not to play."

He laughed a dark sound that I interpreted to mean I was dead-on. We fell into silence again as the questions bounced around my head.

"So you're completely done with football? Chae said the guys want you to play for the local high school."

"No offense," he said. "It's all anyone asks me about and I don't wanna talk about it. It's personal."

"Sure, no problem." The invisible walls surrounding Beau were firmly back in place. I understood better where the pain I sensed in Beau came from. I managed to stay silent for maybe as long as thirty seconds. I had a problem; I liked to talk and needed him to tell me everything. "Am I headed in the right direction?"

It took a second, but he finally let go of his direct stare outside the passenger window and looked around. "No, sorry. I live the other way. Do you know where Sea Springs Bed & Breakfast is?"

"I've barely left the resort."

"Right. The resort. It's why I ended up at the party tonight. The local group fightin' your dad had a meetin' tonight. I can't listen to another second of how badly they don't want your father's company here." He glanced at me. His arms crossed over his chest. Sincere frustration laced his tone.

Finally, a breakthrough. I loved my family's influence in this town even more now.

"Yeah, my dad's out for blood. I don't think he's ever had this much resistance in business before." He grinned as he considered his father's exasperation. "The twenty-four-hour picket line was genius. They never stop coming."

"From what my grandmother says, it sounds like your dad's only goal is to put them all out of business," he said and turned away again. "My grandparents can't stay operational if it continues like it has."

Oh, no. We were taking a conversational turn in the wrong direction. I had to find some way to salvage it.

"Who's the guy that's been all over the news? They've been all over him for the last couple of days. They want to kneecap him," Beau said. I felt his eyes continue to stay on me. "Their words, not mine."

How did I answer? I wanted to use anything to help my cause, but I liked my kneecaps.

"It's you, isn't it?" he asked at my pause. "Nah, that doesn't make sense. He's a lifeguard and saved a kid from drowning. From what my nana says, the media keeps covering it, making him out to be a hero to Sea Springs or something like that."

I barked out a laugh.

"It is you," he accused.

"I think so," I admitted. "But I didn't save anyone. It was by chance that my picture was taken while your grandparents' group was picketing. It's the first positive thing said about the resort. My dad's publicity team got a hold of it and blew it up."

Seconds passed as Beau continued to stare at me. I couldn't read his expression.

"What?" I asked when nothing more was said.

"You have a Ferrari and your parents own the resort. Your dad's like a trillionaire..."

"Yeah, I guess. Not a trillionaire."

I exited the highway and took the turn to go the other direction.

"The truth is my dad didn't set out to put anyone out of business. This area has had a surge in vacationers over the last ten years. Many of those years, the growth doubled. If it wasn't my dad, it'd be someone else, maybe far worse." Beau nodded and settled back into the seat.

What did that mean?

"Are you quiet or are you angry?"

"I'm not anything." He shrugged. "Mobile's grown crazy like that too. This whole deal between the resort and the locals has gotten way too mean and there's no going back from here. They should've found a way to work with your dad. Her group was never gonna win. And now they're out of money."

"I agree with what you're saying. My dad's lost his mind too, and I'm not sure he'll ever recoup all the money he's had to spend."

And here we were again. Beau silent, his focus turned to the road in front of us, staring out into the dark night.

"Is today really your birthday?" I asked.

"Yeah."

"Did you get presents?"

He grinned; his body visibly relaxing. He dropped his arms from his chest. All good signs we'd turned the conversation around. "Yeah, that bike I was on that I wrecked in front of you."

"Oh no." Seriously on the *no*. I kept landing us in bad dialog after bad dialog. "Did it get messed up?"

"It's fine. I get roughed up more in a game," he said and turned toward me again. "But I did a badass somersault over the handlebars. The brushes stopped my fall. I nailed it. Makes me think I should have a career in stunt work." Beau was clearly making fun of himself, yet he said it with hints of pride. For me, if I had received a single scratch, I'd have to be checked out in the emergency room. "I also got a cell phone."

He reached into his back pocket and pulled out a new Nokia. "My dad always thought I was too young for a phone. Apparently, my mom doesn't. That's the cool thing about divorce, I guess."

"Well, happy birthday." It gave me a chance to look at him again, if only for a few seconds. I sensed we may have had a breakthrough and moved on from the awkwardness.

"Thanks. Take the next exit. There'll be all residential roads from here."

I did as instructed, feeling far better about the trip as I left the highway. The speed limit shifted to thirty miles an hour once we were back on the frontage road. Now all I had to do was find a way to keep Beau in the car for as long as I could.

9: The Night Whispers
Beau

Something about the dark, quiet night, mixed with the soft feel of luxurious leather, and this guy with his sexy cologne sitting next to me lulled my senses into a place I hadn't been in a long time, —comfortable.

Since I rode with the enemy, I risked a lot. Images of my grandmother with a shotgun played through my head. There was about a fifty/fifty chance on whether she'd shoot me, but Dash definitely had zero percent chance of coming out unscathed.

I threw a joke when I should have been anxious. All Dash's doing.

I managed to keep my humor on the inside as my cock strained, pulsing against my jeans every time he opened his mouth to speak. His smooth tenor sounded so intimate. Alluring, mixed with lots of fairy dust.

Dash was friendly, easy to talk to. Even though he did most of the heavy conversational lifting.

He wasn't like anyone I'd ever met before. Genuine, responsible, and respectful of the world's boundaries. Qualities I'd never known anyone my age to have before.

Maybe all wealthy people acted that way, but I didn't think so.

"You like to do what's right?" I asked.

"I don't know about that," he hedged then gave me a side grin. "That's a lie. I'm generally aware of what's right and what's wrong. I try to stay on the right side of things. Sometimes, I fail."

I nodded and turned toward him as much as my seatbelt allowed. "Like volunteering to drive me home?"

"Exactly," he said, letting the word drag out as he nodded.

I got it. I tried to do what's right. My rebellion came by climbing out my window at all hours of the day and night, but I generally stayed close to home.

"Take the right then the next left," I said, when the lights from the convenience store came into view.

"You don't have to be home right away, right?" Dash asked, flipping on the blinker and gently applying the brakes as we approached the four-way stop. He continued to slow, preparing to pull into the convenience store's parking lot. "I really need to use the restroom."

"They're around back, but you need a key," I said, scanning the parking lot. I didn't recognize the few trucks or guys, who rested their forearms over the back of one truck's bed.

If those guys were locals, my concern for Dash's well-being spiked, and I pointed a finger to drive around the side of the building. "Why don't you park around there and let me go get the key."

The implication wasn't lost on him. He took a wide curve to park in the back of the lot.

Dash came to a stop and lifted in his seat to extract his wallet from his back pocket. He thumbed through the bills, more cash than I'd ever seen, and pulled out a twenty, handing it to me. "Can you get me a Coke? And get whatever you want."

I didn't take the money as I reached for the door handle. I had my birthday money on me. It wasn't much but I could buy us drinks.

Dash's hand darted out, gripping my forearm, keeping me from leaving the car.

That sizzle happened again, searing me from the inside out. Excitement rushed through my veins as desire raced along my nerve endings. Goose bumps sprang forward.

I couldn't hide my body's reaction as the breath I held released in a simple sigh. No way he missed it.

The rawness of my response flushed my cheeks, warmth creeping up. My uncertain gaze skidded to his.

"Let me make sure the overhead light is off." He didn't immediately release my arm, but it also didn't linger. The wild fluttering of my heart locked me there, staring at Dash. He broke the gaze and hold, something I'd never be able to do, and reached for the overhead light. "Take the money. You're taking the risk of being with me. Let me buy you a soda for your birthday."

The twenty was back in my line of sight. In auto mode, I accepted it. I certainly couldn't think properly while in the middle of my acute physical response. Luckily, the fresh, sultry air helped cool my heated skin and cleared my head, but my cock remained stiff as a board. I had to adjust myself as I started for the store's entry.

Dash's touch was like a Louisville slugger's grand slam to my libido. I wasn't even ashamed of my reaction. Every other time I had the slightest physical attraction toward a dude, I immediately went into flight mode. Forcing a turn and burn out of there as quickly as possible.

I rounded the corner, scratching my jaw. I felt real stubble there, at least in a small patch. My shoulders firmed up, squaring, and I grinned at how truly comfortable I was.

"Brooks. We wondered who parked around there," one of the guys standing at the truck's bed edge said. The outside lights from the store made it easier to see their faces. I honestly didn't remember any of them. They looked quite a bit older than me.

"Hey." I lifted my chin. Hard to come off as cool with the grin etched on my lips. It might be permanently there from now on. I tucked my hands in my front pockets, pushing the cash inside, and hopefully, hiding the full hard-on in the front of my jeans.

I made quick work of buying our drinks and grabbing the key from the attendant. I ignored the guys, only giving another nod, because it seemed like the thing to do, and I started around the building to the car.

"Hey, Coach wants you to come play for us," one of the guy's said, his voice moving closer. I stopped in my tracks and looked around. The guy was taking long strides toward me. Nothing about him jogged any memory. Crap.

"Yeah, I heard. I'm thinkin' about it," I said off the cuff, hoping it would be enough. It wasn't. He kept coming toward me, making me pivot on my heel, heading toward the nameless guy, putting space between the locals and Dash hopefully still inside the car.

"What's there to think about?" he said, knocking me in the upper arm when I got within reach. Thankfully not the aching one.

Not a conversation for now. I cocked my thumb over my shoulder. "I gotta go. Someone's waitin'."

His stance changed. Now, he appeared in on a secret. "Nice ride. Those rich bitches from the resort sure like to slum it over here." He slapped my arm and gave me a weird wink where both his eyes closed instead of just one. I didn't care for the way he lumped me into the slums.

I nodded, attempting some form of comradery, then pivoted again. "Seeya around." My strides were long and purposeful. I carried Dash's can of Coke and my Dr. Pepper, the restroom key dangling from my hand. I continued around to the driver's side, fully aware of Dash watching me the entire time.

Whatever change was happening to me rippled over my consciousness. Confidence built at lightning speed. I felt alive. Dash's door opened, and I handed over his drink between the car and the door, while he continued to sit behind the wheel.

"You know those guys?" he asked.

"No, but they knew me, and they think you're a hot resort girl."

His brows wrinkled as I quietly chuckled.

"I didn't correct 'em but I'll stand here until you're done. There's a drop box that you're to put the key into. It goes back into the store. They said don't be gross about it and they sanitize."

Dash's brow wrinkled further, taking the key between his forefinger and thumb. That made my laughter grow louder. Of course he wouldn't get the practicality of an old school restroom drop box.

I followed like a bodyguard as he went toward the back of the building. Something protective rose inside me. I'd be the sentry to guard his door.

My purpose felt damned good.

A parked car on a tree-lined street with the moon filtering through the branches made magical things happen. With my head rested against the head rest, I turned toward Dash. I was relaxed and having a good time. He sat at an angle, facing me, as far as the steering wheel allowed. The radio played the only pop-rock station around.

Twenty questions turned to fifty or even more the longer we sat together. I didn't want to leave.

"What position did you play?" Dash asked.

"It's my turn to ask a question," I countered and lifted a brow when he started to shake his head, an argument on his lips. I knew that with all certainty because he'd done that very expression every time I inserted a question.

"Go ahead then," he gave, but I could tell it didn't come easy. "But it's noted that anytime I bring up football, you change the subject. Do you really not like it anymore?"

"Again, my question."

His smile that charmed me grew bigger. At different times tonight, I noticed different things about him. Right now, he looked like the after shot of Captain America. He was beautiful with the way his hair swept off his forehead and his strong jaw highlighted his wide plump lips. I liked his smile a lot.

"I get the impression you're older than you said."

The musical cadence of Dash's laughter made me want to kiss him like I've never wanted to kiss anyone before. I watched his mouth move as he explained a question I didn't ask. "I'll really be sixteen on July fourth. You already know that part, but I'll graduate from high school in December."

Since his lips were the perfect blend of fleshy and plump, it was hard to concentrate on his words. Luckily, I caught the tail end of his explanation. "Explain further."

"I have a high IQ. I skipped a grade in elementary then tested out of other classes. I'll graduate in December with my associate degree. My plan is to take a gap year then start at SMU in the fall." His finger twirled in a circle that I took to mean time passing. "I've already been accepted." His gaze danced as he rolled his eyes dramatically. "I could have skipped more grades, but I didn't want to rush my life. I felt like I needed to stay in my age range even though I've never really acted my age. It made sense to me at the time."

Dash clearly thought his explanation was silly, grinning and laughing, but I didn't see it that way. A million questions ran through my head. Did he make those decisions about his future, or did his parents? It all seemed so reasonable and mature.

"Who do you get your intelligence from?" I asked, not readily diving deeper until I knew more.

Dash's surprised gaze landed back on mine. "No one's ever asked me that question before. I'm not a hundred percent sure. I'd guess my father's side of the family. They're all successful for generations back. But my motivation's different from the rest of my siblings. Right now, my goals are pretty simple. I want to practice law at a big firm. Get some experience and clients under my belt then go out on my own. I want to work on pro bono cases to help those in need, but I understand I'll need capital to make it happen.The rest of my family works for my father's company. All of them do. They had me later in life. I'm the tenth one—it's the meaning of my name. Dasham means ten."

"Mmm. I've only ever been an only child. I don't know what it's like to have brothers and sisters."

Dash's goals and family dynamic fascinated me.

"So if you're too young when you graduate law school then no agency would hire you, right?"

"Absolutely not answering. It's your turn to answer a question," he stated firmly. "What do you like to do for fun?"

"I like to fish a whole lot. It's quiet, and I like the quiet. I think I'd like to have a job. I work any chance I get, and I like the idea of having my own money in my pocket," I said, saying things that I'd never said to anyone before. "But jobs around here are hard to come by."

"My dad has a deep-sea charter fishing service connected to the resort. I bet I can get you a job doing something with them," Dash offered. "They're having a hard time finding locals who want to work."

I was instantly intrigued, and at the same time, I could hear my grandmother's strong disapproval. She'd be mad at me for siding with the enemy. Dash barked out a laugh at whatever he saw cross my face.

"I get it. If anyone found out, you'd be public enemy number one but think about it. I'm sure I could get you hired."

"So do you really work as a lifeguard?" I asked.

His frown caused me to laugh. "Yeah. I'm surprised more people haven't drowned."

"That's why you're so tan. I bet the girls go nuts over you."

That sent Dash into a low groan. It probably wasn't meant to entice but it did. All the fluttering in my belly took flight inside me again. Unfortunately, the alarm on his watch beeped, alerting us of the five-minute mark before I was due home.

"Dammit," he muttered and worked the controls on his watch. "This is the best time I've had in a long time. It flew by."

Of course, I agreed. I turned my head and stared out the front window. From where we were parked, I could sprint across the open field and be home ina couple of minutes.

"Thank you for bringing me home," I said and let that be enough as I reached for the door handle.

"I had a good time." Dash's captivating smile happened again, stopping me from opening the door. He rolled his eyes at something unknown, followed by a frustrated sigh.

"What?" I asked.

His lips mashed together as he reached for his phone in the center console. "What's your phone number?"

"I don't actually know," I answered honestly. It never occurred to me to learn my number because of caller ID.

"Give me your phone." Dash didn't hesitate to grab it before I had a chance to extend my hand. His thumbs raced over the number pad until his phone rang. He made sure the number was there before handing it back to me.

"I'll drive you around." He righted himself in the seat and reached for the key to start the engine. Automatically, my hand reached out to stop him before the car's lights drew attention to us.

The touch made my heart begin its version of the electric slide, all happy and cozy. He paused and didn't move his hand out from underneath mine. I couldn't get my hand to budge either.

"My grandparents' place is right there," I whispered about the old three-story home surrounded by the trees that hid us. "If you drive me, you'll have to go around the other side and I'll be late."

With an inner strength I didn't realize I possessed, I moved my hand off his. My gaze shot to my feet to gain perspective. His skin felt like sat into me. Something I needed to remember for later.

"Which room's yours?" he asked, his voice low and intimate.

When I cracked the door, the cooler night air and humidity seeped inside. The fresh air helped add to the mystique of the night. "Third floor,right side."

"And you've climbed out of that?" Dash asked, astonished.

"I can climb out of anywhere. I lack fear, if that makes any sense. My mom hates it." I put a foot out on the pavement and started to slide out of the seat, very aware of the hard-on pressed against my jeans. I stayed bent at the waist and dipped my head back into the car. "Thanks for bringin' me home."

"Completely my pleasure," he said and sat there staring at me. "Happy birthday."

"It's been a good birthday." My heart made me say it just in case I never saw him again. I cast one last glance then shut the door behind me.

Dash stayed parked on the road until I was at the back door of the house. The wait seemed purposeful. With a quick look over my shoulder, I waved before slipping inside. I knew he couldn't see me, and I couldn't see him inside the car, but tonight mattered in a big, big way. Maybe my secrets weren't as awful as I thought they were. The relief was staggering if not a bit premature. Time would tell.

10: The Climb

Dash

After the best night of my life, I took the main roads back to the resort without even considering the repercussions. Heck, I didn't even remember much of the ride home. Beau hijacked every one of my thoughts, leaving silly grin in on my face.

From the way he tilted his head when he smiled, to that slightly bow-legged walk he had—I'd call it a strut—to the way his fingers felt as he touched my skin... My body tightened painfully. Unmanageable need coursed through me. I needed an outlet that only he could solve.

I nipped at my lower lip as tingles ran like a free-for-all all over me.

Man, the dreams I'd have tonight.

My smile brightened in anticipation as I parked in a reserved spot and took the private elevator up to the penthouse suites. I could whistle a cheerful little tune as I watched the call numbers above the doors rise. Absently, I tucked my hands inside my pockets.

The crazy emotion Beau elicited inside me failed to dissipate. I never wanted it to end. Only to mature in a way that made both of us happy.

The story of our lives played inside my head. I wanted him to be my date to senior prom, and I'd be his date when the time came. He'd be at my graduation and me at his. My plans for my gap year changed. No more traveling the world. I'd spend it in Sea Springs with Beau then go on to college only a year before him. My family's long-standing relationship with SMU could help him be admitted. By then, we'd have enough time under our belts to live together as we finished university. From there, anything might happen.

I smiled at the fantastic plan. The elevator doors opened as the images of us together played out through the various stages of our lives. I walked the short hall to our suite. On each side of the building, there were two private sets of rooms and entrances. We share a floor with my oldest brother's family, Joy's father.

Quietly and methodically, I turned the doorknob and opened the door to be greeted with a dark main living area. That surprised me. I was fifteen minutes late. Back at home, I'd have Amelia waiting up for me...

Another hard truth shot through me. My parents never waited up. It was Amelia there for me every single time.

With more attitude than necessary, I tossed Joy's keys on the closest credenza and made my way to my room. The lamp lights initiated before the bedroom door fully opened.

A coldness tried to creep against my warmth as more truths of my life revealed themselves. I took my phone and sat on the end of the bed. More than anything else, I wanted to call Beau, talk to him until the sun rose, but how did that play out if I read all the signs wrong?

The cold turned colder, eating away at my good mood.

Well, hell. As a rule, I didn't allow myself to curse, but it seemed appropriate here. How had I let tonight end without firming things up between us? Not even a *let's see each other again* commitment.

My heart began a slow, steady thump of uncertainty.

I should call him right now to correct my error.

Pure adrenaline had me getting to my feet, taking a quick look over my shoulder at the alarm clock on the nightstand. Twelve twenty in the morning. Defeat had me taking my seat on the bed again. My eyelids closed. His image was right there waiting for me. This time I remembered the way he looked at me as he bent down to thank me before he shut the door. The backward ball cap framed his face perfectly.

In my recollection, I noticed something I'd missed at the time. He was aroused. In the tight fit of his Wranglers, I saw the evidence outlined.

How hadn't that been my only focus?

Because I liked him a whole lot more than just physically.

My decision was made, I was going back.

First, I went to my window. If Beau crawled out of them, maybe I could too. It seemed romantic to scale the walls to be with the guy that I thought I loved.

Besides the death trap of being on the seventh floor without even a ledge to jump down to, the window didn't have a latch to open. My plan was foiled.

With my parents fast asleep, I still went quietly through the suite, grabbed Joy's car keys, and shut the main door without even a click of the latch.

Motivation propelled me back down the elevator to Joy's car and on the road toward Beau. I didn't get lost in the what-could-happen-if-I-was-caught possibility. It didn't matter, except for the possible halt in my current mission. Less than ten minutes later, I parked on the side of the road where we'd hid before.

With the engine off, I sat in the dark and pulled up Beau's cell phone number. I opted for a text in case his ring volume was turned up.

For the first time in my life, I was at a loss for words. It took forever to tap out the simple message.

"Are you awake?" I pushed send and immediately regretted it, wishing I could take the words back and type something witty and clever instead.

My phone rang loudly in the silence, catching me completely off guard. I answered before the first ring finished.

"Hello," I said somewhat breathily and stared out the front wind shield at where I thought Beau's bedroom might be.

"I'm awake. I'd text back but it costs money." A dim light flashed in the window I watched.

"Yeah, I was afraid to call so late if your ringer was turned up loud," I explained. "Can you come outside? I'm parked on the road where I dropped you off."

Long seconds passed before he responded. “Is anyone with you?”

“No, I’m alone.” After several seconds of silence, I added, “I can come closer to your house.”

“Give me a minute,” he said quietly. I heard some rustling in the background, his voice going lower. “I gotta be quiet.”

“Okay. Do I come closer?” I offered again.

“No. I’ll be down in a minute. I gotta get dressed.” The call ended. My gaze fixed on the third-floor window. It took a few minutes before Beau’s shadow appeared in the window then started across the roof. He stayed low and moved quickly until he jumped from the third floor to the second, then down to the first. It was impressive.

I reached for the visor and stopped just shy of bringing it down. The lights on the mirror would put my vain side on full display. Instead, I turned the rearview mirror and pushed my hair in place.

Beau sprinted across the field. I got out of the car and went to standby the passenger door where the cluster of trees was thickest, easier to avoid prying eyes.

Another advantage to this side of the car was the eerily dark night aided in what I planned to do. He never slowed until he was a few feet from me.

He wasn’t out of breath, and his hair was free of the ball cap. The loose strands took on a windblown style. I liked it a whole lot.

“Hey,” he said, walking the last three or four steps to me.

“Hey.” I repeated a word I never used. “Did I wake you?”

“Nah. Not really. What’s goin’ on?” he asked, his hands going to his waistband.

All the confidence I had started with crumbled into a realization that this was a really bad idea. I had no idea how to begin. “I, umm.” My gaze riveted to my deck shoes. Staring at Beau made it too hard to think straight. “I wanted to tell you that I’d put in a good word for you at the docks, if you’re good with that?”

“Yeah. Sure. That’d be great. I guess. My nana won’t like it, but I need to work. Help pay my way if nothing else.”

I nodded and felt my face wrinkle. My nerves were getting the best of me.

"But you don't have to. I'll keep lookin'."

"It's not a problem for me, but that's not why I'm here. I wanted to tell you that I enjoyed tonight," I said and forced my gaze up to his. He said nothing, his face expressionless, giving me no sign of what he thought. "I feltlike we connected... You know..." I couldn't hold the stare and continue. "I feltlike I needed to come back and let you know."

"Okay," he said.

"Wait. Hold on. I'm not saying what I want to say." I took a step backward to lean my butt against the car. I crossed my arms over my chest and forced my spine to stiffen regardless of the sea of doubt rocking through me.

"Look, I'm gay," I tried again. With my shoulders squared, I looked Beau straight in the eyes as I continued, "And I felt like we had a connection. That's why I'm here and what I'm trying to say. Did I get it wrong?"

In silence, he stared at me for several long seconds, maybe minutes, perhaps hours. It felt like days.

"How did you know?"

How did I answer that? Our dialog took on a calculating edge. Did I pretend not to understand? I didn't think so. I sensed truth and honesty from him, also vulnerability. "I didn't know, *know*.I guess I still don't know. In my life back home, I'm out, but not here. No one here knows I'm gay."

He ducked his head, chin to chest, as his strong arms came up and crossed, mimicking my stance. I sensed something akin to hurt radiating from him in waves. Whatever it was, I didn't like it.

"Have I caused you pain?"

"Maybe." He kicked at a rock until he bent and picked it up. The stone sifted through his fingers in a practiced move. "It's why I quit football. Nobody knows. I've hidden from everyone, but I felt like you knew." Beau's uncertain stare pinned me in place, waiting for a response.

"I only knew we got along really well, and I'm attracted to you. I sensed it when I first saw you at the party. Even before then, when you were on your bike and crossed in front of me. I felt like the universe was talking to me. That's why I came back."

"Nobody can know. I haven't told anyone," he said again, as serious as the day was long.

I nodded my commitment to keeping the secret. The anxiety and worry that I was in this alone fell away. Not quite relieved but we had crossed the line-in-the-sand moment. This could have gone wrong in so many different ways. I shook out my arms from the tension formed in my shoulders.

A small smile tugged at the corners of my lips. He hadn't said he was into me too, but at least I wasn't into a straight guy. "Your secret's safe with me."

"Thank you," he said.

"And the other part?" I hedged, needing to know if we had any sort of chance.

"Yeah. I do too." He nodded and looked away. My heart sang even if I did recognize the shame in Beau's expression. Both the intense attraction and his disgrace were new to me. I had no idea what happened next but that was okay. We'd work it out together.

"You sure get quiet," I said and stepped closer, wishing I could reach out and touch him.

"It's weird sayin' it out loud. The world didn't swallow me whole. I figured it would," he said. "I couldn't sleep. I ended up callin' my buddy, Scott, 'cause I couldn't stop thinkin' about you."

I stepped closer again. Beau held his ground.

"I couldn't stay away. I think I was in my room for about three minutes before I left and came back. I tried to climb out my window like you do. In my head, it was a grand romantic gesture, but I'm staying on the seventh floor, and luckily, the window doesn't open."

Beau grinned a giant smile. "Crawlin' out the window isn't for everyone."

"You're athletic. I watched you run along the roof and know exactly where to jump down. When you go home, will you go through the door or back up through the window?"

"I'll climb back in," he said, and I stepped forward again. "I've been in sports for as long as I can remember. I used to rock climb for a club. Ilike the adrenaline of extreme heights."

"Hmm." I liked Beau a whole lot.

Beau's hands went to his hair, pushing it off his forehead. "I need a haircut. I should've already gotten one. I've been going through something the last few months. I usually keep it shorter."

I casually crossed my arms over my chest to keep from reaching out to touch him as I tracked every one of his moves. "I like how you look."

His gaze connected with mine. The smile was back. "You're beautiful," he whispered. "Perfect. Like a dream. I nicknamed you Dash for dashing..."

For as long as I remembered, people had told me I was easy on the eyes. It never mattered more than right then. I wanted Beau to believe those things about me. The warmth of his words seeped through my pores. I reached out, sweeping my fingers down his arm. The simple caress sent an excited shiver up my spine.

Nothing could make me move my hand. I traced the defined muscle in his forearm. But even more important than how it made me feel was that he stayed under my touch.

The contact meant everything to me.

"I like the idea of you calling me Dash. No one ever has."

"So what's next?" Beau asked.

I felt reasonably sure I shouldn't outline our future together the way it had been running loops inside my head all evening.

"What's that look mean?" he asked when I didn't readily answer.

"It's nothing. I'll tell you later." I stepped a half a foot forward, being closer to him, pushing my hand through his crossed arms. They broke free, giving me the opportunity to intertwine our fingers together. "Can we meet somewhere tomorrow?"

"I don't know if that's a good idea..."

Oh no. We were hanging out, for sure.

"Remember, I'm in the same place as you. We'll be friends. I want us to be friends. Nothing overt. I promise." Beau's fingers tightened around my hand then shook me off.

"You need to know, I'm not ready to...you know."

Of course, he wasn't ready. Look at the space he'd put between us at the very suggestion. "We'll take it slow. Come to the resort tomorrow. I'll get off work about two. You'll blend in there where I stick out over here. We can go to the docks, and I'll introduce you to the manager. We'll get to know one another."

"Okay. Maybe we could go to the beach. Everybody seems to have forgotten it exists anymore." He hooked a thumb over his shoulder. "I should goin' before I'm caught."

I wasn't sure I believed him, but I also didn't want to push past his comfort place.

"Yeah, me too. I'll go wherever you want to go. I have no plans."

He took a step backward, still staring at me. "Be careful goin' home."

"You know this matters," I said seriously. "It's not a fling. It's gonna be hard shaking me off."

I got the grin I liked so much before Beau took off running across the field. Much like earlier, I watched him until he jumped, parkour style, onto the roof. He lifted a hand then climbed through his window.

Becoming a stalker might be an issue for me because I was absolutely in love. Hardcore love.

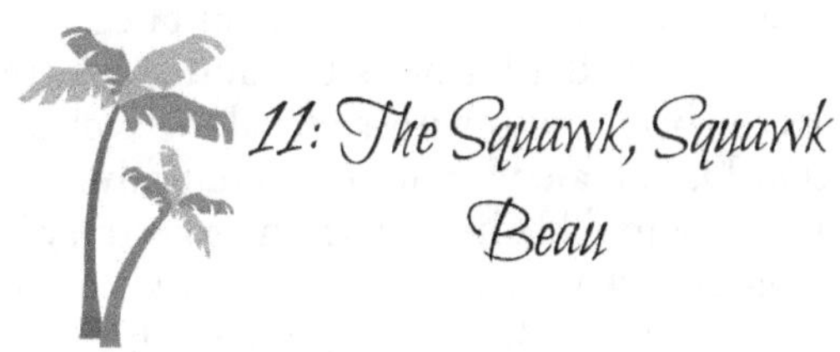

11: The Squawk, Squawk

Beau

Something about the way the seagulls squawked in the distance and the sounds of the waves pushing back and forth against the shore lulled me into a good, relaxed mood. The warm sun, and just being outside had to be factored in too. Today was everything for me.

I ran over the sand, soaking wet from the waves, until I dropped down on a large bath towel from the resort. I absently dragged a smaller one over my face then my hair. My gaze locked on Dash, still in the ocean, swimming the freestyle stroke back to the shore.

As hard as it was to admit, Dash the Perfect did have a flaw. He wasn't much of a swimmer to be a lifeguard. I might have drowned waiting for him to get to me.

The credit for my good mood had nothing to do with the sounds of the beautiful day. It rested solely on the guy in the water coming toward me. He was dazzling, stunning to spend time with. Today's obsession? His mouth. His jaw encased a set of perfectly formed, fleshy lips.

I started the day awkward and unsure, worried about someone seeing us and coming to correct assumptions, but his genuine good nature soothed any uncertainty. He showed me we could pull off the appearance of friends while getting to know each other on a different level.

He did manage to get me a job at the fishing charter service. My position was grunt worker number two. Meaning, they'd assign various duties for my shift when I arrived. Perfect for me.

Dash trudged through the shallow water at the shore, his swim trunks hanging low on his hips. He had a badass tan with not a freckle anywhere. Not me. I hadn't been in the sun this way for years. I had a farmer's tan and a splattering of freckles across the bridge of my nose and along each shoulder. Something that Dash teased me about mercilessly.

"Jeez, you can swim." He huffed, trying to catch his breath while dropping down on his towel, exhausted. He lounged back on his elbows. When that proved too much effort, he laid down fully, draping his arms over his face, covering his eyes. His chest pumped up and down with each breath. My lips quirked at such a dramatic display.

I reached for the other smaller towel and tossed it over him, chuckling. "I win."

"Remind me to never suggest a race with you again. You're a warrior competitor. How did you swim so fast?" He lifted his arm enough for me to see the anguish on his brow as he still struggled to breathe.

"My buddy back in Alabama, Scott Lee, lived next door to me for all of my life. Everything we did was a competition. We played every sport together, challengin' each other. I hate to lose, but Scott hates it more which made me try harder. I got to where I won most of the time. It bugged the crap out of him." I spoke the absolute truth except for admitting the true joy I had from watching Scott throw his baby fit when I beat him. Life didn't get much better than that, as potentially demented as that might sound.

"You could give me a break. At least pretend I was close. You left me in the dust. I think you were back on shore before I took my first stroke." His arm dropped back over his eyes.

"I did give you a break," I said, trying to hide my laughter. The appreciation for my efforts fell flat when Dash's small towel hit me in the face. It only made me laugh louder, and I reached for a bottle of water. "I decided if I had to wait for you to save me, I'd probably drown."

"Haha. My guy thinks he's funny..."

I barely got the swallow down and had to pause before taking another drink to let the burst of laughter free.

He moved faster than I gave him credit for as he lifted and squeezed the plastic bottle, water splashing in my face. I was so unprepared, I took the liquid in through my mouth and nose, causing me to bend away as I coughed and choked it out. Dash's laughter rang joyfully while taking the win away from me.

"Don't worry. I'm a lifeguard. If I can get to you, I'll save you if you drown." Playful condescension laced Dash's tone. A towel was tossed over my head. He enjoyed himself immensely and got me real good. His infectious snicker had me laughing again as I wiped the towel over my face. I gave him a side-eye where he was sprawled out on his towel, hands underneath his head. Grinning at me like a Cheshire cat.

It was hard not to stare. Dash might not be fast, but he was mouthwateringly fit.

"Tell me something about you," he said, then closed his eyes.

"I can't imagine there's anything I didn't say last night." I wadded the smaller towel up and shoved it behind my head as I lay back too.

"What's your favorite color?" he asked and shifted on his towel to lay on his side, head in hand. "I like learning about you. Since you're stuck in my head, it gives me more to think about."

"My favorite color?" Why would anyone want to know? I gave him a critical stare. One eyebrow arched as I contemplated my answer. First, I assessed the question. It seemed obvious enough. Second, how did I answer? Was there a trick to it?

"Sure. They're details everyone in a relationship should know about their partner." Dash gave me an absurd look, like I was the dumbest person on the planet for not already knowing. All the attitude coupled with the teasing smile didn't help to make his point.

"We're in a relationship?" I asked and closed my eyes. Hopefully, I succeeded in a nonchalance I didn't feel as I tried to hide my body's reaction to such news. It went instantly haywire, my heart doing a free fall in its excitement. We'd gotten along beautifully today. If that held...

"Yeah. You don't agree?" The way he said it had me cracking a lid at him. This time, his I'm-crazy look held sincerity.

I let the idea of a relationship bounce around my head. In my silence, I lifted my brows as if I thought of something good then lowered them like I'd had a bad thought.

I kept him on the hook. "I don't really think about color. I have a lot of browns..."

"Omigod, you can't say brown. That's nobody's favorite color," Dash replied. I couldn't help my burst of laughter at his passion over something so silly.

"Calm down. It's probably blue, I guess."

He shook his head again, and as if he were speaking to a simpleton, said, "There's a wide range of blues. Narrow it in for me."

I paused, trying to envision the different colors and how I might feel about them. Brilliance popped into my mind as if I were an actual genius. Seriously, my game might be the smoothest around. "Whatever color of blue your eyes are. That's my favorite color."

"Oh my God." A fistful of sand landed on my belly. "You took my line! I was just setting it up for a better landing."

Oh man, Dash knew how to give a good time. My amusement grew when more sand was flung across me. "I win, again."

He dramatically dropped down on his back, his arms crossing tightly over his chest. A firm pout came to his face.

"So what's your favorite music?" I asked. "I listen mostly to country."

It took several long moments for him to participate. "I listen to anything but country." We both turned our heads toward each other in unison. "Country music's too sad. It's like a Disney movie. Everybody has a broken heart."

I saw his point. I listened to country music because everyone around me did. "You aren't wrong."

"Whew, I was beginning to think we weren't as compatible as I originally thought."

Insecurity shot through me at warp speed. After years of pent-up self-loathing and worry, Dash had wiped it all away in a few short hours. But not any longer. "I'm open to other types of music if it's a deal breaker."

Dash's grin grew bigger. He'd been teasing me, and I fell for it. I tried to play it off as indifference. Who knows if I was successful.

"As long as I don't have to listen to it..." I quipped.

But the uncertainty coiled around my heart, refusing to give an inch. My brow wrinkled as I locked my head faced forward into the sun. The reminder of the oppression I had always lived under was too much. It took me to a dark place I never wanted to know again.

I was too edgy. I bent at the waist, reaching for the bottle of suntan lotion, squirting a sizable amount in my palm. I didn't really need it based on the time of day, but I wanted the distraction.

"Do you want me to rub that on your back?" Dash asked, sitting up too.

I didn't readily respond because the self-doubt tasted like acid on my tongue.

"Why aren't you answering? I was kidding about our incompatibility." He adjusted his position until he moved into my line of vision. "We're tucked between the dunes. It's a private beach. We can't be spotted."

I had to find a way to calm down the panic building inside me. He grabbed the lotion from my hand and squirted the cool liquid directly on my back. I arched away from the cold. His hand followed, swiping roughly up and down my back. My uncertainty spun between Dash's hand being everything and nothing I deserved.

"You sure get awfully quiet. I'm sorry for whatever I said that freaked you out. It wasn't my intention." He tossed the lotion to the side and dropped back down on his towel. "You've mentioned Scott quite a bit. I have a good friend like that too. His name's Chandler. We've been in school together since preschool, so maybe three years old. We got dicey when I told him I was gay. It didn't last. A few years later he came out as bi."

"Did y'all date?" I asked.

He chuckled and kept his eyes closed. "No. Absolutely not. All our friends believe we have, but we haven't."

Chandler. I marked his name in my mind then took a conversational turn. "Your life's more accepting than mine. I can't imagine tellin' anyone. I can't believe I told you," I said, and turned, sitting crisscross on the beach towel, directly in front of him.

"It has to be lonely and painful to not be able to live your true life." The gentle tone he used made me feel like I wasn't hiding my insecurity. He shifted until he took on my stance, sitting in front of me. The frontal assault of how handsome he was paired with all that confidence helped settle the newest ache in my heart. I stared directly into his blue depths.

"I quit football because I got a hard-on in the locker room. I played varsity as a freshman, and the guys were all older than me. More developed. Like men. It turned me on, and I couldn't control it."

"Yeah, that sounds like it'd be a problem." Something akin to compassion crossed Dash's brow, turning him serious. His fingers reached out to caress my thigh. I couldn't let it happen. I wasn't ready for him to touch me in such a semi-public place. But the comfort he tried to give didn't go unnoticed. It was nice that he understood.

"I played Lacrosse, and even with me knowing everyone in my school and my parents being wealthy, it wouldn't have been good for me if anything like that happened." His lips mashed together. Sorrow crinkled the corner of his eyes. "I guess your father's a homophobe."

"My father's a sexist, racist, violent guy. He's a local celebrity back home. It didn't go well when I quit. If I told him why, it'd been far worse. He'd've put me in a conversion therapy program, for sure. The more difficult, the better. He likes to toughen me up. But me quittin' ruins his plans for my life that he's been workin' on since I was young. I'm to play football in college. He and I are a package deal. We go together all the way to the NFL. He's ambitious, eventually becomin' a head coach. He'd pick Dallas if given a choice. He's crazy arrogant."

"It's not about you. It's about him." That was the one thing no one ever recognized. People thought I was a phenom player, dedicated to God's sport, wanting to go all the way.

"I think he feels like I'm the example of what he can make of a player, if given a chance..."

Dash laughed a harsh bitter sound, stopping me from saying anything more. "What a narcissist. If you have natural talent and quick reactions, that's on you."

"Yeah, no. He doesn't see it that way, but that's not even the problem. Imagine what would happen if he heard I had a hard-on in the locker room?"

Dash laid back, arm under his head as he stared at the sky. "Yeah. That stinks. I'm sorry you're going through that."

"My parents divorced over me quittin'," I explained, dumping it all out as if Dash asked for my sordid details. "It's why we moved so far away. I haven't talked to my dad in months. My mom's been through a lot."

"How's she gonna feel when she finds out the truth about you?"

"I don't know. She's intuitive and was a teacher for a long time. She's not like my dad, but I think she'd worry for me." The guilt had my shoulders tensing, and a deep exhale escaped. We stayed quiet and stared at one another.

"You wanna know my current pain?" he asked and only waited as long as it took me to nod. "There's a website dedicated to me. My dad's PR team found it. He said reservations at the resort are way up. Some weeks this summer have filled to capacity. He stressed the importance of me being on point all the time. It's weird, and I don't like it."

"Like what's on the website?"

"I'm not sure the purpose but it shows candid pictures of me around the resort and there's an email address to send pictures to."

I laughed at his obvious discomfort, but I also got it. The guy was so freaking handsome. I'll be searching for the website myself. Pretty cool resource for the long, lonely nights. "You're a really nice lookin' guy. You could be a model or something."

Dash's good nature was back. "I think, under normal circumstances, my parents would generalize me as a failure because I don't have greedy capitalism as my life's goal, but now, they're happy with me, like next level happy. It's weird. Even more weird is that I actively don't want their disappointment." He flipped out a finger to point, pausing my next question. "I was an accident, a late in life baby. I have a brother that could be my dad."

"I wondered about that. I got the impression your father's an older man."

"Yeah, he's a good guy. Travels a lot, but he loves me. Did I tell you I'm already accepted to SMU's Dedman School of Law? It's not a choice. My dad took care of my enrollment when I first showed interest." He rolled his eyes. "Academic achievement isn't the lynchpin for my acceptance. I'd get in anywhere for my family name."

"The mustangs," I said and grinned. Of course I knew about the university and the scandal that destroyed their football team. The only death penalty given to a college in the history of the sport

"Switching topics. Rate the date so far." His fingertips caressed quickly over my knee. So fast, he removed them before I had a chance to process what was happening. My body was engaged from the first touch, sending a quake over me. "No one saw me. Remember, I'm hiding too. And I'd give it a ten out of ten."

My cell phone rang. It was still so new that the sound of the ringtone had me looking around until I spotted my phone. My mom's number came across the small screen.

"It's my mom." I lifted a finger to my lips as I answered.

"Hi, Mom." I waited, hearing nothing for the first several seconds.

"Are you there?" my mom asked.

"Yeah. I'm here," I said, raising my voice as if that might help.

"Where are you? Mom's cooking dinner. Does she set you a plate?"

"No, I'm at the beach. Eat without me." I stuck my fingertip into my ear to better hear her. I'd tuned out the constantly moving ocean and screaming kids, but the squawking seagulls were a bitch to hear past. Put all three together and they were a wrecking ball to clear audio.

The cool part about the cell phone, I could openly stare unabashedly at him as he stared right back at me. "I got a job today. It's only eighteen hours a week, but that's all I can legally work at my age," I explained, repeating the information I learned today.

"That's great. Where?"

"I'll tell you when I get home. I'll head that way soon. Don't tell Nana. She won't be happy."

Dash suddenly bolted up to his feet in outrage, shaking his head no in a silly, exaggerated way.

"Beau. You can't..."

Yeah, I knew she'd figure it out. She was a brain ninja like that. And here we went about the evils of the only company who'd give me a chance.

"Mom, I went all over the place. No one's hirin'."

"Beau, I've told you...hiring. There's a *g* in the word. Say it properly."

I ignored her and kept going. "This is the only place who's will-ing to take me on," I said and turned away from him. "We'll talk about it when I get home. Don't say anything."

Her tone turned teasing. "You can bet I won't say a word. So when did my boy become sociable? You're at the beach. With people?"

"Ha. Ha."

"Well, get home as soon as you can. I need to go to bed early. It's been a long day. When did summer school kids get so bad?" A long yawn followed.

"I think that's the definition of summer school kids..." I cast a quick glance up at Dash who stood like a giant over me, hands fisted at his waist. "I'll be home soon."

Dash's brand of intimidation didn't work, so he amped up the dramatic horror on his severe facial expressions. I had to laugh, my mom forgotten. He came closer, really close, and bent to whisper into my free ear. "Stay longer. I'll take you home."

With his lips against my ear, my initial visceral response sent all the feels washing over me. My brain blipped, knocking away thought for a few seconds. My heart went the other way, connecting hard with how badly he didn't want me to leave. Honestly, I felt the same way, meaning I needed to gain perspective ASAP. We'd had enough time on our first date.

"Were you talking to me? I can't hear you. The seagulls are loud..." My mom pulled me back into the here and now. I'd need to thank her for that someday.

"I'm here." My voice was rough and ragged. "I'll be home before dark. I'm hang-ing up now so I don't use all my minutes." Brilliant thinking on my part. I didn't wait for her acknowledgement and ended the call.

A new, interesting finding about Dash? He didn't take disappointment well. Dash was so dramatic. He stood to his full height, whipping his beach towel up with him. The sand landed all over me. He had to know.

Man, we fit well together, and I laughed, making matters worse.

12: The Love Comes to Town

Dash

I didn't know why I'd thought we'd have the rest of the day and night to be together, but I had. And even if we didn't set our itinerary in stone, I still wanted it to happen.

Whatever amount I'd been attracted to Beau last night, it soared off the charts today. I mean, in the deepest depths of outer space.

All that silly planning I'd done yesterday about our futures firmed into an impenetrable tapestry inside my head. I was so taken with him that a life of commitment and monogamy was something I was ready to sign up for, right that minute. Except I couldn't very well sign along the dotted line if he wasn't there to sign with me.

"Are you mad?" he asked.

Yeah, I was mad at the world. Screw that, I was mad at the universe. All the matter and space that played its role in allowing today to come to an end.

"No," I lied. "Disappointed. I liked spending time with you." I wadded up the towel and threw it toward the resort's bin. We were isolated from the world on a small, private stretch of the beach my family negotiated into their deal. When I began to gather the rest of our things, Beau stood. "I get it. You have to be at orientation training early in the morning."

"Can you come to my house tonight?" he asked. "Or we could meet somewhere."

“No, I’ll come to you.” I instantly set my aim as if I was on the free throw line as I tossed the towel toward the bin. Alas, it fell short again. I guess basketball was harder than it looked.

Now, I’d have time to shower. Polish myself up to look my best when I saw my guy tonight.

Beau. The name echoed through me. I liked that he was tall, taller than me but not by much. I also grooved on being able to tilt my head this way or that to better read his expressions. “What time should I be there?”

“My mom’s goin’ to bed early. Probably any time after dark,” he said and bent to pick up his towel, wadding it between his fists. “There’s an alcove in the middle of the trees where we parked. We can hang out there.”

“Do I need to wear hiking boots or anything?” I asked, weary of the conditions. Hiking trails were one thing. Treading through forestry was quite another.

“No. It’s a simple walk, but we can hear anyone if they come out there, givin’ us time to escape.”

The sunshine in my heart was back. The smile I’d had all day returned to my lips. “Yeah, I’d like that. I liked today. I said that already, but I really did.”

“Me too,” Beau grinned and bent around me to toss his towel away. It made it inside the bin. No matter what his father said, his athletic talent had to be natural, I’d bet my car on it. We still had a ten-minute walk to reach his bike locked at the dock. I’d enjoy every last second.

Well past our agreed upon time of nightfall, I rolled to the edge of the road close to the trees and contemplated my next move. I assessed Beau’s house. All the lights on the third floor were turned off. Should I call it a night and meet up again with him tomorrow? A resounding *no* screamed through my head in an amped up stereophonic sound. We had agreed to meet, and he should be the one to turn me away.

After the longest dinner I’d ever had with my family, I decided I needed a grand romantic gesture to help ease my tardiness. I strategized, working through scenarios in my head. Romance meant sweet and personal, an effort I wanted to make every day to always ensure Beau felt special, loved, and wanted. So I'd start today with throwing rocks at his window, urging him out to spend time with me.

Sitting here in the dark, watching Beau's window, I saw the holes in my plan. Could I accurately aim to get the rocks in the proper third-floor window? Honestly, I didn't know how well I'd do.

If determination gave me a physical edge, I'd succeed easily. I cut the engine to Joy's car—that I technically stole again tonight—and started across the field. The high grass and uneven terrain made the walk harder and longer than expected. He had made it look easy, bouncing on the ground as if it were a gymnast tumble track.

It was far from that.

A new complication arose when I finally got to the house and the dogs around the neighborhood began to bark. Fearing I'd be caught, I crouched, getting as small as I could to prevent being seen.

I stayed low and did my best Donald Duck waddle to get closer to the house and decided to do a test throw with a tiny pebble to see how high I could get. Surprisingly, it wasn't a bad throw. I could easily reach the window and reared my arm back to make my aim. I let the small stone fly. At the same moment, the window opened and a leg started through the frame. My grand romantic gesture hit him in the chest. The startled expression he gave proved he hadn't known I was there.

About a second later, he spotted me on the ground and tossed out a hand that I interpreted to mean, *what are you doing?*

"Sorry," I whispered loudly and stayed in the shadows as I went to the first-floor ledge where he'd dropped from last night. I swear, Beau was half ninja with the easy skill he used to get where he was going.

He landed on his feet right in front of me. "Why'd you throw a rock at me?"

"If I could have made it actually hit the window, I thought you'd think it was sweet and excuse my late hour," I whispered back as we retraced my steps toward my car. A damned rut got me. I lost balance, stumbling in front of Beau.

He reached out to help me, meaning he'd voluntarily touched me. His hand circled my arm, sending instant goose bumps springing along my skin. My guy kept hold of me until he turned me in the direction he wanted me to go and I was securely back on my feet.

His skilled hand caressed over my shoulders and down my back before letting me go.

My cock grew harder, stiffer until that part of my body began to revolt with frustration at how patiently it waited for the same touch. "I brought a blanket and a couple water bottles. They're in the trunk."

"We'll go in right there." He pointed to a patch of thicket that showed no discernable entry. "There's an open patch a couple of feet in."

"Do we really have to trek through the brush where bugs and spiders hang out?" I asked and slowed my pace. "I brought mosquito repellent too..."

He laughed at me this time, not with me. "I think snakes and an occasional gator might be the likely irritants..."

I stopped dead in my tracks. Beau walked into me from behind, bumping me forward. Whatever look I had on my face when I stared at him over my shoulder caused his soft, mocking laughter to increase.

"You're funny," he said and started around me.

"I'm not going where snakes and alligators hang out." I refused to budge. "We can hang out in the car instead. I'll drive farther down the road."

"I was kiddin', but now the bugs and spiders are less annoyin', right?" Beau kept going toward the overgrown trees. My eyes landed on his ass. He needed to always wear Wranglers. They showed his sculpted butt. The strength of his walk with the way his legs slightly bowed really did it for me.

Of course, I had no choice but to follow. I made a pit stop by the trunk, grabbing my bag of essentials and quickly sprayed my legs with the bug repellent. Hopefully its power included keeping spiders away. I hated those things.

He looked back at me before stepping into the trees. I wished he had waited for me. But again, I was destined to follow wherever he led and started for the trail. Three steps in and I was surrounded by utter darkness. I needed time for my eyes to adjust. The exact amount of time for a creature to grab me and eat me up.

Where did I go?

Where did he go?

I tried to listen for a sound to indicate a direction, but heard nothing, and started forward. At some point I had to reach the middle.

An eerie vibe of the shadowless darkness sent a shiver down my spine.

New next rule in our relationship, Beau was never to leave me to my own devices when we were outdoors.

"Boo!" Beau suddenly, and loudly, dropped down in front of me.

I dropped everything I held and stumbled backward, trying to get away from the threat. If I managed to stay on my feet, I'd run for it. Instead of sprinting away, I screamed a high-pitched sound, kicking and punching while trying to stay on my feet. It wasn't easy or graceful.

Luckily, his loud cackle penetrated my very serious flight instinct. He had truly frightened me.

With eyes as big as saucers, I bent to catch my breath. I needed a minute and sent a prayer of thanks for not wetting my pants.

Beau had other plans and reached for my bicep to keep me upright, creating a whole different layer of problems to my current emotional breakdown. His touch caused desire to ripple over me in waves. My heart continued to thump wildly, my breath pumped in and out. I hoped I didn't hyperventilate.

I must have appeared as frantic as I felt because Beau barked with laughter.

"I'm sorry." His over-the-top humor implied something altogether different.

My racing heart thumped violently against my rib cage. "You're not sorry at all," I shot my accusation back with all the venom I could muster—it wasn't much.

"I am, but your face is totally freaked out. I didn't think I'd really scare you." He bent to pick up my bag. Everything had fallen out, making him stuff the blanket, bottles of water, and bug spray haphazardly inside.

He grabbed my arm again and led me through the trees like an expert.

"In the future, let's keep the scaring inside, like in a haunted house, or daylight, or not at all."

"Got it." I didn't think he did with the happy laughter bubbling out when he agreed.

A few steps later, we walked into an enchanting, soul-filling moonlit stretch of green grass about twenty feet wide. Somehow the dark night faded, and the moon lit the center in a soft glow.

"Does everyone know about this place?" I asked, turning a full circle, taking it all in. The scary forest transformed into a captivating fairy tale where peace and harmony hung out freely, waiting for us to arrive.

"Everyone who lives around here does, I guess. The guy who owns the property from where my grandparents live, all the way the other direction, wants to keep it in its natural state. Even if he builds a house, he's leaving all this alone," he explained and flipped out the blanket in the center of the clearing. It floated to the ground as Beau dropped down too, tossing the other items aside.

"So this is all private land?" I asked, closing the distance between me and Beau.

"Yeah. The owner lets the local Boy Scouts clubs camp out here." He patted the blanket beside him. "Come lay down and look up at the stars with me. You can see so much better here than in the city." Regretfully, he took his gaze from mine as he pointed up to the sky. "You know what that cluster is?"

Ah, the perfect invitation. I followed him down, laying inches away, eyeing which constellation he tried to draw my attention to. "Scorpius? I like mythology."

"I was testin' you," he said and steered me toward another cluster. "What's that one?"

I rolled my eyes, turning toward him. "The Big Dipper. I think I learned about the dippers in first grade."

He gave a quiet chuckle and searched the sky. "How about that one?"

Again, I followed his pointing finger.

"Did you forget I'm smart?" I asked and turned my face back to his. "It's Big Bear that encompasses the Big Dipper. Duh."

He didn't try again. We stared at each other for several long seconds.

"I like looking at you."

"You say things like that all the time," he muttered.

"Does it bother you?"

"No," Beau said quickly then changed his answer. "Maybe. I don't understand talkin' so freely. I need to get better at it, I guess."

I gave another ridiculous roll of my eyes for dramatic effect. "Oh, right. You have to be used to people telling you how hot you are. Your body's like a solid muscle..."

Beau laughed at me and turned away to stare up at the sky. "No one's told me I'm good lookin'. I had a friend back home that developed a crush on me, but she just kept sayin' she'd be my arm candy when I went to the NFL, and she wanted to spend all my money."

I barked right out loud. Who said things like they plan to spend all of someone else's money?

"Let's share rosters," I said. Beau's head whipped toward mine. If I gauged the confusion on his face, he'd been very serious when he said he wasn't ready to take the next natural steps by being my boyfriend. I didn't let it go. "What? It seems like an important relationship question."

"How many people have you been with?" Beau blurted.

"Like penetration?" The expression on his brow turned intense and vulnerable.

"Yeah, I guess."

"Zero. I told you that last night. I was seeing if you paid attention." The instant relief of Beau rolling his shoulders, pushing away the tension said it all, in my opinion. I decided having sex was most likely a big decision, that neither of us would go at willy-nilly. "I've kissed a few guys. My first time was about four years ago when I played spin the bottle at a school party. I've done some heavy...petting, I guess that's what I'd call it. It was a guy who came home from college last year during Christmas break."

"Do you see yourself as a top or a bottom?" he asked.

"Versatile all the way." With all certainty, I wanted to go both ways.

"Why didn't you do it with the Christmas dude?"

"I don't know. I feel like the first time needs to be special. If I'm going to remember it for the rest of my life, I at least want him to be someone I care about," I said, trying to explain my reasons without sounding like a dork. "Is there really no one else for you? No girls in your past I should know about?"

"I've done nothin'. I've known about my twisted ways since I was young. It's only in the last couple of years that it became a problem. I've been freaked out about the repercussions. It's made me close up, puttin' space between me and my life. Then you came along and changed everything."

"Yeah, that same connection is what drove me back here last night. Can I kiss you?" I asked.

Beau's gaze skidded to mine again. The passion in the stare was palpable. His chest rose and fell steadily, letting me know how much he cared. He answered my question with action. It was funny to think he kept himself hidden, because I could read him like a book.

Boldly, or at least it felt that way, I turned to my side to place a hand over his heart. His gaze stayed fixed on me. "We can wait. I'm just really, really, into you. I didn't even know I was unsettled in my life until you came barreling in, changing everything for me."

His palm rested on top of mine, his fingers circling until he held my hand. I liked it a lot. This was a hand I was determined to hold many times over. The tingles were back in full force, making me scoot over to lean in. His actions seemed invitation enough, but he also had me doing all the initiating.

Seconds before my lips landed on his, I took a deep breath in, taking Beau's scent into my soul. He smelled the same as before. Outdoors... No, that wasn't right. I couldn't put into words what the fragrance was, except it mixed with mine and became one.

I closed my eyes and touched my lips to his. Fireworks exploded behind my lids. The sultry evening turned red hot in all the right ways. His hand held mine. His other extended around my back, keeping me close.

When the tip of his tongue poked out, caressing over mine, my life was made perfect, and that was before his lips parted, letting me inside. The beauty of our surroundings added to the delicious warmth seeping over me. My entire body tensed and strained.

I was lost to Beau Brooks.

13: The Mom
Beau

My mind went numb, coasting on the feels as instinct took over. The small amount of control I had was lost when he swiped his tongue fully inside my mouth. The sexy, competent move came with a parting of my lips, doing a deep dive into the farthest reaches of my mouth.

My cock punched against my jeans, wanting desperately to be involved.

Jesus, the way my body responded created chaos inside me. My nipples hardened, my belly quivered, and all I wanted to do was wrap myself around this guy.

I found what I was missing in a big, big way. Desire, compassion, and being wanted was such an overwhelming turn-on.

A primal tug bonded me tighter to Dash.

All I knew for certain was I never wanted this to end. The pain and suffering of my life faded, leaving behind the indentation of a nice size, hard as hell cock, pressing into my thigh.

He wanted me as badly as I wanted him.

Tingles shot through me as Dash moved, coming down partially on top of me. His elbow held him in place on one side. His other hand, still in mine, began to caress across my chest, skimming one of my nipples on its path down my side. I was forced to let go as he crawled further on top of me and shoved his hand under my shoulder, to help stay right there. All the while, the hot, sensory-destroying kiss continued.

There were no awkward moments. I followed his lead, turning my mouth the same direction he went. We were on fire as the kiss turned carnal. His tongue danced against mine in a clash of tongue and teeth. My cock never let me forget it was there, needing more than I was giving.

That physical need fueled me to wrap my arms completely around him, fusing our mouths together.

I slowly rolled him to his back, following where he landed. I pushed a knee between his thighs, never wanting to lose the feel of the evidence of his desire. His arms wrapped around me, his hands gripping my shoulders, keeping me flush against him, right where I wanted to be.

The only problem I had was the pesky need to breathe. My head fought the urge. I'd been trained to hold my breath, I could last awhile, but it seemed my time was up. I didn't want to let go. Never. In this moment, I could die happy from a lack of oxygen, if only my body's natural instinct for air didn't overpower me. As I detached from the kiss, sucking in gulps of air, his hips drove upward, arching hard against me.

I stared down at him, taking it all in. In his current state, he was majestic. A hooded brow, plump, fleshy lips swollen from my kiss, his hair in disarray from my touch.

"I'm sorry," he whispered as his hips rolled against my thigh again. As I watched him, I knew sex was where we were headed. I had a lot to figure out first, but when the time came, we'd make love because I'd been swept completely off my feet.

"Don't be sorry," I said quietly, my hand reaching for the top of his head. My fingers slid into the silky strands. My current quest was to log every touch and feel into my memory, so when I drew this moment forward in my mind, I'd have the full experience again.

"I'll get a hold of it," he whispered, at the same time his hips did a far less forceful thrust. "I'm sorry. I'm very attracted to you."

We needed to slow this way down. I leaned in to place a simple chaste kiss on his lips.

Dash opened, wanting to take it deeper, but I held back. Self-doubt sent a small niggle skirting around my stupid brain, reminding me how teenage guys really were. Scott would do and say anything to get laid, and that was fine I guessed. I only needed to wait until I was ready. After this kiss, it wouldn't be long. I leaned farther back even as his strong arms and hands held me tightly against him.

"Don't leave. Let me hold you. I can't get my arms to let you go," Dash said.

Breaking free wasn't a problem, but I liked the idea of staying as close as possible for as long as I could.

"I'm way too into you too," I said again—like every other time we were together.

Dash's hands slid over my shoulders into my hair, sifting through the longer strands at the base of my neck before pushing the blunt tips of his fingernails up over my scalp. It felt mesmerizingly good. His voice was deep and husky as he continued.

"You know I like to talk. And I like to define things. Understand what's happening." I absolutely knew if given a chance, he could handle the heavy lifting of all the conversations, twenty-four seven. He was good at it too. "You have no idea how into you I am. I'm planning our entire lives together. You're going to my prom then I'm going to yours. You'll go to my college where we'll live together until you graduate and I finish law school. I want to do good in the world, and I feel like you feel the same way. We'll have a commitment ceremony, but for the record, my heart's already done that. We'll travel, have children if you want..."

I'd never thought of a full life in that way. Dash laughed at my expression. The shock in my mind had to have reached my face.

"I'm scaring you. I can see it in your eyes, and I don't mean to. I only wanted you to know that you're truly not alone in what's happening to us. Since the moment I set my eyes on you, you're all I've thought about. I don't understand what's going on with me and you but saying it out loud makes it easier to cope. I feel like we knew one another before we ever met. Like you're supposed to be with me."

He laughed again, probably due to the heated flush on my face.

"I've said too much. I'm sorry. I'm not like this at all. People tell me I'm too practical. My feet are planted too firmly on the ground. Imagine their surprise about me saying we have a celestial connection."

"I don't disagree, but I'm more skeptical, I guess, and decided to take this one hour at a time," I said, feeling the silence building inside me, keeping me from saying more, I needed time to think.

"Kiss me. Curl my toes again. You can be the guide to where we go from here. I promise, I don't need more than you're willing to give." Dash brought his hand forward, sweeping the hair off my forehead, but the unkempt style had it falling right back again.

"I'll cut it," I murmured.

He stared at me, seemingly taking in every part of my face.

"Don't change a thing. You're perfect." Dash lifted his head, his lips parting as he sought mine. I met him halfway for another soul-searing kiss.

One week later

"Brooks." I released my hand off the pressure washer lever, instantly stopping the spray, and glanced over my shoulder to my new boss, Guy. His gruff, loud voice held authority, and carried all the way to Mexico, I was certain. "Finish what you're doin' then mop the patio then take off. I'll log your hours in the mornin'."

"Got it," I hollered back, lifting a thumbs-up high in the air just in case he couldn't hear me.

He didn't pay any attention to my response as he locked the back door to the charter boat office. I waited to see if he had more to say. Sometimes his directive came in two barked sections, minutes apart.

As Guy fisted his keys in his palm, he pointed a finger at Dash who hung out in his normal spot, sitting on a ledge at the end of a retail leasing complex, facing me. "Your old man doesn't need to know I'm leavin' early."

This was a regular conversation between the two of them. Dash grinned from his perch on the property's edge, his feet dangling, his arms hanging over the bottom rail. "Got it." He gave his own thumbs-up to drive his oath home.

Guy checking out before the end of his shift was a daily occurrence. He hadn't been caught yet, which probably meant it didn't matter to anyone in charge.

As expected, Guy finally remembered he had more to say and pivoted around, walking closer to me. "We're shorthanded on the booked charters next week. You'd have to be here by five in the mornin' and stick around to do your afternoon duties."

I wasn't a hundred percent sure, but I felt like there was a question in there. "Yeah, I can do it," I said, beaming. I'd be out in the ocean, helping people fish, or probably just doing work no one else wanted to do, but still a dream come true.

"Will he be paid overtime?" Dash called out, inserting himself as my acting manager.

I shrugged at Guy's burst of irritation as he swung his head toward Dash. "Yeah, I guess so now. And this is between me and my employee. Stay out of our business."

Dash nodded approvingly and shot out his own thumbs-up. When Guy turned his exasperation back at me, he whispered loudly. Dash had to have heard. "Don't you have any less annoyin' friends?"

I don't know why the question tickled me so much. Maybe due to this perpetual happiness following me everywhere I went. I snickered because the answer to his question was *no*, I didn't. Dash and I spent all our free time together, and I wasn't looking to change my circle of friends.

"He's just lookin' out for me," I finally answered pretty lamely and did my best to hide my joy. Guy rolled his eyes then pivoted on the heel of his old work boot. A perfectly executed move for someone with a sizable beer belly that made him as tall as he was wide.

"We'll need to cap your time at thirty-five hours next week. You're gonna work more than that, but I'll catch up the next week. No one needs to know you're workin' that much."

"Sure, it's not a problem. Thanks for the work." I started the sprayer back again.

Guy started for his truck with a carelessly given backhanded wave. Once he'd made it to the front parking lot, I finished the last section of the dock, keeping one eye on Guy's truck until he left. My hand lifted off the nozzle as my excited gaze flipped to Dash. "I'm makin' two hundred fifty dollars next week to fish."

"And maybe that same amount the next week," he piped in. "I'll keep up with your hours and make sure they pay you properly."

The idea of Dash managing Guy through the payroll process made my heart smile. The gruff, grumpy old man already had a distaste for office work. He was sure to be driven crazy by Dash watching over his shoulder.

"What's your schedule next week?" I called out, bringing the hose back up to the porch to finish cleaning there. Missing Dash might be the only downfall to fishing all day.

"Same schedule. Monday, Wednesday, Friday. I'll head over here when I see the boat come back in."

"Cool." Problem solved. Dash always had all the answers. I quickly lifted the nozzle and pressed, sending the high-power spray of water in his direction. I honestly lived to tease that guy. This round ensured a mess to his perfectly styled hair.

I got the normal reaction, a squeaky yell and a quick duck with nowhere to go. When I began cleaning the porch in earnest, my mind wandered to the idea of being paid to fish. Jeez, that'd be my best life. A more intriguing snapshot flitted around in my head. Dash with me on such a boat.

Maybe we should stick with my brand of fishing first. He was a little bit of a baby. Clearly he'd had a pampered life, but he was also weirdly grounded. He innately understood the heartbeat of the world and showed great compassion for everyone and everything. I didn't mind doing the odd little tasks like killing whatever bug threatened him...

A loud whistle pierced my scattered thoughts, and I glanced in Dash's direction. My hand lifted off the nozzle to better hear as he began to get to his feet. He pointed me toward the parking lot and started that direction. I instantly knew the car. My mom. Anxiety hit hard, showing the cracks in my happy place.

I absently dropped the hose to the pavement as I started in her direction. "It's my mom."

Dash's sure steps stumbled as he swung his head in my direction. "You sure? Not a potential client?"

"I'm sure." I kept going, lengthening my stride, trying to get to her before he did. I thought I might until he squared his shoulders and began walking with purpose as he ran his fingers through his hair. Like always, he held all the confidence in the world.

My mom pulled into a space, closer to him than me, letting the car idle as she opened the door and stepped out, looking all vice-principally in her pantsuit and small heels. She was pretty, at least all my friends back in Mobile thought so. They all talked about dating her which creeped me out.

"Hi, Mrs. Brooks. I'm Dasham. Beau calls me Dash," he said, boldly, jogging the few steps separating them. He stuck his hand out to shake hers. Man, he had manners game and didn't mess around. He appeared respectful and interested. My mom ate it up.

"Hi, Dash." She gave him her real smile, not the practiced one she reserved for her students and their parents. He didn't hesitate to give a genuine one back. "Call me Linda. I wanted to stop by and see where my son's spending all his time these days."

Most likely she meant with whom, instead of where, but tried to save me any possible embarrassment. I'd told her as much of the truth as I was willing to tell about my employment and my friendship with Dash, highlighting that he was the resort owner's son.

I kept going until I sidled up next to her side, also facing Dash just in case I needed to tackle him to the ground to offset anything contradictory he might say. My mom leaned in, like she always did, lifting on her tiptoes to place a kiss on my cheek.

"I wanted to see where you work, and I wanted to meet your new friend."

"That's him," I explained and pointed to Dash. "And that's the charter's office. I clean up after everyone. The boats are at the dock, I already went over them." I absently hooked a thumb toward the ocean as if the boats might be located somewhere else.

To her credit, she did glance in the directions I pointed, but Dash obviously held all her curiosity. "So you're the one everyone's talking about?" she asked, clearly paying attention to the local news.

"Sadly, I believe so." Dash's charming side roared to the forefront as his chin hit his chest. "The attention wasn't anything I encouraged but the hype's beginning to quiet down now. The girls aren't following me all over the resort like they used to. I think my fifteen minutes has come to an end."

"Well, that's too bad. Beau needs to meet someone new." She bumped her hip against the side of my body, happy with her tease. "Having a girlfriend..."

"Mom," I cut her off and rolled my eyes. When I knew she was watching me, I exaggeratedly mouthed the words I'm sorry to Dash.

"No, it's good," Dash said assuredly, winking at my mom. Who did that? Who executed a perfect, playful wink at fifteen years old? "My mom says those same things to me."

I doubted that.

"Where do you live when you're not here putting the fear of God into the locals?" my mom asked.

"Mom," I started only to have Dash shake me off again.

"In Southlake. It's a suburb north of Fort Worth," he answered, tucking his hands inside the front pockets of his walking shorts.

"I'm not as familiar with Texas as I should be. I need to get better." My mom wrapped an arm around my waist, knocking mine to place around her shoulders. It took a second, but I finally followed through.

"Texas is so big, it's hard to know what's where." Just like that, Dash had my mom eating out of his hand.

"There's more to why I'm here." She glanced up at me, finally, and lifted a hand to shade her sunglass-covered eyes from the bright angle of the sun. "I also come with news. I found a house and put in an offer. I wanted you to see it first, but I had to act fast. It's close to my school. A pretty three-bedroom cottage-style home. A coworker's grandmother is selling."

"When would we move?" I didn't care in the least about seeing it. My concern was the at least twenty-minute drive from the beach to her high school. I didn't think Sea Springs had a transit system. It'd take forever to get back and forth on my bike.

"We have to wait until right before school starts. They need to move her into a facility then move her belongings out. The homes around there get snatched up quickly. I'll take you to see it as soon as you have time off from your job," she said excitedly.

Her happiness made me happy. Since I was currently in a day-by-day existence, I let the worry go. Let it work out like it's supposed to. I'd figure it out.

"Who was the coworker?"

When she met me with silence, I gave her a funky side-eye. The expression she gave had me instantly knowing the deal. "Mom. That part of my life's over. I don't want to play football anymore. I'm out of shape. I haven't conditioned..."

Dash sucked in a sudden breath, then began coughing and laughing at the same time.

"I am out of shape. And football's all anyone talks about with me. It's why I spend so much time over here."

I was on a long-winded, rambling denial, and I just stopped speaking, shaking my head *no*.

"Son, it's not about you." At her statement, I gave her my best skeptical look. "He's the varsity baseball coach. He's invited me to dinner on Friday night, and I'd like you to be home to meet him."

Wait. What? My mom had a date with a dude?

She was barely two weeks shy of being divorced.

"Mom. It's gettin' weirder."

"Put the *g* on the end of your words, son." Her brow lifted at me with her incessant reminder.

"Getting," I repeated properly, trying my best to shake off the creepiness in the conversational turn. Of course, she wasn't ready to date. She needed to concentrate on being my mom first before finding her way back into the world. Not dating some sex-crazed, ego-maniac coach. Heck, that was what got us to Sea Springs here in the first place. Her lousy taste in men.

I started walking backward toward the dock, waving her off. We'd certainly talk about this later. "I gotta finish up. We'll talk later?"

Dash gave me a questioning glance, clearly not ready to let this time with my mom go.

"Dash, it was very nice to meet you. Made better now that Beau has a friend who can speak in complete sentences. I believe that's a first in my boy's circle of friends." Some might call what she said a joke, but it wasn't.

"It's nice to meet you, Mrs. Brooks," Dash said.

My mom moved backward a couple of steps. "The three of us need to have dinner soon. My treat. And please call me Linda. Mrs. Brooks is my ex mother-in-law. She wasn't a pleasant person."

He rocked on his feet. "It's a respect thing so we'll have to see how it goes. Beau's a great guy, the best friend I've ever had. Now I see where he gets it from."

Her smile brightened. She pointed to Dash as she looked at me. "Keep him around."

Oh, yeah, exactly what I intended to do. I nodded and waved when she dropped into the front seat and shut the door. My thumb hooked over my shoulder as I stared openly at Dash. "I'm gonna put everything away."

He stayed rooted where he stood, waving as my mom backed out of the spot and started out of the parking lot. When she left, he slowly turned, looking lost in thought as he walked back to his perch on the side of the building. "Take your time. I'm great. I think she liked me."

14: The Baby Back Ribs
Dash

One week later

The idea of quiet relaxation while being in the wide-open wilderness always intrigued me. Mainly due to my recent discovery that all the things that wanted to bite me, lived freely outside, mainly in the dark. Yet, here I was again.

I stared at Beau's grandparents house. It was eerily quiet. The only lights on were on the first floor. If they had guests staying in the B&B, it was hard to tell. An inkling of guilt always hit me when I had time to just stare at the houses in the neighborhood. I unwittingly played a part in the downfall of this community. It went against everything I believed in, but I didn't have a say in any of it.

The front door opened at the same time my cell phone rang. I reached for the phone while watching Chae walk down the front porch steps. What I assumed was Beau's grandmother followed her down. I saw where his mom, and then Beau, got their looks. She was tall, thin, and didn't look her age.

I wasn't sure what to do. Rationally, I understood, if I could see them, they had to be able to see me. Beau's worrisome feelings had me ducking my head to keep unwanted eyes off me. "Are you there?"

Phone call. Joy. Right. "I am," I said quietly as if someone might hear me.

"Dasham, where's my car?" Her tone held zero warmth and was full of accusation as if I was nothing more than a common criminal.

And did she really not know the answer to her question? Then how did I respond? Surely not with the truth, especially if she was with our family.

"Can you just cover for me? I've got a week until my birthday then I can drive my own car." Seemed reasonable. Definitely the truth. If I wasn't in such an awkward position, I'd pat myself on the back.

"I need my car to go see Donny," she hissed angrily.

"Then take your brother's car, or your dad's. They won't notice."

"If I get caught, you're going down with me."

"That's fine," I said and lifted my head enough to see Chae looking in the direction of my car. Beau's grandmother turned, following Chae's interest.

Oh hell, please don't let them start toward my me. Please.

"I'm done, Dasham. This is the last time. Take someone else's car from here on out." Oh yeah, right. I'd never do that. She was the rebel, not me.

"All right," I said, knowing I lied. At the same moment, Chae started toward my car. Beau's grandmother waved goodbye before heading back up her steps, inside the house.

"You're speaking so weird, like in code, or worse, like you belong here. Pretty soon you're gonna start saying, 'ain't' and 'y'all' and 'fixin''."

We were done. I ended the call. As funny as a strong southern accent was, Beau spoke that way. I found it charming and delightful.

As Chae came closer, I lifted in my seat. We stared at one another. Something akin to speculation locked on her face. Hmm. Her purposeful stride never stopped until she reached my car. Out of habit, I lifted a finger to disable the overhead lights then unlocked the doors—because who sat in the wilderness with their doors unlocked?

She dropped down in the seat as if I'd invited her.

"You need to know that the neighborhood's noticin' you here every night. They're startin' to figure out that it's you, Dasham Richmond. They're questionin' what's goin' on. What's your angle? They're so consumed with stoppin' the expansion that they haven't figured out you're here only for Beau. Which is weird, because everyone outside of this neighborhood is questionin' how tight you two are."

I weighed her words, letting them filter through my mind. "How do you feel about Beau and I spending time together?"

"Y'all are safe with me. I figured it out the night of the party—you had to know I did," Chae said and turned in the seat to face me. I started to ask why, but she lifted a hand to stop me. She had more to say. "You had three of the prettiest girls from our high school surroundin' you, and you weren't interested at all."

The protective juices I had for Beau reared forward. I instantly built a claim to rebuke her notice. Her hand extended again, this time closer to my face.

"Let me finish. Beau's the same way as you. In all these years, he's never paired off with anyone. Not even a childhood girlfriend. I think he can hide pretty well because all anyone thinks about him is his athleticism. What I see is a scared guy. His dad's an ass, but that's not it. He's always been that way. When Beau was a kid, we all hung out all the time. We'd leave first thing in the morning and not be back before nightfall. His dad rarely came here with them. When he left the party with you, I knew for sure."

Her explanation was like a blow to my psyche. I'd tried hard to come off as a buddy to Beau. Something close to an instant camaraderie and rapport with him. But she was right, we were together every free minute we had. I quickly processed my thoughts, and my only worry was with Beau. Would he pull away to keep his pretense in place?

Chae's door jerked open, startling me. Anxiety pumped through my veins, because I was still a big baby about being parked on such a deserted road, fearing the inevitable moment the bogeyman came. My thoughts zipped over me in rapid-fire succession, trying to rapidly plan my escape.

"It's Beau," Chae said, all breathy from her own fear.

Normally, if Beau was in the vicinity, I sensed him but not that time.

He bent to look inside the car. Clearly, based on expression, he was as uncomfortable and unsure. "What's goin' on?"

His worried stare went to Chae. "Get in the backseat. You're lettin' the mosquito's in." Her forceful snap put Beau into action. Within seconds, he shut the back door and popped his head through the center console.

I lifted the steering wheel to get more room to adjust in my seat. A consuming need had me staring at him. Hopefully, my words and body language conveyed support as he learned our latest obstacles.

"Chae knows, but she's known from the beginning. It's why she introduced us…" I explained into the quiet inside the car.

"How did you know?" he asked, interrupting me.

"He's got more to say. Let him finish then I'll answer anything you want to know." Chae hadn't turned to look at Beau, instead adjusting her visor mirror to better see him.

"Chae seems intuitive. She knows you well and your lack of engagement with the opposite sex put it all together after I showed interest at the party."

Beau nodded. His brow wrinkled as he sorted through what I said.

"But that's not the concern. The neighborhood has noticed me parked here. Apparently, they've connected the car to a Richmond. She thought we should know. Also, the townspeople say we've gotten close quickly."

Chae piped into add, "They're noticin' y'all together all the time," she explained. "I don't know if you've heard but the local's group is filing bankruptcy. Many individuals are too. Your grandmother told me tonight that she had to let me go because she and your paw are goin' to go to an attorney tomorrow to look at their options."

In my world, secrets were held close. Down here, everybody told all their life stories to anyone who listened, meaning gossip and speculation would only thrive.

"I'm sorry," I said, my focus still on Beau.

"We're for sure movin' in that house she wants at the end of the summer. You'll be back in Southlake by then," he said to me. "With the way everyone around here thinks they're losing everything, my mom made sure she had extra space for Nana and Paw. I can't imagine any gossip about me and you can penetrate their worry," Beau said, then lifted his stare toward Chae's mirror. "Don't repeat that."

"What did you think about the house and the guy?" I asked about the reason for Beau's late arrival. My guy had stressed about meeting his mom's new potential boyfriend. I called him a boyfriend because she spent some part of every day with him, like I did with Beau. But he insisted the guy be called Coach, who was only a friend.

My overprotective bear.

"It's hard to tell about the house. The woman who lives there has way too much stuff for me to see my mom's vision, but it's close to school so I can walk. The guy tried his best to be nice to me which seems all right. Never asked me about football. But they seriously need to take it slow. She's been through a lot."

"Was he handsome? Your mom's pretty. She needs a nice-lookin' guy to be nice to her," Chae added, finally turning her head as far as she could to see Beau's response. "She's just the best and wants more kids. She's young enough..."

"What? She doesn't want more kids. I'm fifteen years old. That'd be weird to have a little brother. Or worse, a sister. I know what guys think. No."

Chae and I both exchanged a smile at his possessiveness before she settled back in her seat.

"I came here early because I mis..." I let the words trail off, not finishing the sentence. The constant devotion tumbling from my lips might embarrass Beau in front of Chae, making me clamp my mouth closed.

"They kept talkin' at dinner. They wouldn't stop. And I had no reception on my phone."

"Did you play *Ninja Assault*?" Chae asked, knowing something about Beau that I didn't. "He's a beast at the game. He's been playin' for a while."

"I had to walk across the street to CC's Pizza to find the game. All these new restaurants comin' in are too fancy to have an arcade area," he explained.

"Did you get top score?" I asked, already knowing the answer in my heart. Being with Beau meant I'd never win anything else for the rest of my life.

"Absolutely, he did, and I wasn't even there," Chae clapped out before Beau could answer.

My love only nodded. Maybe his chest swelled with pride from the win.

"The high score was low. It wasn't hard," he said, downplaying his achievement. I fought my grin. My strong competitor.

"So how are you with everything?" I asked.

"I don't know, but not bad," he said, his fingers now held his attention as he fiddled with them. "I've been a private person for a long time, but I'm pullin' out of it."

If I interpreted his look accurately—his gaze said what Beau never did—I was his reason. Too bad Chae was there, or I'd jump in the backseat and make out with him for the next five hours with all the love and hope I saw in his eyes.

"So you have money?" she asked me.

"Yeah, I guess." I hedged, worried about her direction. I didn't have enough to save Sea Springs from financial ruin...

"There's a new Chili's in town. Wanna take me and Beau?" she waggled her brows, talking as if Beau and her were in on the secret. "They stay open until two so we have hours until they close."

Okay, that sounded fun. It'd mess with my make-out time, but we'd be out in the world with Chae as our buffer.

"You in," I asked Beau.

"Yeah, let me text my mom," he said, reaching in his back pocket for his phone. "To see if I can stay out longer."

"I'm in too." I sat straight in my seat and started the ignition.

The small circle of people who knew about Beau had grown by one. A step in the right direction by my estimation.

15: The Boat

Beau

In that minute, life was as right as rain as it could get. I walked along a path at Mud River's edge, trying to balance myself along the rough terrain. Dash walked step by step behind me, complaining nonstop about every second of the trek we made. My guy was a city boy through and through.

"I'm carryin' all the gear. Just walk in my steps, or stay here, I'll come carry you on my back..."

"Ha. You're so funny. Why do we have to come out here to fish? I don't think I even like fishing. It seems really boring," Dash complained irritably.

"Stop," I said, and did that very thing, glaring at him over my shoulder. He came to a sudden halt too. His foot slipping off the rock I stood on, landing straight into the river. "It's the opposite of boring."

"I got my foot wet. How long is it gonna take to dry?" His frustrated gaze bounced between the shoe and my face then back down at the shoe again. His index finger pointed me in that direction.

My laughter rang loud. "Fishin' isn't boring. It's one of the things I wanna do when I grow up." Wet shoes were just part of the fun. I started forward again. We had about twenty feet to go to reach my secret fishing hole. "Fishin's relaxin' in a way I can't explain. The most relaxed I've ever been."

"I bet I could come up with a thing or two more relaxing," he quipped, and I completely ignored him.

"A person unplugs around the water. It's quiet and peaceful. No judgment or anger, just calm. When a fish takes your bait, you're launched into immediate exhilaration as you try to hook the fish and reel it in without it getting away. I love everything about it. I wanna get some money saved then come back down here and figure out how to start a charter service. Well, I guess maybe not down here now," I said, teasing Dash about the resort. "Somewhere that still has mom and pops."

At the end of the rocks, I leaped to a patch of dirt, mixed with sand. My quiet place.

"I wanna be a UPS driver until I save enough money to buy a deep-sea boat. Ever heard of anyone wantin' to do that for a livin'?"

I set the tackle box down and the poles against it. By the time I turned, Dash had gone past me toward the short, abandoned boat dock, with a row-style canoe tied to the end. "Does that work?"

"Work like rows itself? No. Floats? Seems like it."

I believe he saw the humor in my answer, but instead of a silly reply in return, Dash gave his charming, maybe edged with hints of wickedness, smile. Oh man, that smile sent my toes curling.

"To answer your question, no, I've never heard of anyone ever wanting to be a delivery driver."

"You're not hangin' out with a good crowd then," I said, sauntering over to him.

"I'm not?"

"Nope. Doesn't seem like it. In my world, that's a great job. UPS is union." He immediately shook his head.

"The world might swallow my father up whole if he heard your excitement." Dash slung the backpack over his shoulder. He had a way of easily unzipping it without placing it on the ground, probably because he used it so much. As expected, he pulled out a towel that he called a blanket and a packet of bug repellent wipes. Two water bottles had to be in there. He always toted them around, but we never drank from them. "Wanna try the boat first?"

"What? No. I have to show you how to fish first. It's harder to balance and learn on the boat. It's not really a fishing boat," I explained, and he still paused before dropping the towel down.

"But the boat seems more romantic," he said and hooked a thumb over his shoulder.

Ah, I was learning my guy too well. Maybe two weeks of spending every day together taught me a thing or two. I let my eyes roll and dropped down to the tackle box, flipping the clips up. "You're just tryin' to make out. It's all you ever wanna do with me. I'm a piece of meat to you."

Dash barked out a harsh sound, maybe a laugh, but he didn't deny it.

Silence held between us as I pulled out the small tub of worms from my tackle box that I'd dug up this morning. We were going preschool learning today. Dash was getting a bobber. I decided on that approach because he was only here for me. Everything we did was for me, keeping me hidden away and safe from prying eyes. And secondly, I really liked the idea of making out with him too. If I gave in now, we'd be inside that boat, like I planned, floating around until we hit the ocean before we resurfaced.

The warmth that was all Dash spread through me, hugging my heart.

"You're not listening to me," he said. Not only was I not listening, I hadn't even heard his approach. His tennis shoe covered feet came into my peripheral vision. I bent my head as far as it could go and still barely saw his face.

"You don't know that," I quipped. Man, my joking game was on point. I dipped my gaze, using my index finger to retrieve a single worm.

"Then what did I say?"

Of course, the obvious question to my question. Instead of answering, I did something to ensure Dash's horror as I began setting a portion of the worm on the hook. From splitting it in half to threading it around the hook, Dash set off in a stream of *ewws* and *disgustings*.

"Did I tell you that I'm the Mobile County skipping rock champion two years running?"

"No. That's why you're always picking up rocks and throwing them."

"Yep, I'll thread the hook until you're ready to try..." I said. Dash took a giant step away.

"I'll watch you fish," he shot back and took a couple more steps backward.

"No. You'll like it. I promise," I said and followed him. "Put the stuff down. We'll use it on the boat. Come try." When he was still hesitant, I decided to show him with a first cast. I threw the line, letting it go until it landed in the water about where I wanted it to.

The bobber sank then popped out of the water. About a minute later, the angler began to move. Since I was at one with every fishing pole ever created, I knew the feel and quickly jerked the rod backward, setting the hook. I had it and began to reel the fish in. The excitement drew Dash to stand right beside me.

"Get the net." I didn't really need it, but I wanted his involvement. Strangely, he stayed quiet and was back in a second. "Here, you take the rod. It feels like a nice size."

He did, holding the rod in a death grip.

"It's probably a cat. Be careful with your line. There's a balance you have to find, you need enough drag but not..." The fish jumped out of the water, showing its size. Dash gave a holler in excitement. I took a backseat and let him go. He had it from there.

"Don't you lie to me," he teased. "This boat's awfully clean to be abandoned here like this. Know anything about that?"

My grin grew bigger, yeah, I knew plenty about it. My hand trailed under the hem of Dash's shirt, giving my fingertips the skin on skin contact they craved. How we'd managed to stretch out over the bottom of a handmade canoe, made about forty years ago, spoke more toward our willingness to be on top of each other than anything else.

"We're just lucky I guess." For me, I lay with my face toward the sun, my other arm tucked under my head, where my wadded-up T-shirt was too. A vintage AM radio played quietly from an old local country music station. The twang relaxing as the boat gently rocked.

"Really?" Dash laid at an angle on the side of my body, his cheek on my chest, a knee positioned between my parted legs. His thigh casually brushed against my hard as heck length. I no longer even attempted to hide my desire. I'm not sure he ever did. But we hadn't gotten much past a hot and heavy make out session.

I lost the question he asked when his fingertip lightly caressed my nipple. Dang, he made it so sensitive. The bud tightened with tingles of desire shooting from my nipple all across my body.

"I'll take your silence as an acceptance of my discovery."

"Mmm," I said and closed my eyes. The visions of Dash were right there waiting. I gave a small smile remembering his excitement of reeling in one fish after another. And his frustration when I'd let them go back in the river. Whether he liked it or not, my guy was a natural fisherman to his core.

"I like when you smile like that. I like to think you're thinking of me," Dash murmured. I dropped my chin and cracked my lids to see him staring down at me. He rose enough to place a series of small kisses on my lips. The boat rocked at the disruption of our balance. I didn't care in the least, but he did. He lifted and stayed still until it stopped moving.

"We're good. We're evenly spaced. Kiss me again." He didn't do that, but the hand that had played with my nipple caressed down my chest and over my tummy. It slipped under the waistband of my cargo shorts. Not the first time his fingertips had touched me, but my body gave the same over-the-top reaction as every other time. He skimmed my tip, massaging there in small, circular strokes, spreading the leaking bit over me.

Even though I'd denied wanting to take our relationship to the next level, claiming we needed more time, I was truly ready.

"Is that for me?" Dash whispered and pushed his hand lower. That was new. It felt too good, better than anything I was able to do on my own. My body bowed as my eyes rolled into the back of my head. He lifted above me, pressing his lips against mine. "Do you trust me?"

How could I retain anything asked when the heel of his palm used pressure, rising and falling over me? He used both knees to spread my legs apart as the tip of his tongue lavished the shell of my ear before pushing inside. The quiet whisper was almost my undoing. "I love you. You have to know."

His hand gripped my length with purpose in every tug. My eyes opened, my head tilted, my gaze searching his. The words he spoke were etched on his face with certainty and strength.

My heart thumped wildly against the knowledge that he plotted every moment we were together, making sure it was special until he got us right here together. I gave small shallow puffs, my mind reeling with the pleasure below.

"I love you too. I have since...you know."

"Me too." Dash moved carefully between my thighs, most certainly trying to keep balance. "My birthday's in a few days. I want us to make love. For that to be my birthday present from you." He deftly shoved his shorts down past his butt, springing himself free. My hips pumped back and forth while he unzipped my shorts and pushed my underwear low. Seconds later, he had us in his fist, jacking us off together.

Oh, Jesus. I was gay. I was so gloriously gay. My breath panted, and my vision blurred. The moment had me dropping my head backward, imprinting the size and shape of his cock, down to the lines and veins running over it, into the deepest recesses of my mind. I'd never seen anything so beautiful in my life.

"You and me. In my room at the resort. I'll slip you in," he said, all breathy and husky. "Say yes."

He pumped his fists up and down like a pro. The friction spoke of decadence and wickedness in the best possible way. My body coasted on pleasure, finding the freedom to love all the different layers of me.

From head to toe, every muscle in my body tightened and strained. I wasn't breathing. I had to breathe. But staving off my release took all my energy.

My hands reached low, needing to feel him. Dash guided me and clutched my hand in his, holding us tightly together. It all became too much. Survival took over. I exhaled in a whoosh and took a deep cleansing inhale. From there, my breath came in short shallow puffs. My world turned into vivid technicolor.

"Look at me," he instructed. My balls tingled, my hips arched forward and stayed locked there.

I had no hesitancy when I opened my eyes and reached out for Dash, cradling his face in my palm. Sweet agony mixed with the most delicious desire.

"These weeks have been the best of my life. I love you," Dash repeated.

How could he hold enough thought to form coherent sentences? "I can't hold it..."

As I looked down the length of my body, I watched our heads bound together, dripping. Dash's need was as great as my own. His lips came down on mine, his tongue pushing inside my mouth, taking what he wanted. My hips arched one last time before my release barreled forward. Oblivion surrounded me. A perfect moment in time. I found perfection. Sleep pushed me under.

16: The Reality

Dash

The muted voices from the living room, quietly filtering through the closed bedroom door, had me paying more attention there, then gathering my gear for my next shift at the swimming pool.

Quietly, I opened the door to a small slit and surveyed the scene. Based on the loud conversation, I'd thought others were there with my father. But he was alone, sitting at the dining room table in full business attire. He always overdressed for such a warm, sultry climate. How did any deodorant stand up against all those clothes?

The waitstaff worked quietly, setting breakfast at the other end of the table. A telephone was placed to one side of him. Tom, one of my father's senior advisors, spoke from the speaker. A set of blueprints was sprawled out before him. I stared at them, trying to remember if I'd been told of any new architectural plans. My curiosity got the best of me, and pushed open the door. Whatever discovery I had to solve needed to be done in the next ten minutes, since I was due downstairs.

My father noticed my entrance, causing him to pause mid-sentence and push his seat backward from the table. He stood, joy evident as he gestured me over. "Tom, Dasham's here."

As I surveyed the blueprints, I interjected, "I won't bother you. I'm headed down for my shift."

The hearty clap on my back and wide grin made me forget everything else as I openly stared at him. My father was rarely happy. I needed some sort of explanation. "Son, you've fulfilled your duty. Your efforts are greatly valued. We appreciate your service, but there's no need to continue with the charade. We've done it."

"Okay," I said, then paused. The confusion sparked a whirlwind of possibility. "Can we rewind? What duty?"

Both Tom and my father chuckled at me, most definitely not with me. My dad threw out a hand to shake mine. With hesitancy, I reciprocated the pumping grasp. I wasn't sure I'd ever been in a situation like this.

"What's happened?"

"The local group opposing the resort has officially declared bankruptcy. They're done. The picket line's down by half today. We anticipate dissolution by end of day."

Regret tumbled through me. The stories Beau and Chae had told of the area's past vitality and vibrance must have deeply affected me. What would become of those small businesses? They were bound to fail.

"What's that for?" I asked, nodding toward the blueprints. A dawning understanding twisted my gut. There was no one more ruthless than Tom. He certainly wouldn't give the locals time to absorb their losses and recover. He'd strike swiftly, like a cobra, injecting venom into the wound.

"Tell him, Tom." My father wrapped an arm around my shoulders, clasping me in place. Somehow, I'd landed in his private inner circle of confidants, and I wasn't entirely sure how I ended up there.

"We have the plans for the next phase in the resort expansion," Tom explained. "It's massive and ambitious. We're building a four-hundred-acre amusement park and a two-hundred-room extension to the resort. We've signed national restaurant chains and large retailers who have waited for this day."

If my father succeeded, other large hotel chains were destined to follow.

"Son, you've been an instrumental part in changing the reputation of the resort." My father deftly flipped the bound pages of the blueprints back to the second page.

"Is his silence a sign he's waiting for a financial payday? If so, he'd be a true Richmond," Tom said.

My father burst into an uproarious laughter as if that was my angle and gave me a hearty pat on the back.

The plans outlined the significant expansion of the resort, tripling the current size. I bent in to examine the blueprints more closely. There appeared to be a Las Vegas vibe, dazzling displays of lights and attractions, which seemed excessive for the tranquil beauty of Sea Springs. The proposed amusement park had multiple roller coasters, a big water park, a multi-screen theater, and a large digital arcade. It was a lot to take in.

"Will the city approve?" I asked.

"The governor's in our pocket, young Richmond. You have a lot to learn," Tom declared proudly.

"Where's all this land coming from?" As I spoke the words aloud, I knew the answer. It wouldn't be good. The land surrounding the resort was all owned by those who fought the resort in the first place. The expansion was destined to destroy them.

"With the bankruptcy, we can acquire the surrounding properties for a fraction of their value," my father explained as if teaching me a valuable lesson. My heart plummeted. A strong sense of empathy washed over me.

"I'm needed on another call," Tom said. "Well done, Dasham. Jack, we'll talk more tonight." The call ended abruptly.

Oh no.

"Go change your clothes. You're finished with that absurd job. I've had breakfast brought in. Change and join me."

My aversion to pretense and privilege had only grown stronger since my time in Sea Springs. After all the attaboys I'd received, perhaps it wasn't a coincidence my photo was taken. Maybe my father intentionally exposed me to all the publicity.

The thought of his cunning manipulation made my stomach twist. My actions had harmed Beau.

However, my father still had the ability to help Beau's family. I needed to be candid and ask for his help. Despite everything, my father wasn't a monster.

"They'll be shorthanded without me," I said absently, but also didn't argue for the integrity of working until they found someone to replace me.

"Your sister's removed you from the schedule," he said, while rolling the plans up. "Change quickly. They've prepared the leek and prosciutto quiche you enjoy. It's best served fresh."

All right. His clear joy had me taking a deep breath. I'd never seen him so happy.

I made quick work of changing out of my clothes, relieved to never have to wear my lifeguard's uniform again. Instead, I slipped back into my usual attire—polo shirt and plaid walking shorts. I searched out my deck shoes, sliding them on before having a quick check in the mirror.

The smells coming from the interior of the suite had me moving faster. The last few weeks had me suffering from acute insomnia, and an advanced eating disorder. I was never hungry and had a general lack of motivation for anything other than being with Beau. Yes, after yesterday's intimate encounter, I was now ravenous. My teenage guy appetite was back. I planned to eat the entire quiche by myself.

Besides, I needed fortification to be ready for the best birthday of my life. The sweetness of love overpowered everything. I was such a dork. Soon I'd be writing sonnets to Beau's inner beauty.

"What would you like to drink?" a server asked, drawing me from my mental rough draft of said sonnet. My father was on another call, phone to his ear, gesturing me to the seat at an angle to his.

"What're my choices?" I asked, glancing over the spread of food. My stomach growled a loud grumble.

"I believe we have everything available. If not, I can call down and have anything brought up," she explained.

"How about some pineapple, orange, carrot juice?" My favorite juice from my travels overseas. I took my seat, with the napkin barely in my lap, before reaching for the quiche trowel.

I ate a few bites of the quiche, staying silent until my father ended the call and I heard the door click close behind the waitstaff. We were alone. "Is Mom joining us?"

"No. She's planning our trip home. We're leaving after the Fourth of July festivities. We'll be home before nightfall." He mirrored the energy I had toward our meal, digging in as if he hadn't eaten in days.

"Can I keep the car?" I asked and went at my plate in the same way. With my mom not popping in at any moment, I didn't have anyone to correct my eating habits.

"You deserve it. You were a natural out there and handled the press like a pro. I'm proud of you." He reached for my hand, giving a soft squeeze.

The surprising caress caused me to accidentally swallow a bite the wrong way. I coughed and grabbed my glass of juice, my napkin in the other hand. Honestly, my father's ensuing chuckle seemed a bit out of place for such a potentially hazardous moment.

"I'm sure we'll have something for you to unwrap on your birthday. Don't think I've forgotten." He winked at me, reaching for his coffee.

I took a moment to compose myself and breathe properly again, then put forth my next request. "If everyone's going home, I'd like to stay until school starts."

"Why?" My father's brow wrinkled, his expression confused. "I heard Chandler's family's returning early too. Why stay here?"

With no time to contemplate the various scenarios I could use to answer, I placed my fork beside my plate while Beau's mesmerizing face occupied my thoughts. The time had come. Let the consequences fall as they may.

"Maybe Chandler can come visit me here, or not. But I have something I need to share with you. I've met someone special, who's become important to me."

Perhaps it was the seriousness of my tone or the way I relayed the information, but my father paused, placing his fork on the edge of the plate, watching me closely.

"I've noticed you've been preoccupied lately. Joy's mentioned you've been using her car." Curiosity set his brow as he reached for his coffee cup. "How did you two meet?"

"He's from here. His name's Beau, and I'm really into him." The truth of my words left me suddenly vulnerable. "I like him so much. He's different from anyone I've known. Intelligent, athletic, and very nice-looking. He captivates me. My world revolves around him. He's all I think about. He took me fishing. I told him you'd be shocked he got me out there." I kept my steady gaze on him as he nodded his understanding.

"You've lost weight. Eat before it gets cold."

"Dad, I'm all mixed up. I came out here starving and now I can't imagine putting another bite inside my mouth. He's so special to me. My stomach's in knots, but in a good way, I suppose. I know I'm not making any sense."

"I understand, son. Everyone goes through first love madn ess..." He sympathized in a trivial sort of way, causing me to interrupt him.

"I truly love him, and he loves me. I have our future mapped out..." My dad gave a condescending bark of laughter as he began to finish his breakfast with purpose.

"What's this Beau's story? Did he see you on the news?" My father raised a critical eyebrow. "Weren't you supposed to be encouraging the girls, not the guys?"

"We met organically," I assured him. "We've been seeing each other in secret. We both need to be discreet. His father's a football coach in his hometown in Mobile. He played football too but doesn't any longer. It sounds like his dad wouldn't accept him. Maybe he's abusive, I don't know. But he lives here now with his mom. His grandparents own a nearby B&B. He never believed in their fight. He's reasonable."

I glanced down at my plate, unable to hold my father's increasingly disappointed stare.

"I have a request. Please don't destroy them. I haven't met his grandparents. You're the first person I've told about our relationship. They've spent their whole lives here. They have nothing else."

"Who are they?" he asked.

"His last name is Brooks. I believe his grandparents last name is the Vibrock—"

He interrupted me with a loud burst of laughter. It didn't sound good. "You're asking too much. That old woman deserves everything that's coming for her. She spearheaded that group. She's responsible for this community's demise." My father pushed his plate away. "I've had to leave my business and spend a month here. Do you realize the cost of bringing our entire family here to live on this property? You're asking too much, Dahsam. These people here are different from who we are. We don't belong with them, and they don't fit with us." Aggravation grew as he shook his head in frustration. "I know you think you're in love, but it's not what you believe."

My hand extended in an effort to silence him. I refused to listen to a negative rant that belittled what Beau and I shared. I didn't have blinders on to the obstacles in our way, but I was fully committed to doing everything possible to ensure Beau and I stayed together.

"Please." My single word response was the counter I gave to his argument. "If I've in fact contributed to your win, I request my payment go to keeping Beau's family from losing everything. They're good, honest people who got caught up in trying to save their small business. You, above everyone, understand the passion that goes into keeping your business afloat. Please, for me."

Crazy tension filled the space around us. Silence reigned.

"I'll see what I can do," my father finally bit out. "I'm not promising you anything, but I'll look into it. I always believed Chandler would be your one. His family suits us better. Not some hillbilly from Sea Springs, Texas. Dasham, you test every boundary."

There was nothing left to say. I mimicked him, crossing my arms over my chest. Mine was more to hold me together. I hadn't anticipated him to go so low by bringing in class divisions.

His chair scraped against the tile when he abruptly stood, placing a hand on my shoulder. I resisted the urge to pull away from the touch. "Don't worry. I'll handle it. Today's a day of celebration. How was your experience as a working-class man?"

I decided to believe him. Regardless of the pain he caused, he hadn't let me down yet. Even then, it took a few seconds to clear my head. "How do people live off such a low wage?"

My dad gave a commiserating chuckle. "It's a fair wage. Industry standard."

"But aren't you the creator of industry?" I set the napkin beside my plate, done with my meal.

"Now you're catching on, son."

I didn't understand his response, but I didn't need to. I also stopped actively listening as he carried on.

How much did I tell Beau? I'd wait and get us past the holiday. Maybe allow all this to play out, while I kept guiding my father to save the day.

17: The Sweet Sixteen

Beau

July 4th

The moment was just as ideal as I imagined it to be, and my expectations had been high. Making love with Dash fulfilled me physically—man, did it—but the emotional elements cinched me to him like a life force, holding us together.

The whole adventure was made better with Dash's pretty face and hooded brow staring up at me, encouraging me to continue as his length bounced with every one of my thrusts. I prayed I gave him as much pleasure as he gave me.

I had also studied for today, implementing my newfound knowledge. I prepared him for what was to come.

Then, as we grew closer to the end, I somehow managed to get him off with my fist. My instincts were razor sharp, but it was all lost when my hips began to piston wildly. I couldn't hold them steady. My release came with a carnal sounding growl.

What I needed was a quick catnap, then to figure Dash out. Make sure he liked bottoming as much as he seemed to. I fell on top of him and gathered him in my arms. My eyes closed as my forehead hit the pillow and darkness edged in the periphery. Visions of Dash during the act played like a slideshow through my head.

He held me close, keeping me wrapped in his arms. My guy was a cuddler, and a talker. The embedded image of seeing

Dash naked stirred me, I tingled to life again. I had no idea I'd recover so quickly, wanting to do it again, and again. I grinned into his hair.

"I can't breathe." His husky tone hissed, sending a chilled shiver running through me. The labored puffs against my neck spoke to the truth of his struggle. Even then, I didn't want to let him go.

Apparently, he didn't feel the same way, and wiggled out from underneath me. After the briefest struggle, I eased my hold to let him go.

"I'm sorry," he murmured, rolling to his side next to me. The palm of his hand rested on my cheek. "I contemplated death so I didn't have to move, but I wanna live so we can do it again."

Oh man, my guy was sweet. I stayed still, staring at him, our faces close to each other. The quiet between us felt peaceful, a feeling I cherished. His thumb gently swept across the skin underneath my eye, tenderly caressing there.

"Did you enjoy it?" I whispered.

"So much," he said quietly, giving One of his many dashing expressions that enchanted me, fitting of the nickname I gave him. "You have the grace of a wildcat. It's entrancing to watch you move. Your muscles are fluid together... Promise me you won't cut your hair. Let it grow for me. I like running my fingers through it."

Then he did that very thing, moving the long pieces off my forehead and face. They probably didn't stay where he put them, which was fine, since it meant he'd touch me again.

I took in everything about his face. His lips looked plumper than usual, probably due to all the kissing we did. He also kept his bottom lip between his teeth as we made love. "Did I hurt you?"

"Hurt me so good," he teased, his tone sated and relaxed. The thigh he had wrapped around my waist tightened as he came closer, enough to press his lips tenderly against mine. "The way you dropped to your knees and swallowed me deep was a major turn-on. I think I'll remember it always."

We were inches apart, but I couldn't hold his stare and looked down at his chin. "I didn't know what to do. When I was digging through the junkyards, I found an old box of VHS tapes. One was gay porn. I secretly swiped it and watched it. I tried to pick the sexy parts out that I thought you'd like."

His giant grin had me doubting the wisdom of revealing that truth.

"I did the same thing." His lips reached out to touch mine again. "I told you I wanted to do both ways, but I picked bottom first because it looks so alluring. You didn't disappoint. That prostate rub, so good." My gaze lifted to his again to gauge the truth. "I guess it was selfish. I should've let you go first. That just occurred to me. I'm sorry."

The worry had me feeling special, but I wasn't ready to bottom. Someday, not now. I trailed a finger down the bridge of his nose to flick his bottom lip.

"We should shower. I'm a mess. I felt you coming inside me," Dash said.

"We should've used a condom," I murmured.

He shook his head hard at me, looking like I was the dumbest person on the planet.

"I felt the pulsing when you came. We were one person. Condoms aren't for monogamous relationships. We won't ever have to use them..." Dash stopped speaking and rolled away, off the bed. "I feel energized. The room seems brighter and bigger doesn't it?"

He went to the en suite bathroom. The term Dash used when giving me a tour of his room before tackling me to the bed.

His warmth was missed.

I stared at the ceiling. He called the decoration up there ornamental. I called it fancy. The entire room was stunning and spacious. The bed might be the most comfortable I'd ever slept in, though I hadn't actually slept. His perfect ass bounced as he jogged to the bathroom. "I think we should come out tonight at the fireworks show. Nothing's going to change between us. Might as well get it out to the world."

Those words didn't freak me out like they should have. With my eyes closed, I thought of the only obstacle we had in our way: my grandparents. I figured they'd disown me for being with Dash Richmond more so than being gay. Probably my father was too far away to know anything about it. Besides, what could he do? My mom had put me in a safe place.

"Are you paying attention?"

No, I wasn't and popped myself up on my elbows to see Dash poking his head around the corner of the bathroom. My heart skipped a beat. His disheveled hair, his pouty lips slowly returning to their normal size, his gaze adoring as he stared at me… How had I gotten so lucky?

"Yes, I did. I think we should wait until my grandparents calm down."

He gave an exaggerated eye roll and disappeared. The shower faucet flipped on. The unexpected sound of pitter-pattering feet came running toward the bed. They didn't stop until he jumped directly on top of me.

"Umph." I jackknifed up, my hands covering my privates, the last part of my body I wanted to hurt right now.

Dash playfully bounced us on the mattress.

"Quit turning me down. I refuse to hear *no* another day." His smiling expression was in direct contrast with the severity of his tone. "I told you my dad's gonna take care of your grandparents. He promised."

Yeah, I had all sorts of responses to give. Where did I even begin? I confidently lay back, tucking my hand underneath my head, saying the first of my counterargument. "If you want me to spend the night with you when your parents leave, my mom better not find out about us. She'll never allow it."

Understanding dawned and his expression changed. He leaned back on his heels, his shifting eyes giving a peek into his mind. He quickly went through the different scenarios to find any other possible angles. He was so smart. I'd gotten to know him well. Seconds later, I saw the moment that I had him.

"I win."

"Perhaps you did or maybe you didn't," he remarked, the gears in his head whirling again. "So you're saying you'll spend the night with me after my parents leave?"

"If my mom says it's all right," I answered, but I'd probably sneak out. We both knew I would. "But she might want to talk to your parents."

He looked horrified at the suggestion and scooted around on his ass until his feet were back on the floor. "I need to shower. Stay here, just like this."

"I won," I called out to drive the win home.

"Not yet." The sound of the shower door clicking closed echoed in the quiet of the suite.

I often couldn't believe how well Dash and I connected. After today, I'd describe us as missing pieces to each other's puzzles. Once I was comfortable with Dash, we'd never had any awkwardness between us. Not in our first time to hold hands, not during our first kiss, and not after today.

Rolling out of bed, I took account of my body. How had everything about me changed yet stayed the same? Sex might honestly be my new favorite pastime. My brain switched gears as I went for my T-shirt. How hadn't I hurt him? And I could swallow, I was sure of it.

If Dash and I were innately close, then bathroom privacy was likely a non-issue. Somehow, that made it okay to at least join him in the bathroom. I grabbed a hand towel and washed my chest and my junk then ran water over my hands and through my long hair, pushing it off my face as Dash opened the shower door.

Dash was uninhibited with his body. Which eased me with my own. I watched him through the mirror—a mirror that came with a defogger. Seriously fancy. He was the image of perfection. And here I was again, committing his body to memory.

"Toss me a towel."

I did from the stack below the sink.

"Since you're dashing all my hopes and dreams..."

"Dash, is my word, and I'm only being practical."

"Practicality doesn't belong in our relationship," he said and ran the towel over his body. "So here's my counter. I want some sort of PDA tonight to let me know you're thinking about me on my birthday. Then spend the night tomorrow after your shift as my birthday present."

I cut him off, going for my underwear and shorts while pointing to the gift sack sitting on Dash's desk. "I brought you a present. You haven't opened it..."

He continued as if I hadn't spoken. "You can shower here when you get off work. My parents are leaving this evening. Amelia's coming in the morning. She'll believe you're my friend. Then as soon as my dad talks to your grandparents and they agree on a plan, we come out. It's a safe plan no matter what argument you come with."

He slung his damp towel over one shoulder. The other one propped against the door frame. The *David* had nothing on Dash. Overwhelmed, I took a seat on the edge of the bed. I'd grown so hard so fast I rammed the heel of my palm into my groin to stop the insanity.

"We'll talk about it when you're dressed. You're making it hard to think straight," I said.

His sweet smile and soft chuckle had me unsure of what he'd do next. Luckily, he ducked behind the door. "Maybe I need to stay like this in front of you all the time. It might give me a few wins every once in a while. Let me dry my hair. Then we're going for a ride in my Ferrari."

I dropped back on the bed as the hair dryer roared to life. My hand came to my heart. I was way over my head with that one.

18: The Moment
Dash/Beau

One week later

What a difference a month made.

A single moment had changed me to the core. Being in the right place at the right time began to look more like destiny than chance. The way life aligned for me, locking into place, had me considering all the challenges Beau and I faced. One by one, we knocked them down together.

If the resort hadn't faced its difficulties, if his grandparents hadn't put up such a fight, I might not have ever met Beau. Yeah, fate took on a tangible meaning in my life. It became real and fluid, and I'd appreciate it every moment for the rest of my life.

"Amelia's nice," Beau said absently, staring out the passenger side window. We held hands as much as I could while handling the stick shift. Apparently, my selfishness knew no bounds. I did my best to occupy all our time, keeping Beau to myself. The idea of parting with him to complete my fall semester took on a bleak, desolate outlook.

When had I become so emotional?

I couldn't ask that same question about becoming controlling, I'd been that since birth.

"She's having a well-deserved vacation. I'm in a place that takes care of everything for me. Her tan's coming on strong.

I'm also sure she didn't need to come here. I'm responsible and honest..." Beau interrupted me before the outrage tumbled from my lips again.

My only real issue with Amelia was her keen eye. She knew me and watched me closely. And that was technically okay too. She approved of Beau. She hadn't forbidden Beau's nights spent with me. She stayed discreetly away, never in my way.

"Says the guy who stole his niece's car every night to come see me."

All right, mister. One eyebrow cocked at the refute. Clearly, we needed to make a few new rules. When I launched into a baseless complaint, Beau should agree with me instead of introducing reason and truth into the mix.

When he glanced at me, he said, "I win."

"You always do. It's very annoying," I remarked sharply, downshifting to take the turn to his house.

He casually shrugged me off in the typical air of competitive arrogance, causing me to laugh. I guessed facts were facts.

As we drew closer to Beau's house, I noticed three police vehicles parked in front of his grandparents' home. My gut sank at the possibilities, none of them were good. My father said he'd help. "What's going on?"

Beau swung his head toward the front windshield and reached for the cell phone in his back pocket. At the same time, the front door opened. A commotion spilled out into the yard.

"That's my dad," he said in that fearful way he used when speaking of his father. "Drive to the house. Hurry."

The tension in the car escalated in the few moments it took to arrive in front of the home. We watched his grandfather grasp his father's forearm then get shoved several feet backward until he tumbled hard to the ground. The police, who had created a u-shape around the front porch, finally intervened, attempting to manage the growing volatile situation that had Beau visibly upset.

Without hesitation, he leaped from the car before I came to a full stop. He left the door wide open as he sprinted toward his grandfather. "Keep your hands off him. His heart's weak."

He bellowed with a vicious voice. Maybe the meanest I'd ever heard. "Get away. Why're you here?"

"That's him. Put him in my truck."

I stood corrected. His father was loud, commanding and sounded like a demon from the depths of hell. Beau evaded one officer to get to his grandfather's side. Tears streamed down his mom's face as she spoke urgently on her cell phone, requesting an ambulance. Her gaze fixed on me.

I broke the boundary lines I hadn't yet crossed and hurried to Beau's grandfather's side. He was unconscious, with his wife kneeling on the other side of Beau.

I hadn't paid much attention in health class, but with the blood near his head, I remember the teacher telling us to elevate the head and shoulders slightly. I removed my polo shirt and wadded it up to place under his head, hoping I wasn't making everything worse. "I believe he should lay still and his body straight, just in case there's a spinal cord injury."

"I'm sorry," Mrs. Brooks said, drawing my attention to her anguish. She passed the phone to her mom and came to Beau, drawing him up. Her hands covered each of his cheeks. They stood inches apart.

Her words tumbled out so rapidly it was hard to understand. "Your dad has a legal order to take you back to Alabama. They know about you and Dash. They have photos. I'll fight this Beau. I promise you." She circled her arms around him, hugging him tightly. "Do what he says. Don't be defiant. He's promised not to hurt you. I'll be back with you in Alabama as soon as I can get there."

"I'm goin' back to Alabama?" He stared at his mother in utter confusion. My brain blipped as I tried to grasp the seriousness of what was happening to Beau.

"Son, this doesn't have to be difficult. It'd be better for everyone if you voluntarily got inside your father's truck," an officer said with empathy, keeping a courteous distance from Beau and his mother.

"Fuck that," his father yelled and pointed to the truck between the patrol cars. "Get in the fuckin' truck. I'm tired of all this. You're legally in my custody."

He held a file folder in hand with a picture of Beau and I at the Fourth of July fireworks celebration. I'd purposefully stood behind him, admiring his ass. I hadn't let up on my request for a PDA. Reluctantly Beau placed his hand between me and him. The handhold had only lasted about fifteen seconds. Who had been there to take our picture? I hadn't seen any photographers for days.

The fault of the day rested solely on my shoulders.

It was hard to believe the promise of no abuse as Beau's father stalked toward him, rage on his face. "Get in my fuckin' truck. I'm not sayin' it again."

"What about my stuff?" He set his shoulders and feet, readying to battle, but the glance he gave me spoke of sorrow and regret. He knew he was out of options.

Oh no. My palms began to sweat as the understanding that Beau was leaving me forever seeped past my rapidly building barriers. My anxiety spiked into the stratosphere, making me breathy and scared.

"There's nothin' here you need." He gripped Beau's bicep to drag him across the yard. My guy stumbled as he held my stare the entire way. How did I tell him that I loved him? I'd wait for however long I had to.

"Stay the fuck away from him." His father aimed his disgust and anger toward me as he yanked open the truck door. I'd started toward Beau without even realizing I had. His father's vicious sneer had me halting. I didn't want to make this more difficult for Beau than it already was. "Whatever this was is done. If you contact him, I'll get a restrainin' order and press harassment charges against you. The papers are ready to be filed."

"Take care of my paw, and my mom," Beau called out, his voice cracking before his head was shoved from behind into the backseat of the pickup.

I nodded, watching the tears well in his eyes. My heart darted across the lawn, going with Beau, wherever he was being taken. He stared at me through the window of the truck as the engine roared to life. I jogged toward him as I absorbed a death punch to the center of my chest. He continued to stare at me, turning his head to look out the back window until he couldn't be seen.

I was stunned and dropped my hands to my knees, keeping myself upright as I gasped for air. I needed to call my father. He was powerful. Surely he could do something.

Until then, I had to do what my love asked. When I started back to the yard, I found Beau's mom behind me, taking me into a loving hold. The police finally stopped the charade of protection from this family and began helping Beau's grandparents.

"I'm sorry," she muttered with tears in her voice. "I don't know how he got hold of that picture. I didn't see it anywhere in the news but be sure that I'll fight to get my boy back. I promise. His dad won't hurt him. He's just loud and intimidating. Beau knows how to handle him."

Her words appeared to reassure herself more than me. I held her tighter as the sounds of the approaching ambulance grew closer.

What happened now? With the way my heart thundered and darkness crept into my vision's edge, I began taking deep gulps of breath to stave off the pending hyperventilation.

Seeing Dash running toward me with tears in his eyes broke my heart more than anything else. Thankfully, my mom had gone after him. She'd give Dash comfort. She was just that way.

With zero emotional support to cling to, I was returning to a life I no longer wanted.

Beau

"I shouldn't have let you leave. I messed up," my father said, staring at me from his rearview mirror. I refused to look up. Instead I did the exact opposite, bending to stare at the floorboard. "When you quit football, it never occurred to me that you were havin' queer tendencies. Then it all clicked in place. I did this to protect you. Being queer ain't no way to live your life. It'll only cause you pain. If you'd've talked to me, I could've helped you navigate all this. Curiosity's normal for any kid. You aren't the only one I've had to help over the years."

Since I hated that man, I refused to appreciate the gentle tone he used in his horrible explanation. Honestly, I expected him to be kicking my ass all the way to Alabama.

"You're too much like me not to be angry as hell right now," he said. "I haven't shared this with anyone except my girlfriend. She lives with me and plans to help get you right again. I've spoken with the pastors at The Rock church. They've offered a few avenues to help your recovery. We'll start with the easy way then progress as necessary. I've designed a strict schedule to get you focused and ready to play again. That, and I've put you in harder AP courses in school. No more breezin' through life. Everything I've done will help keep your mind occupied. You're also startin' counseling a few times a week. Not with one of those feel-good therapists. We're gonna target this head-on. You'll get past it. Got it?"

Of course I didn't respond; I was barely hanging on.

"If you're a jerk about it, I promise it'll be harder on you. A man needs to be with a woman. That's the way it was intended. The counselor's gonna help you learn the tools to cope with your urges. Eventually, you'll figure it out, I promise you."

I let go of an unsteady breath and continued to stare at my tennis shoes. "What's gonna happen to Mom?"

"You'll have supervised visitation once she meets with your counselor, but that's gonna be damned difficult with her so far away. Until then, she can call once a week. Those calls will be monitored too. She's let shit happen under her watch that shouldn't have happened, per the court's emergency ruling. There's also no communication with that kid you were with, got it? You initiate a conversation or try to maintain any sort of relationship, there will be significant repercussions. You hear me?"

Anger raged through me so intensely my mind and body went numb. My fingers trembled. I slammed my forehead against the back of the front seat. I'd tasted a life of freedom. I wasn't going back.

"Challenge me on this and find out, buddy." His sympathetic tone turned harder and unyielding. "You better get used to the idea of spendin' all your time with me. When you were little, you wanted me and you to move through life together. I abided by your wishes. Do you know how many offers I've turned down from the NFL in order to stay home with you? I'm damn sure not gonna let a bunch of hormones get in our way."

Why did he always tie me to something I supposedly said when I was four years old?

And whatever. He'd never turn down the NFL. That was a lie.

He turned up the radio, signaling an end to our conversation. At the same time, I felt the vibration of my phone in the pocket of my cargo shorts. I glanced at my father who hadn't seemed to notice. The first chance I got, I had to turn it off to better help hide it and save the battery. If he found the phone, I'd never be allowed to keep it.

A world that Dash had turned bright dimmed back into the state of oppression I'd always lived under. A tear slipped down my cheek, already mourning the life I was leaving behind.

After consuming more beer than I'd ever seen him drink, more than he used to drink in a week, my father passed out hard. The remote control tumbled off his belly onto the king-sized mattress in a motel approximately six hours from Mobile.

I was relegated to the other side of the mattress, with one wrist cuffed to the headboard as a consequence of all the sneaking out I had done over the years. That was another thing I apparently had to get used to. I feigned sleep almost immediately after arriving. I needed the rest because I'd start conditioning and training the minute we arrived home tomorrow. He claimed I'd grown emotionally and physically soft since I'd left his care.

The tears I'd fought for most of the day began to silently fall as I reached for my cell phone.

With deliberately cautious movements, I pulled the phone free. I only had a small amount of battery remaining as I quietly worked the keyboard to open my text messages. All the while I kept track of my father's snores.

He sent three messages. Shamefully, I opened his first.

"Be safe. I love you. Do what he says until I can get my dad to help."

"Ur mom caught me up on your dad's emergency court decision. We'll figure this out. Just wait for me. Don't lose hope. I'll wait for you forever."

How long was forever? Years might go by before I could even talk to him again. This phone just became more of a lifeline than ever before.

"I'm sorry to say, your grandfather isn't doing well. He's in a medically induced coma with a ventilator. Your grandmother's by his side. I'm worried about you. Text me when you can."

I understood it might be silly, but I touched the small screen, seeking a connection with Dash. I wish I had a photo.

It took me a moment to craft my message back to him.

"I'm okay. My phone's hidden. I'm sorry. It's gonna be difficult here. Don't wait for me. Thanks for looking out for my paw. I'm turning my phone off until it's safe. IDK when that's gonna be." I ran out of texting space and pushed send as tears again streamed down my face.

We'd only had a month together, but man, what a difference thirty days made to my soul. Dash was too shiny to be stuck with a guy like me. *"It's best for you to go on. I'll always remember you."*

I pushed send and wiped a hand over my cheeks then under my nose.

I quickly opened my mom's text as my father mumbled something about a red barn in his sleep. *"Do what he says. I love you. I'll be there as soon as I can."* I wondered if she knew the hoops she had to jump through to be with me again.

I typed number by number as quickly and quietly as I could. "*Me too. I'm sorry about Paw. Tell him I love him. He's a great paw. Keep my phone on.*" I pressed send. My father woke in a stupor, stumbling from the bed to the bathroom. I clicked the button to turn the phone off and managed to get it tucked back into my pocket before his return.

My life was over. My mom couldn't help me. I didn't know how I knew, but I did.

Fear, sorrow, and sadness caused my empty heart to turn to stone.

19: The Cuffs
Beau

Three months later

"Seriously, dude, how long you gonna be grounded?" Scott asked, quietly shutting my bedroom door behind him. After all these months of being back in Mobile, Scott was still the only person I was allowed to see outside of school and those visits were scheduled and timed.

I looked back over my shoulder at him from my regular seat beside the window. He wasn't the most intuitive guy, but I saw the real worry on his face.

"You're always so fucking sad. Are you suicidal? You look that way. Don't do it. Call me first," Scott plead.

Hmm. I didn't speak—I barely did anymore—and contemplated my death. It didn't elicit the fear it once had. My gaze shifted back out the window. I could see a pretty major Mobile road that allowed me to watch life happening for everyone except me. "Why're you still handcuffed?" Scott asked.

"You know why. It's to keep me from sneakin' out. Which I'd probably do." In my head, I added, "*and run far, far away.*"

Scott came to sit with his ass on my desk. "Someday you're gonna have to tell me what happened. All this ain't right. I feel like it's child abuse."

"It's not if the court says he's right." The tears just beyond the surface threatened to fall.

Scott leaned closer to my ear. "My mom talks to your mom. She's fightin' in court to get you back and says she loves you."

The only secret I had managed to keep from my father was the cell phone tucked in the floorboard of my closet, under a pile of shoes and gear. I plugged it in every once in a while, maybe twice since I arrived back in Mobile. Her messages were there, and those from Dash, promising to wait for me. I chose not to respond. I couldn't find the strength to tell him to go on again, live a good life without me. A teardrop ran down my cheek.

Scott's reassuring hand came to my shoulder.

The bedroom door burst open with force causing me to turn my head away to keep anyone from seeing me cry. It'd only make my life harder.

"This door remains open at all times," my dad barked. Not necessarily mean. That was the weird thing, he wasn't regularly mean to me even though I fully understood the beating waiting for me if I strayed off course.

My dad's entire focus was the constant surveillance of me and drinking more than was healthy. Which was the reason for keeping me handcuffed to whatever furniture I chose to stay in. Between the handcuffs and the newly installed security system, when he passed out, I was safely stuck inside.

During the school week, I trained six hours a day. Two hours in the morning and four after school. More on the weekends. He kept me busy every minute of the day. Since beer was the only alcohol permissible for the coaches while on the field, the cocktails continued once he got home. He and his girlfriend drank freely while they stumbled their way through reading the bible to me every night. My demons be damned.

The fun thing we were doing together now was watching free straight porn. He was so gross.

"Yes, sir. I forgot." Based on his expression, my dad clearly didn't believe him.

"Come on. You're done for today."

"I'll see you Monday," Scott said, then tried his best to divert my father's attention. "Pretty sure the Titans are going all the way this year."

"Are you nuts?"

It was then I saw the man following my father into my room. Scott's save had failed. I got an angry finger pointed at me. "I'm gettin' tired of the mopin'. Show me you're gettin' better, or we'll have to move to other options. You aren't gonna like 'em. This pastor's gonna talk to you and you're gonna respond. You hear me?"

Scott had to have heard, but I don't care. A set of blue eyes that remained just below my closed lids was my only happiness. I turned to stare back outside the window, knowing all he really cared about was this season's playoff games. If I performed, he wouldn't send me off somewhere to deteriorate.

20: The Anniversary Dash

Nine Months Later, the Fourth of July
Southlake, Texas

I scrolled through the countless unreturned text messages, wishing for a sign from Beau.

Today held meaning. My birthday and the day I first made love to my guy. I missed him so much.

"Come on, douche," Chandler said as he pushed open my bedroom door uninvited. "Get your ass moving and bore everyone downstairs while you blow out the candles."

He wasn't wrong about the energy surrounding me these days. It had been a full year since I last spoke to Beau and all I seemed able to do was wait for his reply to any of the dozens and dozens of texts I sent.

Like I lectured myself many times, I wasn't a quitter. I knew what I wanted and had to stay the course. Strength built quickly. I had to be steady for when I saw my love again.

With a practiced move, I flipped open my phone and quickly typed a message—an anniversary text, or at least I liked to believe we committed to a lifetime together one year ago today. *"Today's meaning is more special to me than my birthday. Last year was the best time of my life. I miss you. I'll be here. BTW, my father hasn't had any luck in your case. He's still trying. I'm waiting. Take your time."*

I reread my words, ensuring I wrote with no acronyms. He deserved complete sentences. After hitting send, I waited a second or two before closing the phone to let the text go through.

"Buddy, you need to move on," Chandler said, placing a hand on my shoulder, staring me directly in the eyes. Unlike my family, he never pushed me past my limits until right now. "If it's meant to be, then let it happen. You can't stop living your life. He wouldn't want that."

I was certain about that. The final message Beau sent encouraged me to forget him. An impossible feat that gutted me at the very idea. I deleted it from my phone. He'd come to me. He had to. I saw no other option.

I nodded to Chandler in understanding, fully aware I controlled my world. If nothing else, my focused insistence had to bring Beau back to me.

21: ... Beau

July 5, One Year Later
Mobile, Alabama

I was nothing short of pissed off as I raced up the stairs at lightning speed to grab my overnight bag from my bedroom. It had been nearly two years since I'd been allowed to spend unsupervised time with my mom, and my stupid old man purposefully kept me out on the football field, letting her wait.

He was such a fucking dick. Since she'd moved back to Mobile, both of us had bent over backward, following every one of his ridiculous rules, and still he was such a giant motherfucker all the time.

My black heart hated him on an unhealthy level.

And all the bad words I used stayed in my head, ready to unleash at any given moment. Except, I never said anything aloud. The resentment I harbored toward my life was ruining me and I was only seventeen.

Why was the age of majority nineteen years old in the state of Alabama? I still had two years of his bullshit. But that information came from my father, and he lied all of the time.

In the entry of my room, I quieted myself and headed for my hiding spot in the floorboard of my closet. Despite the constant surveillance, I'd somehow managed to keep my cell phone from being found.

I tucked it inside my bag, slinging it over my shoulder. I ran down the stairs two at a time, making a beeline for my mom's car parked at the curb. Hopefully, we'd be heading down the road before my father returned from the garage with a bottle of liquor in hand. I refused to participate in one of his humiliating pat downs again.

The godlike authority he held over me and the way I weakly complied was the most embarrassing part. Well, that, and the peer-pressured kiss I'd given Katie on the field when we were crowned homecoming king and queen. My father had beamed at me with pride.

The disgust that shamed me flipped around on its axis when I jumped into the car with my mom, bringing my bag down into my lap.

"Go, go, go," I urged before fully shutting the door. My gaze fixed out the front windshield, to avoid seeing my dad if he came to the front porch.

My mom didn't take my bait, driving away at a normal speed. "I have the car charger plugged in."

She remembered. Each minute I waited for the phone to power up might be the longest of my life. As much as I lectured myself over what a loser I turned out to be, that Dash and I had no chance at a real future, and never really had, I still wanted to hear from him.

When the phone powered up and I accessed the messaging app, I saw the reality of time and distance. Dash's messages had stopped coming in regular intervals, but there were still a couple of new ones since the last time I checked.

"I liked him," my mom spoke softly.

I didn't respond. My treatment kept my homosexuality buried inside. "I should keep this at your house now."

"Maybe we can upgrade your phone."

The resources she'd spent in paying for my Paw's funeral, moving back to Mobile, court battles, and child support had her juggling multiple jobs to make ends meet and pay her debts. It didn't allow room for anything frivolous.

"I don't wanna lose the texts." I finally answered with the truth and pressed the option to read Dash's text messages that I used to pretend were love notes.

My mom reached a hand over to hold mine.

Close to Christmas, he sent, *"I miss you. You're the best friend I've ever had. I'm waiting."* I wondered what happened to make him choose those particular words?

The other one came yesterday. *"Today's our second anniversary. What a great day. I love you. I'm waiting."*

Those words caused swift and unyielding pain to slash over my heart. So much so I absently lifted a hand to my chest, rubbing there.

The voices in my head resumed their constant mocking. Dash wouldn't want anything to do with me if he saw the cowardice, loser trash I'd let myself become. Our fleeting summer romance had left my life in shambles and was long over. Shame replaced the pain, luckily numbing me. I welcomed the feeling.

I stuffed my phone in the cubby and tossed my bag in the backseat.

"You okay?" she asked, and I nodded.

"You ever gonna trim that hair again?"

"Probably not. How's Nana?" I asked, shifting the topic. The only reason I kept my hair longer was due to Dash's preference which made me into an even bigger loser.

"She's good. She's waiting at the apartment for us. She can't wait to see you."

"I miss Paw." My actions had caused his death. They'd lost everything. My grandmother had to move to Alabama with my mom. I stopped the thought before the spiraling began.

"Me too, babe. But let's focus on the plans I have for us tonight. I thought we could start at CC's Pizza so you can play *Ninja Assault*. I have a bag full of quart..."

"Excellent," I butted in, cutting her off. "I haven't played since I came back."

My thoughts shifted to *Ninja Assault*, wondering if my top score was still intact.

"Then I thought we'd have movie night. You pick the movie. I baked your favorite brownies. Then tomorrow morning, we have an early start. I booked a fishing charter to take us out. I'll have you back home before time."

"Mom." The word was said with happiness and reverence. "I haven't been fishing since I was in Texas. Dad never goes anymore. He spends all his time partying and drinking. It never stops. He drives to work with a bloody Mary as his breakfast."

Her jawline set firm, a frown carved into her face. It took several quiet moments until she shook her head, freeing the expression. "Let's focus on the next twenty-four hours."

"I'm working on my vocabulary for you," I said, trying to lighten the mood.

"I noticed. I'm proud of you."

I nodded and reached out to take her hand. She'd been handed the blows just like me. Life had to get better. It couldn't be worse.

22: ...
Dash

Another ten months later
Southlake, Texas

At my college graduation, I sat on stage waiting to give my overly pre-rehearsed speech, staring at the sea of families who came to support their graduates. However mine wasn't among the throngs there at Moody Coliseum. Their failure to show might actually be my fault. I couldn't remember if I'd mentioned it to them or not.

Since moving out of my childhood home, I hadn't seen much of my parents. My mother lived full time in Paris. As for my father... Well, he was everywhere, all the time. Both seemingly forgetting that, at eighteen, I was barely of age in the state of Texas.

I didn't care.

While listening to Herb Kelleher of Southwest Airlines give his commencement speech, I casually crossed one leg over the other, trying my best to stifle a yawn. Over time, somewhere in the last two years, I had learned to appreciate a good, relaxing happy hour. A time of day Chandler claimed was somewhere between two in the afternoon and six in the morning.

Although I wasn't aligned with his schedule, I did embrace the moments of unwinding that helped lift the weight I'd been carrying for years.

Maybe my lack of caring was due to another timeline accomplishment that I wanted with Beau, and missed again. His name vibrated through me, taking my breath away. My obsession with him had faded over time.

For my own mental health, I had stashed him away until he came back to me. In the meantime, I took life head-on, focusing on building my life in such a way that I could always support us. I admitted it seemed silly. The likelihood of him coming for me seemed smaller by the year, but I wasn't ready to let go of the dream. It hurt too bad.

I texted him this morning, letting him know I was graduating. My mind blocked everything out as I imagined staring at him, sitting out with all the families, watching me achieve my goals. Tears gathered in my eyes as everyone faded, leaving only Beau there, smiling at me.

Suddenly, an elbow nudged my arm, snapping me out of my Beau-induced thoughts. The world and my obligations zipped back into place. "They called your name. Go give your speech."

The audience's laughter had to mean they'd called me a few times. I stood, looking around for my notes until I patted my gown. The woman sitting next to me saved the day again, reaching below my chair for the index cards.

"Thank you." I had a five-minute speech to give. Yeehaw.

23: ...
Beau

2004
Samford University, Birmingham, Alabama

"Man, do you ever fucking speak?" I slowly lifted my gaze from the textbook in my lap to my roommate, Brock. A guy who had more personality and confidence than anyone had a right to have. He was borderline arrogant. My brows dropped at his tone, and I pulled an earbud free, letting the music still play in one ear. The earbuds and MP3 player were a graduation gift from my mom.

As a football player, I was required to live on campus. Apparently, living outside my father's constant attention hadn't changed too much for me. I didn't talk much, I was unsociable, and I performed like the monkey he'd trained me to be. Well, I wasn't entirely out of his sphere. My jerk of a father continued to impact my daily life as the new director of football operations for the college I attended.

Every time I considered his new position, I gave an inner chuckle. Despite all his local boasting about where the pair of us might land, how he wouldn't settle for anything less than an assistant coach position, he was the lowest coach on the totem pole...

The laughter bubbled out, probably making me look psychotic to Brock.

The only institution to extend me and my father an offer was Samford University, a Christian college in Birmingham, Alabama. The darkly hilarious part was that my father struggled with alcoholism and found himself in a setting that prohibited alcohol on campus and required their staff to project responsibility and restraint all the time.

"What?" I asked.

"Your cell phone's going off." Only after hearing the next ding did I register the sound. I leaned toward the well-worn dorm-assigned end table and grabbed the cell phone my father had gotten for me. I was only allowed the phone and a driver's license once my father received his first DUI and needed me to pick him up. This phone, like my other, had limited minutes a month, all in which my shitty old man used regularly. His latest DUI resulted in a forced breathalyzer. He'd been damn mad about that one.

But that wasn't the phone that dinged. It was my other one. The one that connected me to Dash. When I opened it, I saw a series of texts from him. Man, he was a dog with a bone, never giving up after all these years.

I started from the bottom and read up.

"I wish you'd text me back. Let me know you see my messages."

"You had to have graduated this year. I celebrated for you."

"I'm having a weak moment. I'm lonely. Am I waiting for you by myself?"

"I've never been with anyone but you, but it's getting harder."

Jealousy struck hard and fast, momentarily blinding me. He better not be with anyone else with all the waiting he said he was doing. After a moment of fire building up from my soul, I continued to open his messages.

"Please let me know if you see this."

"I'm sorry. I've had a little bit to drink. My roommate goes at life hard. People are in my house all the time. It's tough to stay detached."

"I'm still waiting. No pressure."

As I stared at the phone, an overwhelming need had me slowly creating a text back. He had to move on and let me go. What we shared wasn't real. Only the lovestruck feelings of two adolescent boys. After all these years, and everything I'd been through, I didn't know who I was anymore.

"I get your messages. It's helped me knowing you're there but now you need to hear me. Move on with your life. I'm not the person you knew. No one likes me anymore. I don't like myself. Go on without me."

I pressed send, mainly due to the frustration of having to use the number keys to slowly create the message.

As I sat there, pondering the emptiness inside me that kept me from feeling much of anything, a small spark of love ignited in the tiniest of flames. Another message appeared as if Dash felt it with me too. *"I needed your message. You're wrong. Take your time. I'll always want you. I'm waiting. It can't be much longer."*

I marveled at his unwavering devotion with me being just as determined to stay away from him. I'd ruin his life and ruin the happy memories I still clung to.

"I'm gonna go work out." I dropped the book and phone to my mattress as I rolled from my bed.

At the door, my roommate's newest girlfriend was standing there, hand poised to knock. "Omigod, you're huge. How tall are you?"

I didn't answer. Instead I twisted to let her in as I stepped out.

"Nah, I'm good. I'll catch you next time," Brock called out as the door closed behind me.

See? I'd been rude. I'd lost myself with no chance of learning to live properly again.

24: ...
Dash

July 4, 2005
Sea Spring, Texas

"Dude, come on," Chandler's voice echoed from somewhere inside our hotel suite.

Sitting on the bed's edge, I took a moment to get my anniversary text out of the way.

"It was your idea to take a charter out. Everybody's waiting for us," Chandler said closer to the door. "Apparently the fish guys don't like to be late on the water."

"Go. I'll catch up with you," I mumbled and began to type. *"Happy anniversary. This is year five. I love you. I'm waiting."*

Short, sweet, and to my point. I tapped the send button. I was going fishing for my birthday. A burst of laughter slipped free as I opened the door to an antsy Chandler. He'd probably die where he stood if he had any idea this was Beau's thing.

"Why're you laughing?" he asked defensively and glanced down at my fishing attire.

"Get going," I said, nodding him toward the door. "We're late, remember?" I squeezed past him and started out of the suite. We had a birthday to celebrate and fish to catch.

Part 2

1: The Best Friend
Beau

January 2006
Mobile, Alabama

The pace of the procession from the burial site to the reception area slowed as my mom's high-heeled shoes sank in the damp grass with each step she took. We lagged behind the crowd of mourners who'd gathered to bid their final goodbyes. There had to be a thousand people in attendance today.

In the midst of them were both the young and older men who had learned to play football under my father's tutelage. They ambled past us, quietly offering their sincere condolences at my shitty old man's untimely passing.

I'd offer the appropriate nod of appreciation or acceptance, not that I meant either. But it was the only gesture I felt comfortable enough to give since I'd spent some part of everyday begging the universe to end the old bastard's life as brutally as possible. Seemed my requests were heard.

Fortunately, no one else was injured when my father blew through a red light, clipping the back end of a supersized Dodge pickup truck. My father had no chance, driving at full speed in his beater SUV. He was propelled airborne, flipping over and again, out of control, until a closed Starbucks got in his way.

The scene was brutal to say the least. The local police reported that my father died on impact. And perhaps he did. But those same officers said my father's blood alcohol level was *below* the legal limit. I didn't believe that lie. My dad drank all day every day. He'd lost his job at Samford University in Birmingham. He had little choice but to relocate back to Mobile with a suspended driver's license due to multiple arrests for driving under the influence.

I supposed the Mobile PD had shown my father leniency due to his reputation in the city. They usually helped him home instead of formally arresting him. In the end, their grace gave him power, not the help he really needed.

My mom patted my arm, drawing my attention to her. "Son, you're being rude."

"How can they be sorry he's gone?" I whispered.

"You're almost done. Hang on for a few more minutes. We'll walk through the reception then leave. Can you be my big boy for a little longer." She teased me with my old childhood moniker even though I was twenty years old. Happy memories of better times made it impossible not to smile. If I remembered correctly, there was usually a cookie involved to convince me to behave.

I stared hopeful that there was something in the variety of a home-baked chocolate chip treat in her pocket. I loved those things. It took a moment, but she caught on and responded with a dramatic eye roll. "I'll bake them for you when we get home."

"Look at you, sproutin' up like a beanstalk. Seems like you've outgrown your grandad," Arnold Williams, a friend of my grandfather's said from behind me. "How tall are you these days?"

Arnold stared up at me with a good-natured grin. He was thinner than I remembered, more wrinkled, and shorter too.

"He's six-three and two hundred and thirty pounds. Can you believe it, Arnie?" my mom answered for me, again highlighting my lack of communication skill.

"I tend to keep my belly full," I added with a nod, watching Arnold's widening grin. With fewer teeth and less hair, his weathered face creased with amusement. A pang of sadness squeezed my heart, wishing either of my grandfathers could be there today. Had they survived, my life would have turned out so differently.

"I can sure see that." He chuckled, then shifted his gaze toward the parking lot, hesitating before heading in that direction. "It's chilly out here. I keep hearin' that we're warm for this time of year, but I think they got it wrong."

"Thank you for coming today," my mom said sweetly.

Arnold paused, gazing between me and my mom before focusing only on me. With his hands tucked into his coat pockets, his voice got stronger as he said, "You were good to him. He didn't deserve it, especially separatin' you from your mama."

I let go of an unsteady breath. No one, except maybe Scott, ever saw it from my side. Others acted in awe of the athlete my father had created, or in the NFL vision he had for our future, but never for me alone.

A swell of anger built swiftly. I ground my teeth into the flesh of my mouth as a tidal wave of undealt with emotion threatened to pull me under.

Fortunately, my mother came to the rescue once again. "Thank you, Arnold. It's been a challenging few years. We're going to the reception area then taking off. Beau needs to put all of this behind him and begin to live the life he wants."

Arnold patted my bicep and started toward the parking lot again. "You sure do."

We walked the remaining distance to the reception area, which consisted of a giant tent placed close to the family burial plots. It was a true countryside gathering.

As I stood at the entry, I steadied myself, blocking my feelings. No more bursts of anger to contend with. My mom waited patiently at my side.

The crowds of mourners fell silent and shifted their attention toward me. Evidently, my reputation preceded me. I sensed their wariness. Nothing new there. Most people treated me as if I was one quake away from erupting.

Luckily, the strong tangy scent of fresh BBQ waffled through the tent, stealing my spotlight. Scott's father, Mr. Lee, was grill-master of the day. The reigning Dog River Festival champion of Backyard BBQs for two years in a row.

Leaning down, I whispered quietly to my mom, "Don't fix a plate no matter how good it smells. We'll grab something on the way home."

Her nod of agreement clearly indicated we were in sync, like usual. My light in an otherwise dark world. The insurmountably heavy burden my father placed on my shoulders was rapidly lifting in a wonderful and appreciated way. We entered the tent side by side. She effortlessly held the conversation as we did one complete pass of the dining space.

Ten minutes later, we were out on the other side of the tent with a to-go box big enough to feed a family of ten.

Ten. Ten.

Dasham.

Dash.

In an instant, Dash's smiling face appeared vividly in my mind. My beacon in an otherwise lonely, lost life. Dash's piercing blue eyes gave me a source of solace from the moment I was whisked away by my father.

After all these years, Dash still mattered. I wondered now if I could finally let him go.

One Week Later,
Birmingham, Alabama

"What about any of this?" I glanced over my shoulder toward Scott Lee who had his head stuck inside my father's crappy old refrigerator. With the loud knocking the condenser made every time it came on, I was certain it was on its last leg. "It looks foul in here."

"Go in careful," I cautioned, lifting from the backbreaking work of scrubbing the grimy, crumbling forty-year-old linoleum floor. "There might be botulism inside there." I raised then wiggled my yellow plastic gloved fingers to encourage him to grab a pair before diving in. "Glove up. Masks are over there too."

Scott's head peeked over the door; his eyes narrowed as he assessed my level of seriousness. I grinned and nodded my certainty at how disgusting it could get, then cocked my head toward the disposable hazmat suit I'd bought as a precaution.

"I ain't scared of nothin'," he declared boldly and bravely, and swung the single door open wide so I might better see the contents. As if on a death wish, he reached an arm boldly inside, swiping all the old, rotting groceries off the top shelf into the trash bag in his hand. "Your dad's gross," he added. A second swipe resulted in even more clanking and crashing.

"How did your father manage to buy two houses?" Scott grumbled; his head stuck inside the box.

"I don't know, but we're nearly finished with the kitchen." I told the lie I'd been using all week to convince myself to continue going. It was losing some of its motivational power. However, this time, we were in fact closer to the end. "You don't have to stay. You've done more than enough."

"I got four days before I go home. Lauren's havin' a baby shower this weekend. I'm not goin' anywhere around there, or I'll get roped into being a part of that female fest. You're stuck with me until Monday morning. Quit trying to toss me out."

"It's weird you're havin' a baby." A massive understatement but still true. More than that, Scott was genuinely excited about being a dad. Throughout all the years of our friendship, close to twenty now, neither of us wanted to have children.

"Yeah," Scott replied, using his index finger and thumb to carefully remove each bottle of condiments to drop into the trash with a louder clank. "With Lauren. She was supposed to be your girlfriend."

Hmm. I considered the different angles such a statement might mean—none were good—and lifted to visually gauge where Scott was headed. He winked at me.

Okay, another puzzle. Who knew what the wink meant, but I didn't pursue it either.

"She was never gonna be my girlfriend," I said, leaving it there as I surveyed my work on the kitchen floor. The only area remaining to be cleaned was where the refrigerator stood and the dirty section of tile surrounding it.

"Why's that?" Scott prodded.

Well hell. I furrowed my brow at the question I didn't want to answer. My instincts had me tumbling backward into my old self and clamping my lips shut. The bucket of water I used to scrub the floor was a good enough distraction, allowing me time to figure out a reasonable response. I rolled to my feet, grabbed the bucket's metal handle with my fist and headed for the backyard.

Frustratingly, Scott followed me out with the trash bag in hand. How did he not know I was in the middle of a crisis and needed time? And would he now press the issue for an answer?

He trotted down the few concrete steps to the ground, right on my tail. Fuck, warmth spread from my neck to my face even in the chilly weather. Anxiety built swiftly making me feel preyed upon, and unusually vulnerable. I regretted saying anything about Lauren. My defenses lowered too soon with Scott. Luckily, I went one way to toss the dirty water into the overgrown yard. Scott headed in the other direction toward the trash bins.

The precious seconds of alone time allowed me to pull forward my tried-and-true coping mechanism. A practiced tunnel vision to shut out the rest of the world, leaving only the work on this house, and what was going to happen to my mom as my sole focus. The manic thoughts calmed instantly.

As it turned out, my crappy father passed away without updating his will. The only one in place was the one my mother had convinced him to make years ago. I inherited half of his estate that consisted of two properties, investments, and a lot of money he'd saved. The other half went to my mother. Over the last few weeks, I'd developed another new coping mechanism: Enjoying the fact that my shitty old man was rolling in his grave, fist-fighting angry for leaving such a glaring oversight undone.

His personal checking account held enough money to pay for simple repairs to his two homes. I'd hired a professional lawn care company to come on Monday. I also purchased several large buckets of indoor paint and other supplies. My mom planned to join us Saturday morning to help tackle the enormous job of getting this house together to list next week.

I made a mental list of tasks that still needed attention before the 'for-sale' sign hit the yard: Paint the walls, deep clean the carpets, and move the beater furniture to the curb to be picked up.

"So, you really gave up football?" Scott startled the shit out of me. I spun around, bowed up, my fist drawn. Too many years of psychological abuse had me unappreciative of being caught off guard.

Scott lifted both hands in surrender. "Whoa, buddy, it's just me."

There was no way Scott missed the fear that accompanied my wild reaction. I quickly glanced away, pretending to be fascinated with the water faucet on the outside brick wall. The constant drip left the ground underneath muddy and mucky. I carefully turned the rusty knob and let the bucket begin to fill without splashing back at me. Yep, I was a professional bucket filler, and quite possibly losing whatever was left of my mind. "I dropped out of college too."

"I'm comin' closer," Scott announced as his work-boot clad feet came into view.

He didn't push me for more of an explanation about quitting football, a yes would have sufficed, but I gave it anyway. "I don't wanna play anymore. Haven't for a long time. And Samford's expensive, I can't afford to be there if I'm not on scholarship."

"Huh," Scott said.

"What's that supposed to mean?" I fired off while twisting the squeaky knob. With more attitude than necessary, I gripped the handle of the bucket, sloshing water out as I went for the house.

"I wanna know what happened years ago to bring you back to Alabama," Scott said, again right on my ass. Someone had to teach him about personal space. He needed to back the fuck up and stop all the probing. I'd say whatever I wanted to say. At the base of the steps, I turned toward him, my brows dropping as my stare snapped to his. Why dredge up the past? What did it matter? I'd made it clear from the beginning that I wasn't willing to discuss this topic. I was on the defense now, a comfortable place to be.

"Don't give me that look. I ain't scared of you. You're like a brother to me. And I have a theory about what happened."

"What's that, Einstein?" I shot off sharply then promptly headed back inside, intending to ignore the answer. No doubt chatty back there would follow. My only hope was the slow steady thumping in my chest that sounded like a jackhammer to me, not him.

"I'd rather you tell me," Scott said quietly. I remained silent and began to disinfect the refrigerator, spraying more Clorox over the surfaces than was probably necessary. Of course, the dog with the bone over there wasn't going to let anything go. First, came the scrape of a kitchen chair dragged across the floor. Second, Scott took the seat in the loudest way possible, going so far as to let out a grunt.

"My guess? I figure you're into the wood." Clearly Scott meant to ease into the conversation with humor, but I wasn't there with him.

One second, I felt paralyzed. The next, fire whooshed over the length of my body. Heat crept up my neck into my face. A trickle of sweat ran from my right pit. I somehow forgot how to breathe.

"I decided you got away from here and were finally able to be yourself. Your shitty old man didn't like it and used his influence to bring you back."

Damn. His guess was pretty spot-on.

I placed the Clorox spray bottle on the shelf, before I dropped it and made a bigger mess.

Shame had me lowering my head and closing my eyes. The word *deny* flashed in bright neon colors behind my lids. "What're your other theories?" I managed to ask in a harsh, rough sound, dropping to one knee in front of the open door, unable to stand on two feet.

"He's gone, bro. I don't think he ever bounced back from your mom leavin'. Nobody goes at the bottle the way he did without harboring a lot of unresolved issues," Scott explained, revealing how closely he'd paid attention. "He was always a drinker but never like what he became. It all happened too fast. I think he took you from your mom to hurt her. You were the collateral damage."

"Then his goals were met," I mumbled. The strong scent of bleach acted like smelling salts, keeping me in the here and now and bringing me back to my feet. The tendrils of humiliation crawled across my skin, prompting a full body shiver.

"You didn't deny it."

Blinding rage replaced my embarrassment. I grabbed the wet sponge, hurling it into the refrigerator with such force it rebounded off the back wall, landing back into the bucket at my feet. Water sloshed everywhere as I pushed the bucket away with the side of my foot. Fortunately, it remained upright as I slammed the refrigerator door shut. "Jeez, man. It's been a hard couple of weeks. Get off me. I'm lookin' forward, not backward."

Adding to my irritation, Scott remained unfazed. Treating my outburst as insignificant. I wasn't sure I ever wanted to tackle an opponent more than right that minute. "Look, you know I'm good with whoever you are on the inside. It doesn't matter to me. What's important is you need to be you, and you need to be happy. I'll be there for you while you figure it out."

Like surfacing headfirst from a torrent of ocean water, the anger ran from me, seeping from every pore. Dash and my mom were the only ones who had truly accepted me. I stared at Scott, feeling overwhelmed by the emotional storm hitting all at once. My chest heaved as I realized I no longer wanted to hide from Scott. The silence between us was deafening.

Scott neither pushed nor retreated. He remained neutral, with no hint of judgment, disgust, or condemnation. The exhaustion of my life had me settling into the seat across from him. Words tumbled from my mouth without thought, something I hadn't done since I left Dash in Sea Springs.

"When my mom and I left, I met a guy in Texas who helped me with my fears. We ran under the radar pretendin' to be friends. He was good to me emotionally, allowed me to be me in every way. We clicked like you and I do, but I was really into him. My dad found out. It was enough to file for an emergency order of custody and you know the rest." My gaze swept to my glove covered hands. "Does anyone else suspect?"

"I've never heard if they did," he said. "Most people think you're stuck up."

I'd heard the refrain many times before, nothing new there. "Don't tell?" Insecurity laced every syllable.

"'Course not," Scott said. I nodded to convey my appreciation as my anxiety twisted my stomach. "So, this is a guy-on-guy thing? You're not into women?"

"No," I admitted. "I've never been. Since I met the guy in Texas, I haven't been attracted to anyone else." I carefully removed the gloves, finger by finger. "I feel deep shame for bein' this way."

"Why?" Scott asked. He'd used that same tone on me many times, the one laced with how off the mark he thought I was. "There's no shame in bein' gay. I have two uncles who are. You know that. You're an awesome dude. Where in Texas is this guy? You need to go see him."

The image of Dash resurfaced vividly. In this memory, he'd just caught his first fish, going wild with excitement. He was breathtaking. A sense of peace enveloped me from the inside out. I no longer had to hide him from everyone, Scott knew.

"No. I can't. I have no way to get there. I've got the cash in my wallet which isn't much. Maybe after the houses sell and the will's processed. I'm givin' my mom my half..."

"Take my truck," Scott interjected, scooting the seat backward to stand. He dug a hand inside the front pocket of his jeans. "I'll stay here with your mom and keep workin'. Be back by Monday, and we'll head back to Mobile together."

My heart clinched at the prospect. The inner spark I'd buried a long time ago reignited, urging me to go. I recognized the value in Scott's idea. It fit with my current efforts of putting the past behind me. I could move forward with my life freely without wonder or regret.

A simple text message would suffice in accomplishing the same goal.

Scott tossed his truck keys on the table between us. Six fifty-dollar bills followed. "Repay me by bein' my best man. I'm gettin' hitched on Wednesday evenin' at my parents' place. What do you say?"

The surprises kept coming. Married with children. The depth of Scott's love showed strongly in his expression. He squared his broad shoulders. He was manning up to his responsibilities.

"Of course, I'll be your best man, and I shouldn't be goin' to Dallas right now. Let me paint the inside of the house, or hell, we can go to Mobile right now," I offered.

Something horrific crossed his face. "No, I told you. All the women are in shower and wedding mode. My mom invited every one of my relatives. They're stayin' in town until after the shindig is over. You and I don't go back until Monday mornin' at the earliest. Tuesday's okay too." His finger circled around the house. "You go to Dallas. I'll handle everything around here until you get back."

Scott's family was a loud and overbearing bunch. We used to sneak off anytime they came to town. A low-level hum of worry built steam inside me. Had Dash really waited for me? For sure, he wouldn't want me once he learned what a loser I'd become. No job, no education, and no real future. The roiling pit of uncertainty in my stomach was back.

Dash didn't have to actually see me. I could ensure he had a good life, and that would be enough.

"You're overthinkin'. You could be in Dallas by eleven tonight if you get goin'. It's a straightforward drive down I-20." As far as Scott was concerned, the topic was closed. He went for the paper towels and began cleaning the spill I'd made.

I wanted to see Dash at least one last time. I went to the bedroom I'd used while in this house, and packed quickly, tossing a couple of pairs of blue jeans and T-shirts in my duffle bag. Socks and underwear followed. Also my dated cell phone and charger.

If luck was on my side, I'd see Dash, learn the truth of his life, and be heading back here by this time tomorrow.

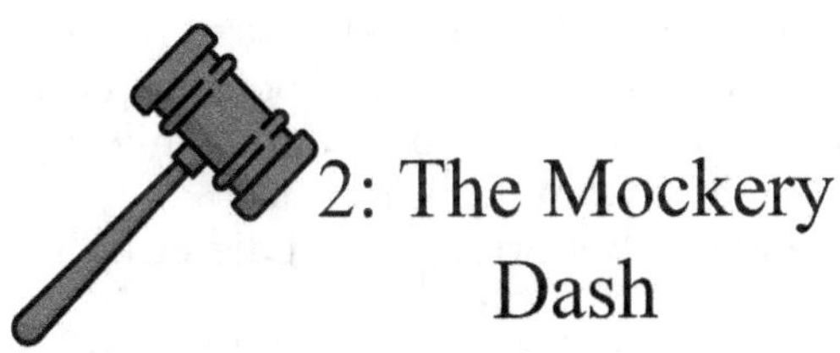

2: The Mockery Dash

Dallas, Texas

Being unexpectedly chosen by my professors to be lead counsel for the nationwide mock trial competition team was one of the most prideful moments of my life. I'd done well in law school, consistently going above and beyond what was required of me.

As a young, determined student, halfway through my studies at SMU's Dedman School of Law, I considered those qualities my strengths. My teammates, in their last year of law school, viewed them as weaknesses, making sure I always remembered I was a trust fund baby. Undeserving of anything since my family name was on several of the buildings on campus.

Like most of my life, I maintained a singular, intense focus while prepping for the competition being hosted at Dedman this year. The rest of the world faded as I spent day and night absorbed in the trial prep.

It all came down to this moment. I stood behind the defense table, the pump of my breath synchronized with the ticking clock on the back wall. Sweat began to form in my armpits, I stood paralyzed as the judge finally delivered the verdict. Her measured words marked the culmination of the final show-down. We won!

A hard-fought battle to the very end against trial teams from all over the nation, and we bested them.

I argued the fuck out of this case. Prepared for every twist and turn thrown my way. A sudden and powerful cheer broke out from my side of the mock courtroom, while a palpable sense of defeat loomed from the other side.

They were worthy adversaries even if I did kick their ass in the end.

A rare surge of pride welled; one I couldn't contain. A wide, toothy grin spread across my face. I hoped to know this exact feeling at the end of every case I argued.

"We did it!" Alexis, second-chair counsel, clutched my arm as she gave a celebratory leap. The rest of the team embraced and congratulated each other.

As the victory unfolded in my periphery, Dr. Harris, my team's mentor, came forward. His hand outstretched to shake mine. He didn't come at me with a smile, but the standard frown appeared less severe.

"You held your composure, Richmond," Dr. Harris said.

"Thank you, sir," I murmured, aiming for humility, but feeling far from it right then. "They're a formidable team."

"Dr. Harris, we're going to Parliament to celebrate. Join us," Alexis invited, shaking his hand. In a first-time move, she looped her arm across my shoulders and beamed at me. "You're legal drinking age, aren't you, Dash? Come along too."

Hmm, was that another jab at my maturity, or an earnest invitation to join in the celebration? It was difficult to tell. My peers had a relentless competitive streak, always ready to point out each other's perceived shortcomings, yet this invitation was a first and sounded genuine. "I'll be there."

"Great," she said. Her grip on my shoulder evolved into a side hug. "I'll welcome you on my team any time."

I doubted her sincerity since she was graduating at the end of this term, but let it slide as she redirected her excitement back to Dr. Harris, breaking protocol by giving him the same side hug she gave me. Stranger yet, he accepted it with one of his own.

"The championship trophy's coming to the place it's always meant to be. Come by the bar."

"I'll be there in spirit," he said before making his way toward the crowd of students pouring into the litigation area.

I took my briefcase and quietly exited through a side door, departing unnoticed. Today had been a triumph. I felt a true sense of accomplishment, but like usual, I had no one to share it with.

Chandler might eventually lend an ear, but his self-centered nature often meant he was only interested if it affected him directly. Since he'd been overlooked for the mock team, he didn't care.

Moreover, my devotion to the silent man on the other end of my cell phone was the real cause of my solitude. My loyalty to Beau created a divide between me and those rare few people who knew my reality. No one, whether friend, family, or foe, understood what motivated me.

I slipped my hand into the inner pocket of my bespoke suit jacket, made for this day. I retrieved my cell phone to report my big news to Beau. Absently, I extended an elbow to push open the building's main door and trotted down the perron.

"Dash! Be at Parliament by seven." Joshua, a teammate, called from the front doors. I didn't break stride until the final step, then pivoted around to shout back, "I'll change then head that way."

"Don't bail," he instructed, leveling a warning finger my way.

My thumbs-up flew high as I started for my car. My complete concentration was back on the screen in my hand, tracing a familiar path to Beau's contact information.

I refused to give up on him even if the situation appeared hopeless. I'd resolved that if I hadn't heard from Beau by summer break, I was going to find him. If I had to abandon my dreams, it was probably better to know sooner rather than later.

My pace slowed, my thumb hitting all the wrong letters until I finally had to stop. I set the briefcase between my feet in order to use both hands to craft a readable message. After reading and rereading the words, making alterations here or there, I pushed the send button. Good. He'd know before anyone else. I slipped my phone back into my breast pocket, close to my heart.

Before my briefcase was back in my hand, a series of dings had me looking around the tree-lined sidewalks, leading to the maze of buildings on campus. The short hairs on the back of my neck stood on end at the uncanny timing. A shiver slithered down my spine.

My heart thumped wildly. I spun around, scanning the kept lawns and stately buildings of the school. Nothing appeared out of the ordinary. Still, I couldn't let it go.

The parking lot, a short distance away, drew me like a bulls-eye. In the distance, I saw a man getting into an older pickup truck. The slanted angle of the winter's sun hit just right to make it difficult to see well.

The creepy crawly sensation intensified as the rumble of the engine came to life. Another shiver quivered over me. The building's front doors burst open. Students and teammates spilled out loud, with excitement. The eerie notion released its hold as suddenly as it had gripped me.

I started for my car again, parked not too far away from where the pickup truck had been. A few weeks ago, I woke to a new Audi R8 in my driveway, technically not available until later this year. My father didn't appreciate its handling and passed it on to me. It drew gawkers everywhere I went. Maybe that was it.

My vigilance became razor-sharp until I slid into the driver's seat and locked the doors the second they shut. If my possible stalker allowed me to survive the night, I'd take action on these eerie feelings tomorrow.

Right now, I had a celebration to attend.

Maybe I'd been wrong about Parliament, a favorite watering hole for many local attorneys. The place reminded me of my dad. Stately and sophisticated with a constant humming vibration of deals being made while others were dissolved. I guessed most patrons, with the exception of the law students, didn't allow themselves to become too mentally impaired. Deals needed a finesse to be negotiated properly. Vodka probably didn't help as well as some may think.

The interior walls, bar top, and tables were steeped in deep reds and polished mahogany. Designed to appear sophisticated and exclusive. Very masculine. A prestigious and expensive networking hub.

I'd never been here before. My future path was set, no need for networking in bars like these quite yet.

"Everybody thinks you're at Dedman because of your family's influence, but you proved them wrong today," Joshua stated boldly, his courage fueled by his alcohol consumption.

I appreciated the straightforwardness and believed most of my peers still shared his opinion—the latter one, not the new one. But nevertheless, I'd showed my worth today.

"We all thought that way," Alexis seconded, noticeably tipsy, raising her glass in salute. "But you set us straight today. Cheers."

With that, a chorus rang out in unison. The roughly fifteen attendees, half my teammates, half their guests, lifted their glasses to the heart of the table before downing what was left of their drinks.

What I hadn't judged properly was my attire. Amidst the sea of crisp, new suits and shiny polished shoes, I'd opted for pressed blue jeans and a relatively new SMU sweatshirt. If the clothing weren't enough to make me stand out, I also refrained from drinking, choosing a club soda with lime instead.

My innate sense of responsibility didn't allow me to drink and drive. The way things were looking, I'd be everyone's designated driver tonight.

I lifted my glass for the toast then dropped an ice cube inside my mouth. I had somehow commandeered the best stool at the table, giving me a view of everyone. The Dedman pride resonated deeply throughout the entire bar.

The low hum of the music began to amplify, signaling it was ten o'clock. Time for the bar to go from sedate to popping. A Madonna hit replaced the previous instrumental playlist. Of course, I knew the song. An essential requirement in maintaining good standing with my gay card. My head began to nod to the beat of the infectious tune.

My simple move seemed to serve as an invitation. Alexis bounded from her stool, grabbing my forearm. I was yanked to my feet. "Dance with me."

I barely managed to get my glass to the table when she tossed her hands in the air and began dancing. The sultry sway of her body aligned against mine. What was I to do with that?

As suddenly as Alexis started, she stopped. Whatever she saw had her standing to her full height, her attention laser-focused behind me. That same weird sensation from earlier resurfaced. I didn't understand it any more than I did this afternoon, but also didn't resist it.

I allowed the feeling to guide me.

Something unseen circled my heart and tugged me forward. My nerve endings sent in flight. A shivery sensation washed over me in continuous waves. Dark shadows encroached on the edges of my vision. What I was able to see came through saturated, vivid, and sharp, all at the same time.

"Damn..." Alexis declared appreciatively, craning her neck to see the front door. "I've never seen his kind here before."

I scanned the bar, searching for the source of my unease and Alexis's delight. My gaze zeroed in on one of the ornate support columns in the open space. My unsteadiness held the focus of two dark blue sleeves poked out from each side of that column.

As I moved closer, the world fell silent.

From the sweep of chestnut colored hair falling onto his forehead, to the strong jaw encasing such a handsome face, my vision began to tunnel. It was Beau. He'd changed. Larger, harder, and almost too gorgeous for my senses to absorb. My heart stuttered to a stop for one, maybe two seconds then began to race wildly as his familiar amber stare met mine. He left the waitress hanging as he zeroed in on me like I did with him. Uncontrolled tears spilled down my cheeks as I broke into a run, launching myself at him, wrapping my arms around his neck, my legs tightly around his waist.

Even with a balancing step backward, I had no idea how he managed to stay on his feet after my forceful impact. Both his hands gripped my thighs, my ankles locked together. Inches from his handsome face, I kept my gaze fixed on his, afraid to close my eyes for fear I was once again dreaming.

My words faltered as I gently used my palm to brush aside the long strands of hair from his forehead. Through all of the tortuous time and distance, nothing had changed. Beau was with me again.

"You came," I whispered seconds before my lips crushed against his, my eyes closed as my tongue insisted on entry into his mouth. He opened, and I swiped forward, executing the perfect deep dive all the way in. My arms tightened possessively around his neck, determined to never let him go again.

I lavished his mouth, taking everything he offered, which wasn't much. Where I was fully committed, he hesitated. An inner conflict urged me to slow down, but how could I? Full throttle was my default setting where he was concerned. As if he read my thoughts, he gently eased off the kiss, causing my arms to cling tighter around his neck.

"Stand on your feet," he whispered huskily. His warm, sweet breath coated my lips. The deep tenor of his voice vibrated through me. The masculine tone had changed too.

"No." And I didn't. Instead, I buried my face into the crook of his neck. The scent of an enticing cologne mixed with a fragrance that was unmistakably him. "Not ever again."

Sadly, he didn't caveman out. Sweeping me from the bar to have his way with me, or me with him. Instead, he leaned forward, letting go of my legs. My feet dropped as his strong hands gripped my biceps, pulling my arms from his neck.

It was now evident that strength also had to be added to the list of his physical changes.

We faced each other. I had to tilt my head back to meet his gaze. "I'm uncomfortable here. Can we do this outside?" he asked softly. Warm honey couldn't be sweeter than the tone of his voice.

"Yes, of course," I said, my stare locked on his. "I need to close out."

"I thought you might," the waitress said, materializing beside me. She extended a small black tray in the gap between our bodies. I hastily added a tip and signed my name on the sales receipt.

"Let's go." Beau nodded over his shoulder and stepped aside to let me pass first. I swear, his greedy eyes tracked me the entire way. I'd forgotten to collect my credit card which the waitress tucked into my palm as I started for the exit. In the same absent-minded manner, I barely remembered to grab my overcoat hanging off a hook beside the door.

The brisk night air cooled my heated skin, helping to untangle my jumbled thoughts. "Of all the ways I pictured our reunion, I never imagined it like this. I thought you'd send a text. My car's this way," I mentioned, looking back at Beau. He wasn't there. With a perfectly executed pivot, I turned around to find him leaning against the hood of a truck close to the entry.

"Mine's here," he called out with humor, watching me. I never wanted his stare anywhere but on me for the rest of our lives.

On closer inspection, I recognized it as the same truck parked in the school's lot.

I had sensed him without understanding what I was seeking.

"You were in the parking lot of my school this afternoon," I said, beginning to head his direction. My need to be alone with him fueled every step I took.

"Let's talk in the truck," he said. I heard the locks release as he climbed into the cab behind the steering wheel. I took a steadying breath as I realized much of our relationship had been defined inside one vehicle or another. As he closed his door, I opened mine, carelessly tossing my cashmere coat in as I hoisted myself inside.

"You cold? I can turn on the heat," he offered.

My ass shuffled across the leather seat until I was so close to him that I had to tilt my head to better see him. The distance still seemed too far, and I reached for his hand, clasping it tightly with mine. Peace and calm blanketed my spirit.

"Why didn't you tell me you were here?" I asked in lieu of answering his question. His handsome expression became unreadable, stoic, and stern. He didn't answer. Beau was still the most beautiful guy in the world, but the rigid set of his jaw and the possible permanent crease in his brow, made him appear harsh and distant. Life had changed him.

A chill unrelated to the weather emanated from Beau as he chose his words. Another change from the youthful guy I used to know. "I don't know what it is about you that compels me to make one bad decision after another," he said, shaking his head briskly, his long hair swaying with the gesture. "Earlier today, I set out to find you. The phone book didn't help so I took a chance and went to your school. I saw you when you came out of the buildin'. I watched you come down the steps. That should've been enough..." His angry stare remained fixed out the windshield.

"What?" I asked. "You planned to leave Dallas without meeting with me?" The way my mind raced, trying to understand what was happening, had me tightening my grip on his. "I've been waiting for you. I have a house nearby that I renovated to suit us both. I've saved quite a bit of money. You'll need therapy, and I found a therapist who specializes in deconstructing conversion therapy. The idea was for you to come here and stay here for good."

The cab filled with our silence. My heavy breaths fogged the glass. Time stretched, each second lingered until Beau tilted his head toward me. His face bore such anguish, the intensity struck deep inside me. If I could hold his hand tighter, I would. "Trust me, you don't want me. I'm broken," Beau murmured, tapping a fingertip against his temple. "I've lost my identity. I'm not the kid you knew in Sea Springs. I'm damaged."

"I'm not the guy you met in Sea Springs either," I countered. "I've grown and evolved. That doesn't mean we don't belong together."

"You don't get it. I haven't grown. My father broke me. I'm a coward. Life's too fuckin' complicated for me to navigate."

His head dropped, his hand shielding his eyes. I shouldn't have barked out a laugh, but it slipped out accidentally. "Cowardice is not a word I'd use to describe you. You're a strong man. I suspect tough as nails based on the calluses on your palm."

Beau shook his head, giving me a side-eye that clearly stated I was way off base. "Not like that. I became my dad's bitch. He broke me down until I was nothin' more than his yes guy. I'm ashamed of how easy it was for him. Then he died and I celebrated his death."

His pointed glare locked on mine with no sign of sorrow or regret. It also wasn't an empty stare of a man devoid of emotion. An ocean of turmoil churned in that amber stare.

"Good. I hope it was an awful death."

For the first time tonight, Beau's fingers tightened around mine. A hint of a faint smile quirked at the corners of his mouth. "I'm not sure it could get worse."

"I think we should go to my place and talk. It'll be more comfortable while we hash all this out," I suggested quietly.

"I'm already deeper in than I wanted to be," Beau answered, but he continued to stare at me, seemingly soaking me in. He lifted our joined hands as the tip of his thumb brushed down my cheek. I leaned into the caress, memorizing the touch, surprised when he used the finger to lift my chin. He was there close to me, descending until his lips pressed against mine.

The kiss began as a sweet searching exploration. At his urging, I opened, his tongue sliding inside. Quickly, desperation fused the kiss into a swirl of tongue and teeth. I allowed Beau the control, letting him guide us.

He released my hand to curve around my shoulders. He drew me closer to him. Oh yeah, my love wanted me. My arm tightened around him as my fingers moved through his lengthy strands. I loved the feel of his silky hair against my hand. I was finally home, again.

All the feels hit in a breathtaking kiss. My tummy tingled when he devoured me as if his life depended on our intimacy—mine apparently did too. A callused palm cupped my cheek and jaw. The teasing pad of his thumb stroked across my jawline, back and forth, while that wicked tongue delved deeper inside my mouth. Of course I followed his lead, matching him touch for touch as I absorbed the best kiss of my life.

3: The Next Two Rights
Beau

Dash's lips on mine were a beautifully enchanting thing. Everything wrong in my life melted away as I rediscovered the bond that held us timelessly in place. Dash's soft, full lips and sweet tongue caressed against mine, giving me the chance to create the rhythm of our kiss. I didn't hold back. I couldn't. My life's love was here in my arms, doing his best to wipe away the past.

The loneliness I lived with began to seep away at the realization that someone truly wanted me. My inner self-disgust vibrated quietly in the background but having Dash in my arms staved off its distraction. What he brought forward was a star-spangled banner style fireworks show exploding through my head. My body heated with desire.

Dash's palm slipped past my open jacket to rest close to my heart, his deft fingertips stretching to caress my hard nipple. The simple touch set off a cascade of tingles rippling over me. Eventually, the need to breathe won, and I pulled away. His lips followed before his mesmerizing face filled my view. Both of his hands were now in my hair, one gently stroking another unruly lock off my face. The other weaving through the longish length.

"Let's go home," Dash said reverently. Every syllable was laced with the implication that it was now my home too.

"I'm not ready to go the distance," I murmured, drinking him in. I was shit to do anything more than lay my palm on his shaven cheek. Dash grinned his gorgeous smile as my thumb traced his full bottom lip.

"Keep touching me like this at home." He began to scoot from the circle of my arms, and I didn't want to let him go. The further he went, the tauter our invisible connection became. My loneliness reared, creeping in around the fringes.

If I had smartness coded in my DNA, I'd reject whatever he offered. I'd be firm in the understanding that he didn't want me, not really.

Turned out I was neither smart nor firm. Of course, a relationship was out of the question, but I had no choice but to follow his lead. However, I promised the scared guy within me this wouldn't last much longer. Scott needed his truck, and I needed to begin my life.

I started the engine. The truck rumbled loudly to life. "Where do I go?"

"Take a right when you exit the parking lot, then take the central southbound on-ramp. My exit's the third one down." He swiveled in the seat to face me as he fastened his seatbelt in place. "You should know, today was the best day for me. I'm grateful you came. When I won the mock trial this afternoon, you were the only person I wanted to tell, but I was losing hope that you'd come back."

Dash spoke like he used to, filling in the silence until he drew me out of myself. It wasn't going to be that easy this time. My palms gripped the steering wheel tighter.

It bugged the shit out of me that I couldn't manage my emotions better where he was concerned. In every other situation in life, I'd kept my feelings locked down. Tucked so far away that no one ever suspected that I had them. I'd been so effective at keeping them secret, I barely registered they were there anymore. I shouldn't have kissed him like I did. It was just all his prettiness right there in my face. His lips alone were part of my wettest dreams.

My thoughts shifted to Dash's cologne. Damn, he smelled good.

"Are you listening to me?" His sharp tone snapped me out of my reverie.

The last thing I remembered… I scanned the street signs, trying to gauge the distance I had covered. I didn't know for sure. Dash caught me unaware, and I couldn't conceal it.

"I said to take the next exit and turn right at the light." His patience calmed me, and I did as he instructed.

"What else?" I asked.

"Oh, he speaks," Dash teased good naturedly. "Stay in the far right lane and take the next two rights. They come fast. My place is the third one down on the right. Let's see how well you listened." His sarcastic humor, evident since our first date, spoke of lots of things. Mainly, a happy life, which comforted me. Joyful people were rare to find, and no one deserved it more than he did.

The house resembled Dash. I pulled to the curb and surveyed the neighborhood. It radiated grandeur and wealth. Dash's home was two stories, maybe three, it was hard to tell.

The front yard was simply landscaped. Two expansive two-story windows took up a large portion of the front of the home. Designer stone, brick, and wood completed the façade. It looked magazine-ready in a contemporary rustic and expensive way. Nowhere near the squalor I'd lived in the last five and a half years.

"Can I park here?" I asked.

"Pull into the right side of the driveway," he said absently, pulling out his phone. His thumbs danced over the screen at lightning speed as I maneuvered the truck into the driveway. Once parked, his phone vanished into his pocket, now forgotten. His full attention was back on me.

"Come inside. We have a lot to discuss." Dash popped open the truck's door then glanced back at me before stepping fully out. "Open your door, Beau. You're here for a reason. Give us a chance."

Something intuitive warned me that if I entered that house, I'd never want to leave. I glanced uncertainly at my hands spread on the steering wheel. They trembled. Fear of adding additional pain to my life began reinforcing the impenetrable internal barriers I'd created over my heart.

Nothing had changed except Dash was unaware of exactly how undesirable I'd become.

The sudden opening of my door startled the shit out of me. I clenched my fists as Dash approached, boldly reaching for my arm. "I understand you've faced unimaginable situations, but you're here now. You came for a reason. Come inside with me."

I looked him straight in the eyes—the hue of my dreams—and spoke my truth. "If I go inside, it'll only make it harder to leave. You have to realize, I'm not the same person I used to be..."

The shame instilled by my father surged, forcing my eyes shut and my head to bow. It was the jingle of the truck's keys that opened my eyes. The key fob was gripped in Dash's hand. All the man unto myself deal faded as my glare pinned him. "Give me back the keys."

"Come and take 'em." The cocky words accompanied a swagger-filled pivot as if he held ultimate control. And in a way, he did. He rounded the hood and started up the walkway before glancing back with a sly grin. "Is this where I add, I win?"

I had forgotten how persistent he could be in getting his way. Seemed the trait had only intensified.

"You're stunning," Dash called louder from the porch, keeping my retort on my lips. "You've grown into a handsome man despite the scowl you've worn all the way home. You're taller and stronger. Do all those muscles on your arms get heavy?"

I had no choice but to leave the truck and follow, my frown deepening. Dash laughed me off, not something people usually did with me. As I drew closer, I added, "You haven't grown an inch more."

His response was to lift the key fob to initiate the truck's locks.

"All the ways I envisioned this to go..." Dash moved closer to the front door under the bright porch lights.

Before this moment, I hadn't been able to stare openly at Dash. My thoughts drowned him out as he left me stunned speechless. I never imagined he could be any better looking than the young man I remembered.

Boy, was I wrong. He exuded easy charm and effortless sophistication, and his matured masculine features held a captivating allure. From the sweep of his now sandy blond hair, almond shaped eyes, straight nose, and strong jaw framing perfectly plump lips, he made it hard to turn away.

How could I have thought I'd be able to see him and walk away? That drove me to the bar for one last glimpse. The reason I stood in front of him right then.

My savior. The only hope I'd had for years.

"What did you think would happen?" I asked, picking up the conversation from the last thing I remembered hearing. I tucked then fisted my hands into my down jacket issued by the university's athletic department.

"Remember, I have a vivid imagination. My dreams had you hoisting me over your shoulder then going caveman on me. Or I'd do that to you. Either way, neither of us left the house for a month." Dash shrugged and stepped backward to the front door as I grew closer. "That's usually as far as I got. I kept envisioning the different ways we'd spend the month."

"You consider that a vivid imagination?" I countered.

Dash opened the front door. His smile widened as he extended a hand, gesturing me inside first. I stepped through the entry, immediately surveying the open floor plan. It was the nicest house I'd ever seen, but also the oddest.

It had a western vibe yet also ultra-modern. Lots of color, fine matching furnishings and glass walls. I was drawn deeper inside as I cocked my head to look up the curved staircase, sweeping up to the second floor from the left of the entry.

"Those are my roommate's rooms," he said. The front door closed behind me, the lock clicking in place.

"Think that's gonna keep me in?" I teased, casting a quick look over my shoulder.

"I hope I'm what keeps you in," he replied with his usual quick wit.

With deliberate movements, Dash came to face me. He lifted on his tiptoes, cupping the back of my neck. With the pressure he applied, my head bent. Not that it took much effort on his part; I was a willing participant. His body pressed against mine. We stared at one another, internally communicating like we used to do.

"You can do much better than me," I whispered. My gaze drifted down to his lips.

"So you've said for years now."

I dipped, he lifted, our mouths melded together once again. This kiss wasn't exactly chaste. The strength and manipulation of my lips held passion, but I also didn't allow it to escalate. We returned to our silent stare.

His conveyed concern.

Everything I had ever felt for him was back in force.

"I waited for you, but it was becoming difficult." I wasn't sure of his meaning, but I suspect it had to do with sex. My assumption seemed correct, judging by the way his arms crossed over his chest as if struggling to maintain composure.

"You don't have to explain or justify anything to me." Yet it hurt. The pain swiftly lanced my heart. I didn't want to hear more about his sex life and stepped around Dash, heading into the living room. Long windows also lined the back walls of the house. The dark night beyond captured my full attention until I took a full turn, taking the house in from this direction. "What's goin' on with this place? I haven't ever seen anything like it."

Dash's tone regained its humor. "A couple of years ago, the house was a Christmas present from my family," he explained and moved to stand in front of me again. "I remodeled based on something I saw in France. It's an ultra-open floor plan on both floors. In this part of the house, the walls are glass. I thought it was cool. Maybe not as much now as I once did. My guests can't resist touching the glass in awe, which means Amelia have to work full-time to help me keep them smudge-free." He nodded toward the rear of the house. "My area's back there. It's more private."

"Your area has real walls?" I asked and grinned.

"There's the smile I adore. Come back and see."

I trailed Dash through the living room, dining room, and kitchen, all the same space. Tastefully decorated, masculine, comfortable.

"This part of the house is shared space and who knows when he'll be home."

At the hallway's entry, Dash stepped aside and swept out a hand, urging me to go first again.

"I don't know the way," I replied.

"You're a smart guy. You'll work it out."

4: The Side Eye
Dash

My heart pounded so fiercely that I feared it might flatline before too much longer.

What I hadn't said to Beau was that I had never dreamed he'd come to me with such distance, ready to leave me once again.

Had I not felt that peculiar sensation, if Alexis hadn't mentioned the hot newcomer, would we even be here right now? I doubted it which meant he still might walk away. Worry and anxiety took me past my usual resolve. The persistent energy I relied upon that fueled my bullheadedness in everything I did. The foreign feelings left me unsteady and uncertain as I tried to rapidly regroup.

Beau had been through hell. The grim reality showed in the set of his brow, the frown he wore more often than not, and in the way he kept looking down at his feet. His broad shoulders rolled as he took everything in around him.

The university insignia on his jacket confirmed my other suspicions. He'd been playing football. Was it forced, or something he'd grown to enjoy?

"Take a left," I instructed, following him.

"The first left of the night," Beau said, his tone held humor, washing over me like a gentle, reassuring caress, tempering the hysteria rising inside me.

As Beau entered my bedroom, the lamp lights and fans flickered on. He went to the middle of the room, the same move as in the foyer then again in the living room, and took it all in. "Who lives like this?"

"What?" I asked, shutting the door behind us. My eyes rolled involuntarily. I couldn't even pretend like I didn't understand the question. The bedroom was akin to a mini home in itself, complete with matching window panels in the same style as the rest of the house. When the lights initiated inside the room, so did the ones in the backyard, and swimming pool area. "Remember, I planned this house for you to live in too. Let me get your coat." I approached Beau from behind, encouraging his jacket off his shoulders. The T-shirt beneath clung to him with static, not purpose. The cotton was well worn, with a small hole near the hem. It didn't appear to be a fashion choice.

"Yup, I don't believe you." As I always imagined, Beau headed for the windows again. He was an outdoorsman at heart. Being cooped up in a city like Dallas might mess with something essential inside him. That was why I chose such openness both inside and outside of the property.

"You should." I tossed the jacket over the sofa near the window and went to the bar on the other side of the room. "Do you want a drink? I have assorted beers. I can mix a cocktail..."

"I don't drink." The firmness in his voice had my head rising from the refrigerator underneath the granite countertop.

"Not at all?" I asked surprised, having never heard anyone say those words before.

"No, but you go ahead." Beau took a seat on the sofa directly opposite from me. Elbows resting close to his knees, his stare fixed on me. It seemed a pivotal moment, but I had no idea why. As much as I might need a shot of liquid courage, I grabbed two water bottles and shut the refrigerator drawer.

"What made you think about deciding not to drink?" I asked, shaking my head at the confusion of my words while passing him a bottle. I circled around the coffee table to sit near him on the sofa. Both bottles went unopened, mine placed close to his on the coffee table.

"My father was an alcoholic," he said, and I angled my position, bending a leg onto the sofa to better see him. The confession caused pain, or perhaps shame, by the way he lowered his head, staring at his shoes.

"I'm sorry." Except I wasn't. Not in the least. The image of Beau being dragged away by his father was seared into my memory. The worst day of my life. I had no care for that man.

"Don't be," Beau said and tilted his head toward me. "He endangered a lot of people and died a pretty horrific death. He lived a rotten, self-centered life."

I nodded, unsure of the situation, but relieved that I didn't have to pretend sorrow. "He was cruel to you?"

Beau's head tilted down again. He did that more than I liked. "He could've done worse, but it's hard to imagine."

"What was it like?" I asked.

"I spent all of my free time trainin' or conditionin'. Durin' the down time, he kept me handcuffed to the furniture to prevent me from sneakin' out. He drunkenly read from the Bible most nights until he found it on tape. It played in my room around the clock. He had countless girlfriends there keepin' an eye on me, barely dressed. I think that was probably done on purpose too." Beau shook his head as if dispelling some memory. "He kept my mother from me. My grandparents both died. But the worst of it all was the number he did to my head. I'm not right."

"I'm sorry. Your father destroyed my life too," I added. "I emotionally couldn't let you go. I refused to pare us down to first love and let you be a side note in my life. My parents sent me to numerous counselors. I was diagnosed with everything from OCD to PTSD to narcissistic personality disorder for my control issues. The only thing that sustained me was my unwavering belief that you'd be back."

Beau's brow furrowed as he gave me a side-eye. "None of those diagnoses sound like you."

"Thank you." I placed a relieved hand over my heart. "I ignored the negativity. I've always wanted to shape my own world. Our dreams, the connection... It was real to me."

"It was two weeks," Beau said, leaning back in resignation. His hands rested in his lap as he stared at me.

I shook my head. "It was a solid month, but it doesn't matter. I met my one."

"Dash..." His voice carried the same doubt I'd heard so many times along the way.

With a lift of my hand, I stopped him from saying more. "I insisted everyone call me Dash. It took time but I refused to answer to any other name. My parents consider nicknames undignified. I suspect they view me as a complete disappointment."

Beau moved his palm to my thigh, gripping me there. "I don't like you thinkin' bad of yourself. I'll admit that I waited for the times I could check my phone for your messages. I read and reread them every chance I got. You saved my life, but you need to hear me, I'm not that kid anymore. I'm hard and mean and insecure as hell. I don't know my place or where I belong. I quit football which makes me unable to pay for school, so I'm out..."

"I thought your life's plan was to work as a delivery driver until you started a fishing charter service," I said, trying my best to hide my smile at the fun memory. Beau had always had two feet planted firmly on the ground.

The warmth of Beau's palm disappeared from my thigh. "I haven't been fishin' since that day I was with you. My old man kept me prisoner as he drank himself into oblivion." He bent his head again, eyeing his fists worrying together. "I turned into a coward. I never bucked him. I'm not sure I could be more disappointed in myself."

This big strong man felt small inside. What a waste. I edged closer. The draw we shared demanded I be as close as I could get. Hell, I'd crawl in his lap if he'd let me, but instead, I covered his hands with one of mine.

He eagerly adjusted until he held it between both of his palms. "It's like this." He nodded to our joined hands. "I only touched you to offer comfort. Now here I am, not lettin' go."

"I don't want you to let go. Much of what you've said resonates with me," Dash said. "I'm honestly a mess. It's worrisome how much influence you still hold over me. I knew happiness today. I haven't experienced it in years."

Beau nodded. "You seemed happy. I watched you trot down the stairs. You were wearin' your suit. It fit you perfectly. I doubt anyone could look as good as you. You command your life. It's really quite somethin'."

"You were there today? When I texted you about my win, a strange sensation overtook me. I felt you there. Just like tonight at the bar."

His grip tightened around mine.

"Congratulations on your victory." Beau grinned proudly at me with his second genuine smile of the night. Lost in what I wanted most in the world, I moved forward, filling the gap between us.

"You're beautiful to me," I whispered and nestled my cheek against his chest, memorizing the rhythm of his heartbeat.

Beau's rough palm cradled my face, his fingers weaving in my hair. He used genuine tenderness in the way his thumb stroked from my temple to my forehead. Time stood still.

"What about those absurd labels the counselors tried to put on you?" he said defensively.

I chuckled and closed my eyes, letting his touch heal the sorrow of the last many years.

"Don't worry. It's all things you're aware of. I'm a control freak. Stubborn and determined to live my life on my own terms, and I've chosen you. If that's considered insanity, I'm good with it.

This moment would go so much better if Beau dropped the resistance and let me in.

"I should go," Beau started. "I gave myself twenty minutes here before I needed to head out. We get along so well that if I stay longer, it'll hurt too bad when I leave. I barely survived losing you once." Those painful words were uttered as a whisper. His thumb continued tracing various parts of my face. The swipes seemed intended to memorize contours.

I tilted my head to better look him in the eyes. His hands remained on me, his fingers gently cradling the back of my neck. "I was shattered when you left. Everything was gone in an instant. The only way I could deal was by planning for the day you returned. When designing this house, I put the western motif in for you. These back walls retract for easy access to the swimming pool. You loved the water."

The pain surging through my heart threatened tears. I never cried, except over this guy. "If you leave, I have to go with you. If you agree to stay, I have a year and a half of law school left then we can move wherever you want. Please don't go. Please."

"I've gotta go back. I have Scott's truck. I was in the middle of gettin' my father's Birmingham house ready to sell when Scott encouraged me to come see you to put this part of my life behind me..."

"Scott knows?" I asked, astonished. If people were aware, why hadn't he come sooner?

"I guess he suspected for a while. He only said anything yesterday. I went dark after leavin' Sea Springs. I cut off contact with everyone. He was the only friend to stay in my life, and I made that damn hard for him. He surprised me when he showed up to help clean my father's properties. He's been a true friend. I need to return his truck. It's the right thing to do," Beau explained.

The continued peeks into his life were hard to digest. I rested my head back on his shoulder, adjusting until my face nestled into the crook of his neck. His cologne was nice. My lips pressed against the warm skin there. "It's late. Leave in the morning."

I intended to go with him. The timing wasn't good, but if we dropped the truck off, then maybe the turn around trip might take forty-eight hours? I'll be able to attend classes on Monday. Seemed doable. "Get up early. It'll be a safer ride and only a few hours difference."

A clever idea.

"I don't know. My mom's gotta be there with Scott by now. I figure if I can put my dad behind me, then I'll be better able to go find a job, buy a truck, find a place to live."

"Dallas has large corporate hubs of all the major delivery carriers. I'm sure I can get you an interview, or you can finish your undergrad here too. I'll get you into SMU with no problem."

"Dash..."

"No," I said, placing my fingers on his lips. "I anticipated you'd need help when you came back. I have resources ready for you."

"You can't fix everything..." he mumbled because I pressed my fingers harder this time. I made sure to align my face to his so he could see how serious I was.

"I'm confident I can. Especially in this situation." I pushed off the sofa, getting to my feet, drawing Beau reluctantly up with me. "Get some rest before you go—it sounds like you need it. My bed might be the most comfortable on the planet." When he didn't immediately refuse, I raised his T-shirt as high as I could reach. He did the rest as I assaulted him with my prying eyes. Damn, how did all that toned muscle get there?

My body was set alight, and my toes curled, as I thought about all the ways Beau could toss me around... Why weren't we having sex right this minute?

I didn't want to push too hard. With my gaze pinned to the floor, I forced myself to think of unpleasant things. War. Extremism. Poverty. Tomatoes. Sour Cream. Tomatoes mixed with sour cream... There we go. I started for my walk-in closet, tugging the sweatshirt over my head. "I have an ulterior motive. I want you to hold me and let's talk about nothing. We used to do that so well."

"We used to talk about everything," Beau said, luckily not detecting my wayward thoughts. "Nothin' was out of bounds."

"I have athletic shorts and an extra toothbrush in the bathroom," I called out just short of banging my head against any of the wood inside this closet. Wood. Jeez-us.

My sweatshirt hit the floor as I began to search for my athletic shorts, not an article of clothing I usually wore. The drawers opened and closed with my touch. Of course the last one held what I was looking for.

"Quite a closet. I've never seen anything like it." I navigated the jeans button through the slot and lowered the zipper. My hand reached for my cock, aligning the tip to peek out from underneath the waistband of my underwear. I hoped he liked what he saw as much as I did.

"How many suits do you have?"

"A lot." With my jeans hanging on my hips, I pivoted around to toss Beau the shorts.

He stood before me the same way except my hard-as-stone cock was met with not even a plump one in return. My tip dripped anyway. "You can dress in the bathroom. If you need anything washed, I'll drop it in, but the earliest it'll be ready is nine in the morning."

Beau rolled away from the doorframe, the tight cords and muscles all worked together fluidly. My cock hardened tighter which was really pretty remarkable.

"I'm not sure I agreed to all this," he murmured, leaving me standing there. I watched his jean-covered ass pop with each step he took. That bubble butt was perfect. He had a slight bow between his thighs.

I went to the closet's entrance and watched until the bathroom door shut behind him. No question, we'd be versatile as soon as I could get us there. I wanted to know what it felt like to be inside him.

My bottom lip slipped between my teeth. I bit down harder than necessary.

Get a hold of yourself. You have a long way to go.

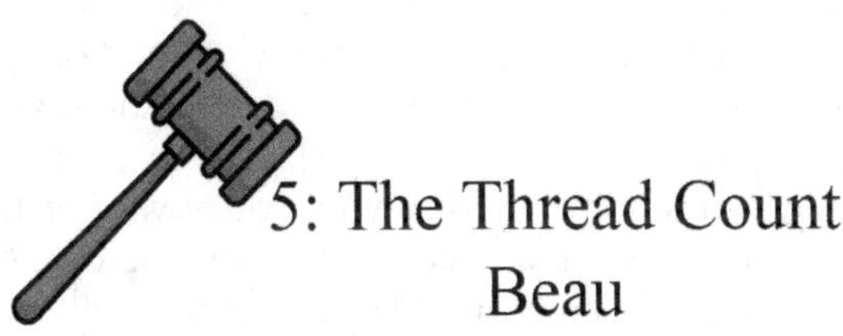

5: The Thread Count
Beau

From the moment I settled into the most comfortable bed I'd ever laid on—even better than Dash's hotel room mattress from years ago—my worries melted away. The instant feeling of relaxation had me digging in to find the exact right spot. Ah, yeah, there it was. The resulting yawn proved the point.

The years of watching my own back had apparently worn me out more than I'd realized. I nibbled at the skin on my lower lip while admiring the intricate patterns of the ceiling tiles. Slowly spinning ceiling fans turned on the opposite sides of the room.

Was this what heaven felt like?

I allowed the notion of finally belonging somewhere—at least for the night—to soak in. I relaxed my muscles, crossed my ankles, and stretched my body from the tip of my toes to the top of my shoulders. I didn't seek the bedspread. I was better than good enough.

Soft, muted overhead lights glowed around the seam of the ceiling and the base of the mounted fans. In the background, instrumental music played quietly. Dash lived a good life.

How I'd managed to get this far into the night was still very questionable, especially since I intended to be en route to Alabama eight hours ago. Nevertheless, I'd cherish this memory, just like all the rest.

Perhaps the universe had guided me on this path of reconciliation to propel me into the future in a healthy way. I was tying up my loose ends.

Dash climbed on the mattress from the other side. His muscular chest and toned arms led to a nicely defined belly, sweet treasure trail, and a solid erection outlined in the material of his shorts. He made no effort to try to hide it.

"I'm sorry. I'm too attracted to you. It'll always be like this when we're together," Dash confessed, maybe due to how intently I stared at said erection. Despite being caught with my eye on the prize, I watched with interest as he used his palm to adjust his cock as he settled in beside me.

"I feel the same way," I admitted, lifting an arm as he nestled against me. He fit perfectly at my side as if that was exactly where he was meant to be.

My feather-light touches along Dash's arm soothed me. He rested his head in the space between my shoulder and bicep. Dash's bark of laughter coaxed me to look at him, prompting me to draw my free arm underneath my head to help hold it up. "What?"

"It doesn't appear that's the case."

I gave a hearty chuckle and solid humph at his absurdity and redirected my attention to the ceiling. Certainly, every person in the world found the man in my arms sexually attractive.

"What's that supposed to mean? I need further explanation. You're making me insecure." I felt his eyes on me.

"Yeah, right. I don't think you know the meanin' of insecurity." A further giggle welled until I had no choice but to let it go, just like the other. Dash insecure. Right. "I got to where I could control my arousal. You made it crucial because you were still all in my head. I guess I got too good at it. It seems like it doesn't work right anymore."

"Really?" Dash lifted to gauge the truthfulness of my words. His eyes narrowed with a wicked glint in his stare. His hand began to slide down my chest. "Can I give it a shot?"

Most certainly not. I was hanging on by a thread. If he managed to bring me up, I might not ever get it to lie down again. With a head shake, I grabbed his hand. There was little doubt the emotions he'd stirred needed to be released, but slowly, dealt with one at a time.

I caught the regret wrinkling his brow. "I'm disappointed. I expected us to be going at it hard."

"Mmm."

"Are you on any of the social sites?"

I barely knew what that was. "No. I don't have access to a computer that often." Another yawn slipped out, turning jaw cracking long this time.

"I didn't think so. I searched for you. I have MySpace and Facebook."

"Hmm," I replied.

"What's going on with the piercings?" Dash asked.

"An initiation deal with the team. All freshmen have it done. I took it a step further, getting my nose pierced. I knew it would piss off my dad," I replied. The good memory of watching him blow his top had me smiling. "I wear these flat tip studs all the time. I'll probably remove them soonish."

"I have employment set after graduation. I've signed the contract. I'll begin working in the fall of next year." Dash's head tilted up to me, maybe for approval, or maybe just in thought. "After this term, I have a year left of law school. I can speed that along and finish sooner if I need to."

"Where're you workin'?" I asked.

"Haynes, Baker, Smart, and Reed. They work for one of my brothers so technically not a self-made opportunity, but most firms in DFW have worked with one member of my family or another. They'll give me credibility as I move forward with my career. Nothing's changed for me. My goal is to help people. I want to offer pro bono services and fight corruption."

As he spoke of his dreams, his fingertip lightly traced the outline of my pec, slowly moving into the edge of my nipple. The simple touch stirred a longing inside me I hadn't remembered was even there. The memory of a young Dash tossing rocks at my window had me tightening my hold, drawing him closer as I tuned back in.

"Money's not really an issue for me, but I'd like to make it on my own. Be self-sufficient and as self-made as possible. Maybe leave my inheritance to our children, or not. I want them to be self-made too."

"Children?" My heart ceased its beat, my lungs stopped drawing in breath. In a whiplash worthy move, I snapped my head up. My eyes had to be bulging out of their sockets. I was never having a child, let alone enough to constitute several. My genetic pool would die with me.

"You didn't seem to be listening. You should've seen the look on your face." His boisterous laugh and teasing glint marginally eased me.

I slid my arm back underneath my head again. Dash propped his chin on his hand. He happily kept my gaze. "I'm still bullheaded. I rarely give in to anything."

"Hmm. I remember you'd sometimes give," I said, easily falling into his hypnotic stare. Dash's charming smile just did it for me, but those eyes were my undoing. I didn't necessarily plan to turn the tables, but I did take the opportunity. "We were only together for a couple of weeks. I guess there wasn't enough time to really get to know you."

Dash's expression grew fierce as he rose above me. It was my turn to laugh. "We had at least a month," he corrected firmly. "Am I the only one who understands simple math?" His strong jaw was set like a steel trap, ready to take on the world if necessary.

"I feel like I win," I said, gently nudging his head down with my hand. It sprang right back up.

"No, you don't win. We had at the very least a long month together. We set forever into motion in those thirty days. I fished and liked it. You showed me how to live a normal life. I shoulder the blame for what happened to you..."

Oh hell no. I jacked knifed up, dislodging him to where he tumbled to his back.

"Dash, listen to me," I said, twisting to look him directly in the eyes. He needed to hear me. "It was my fault the way everything went down. I got too cocky. Yes, you push. You want your way, but it was also the right way. I reached for your hand for the world to see. I was bought into the future you planned. My father showin' up like that... That's on me."

"That's ridiculous." Dash rose as quickly as I had, his chest rising and falling in short breaths. He was preparing to do what he always did, what had me lying in his bed instead of being on the road. He was using reason as he stated his point of view. "I'm the one at fault. You told me no. That should have been enough."

There was no conceivable way I was allowing him, the best man on the planet, to shoulder this blame. I lifted my hand, flinging his words back to him. "If it weren't for the way you went after what you wanted, I'd never have experienced so much. I loved you. I still love you. You drew me out of myself with the way you stayed on me. I reached for your hand. What happened that day is not your fault."

"I don't see it that way," Dash said quietly. His chin hit his chest. His shoulders went slack. He moved until he crossed his legs, sitting in front of me. "I'll admit we're different people now. We've grown, matured, and maybe over the years, I clung to you for the same reasons you clung to me. We've hung on to each other for the hope of a different life. We need to let this happen like it's supposed to. If it doesn't work then it doesn't work, but we have to try. Walking away can't be an option. I know what it's like to lose you. I can't go through it again."

"I don't like me. How're you goin' to?" I whispered hoarsely.

"I don't know the answers except to say, you're here. For you to leave without giving us a chance..." Dash stopped speaking and shook his head, dispelling whatever more he had to say. "Let's go to sleep. You have a long drive tomorrow."

This time, taking Dash into my arms was as natural as sleeping in this bed. When his finger began caressing across my muscles, lulling me into sleep, the smallest of goosebumps sprang up against the touch. A raw reaction that I couldn't hide away. My tight control was slipping.

My eyes closed as I realized I'd never considered Dash's pain. Not really. He'd always been there for me. Never failing to assure me that he was waiting. I hadn't given him the same peace of mind. Luckily, before I fully explored my selfishness, the years of always keeping one eye open, ready for whatever came at me, faded into oblivion. I coasted off to sleep.

Dash's uniquely exotic scent surrounded me, tightening my lax body. I searched for him, patting the bed beside me, wanting my good morning kiss before I started my day. My straining cock hoped his lips agreed to travel lower and take care of my need there too.

I stretched, extending my toes in one direction, my arms the other.

My eyes fluttered open. A long yawn followed as I burrowed deeper into the luxe mattress. I closed my eyes again, remaining that way until the reality of where I was and what I was doing there cleared my hazy mind. This time, I snapped my lids open, my body instantly tensed, and I raised my head to see Dash, fully dressed, sitting in a cozy style chair drawn near my side of the bed. A detail I didn't remember from the night before.

The textbook in his lap held his concentration. Lost to the pages as he turned one over another. He deserved to be on the pages of GQ magazine with the way he dressed: neat slacks and a color-coordinated sweater pullover, jewelry around his neck, bracelets and a watch at his wrists. The impeccable style of his hair, something I'd noticed yesterday, made him seem untouchable to the common man. I lifted further, looking past him to the sunlight filtering through the window.

Damn. I had to hit the road before the day progressed any farther.

In a single motion, I flung the bedspread aside and planted my feet on the floor. I rubbed my eyes, trying to let go of the sleep. "What time is it? I gotta go."

"It's two thirty," Dash said, unfolding from his seat, closing the book. It landed heavily on the bed. "I brought your bag inside." His nod led me to the floor by the sofa across the room.

I stretched my arms above my head, yawning again, sure I hadn't heard him right. "What time?"

"Two thirty in the afternoon," Dash stated calmly, better enunciating each word.

What the fuck? Instantly awake, I got to my feet. Was this a joke? I scanned the room for a clock. Dash stood, wiping at the wrinkle in his slacks.

"I rise early. I don't sleep until two in the afternoon."

"Two thirty," Dash said, correcting me with a broad grin and putting his hands on his hips. "I was unsure what to do. I wasn't quiet while dressing and got up about eight this morning. I called your name several times and shook your foot and arm, but you turned away and stayed asleep. I decided you needed the rest. I've been sitting here studying since. Do you want coffee?"

Shit. "I gotta get on the road." I started past Dash to grab my duffle to dress.

"You can shower. It's ready for you. I've packed. I'll gather my textbooks..."

"Where're you goin'?" I asked, tossing the strap over my shoulder. Dash had bent to gather two books off the floor when our eyes locked.

"I'm going with you," he said as if I were the dumbest person ever and stood to his full height.

"No, you can't do that." For two, maybe three spellbinding seconds, I got lost in all that stood before me. He was just so damn well put together. I gave a forceful shake of my head to clear it of all the nonsense. "I'm goin' back alone. I'm not opposed..."

"No way, Beau," Dash said with authority. "If you leave here alone, you won't come back. Your head's not in the right place." He tossed additional books, one after another on the end of the bed. "I'll tag along as your friend. I promise no boundary-pushing, but in private, we need to discuss the future. A road trip to and from Alabama is a great amount of time to figure it out."

Dammit, there he went again. With a groan, I dropped my head back between my shoulder blades, this time, not near as intrigued with the ceiling tiles as before. Why did we keep going in circles? We talked forever last night. What more did we have to discuss? Nothing, that's what. I left him there and started for the bathroom. "I'm goin' back alone, Dash. There's no place for you there."

"I disagree." Of course he did.

I sent the bathroom door flying shut to end the conversation. I said what I said, and meant it, but never received the satisfying sound of the door hitting the frame's two-by-fours. Dash's hand slapped against the hard wood, bouncing it back on me.

"Give me ninety days. You've said you have no plans yet for the future. Allowing us three months to see if we're compatible shouldn't be a problem."

What? Of course we were compatible. That had always been our problem.

"You can get a job around here. We owe each other a chance at a future."

"You don't owe me anything," I shot back, but dammit if he didn't cut me off again.

"Then you owe me." The condemning words fell like a gauntlet between us.

Well, dammit. He managed to turn the tables on me again. Compassion, as foreign a feeling as happiness, centered me. Pfft. More like knocked me on my ass. I remembered my last thoughts before falling asleep. I hadn't considered his well-being. Always only mine. He was my savior, but I was never his.

Shame triple-timed it to the forefront. I couldn't look him in the eyes, and finally turned my head around, dropping my bag on the bathroom floor. I twisted the shower faucet on the wall. Only a clear half-glass door separated the shower from the rest of the room. It wasn't a small bathroom. Hell, it wasn't a small shower.

"Scott's gettin' married on Wednesday. I need to be there," I explained. "Monday, I have to be in Mobile to finalize the will and handle the money distribution." I lifted my hand to the spray, testing the warmth. Of course, it was perfect.

"That's fine. I need to be back for an exam midmorning Thursday."

"Dash..." I finally ventured to look at him again.

"No, not going to happen. I have zero faith you'll return." He rebelliously crossed his arms as his shoulder hit the doorframe. "Ninety days. It seems a fair deal. If we can't make it work, then you can go begin a life without me."

My internal barriers began to crumble. He'd see soon enough. "I'm Scott's best man. I have to stay through Wednesday night."

"We'll fly home early Thursday morning. I'll handle the arrangements. Is the wedding a formal affair?" Dash asked, pushing off the frame.

"I'll wear blue jeans, probably a nice shirt if I have one. It's at Scott's folks place, next door to where I grew up."

Dash vanished from view. I dropped my shorts and underwear to the floor then stepped directly under the hot spray. The showerhead and hard spray earned itself a gold star.

"So, a sports coat?" Dash called loudly, drawing my attention through the foggy glass half door of the shower. There he stood, in the middle of the bathroom, staring at my naked ass. Of course he'd have no sense of personal boundaries.

"Or a sweater like you're wearin' now," I said just as loud. My palm slashed across the glass to see Dash's slightly raised single brow questioning the sincerity of my suggestion. Maybe he found his answer, and pivoted around, leaving me to finish.

Oh man, he had some quirky habits.

I made quick work in the shower then dried off. I placed my bag on the closed toilet seat. Based on the fold of the ones on top, I guessed Dash had washed my clothes from yesterday. They were placed neatly on top of everything else.

To test my theory, I brought the underwear to my nose. A risky move that proved them clean, then I tugged them up my still damp legs. The jeans and a different T-shirt came next. I tossed my toiletry bag on the sink top. From there, it didn't take more than a few minutes to brush my hair away from my face, shave, and work on my teeth.

A lot of the time, I stared at the hairdryer, the cord wrapped neatly around the base. I didn't usually use a hairdryer. I barely brushed my hair. Had Dash left it for me? Did he want me to use it?

Hell. I shoved my toiletry bag back into the duffle and placed a pair of socks on top.

"What's the deal with the truck blocking my entrance to the garage?" The male voice drew my attention like a lightning crash before the thunder. Instant jealousy fisted my hand as I rolled my head toward the voice. A wall separated me from him.

Extreme emotion ripped through the cobwebs where my feelings used to be. If there was any doubt they were back, it resolved itself in this moment.

Fuck whoever was talking to Dash that way.

Rational never entered my realm as I considered that guy out there to be the same one Dash had been unfaithful with.

I left the bathroom like a bull seeing a red cape, rolling my shoulders, loosening the strain as my biceps flexed. Intimidation was the only thing I had on my mind. The newcomer, who was trim and nice-looking, definitely fitting better in Dash's world than I did, turned that attitude on me.

Seconds later a smirk quirked the corner of his mouth.

A. *Smirk.*

"I'm guessing he came back."

I twisted my neck to keep from snapping his.

"Chandler meet Beau. Beau, Chandler." Who cared what his name was?

"How did it happen? Did he just show up or did you know he was coming?" Chandler asked, eyeing me as critically as I eyed him. Whatever that meant.

"It's only been since last night," Dash said, casually stacking his travel gear neatly together on the end of the bed, seemingly oblivious to the tension. "I've planned to spend a few days away. We'll be back Thursday morning."

"Huh. So it's picking up where you left off..." The beginning of the sentence held confidence that fled with each syllable uttered. Good guess, guy. A real brainiac here. My hard glare continued, watching him watch me. "Is he going to beat me up?"

"No..." Dash finally glanced at me.

"His shoulders just rolled," Chandler warned. "Seriously, dude, it won't take much to knock me out." Right then I issued an oath to myself that I'd never stop working out. I'd lift until I couldn't then do it again. Both of Chandler's hands raised in surrender. "I'm out. I parked in the driveway behind your car."

With a dramatic twist that I didn't like one bit, he left as fast as he came.

My head swiveled toward Dash in astonishment. "Is that who you've been sleepin' with?"

"What?"

I wasn't buying Dash's fake confusion. *Wah*. Dash wanted us to be together forever. Have to have forever, nothing less... Then he fucks that guy?

"No..."

If he went for guys like that, what was he doing with me? "Because you can do better..."

6: The Working On It Dash

I admit, I may have flipped my palm against my forehead in an overly dramatic way, but I had to ensure my brain stayed put and didn't fall out as I struggled to make sense of what was happening. No matter how many times I hit the mental rewind button, I had no idea where Beau's wild accusations came from.

"I stayed faithful to you," I muttered, trying to keep my cool. "*Painfully* faithful. Those were some of the hardest times I've had while remaining loyal to you." The frustration turned to hurt as I consciously absorbed the very idea of him believing I'd been with anyone else. "Why do you think otherwise?"

"Because you told me last night!" Beau tossed out a hand as if throwing my words back at me. A fresh wave of anger ignited. I never said anything close to that. Was he treating me as a simpleton?

My brain might have actually exploded when he went back into the bathroom, leaving me to argue this out on my own. I covered my mouth with my palm, blinking rapidly. Did he just dismiss me after calling me a liar?

"I did no such thing!" I marched toward the bathroom where the madman had gone to hide.

"Yes, you did. You said you struggled with bein' faithful." Beau's arrogantly cocky roll of the eyes grated on my last nerve.

"I struggled mightily. Chandler loves to host a good party. He has people over all the time. I was hit on more than you'd imagine, but I never took anyone up on their offer." My foot stomped on its own to drive the point home.

Beau paused in mid-zip of the duffle bag and glanced at me. "You have guys in your house, offerin' themselves up? What sort of place are you livin' in?"

"Oh my god." This time I flung my hand out, silently screaming my disbelief at Beau. My overflowing aggressive energy needed an outlet, so I paced my bedroom in long strides. The exercise didn't help. My unrelenting hard-on refused to give me a single second's break since the moment I saw that crazy man last night, and he thought I was messing around? Me? "You're suggesting that my years of devotion to our relationship somehow didn't include sex?"

My hands trembled under the burden of the past sixteen hours. I needed to calm down. On a cleansing breath, I tried to approach this from a different perspective. So, what was the different angle?

Perhaps Beau's response wasn't a finger-pointing accusation, but rather a glimpse into his inner turmoil and insecurities. The protective jealousy Beau flexed at Chandler revealed what he couldn't say. Beau cared deeply for me which unsettled him.

My cool demeanor slipped instantly in place. "I'm sorry, I should've better prepared you about Chandler living here. If you don't remember, he's been a longtime friend."

"If these three months are gonna fly, he can't live here," he said, striding past me toward his runners.

"Then we'll move him out." I knew Chandler wouldn't be thrilled with a sudden move. He'd always been my rock, but he also knew I'd move mountains to keep Beau with me. "Chandler can handle his own. He's been my only friend. My age and attitude have been a problem. No one likes a grown-up kid genius who's waiting on the sidelines for his boyfriend to return."

Once laced up, Beau slung the duffle over his shoulder. Did he plan to leave? The bravado building inside me tanked. "We gotta get movin'. If I drive all night, I think we can be there before the mornin'. That'll give me a day to help finish the house before we go to Mobile. Can you make some sandwiches for the ride?"

"Is that all you have to say?" I asked incredulously.

"Probably not. Right now, I need a clear head to drive across a few states. Are you bringin' these?" His head nodded toward my luggage sitting at the end of the bed. He tossed my weekender over the same shoulder with his bag. He fisted my heavy bookbag in one hand, my garment bag in the other. In the doorframe, he shot a quick look over at me, eyeing me close. "You aren't goin' now?"

"I am," I murmured, searching for patience. "But I'm not happy with the insinuation that I'm not who I've tried to be."

"I didn't call you a liar," Beau gently reassured. It mended my tattered dreams together again. "I misunderstood what you meant last night. Then the way he walked into the room seemed overly familiar to me. It rubbed me wrong. I'm sorry."

Interesting. I wasn't a fan of him apologizing either.

The open road was waiting. I approached Beau. He stood frozen, watching me.

An electrifying thrill zapped through me as Beau swooped in for a soft kiss on my lips. He wanted me and I certainly wanted him. A significant leap forward. The garment bag came into my line of vision. "Take it. I don't want it to get wrinkled."

Mark consideration down on the list of good qualities of my adorable guy. It was happening for us. I mentally crafted Chandler's eviction notice.

Birmingham, Alabama

"Hey, buddy," Beau said, heartwarmingly sweet. My guy. His strong rough palm caressed from my forearm to my bicep. "We're here, Dash."

The compact travel pillow under my head might be the best purchase I'd ever made. The small fleece blanket may come in second. I drew it up to my chin, settling into the slight recline of the seat. A yawn followed.

Who knew a ten-year-old truck could ride so smoothly with such relaxing seats?

Wait. Smooth didn't mean still.

My lids flipped open, searching out the front windshield for the time of day. Bad call. Overly bright sunshine assaulted my vision as I pushed up in the seat, righting myself. Apparently, I'd been asleep for hours.

"You snore."

"I don't think so." But how did I know? The relentless sun hit from every angle, no matter which way I turned. I fumbled with the visor to block the blinding light, stealing a glance at my reflection in the dinky mirror.

What I wasn't was a morning person, and I cared about my appearance. And what I saw ensured my morning's bad mood.

The growing facial hair couldn't be helped. I wished I had gotten in the habit of using a handheld shaver. Outside of that, I had a small amount of bed head to contend with. The disheveled style I currently wore took a decent amount of product and time in order to look effortless. I swiftly arranged the wayward strands back in place. "What time is it? And why's the sun so bright here?"

The answer came with a chuckle.

"Around six. I pulled over a few hours to sleep. We made good time. I didn't want to get here too early." A massive yawn interrupted him. "You slept through it all."

Inspecting my clothing came next. I swiped at the wrinkles until I found it best to stand and left the truck. Well damn, even my best wrinkle-free slacks had creases in them. I did a full circle while in the middle of the street. The neighborhood was older, the homes were smaller, and it wasn't nearly as cold outside as Dallas.

"Beau."

I'd recognize that voice anywhere. Linda Brooks, Beau's mother, called from the front porch.

In just five and a half years, she'd aged at least a decade. Her vibrance was gone. The sparkle in her eyes had dimmed, replaced by worry lines etched there and at the corners of her mouth. The past had taken its toll on her pretty face. Yet her love for Beau shone through as she started down the few steps, robe on and coffee mug in hand.

The guy holding the rickety screen door open had to be Scott. He and Beau were similar in dress. What Scott and I had in common was that we both openly stared at each other. His look implied curiosity while I had a feeling mine likely mirrored Beau's with Chandler.

Stop being silly. Scott's generosity brought Beau to me.

I looped around the truck's hood, flashing a grin at Beau's mother.

"Dash, you came." She met Beau with a side hug then bypassed him, heading my direction. "I was worried when I heard he left to find you, and now you're here." She enveloped me in a warm hug. "You haven't changed a bit." The embrace lingered as she pulled back, a curious glint in her eye. "Are you and my boy back together?"

"Mom," Beau called sternly, but his mom and I were on a whole different wavelength.

"I'm working on it," I said, making sure Beau caught every word. "He's stubborn, with walls of reinforced concrete around him, but I've got my trusty wrecking ball."

"Dash," Beau warned.

"Hush, Beau," she said, scolding her son. She looped her arm through mine as she started us up the walkway to the house. "Give him time." Without waiting on us, Beau had gone to Scott, who was at the top step, grinning like a Cheshire cat.

"I win," he teased, genuinely happy. I didn't know how he won, but those words were enough to dig a path straight under Beau's skin.

"You're way off base," Beau scoffed, executing a heavy footed climb up the steps. The slump in his shoulders screamed defeat. I found it oddly endearing because I felt like I was involved. The truck keys exchanged hands.

"No, I'm not. It might be the most victorious win of all time. You're finished. No other wins can ever beat this win."

Scott chuckled happily. Beau clearly had no use for anything more Scott had to say as he flipped around, trotted back down the steps, and side-swiped me and his mom in the direction of the truck's bed. "He didn't win."

Since I didn't have to worry about him leaving—Scott had the truck keys—I continued along with his mom. When close enough to Scott, I extended my hand. "I'm Dash."

"I'm Scott." The sure clasp and direct stare eased any lingering nerves.

"I owe you. I'm not sure he would have come to Dallas if you hadn't intervened."

"That's why I *win*," Scott called loudly to Beau. I probably shouldn't have chuckled. His mother absolutely shouldn't have laughed. She knew all of the obstacles Beau had faced, but evidently, she and I had our flaws.

Beau ignored us as he gathered our belongings.

"I was afraid I pushed too hard after mama-Brooks was worried. Seems all went well enough," Scott said.

If only Scott knew the truth. The intensity of the mock trial had nothing on dealing with Beau Brooks. Beau stalked past like a pack mule, loaded down with primarily my luggage. "Why do we have to talk about this outside? Or at all. Just go inside," he huffed.

I'd give him a break for now, but I wanted to know everything. Much like all those years ago, I was drawn to the familiarity and love within this family. Scott knew how to handle Beau, so I now deemed him my mentor. When Beau held the door open, still holding all the luggage, I went inside, happy to be there.

7: The Ellen's Beau

We opted for dinner at a local Birmingham spot: Ellen's. Named the best burger joint by the local Birmingham newspaper, three years running. We chose to sit on the covered porch, the nearby standing heaters mitigated the slight chill in the air.

I was far past the idea of everyone automatically knowing I was gay because Dash was there with me. My current assessment of the evening landed somewhere between relaxing and easygoing. The chatter between the four of us flowed effortlessly. Dash was the perfect gentleman, just as I'd always known him to be.

He sat next to me in the booth, leaving just enough space between us that I suspected we looked like friends. His half-eaten burger, no onion, no cheese with French fries on the side, all served in a red plastic basket, hadn't budged from the place the waitress had served it.

Manners were natural for him. The expanded paper napkin in his lap looked nothing like mine, which was crumpled on top of my basket I'd shoved to the center of the table. I'd gone at my food like I was on a survival mission and hadn't eaten in a week. It took about a minute for me to figure out Dash was done before I finished his burger and ate the remaining French fries out of his basket.

A jukebox serenaded us with some older country tunes. The kind that made you cry if you listened too closely. Scott had made such progress on the house that we'd had free time this evening.

We hit up the game place next door before dinner. We played Putt-Putt, rode the go-karts, hit some balls in the batting cages, and spent way too much money in the arcades. I was admittedly rusty at anything more than playing football but still managed to beat Scott in two of the four competitions. The loss that hurt the most was *Ninja Assault*. He beat me soundly, officially becoming my former best friend.

My cheeks were sore from all the grinning I'd done tonight. The rivalry between Scott and me came back with a driving force. My old man barely had one foot in the grave, but man, the oppression he'd caused was lifting at lightning speed.

The unexpected thought of my father had a dark vengeance creeping around the edges of my heart, my fingers clenched into a fist. My deep cleansing breaths drew Dash's attention. I ignored his questioning glance and did my best to tamp down the anger threatening to overwhelm me.

My father had no place in my happiness.

Dash did though. He'd been spectacular today. A mix of kindness, wisdom, and a scent that made me want to cannonball into my commitment to him. Even his sweat-soaked labor, weeding flower beds, hauling every bit of junk to the curb, and cleaning out the garage, had a magnetic charm. In mere hours, my mom and Scott had fallen under Dash's spell too.

My head was a total roller coaster of chaos tonight. I tried to refocus my attention on the conversation at the table.

But how? With Dash beside me, I swore I could feel his heartbeat in sync with mine. Maybe it was because I squeezed my big body into the booth, claiming more than my fair share of space. I had one arm casually draped over the booth's back, the other rested on the low partition wall separating the booths.

"You're quiet over there. Does that mean you agree?" Thankfully, my mom's question snapped me back to reality. I raised an eyebrow, needing more information. Her grin widened. The stress of the past was lifting off her too, and I liked seeing that.

"I said, we've planned to leave around five in the morning to allow time to unload at my house, clean up, and be at the attorney's office by ten. You and Dash are staying with me, just in case there was any question."

"I offered to get a hotel room, but she insisted we take her second bedroom," Dash added, his face asking the question that his words didn't. Did he think I actually had a say?

Three pairs of eyes fixed on me. I shrugged and said, "Okay."

"Dash, Beau drifts off while you're talkin' to him all the time," Scott said with sarcasm, flicking a lettuce scrap at me. It didn't go far before falling to the table.

"I feel like he knows that by now, ass. But thanks for lookin' out for him," I added dryly. My mom's contagious laugh had me shooting her a wink. She clearly enjoyed the banter.

"Do you want me there at your meeting with the attorney?" Dash chimed in. "I can review anything you need me to."

"Probably a good idea. Everything played out so bizarre in the end." I kept my eyes locked on my mom, waiting for her approval. "It seems straightforward. The only will found pre-dates the divorce. My mom's the main beneficiary, but he gave me half. What I get goes to my mom."

Her smile, a good mix of sugar and sweet, made me happy. "You need to keep your money, honey. You earned every cent dealing with all that drama."

That wasn't an option. Her debt levels were too high due to the legal costs she'd paid while fighting to get me back. I shook my head, turning to Dash for backup, only to find him smiling at me with the same gooey sentiment as my mom.

"What?" I asked.

His hand landed on my thigh with a brief caress and gentle squeeze. He didn't let it linger. It meant a lot that he tried to respect my boundaries.

"You're giving everything to your mom?" Dash restated what I just said.

"Yeah, I just said that. It can't be the first you've heard about it." My furrowed brow had to show my confusion. "She lost her ability to work in Mobile County. She had to take low paying jobs and work all day and night every day to pay for all the bullshit legal fees that just kept comin'. She took care of my grandmother until she died. Her car's fifteen years old, she rents, and needs a retirement fund."

"He's a good dude," Scott said directly to Dash. "He's changed but it's still there."

"Stop it," I said, feeling a flush rising in my cheeks.

"None of my siblings would trade their inheritance to help either of my parents. They're like buzzards circling, waiting for the end."

I didn't doubt that for a second which made Dash and his desire to be self-supporting more special. The tip of my thumb lifted on its own accord, caressing a small swipe over Dash's sweatshirt. I didn't even consider doing it. But between the two of us, he was by far the better human being.

"Wait, your family has money?" Scott asked.

Dash ping-ponged his gaze between my mom and me, clearly in need of a lifeline. I saved him from his confusion.

"Remember when that hotel moved into Sea Springs?"

Scott nodded but with the way his eyes narrowed, I wasn't sure he remembered.

"His dad owns it and a lot of other things in Texas. I believe he got started in oil?"

Dash nodded, shaking his hand in a "sort of, kind of" way.

"Oh man, that totally clicks." Scott's palm landed on the table with a whack, his smile spreading wider.

"Meaning?" Dash replied. Scott's words hit a nerve. It seemed Dash still tried to pretend he was an average guy.

"I think he means how you present yourself," I answered, cocking my head to better see Dash.

"How do I present? I'm fitting in," he said, lifting both his hands as if he looked the same as the rest of us. All three of us burst out laughing at his absurdity and absolute cluelessness. Dash shot out an elbow, jabbing me in the ribs. "I blend in fine. We're dressed the same, eating the same food. I would have had a cocktail but I'm not sure how Beau feels about it."

Scott's loud bark of laughter couldn't be contained. He drew everyone's attention around us. "Who says cocktail around here? We're country folk."

"You guys, good?" the waitress asked.

"Ever hear the word cocktail around here?" Scott asked.

"Not that often," she said, unsure of her response. She scanned each of our faces, looking for the landmine she'd somehow stepped in. "But yeah, so you play football for Samford, right?" she asked, her eyes landing on me while gathering the baskets from each of us. "You're the one everyone goes nuts for."

As the spotlight shifted to me, my mom knew the drill and grabbed her purse, starting out of the booth. Scott followed. "Used to. I gotta get a job now. It's a family thing."

Dash got my pointed stare. He needed to hustle out of the booth, but he didn't budge.

"Man, everybody's gonna be disappointed." She cast a long glance over her shoulder to the guys sitting at the bar.

Something went down in that exchange, further signaling our cue to roll out of there before I got swarmed with questions. I'd be offered jobs and cash on the side to stay.

"Well, have a good night," she said.

My mom placed tip money on the table. We'd paid for our food up front when ordering. Dash just needed to get hustling.

"I'm about to have an onslaught of people comin' to talk football with me. We need to go." I gave him a solid hip bump. If he fell to the floor, I'd toss him over my shoulder and get the hell out of there. "We'll get trapped."

"Where're your mom and Scott?" Dash asked. A snail moved faster than him. He checked his clothes, shook out his jeans, completely unhurried. From my peripherals, I caught the waitress with the guys. Gasps ensued.

I grabbed Dash by the elbow, pulling him out the front doors with me. We were loading in my mom's car in seconds flat. I swear the entire restaurant watched us leave.

"I have plenty of space over here. It's gotta be more comfortable than that cot," Dash suggested. His hand patted the fancy air mattress I'd splurged on at Lowes today.

"I'm fine," I lied. Anything had to be more restful than this old army cot.

"Clearly not," Dash pointed out. The mattress didn't make a single noise as he lifted, propping himself up on an elbow. "Your legs are dangling off the end. Your arms would too if they weren't crossed over your chest."

"Go to sleep. We gotta get up early." I understood I was being difficult for no reason. It was just where my head was right then.

"You've been awake for the majority of the last thirty hours. You're not falling asleep because you're uncomfortable. Hop on the air mattress." Dash scooted to the farthest side. "Well, don't hop or I'll go flying, but get down here. I'll keep my distance, but the fact you don't want inside this bed with me concludes that you may not want me to keep a distance, and it scares you. Don't be afraid. You'll sleep better here." He patted the bed again annoyingly.

He wasn't wrong, but when the desire floodgates finally burst, it wasn't going to end well for either of us. Well, it would end good. Great actually...just not here.

But his words still had merit. I rolled onto the mattress pressed directly up against the cot. I grabbed my pillow, tucked it under my head, and Dash covered my body with blankets. He faced me, a hand tucked underneath his pillow. We were maybe a foot apart.

"I rented us a car in Mobile. They'll deliver it once we get to your mom's place." Although he whispered, it wasn't quite the right bedtime conversation to lull me under.

"She said we could use her car," I said, trying to understand how a rental car might be delivered like that.

"It'll make it easier if we have a car. I could also get a hotel room."

"You'll hurt my mom's feelin's. She's excited you're here." Dash eyed me, probably trying to decide how much truth was in my words.

"I'll give in on the hotel room if you agree to sleep in the spare bedroom with me. It seems too disruptive for you to take the living room while I have the entire bedroom to myself. I haven't seen her couch, but I know you're too big for it. You won't be comfortable."

"I'll be fine," I murmured, happy for the chance to stare openly at him. Other than the side of his face being distorted by being smushed into the pillow, I enjoyed the scenery.

"We're full circle. And you won't be fine," Dash countered. "You take the bed. I'll sleep on this air mattress." We'd been quiet, talking at a whisper or little above, but that sweet guy caused me to burst out with an involuntary bark of laughter. He brought his hand to my mouth, shushing me. His gaze flitted to the hall where Scott had taken one of the two bedrooms, then down the other direction where my mom had taken the second bedroom. "Stop laughing. I mean it. I'll sleep on the air mattress."

"No, you won't. It's a ploy to get me in there with you."

He pulled his hand from my mouth, and I got a critical stare.

"Pretty full of yourself, aren't you?" Dash gave up the pretense of staying away and inched closer. "Besides, you gave me ninety days." His gaze dropped to my lips. "It's not going to happen for us if we don't share space."

He wasn't wrong, and it wasn't taking ninety days. More like one day. I draped my arm around his waist, wanting the kiss he hinted at more than I wanted anything else, but he was right, I was tired and needed sleep.

"A small goodnight kiss," Dash urged.

I met him halfway. A hair's breadth apart, I whispered, "Thank you for today."

"You're welcome." His breath coated my face, driving me forward to capture his lips with mine. He tasted so damn good, making my dreams into reality once again.

Dash honored his word and kept the kiss small. As he pulled away, his warm palm came to my cheek. His skilled thumb swept over my jaw. "Sleep, big guy. Tomorrow's coming."

I fell asleep with the taste of Dash on my lips.

8: The Crybaby Dash

Mobile, Alabama

"You're a crybaby," Beau said.

Hmm. I felt his playful gaze directed at me but didn't turn to look. I drove, and Beau acted as our tour guide as we made our way to the legendary Dog River. The place where he spent his happier childhood years.

"About what this time?" I asked, taking one of the many curves on this long and winding road.

"My mom was convinced you needed me in that bedroom with you," he said as if only now remembering the theatrics I'd used last night.

It had worked like a charm, and that was all that mattered. Not to mention, I was now a player in Beau's game that I completely crushed. "I win."

Beau swung around in the seat, rocking the car in all his abruptness to face me. "Stop claimin' victory when it's not honestly earned. Manipulatin' and lyin' to my mom about a made-up fear of spiders doesn't count as a win. It's not a win. I only gave in because she was goin' to sleep in there with you if I didn't. What happened to takin' this slow? Buildin' into things? Not pushin' so hard?" Beau asked. Again, I felt his glare on me. I didn't look.

"Regardless of your perspective, it's still a win per the rules of the game as I understand them. That's a five-time streak by now, right?" This time I did take a gander to see if steam came out of his ears when he hit boiling point.

Beau scoffed. "You don't have five wins. You have no wins by my records. By *your* shady set of rules, you might have two." He settled properly in place.

"Not true. I have three wins," I fired off, protective of the few things I'd been allowed to get right. Beau stared at me silently causing me to look closer between the road and that handsome face that held hints of anticipation and...ambush? *No.* I'm ashamed to say it took a minute.

Dammit, I fell for the bait. "Omigod, I was rounding up to five, not being literal."

"See? You don't play by the rules. You lie. I win."

Oh, I marked his smugness in my head. When the time came, he was absolutely being repaid.

"Take your next right, about a mile ahead."

He'd better be glad that I'd had such a nice day that I let it go. We had first tackled the attorney, then took a scenic tour of downtown Mobile. Dallas was landlocked from every which way. I liked the way the city of Mobile sprawled close to the Mobile River's edge. We walked around a park, took in the sunshine, and enjoyed the fresh air. No jackets needed, which was maybe the best part of the day.

Sadly, I played by Beau's rules, keeping my distance as he talked and shared his life. Spending so much time together, it was remarkable how we had no awkward moments. We were always so fluid together. Maybe. He sure liked to give me a hard time, but I decided that had more to do with everything he kept bottled up on the inside.

Overall, Beau's barriers were crumbling, his defenses melting. He watched me when he thought I didn't know. He listened when I spoke. When we did share an exchange, I saw the love and devotion he tried to hide. He made my toes curl. I was living the best version of my life. My dreams were coming true with every minute we spent together.

"When they built this road, why didn't they just make it a straight shot?" I asked, slowing down again. "Wait, I know. Because Alabama thinks crookedly."

"Your hair's darker," Beau said as if I hadn't just made the best joke in the world. "The roots are darker."

I nodded and pointed to the only opening in the road. "There?"

"Yup. Drive about four miles then you'll see neighborhoods begin. We'll be close then."

I took the turn as if it were a curve. Beau's hand shot out to the dashboard, steadying himself. "Hey now," he called.

Again, we were on a road with nothing but wide-open land before us. The scenic route didn't have much scenery. "I'm the only one in the family to go darker. I believe they call the color honey. During the winter, I highlight my hair. In the summer, it blonds up nicely."

"Hmm. It looks more brown than honey."

"Omigod. Can you give me a break on anything?"

Beau flashed the grin I loved, sucking me into his handsome face, before throwing me the ultimate curveball. "The rest of your family's super blond. Does the postman have darker hair?"

The accusations flew every time my family gathered together. My father blamed the milkman, whatever that meant. Honestly, I liked the depth of color in my hair. It didn't wash me out. Beau's laugh meant that he'd caught on to my overanalyzing the subject.

"Don't hurt yourself overthinkin' my question. My mom was super blond when she was a kid, but you can't tell now. You could've warned me in some of those text messages you sent. It might have changed my mind."

"I had to warn you?" This time, Beau couldn't keep a straight face. His lips were mashed together until they burst wide again with laughter.

"I'm kiddin'. You look great, like always." In his effort to set up the perfect tease, he'd delayed issuing a navigational checkpoint with only seconds to spare. "Turn left. It's comin' up quick."

I decided to take back control, and whipped the car to the left. The tail end did a little dance, fishtailing us through the turn.

"Hey now, you're gonna wind us into a ditch."

"You navigate and quit worrying about my hair. I'll add more blond."

"Don't change the color. It makes your eyes pop, and your jaw look strong." He gave the compliment so casually I had to look over at him to judge his sincerity. Hmm. I'd lost his eyes on me as they were now focused out the window. "Turn on the second street on the right."

The further we went the more traffic increased and neighborhoods formed. Memories of the guy I used to know, a good guy, a wild child, began to make sense. Beau loved the outdoors and lived life in such a way that he was allowed to run free without too much objection. The image of a younger Beau, his longish hair flying as he sprinted through the field toward me materialized. He grinned all the time and was never winded from his runs. He always wanted to be outside.

Being chained and locked inside might have been the worst thing that happened to him.

Absently, I asked. "Your hair's still long."

"Mmm hmm," Beau said. "My old street is on the left. Drive about a mile to the fourth cul-de-sac on the road to the right."

"What does *mmm hmm* mean? I like it long. I decided it'd be either longer or shorter by now."

"It's as long as it'll grow. I don't do anything with it. It's too short to tie back. I wore a sweatband to keep it off my face when I played. It's kind of annoyin'," he explained, then pointed as if that somehow helped me understand the directions better. "The second street up there. Do you see it?"

"Yeah. If it bothers you, why don't you cut it?" I asked, slowing until I found the road and made the turn.

"You know. The connection."

I saw Scott's truck in the driveway. "Our connection?" My nerves took flight. Scott had promised to keep Beau's secret, at least until after we left the area. Which meant I was back in the closet I'd never wanted to be in.

"The same reason you insisted everyone call you Dash. Hanging on to any connection to what we had."

Since I was in the middle of grappling with the sadness of hiding us from the world, it took me a few seconds of putting the car in park and unbuckle my seatbelt before I replayed his words in my mind.

"I like that reason," I said, and I did. We'd both hung on to the strings that bound us together. A rare admission from Beau. I barely had the visor mirror down when I caught Beau bending back inside the car, his face coming into view.

"I thought you'd have more to say."

I had to ignore our draw, or I'd give my feelings away to Scott's family. That didn't mean I wasn't affected. The silly, sweet grin plastered on my face as I checked my appearance refused to be contained. Most likely due to the butterflies flittering around excitedly in my belly. "I'll have more to say. I have a lot to say about a lot of things."

"Beau Brooks!" We glanced in the direction of the stern voice. A pretty young woman called from the front porch. I assumed her to be Lauren by the large baby bump. She had her long dark hair piled on top of her head. The sleeves of her shirt were rolled haphazardly to her elbows.

I left the car as her hands went to her hips. Scott came from around the side of the house, which I assumed was from the backyard. The guilt in his expression couldn't be good as he scurried forward. Bad, in fact. The butterflies abandoned me in an instant. I stayed between the car and its door, ready to make a fast getaway if this played out like I thought.

Beau remained clueless about what he was seeing. At least he didn't look like a scared deer caught in headlights...yet.

"How're you already so pregnant?" Beau teased; his smile real. He'd become lighter in the few seconds since she'd called him out. Happy to see her. Well, that was about to change.

"Don't even get me started." She started for Beau with no shoes on. Her entire focus was Beau, heading straight toward him. "You have a life alterin' secret and you never tell any of us? We all thought somethin' awful happened to you when you were away. You just stopped bein' our friend. Seriously, Beau? I hurt for you."

She came to an abrupt stop, the hands at her hips turned to fists, her foot stomping as if to drive her frustration and annoyance into the ground. Beau's warm smile faded, along with his happy mood. The color drained from his face as Scott came to her side like a protective papa bear. I wished to shield Beau in the same way but had to wait for my next cue.

"She wasn't supposed to say anything," Scott said with the same care one would use to defuse a ticking bomb. "What the hell, Lauren? You just promised me that you'd keep your mouth shut."

"I'm done with secrets," she said angrily. "We all watched his father abuse the hell out of him. He was blank inside and you told us he was just stuck up." The back of her hand whacked Scott's belly.

"Lauren!" Scott dropped his head and his shoulders at the same time. "Beau. I only started the rumor because I figured out what was goin' on in the middle of tenth grade. Everybody was talkin' about you all the time. I didn't like it, so I said you were stuck up now. What I shouldn't have done was tell big mouth over here."

"You promised you'd keep it a secret," Beau replied lamely.

The ground I'd begun to make crumbled away like sand in a windstorm. I felt him retreating into himself again. Dammit.

"She won't say anything to anyone else. She knows it's your secret to tell, not hers. It's the baby brain and seein' you again. You know," Scott argued and twirled a finger outside of one ear, making excuses for her.

"Shut up, Scott! I'm not crazy." She actually yelled those words, my brows lifting in surprise. I'd never heard that shrill tone in my life. "I told Katie because she's my best friend and he kissed her."

As quickly as my brows lifted, they dropped. That bit of information was news to me and landed like a ton of bricks. It wasn't Scott I should be jealous of, it was Katie?

Without looking my way, Beau lifted a hand, asking for my silence I assumed. Who knew since, apparently, I knew very little about Beau in the first place. Plot-fucking-twist again.

"So everybody knows now?" Beau looked down at his feet. His shame cascading off him. The muscles in his shoulders tensed then rolled. I braced myself for an eruption, expecting his inner lion to be freed for such a betrayal. I placed one foot back in the car, prepared to dive back in and drive him wherever he wanted to go. I would always be his escape route if I could.

I waited.

Then waited longer.

Lauren went to him, fearless and unafraid. She was a confident little thing, and from her short height, she easily caught Beau's downward stare. Her palm rested on his forearm. "We would have had your back. You were one of my best friends. Like family to me. I've missed you. Katie missed you. She won't tell, I promise. We both hurt that you shouldered all this alone."

The touch evolved into a handhold. His chin lifted a small degree as he stared her straight in the eyes. The move made me proud of my guy. He shouldn't be ashamed of anything. "It was always about my father. Not any of you. He broke me down."

"Hmm," she said, strong enough to hold his direct stare which made me proud of her even though we hadn't officially met. "He hurt you."

"Yeah."

I liked Lauren more and more as she took his other hand, holding it tight.

"He made me into a coward. I was ashamed. He had such a grip on me I couldn't have friends. Nobody would understand what was happenin' in my house."

"You're not a coward. Not ever. Only doin' what had to be done to get by." She finally turned my way. "Who's this?"

Beau's tear-filled expression landed on me. It was a challenge to stay on my feet with everything I read there. Relief, love, acceptance, and appreciation were all there. His shoulders released their tight hold, relaxing. My extraordinary guy sent a wave of tingles rippling over me, sharing the freeing beauty of his coming out.

"That's Dash. I met him in Sea Springs."

9: The Masterpiece Dash

The welcoming and relaxed comfort of Beau's old neighbors also applied to the ones he'd never met. The people who'd bought his parents' house years ago allowed us to sit on his former boat dock late into the evening. The homeowners went so far as to bring out a space heater to help ameliorate the chill in the air so we'd be more comfortable.

Scott, Lauren, and Katie joined us. Katie arrived about an hour after we did. I sat to the side, keenly watching Beau's expressions. The tension which I'd believe was his resting face most recently had begun to soften. In its place was a man who thoroughly enjoyed reminiscing over the shared times with his friends.

I found myself unusually quiet, rare indeed for a man who had an opinion on everything. Although Beau and I showed no outward signs that we were a couple, the implication of an *us* was clear. A moment to celebrate. We had gotten so much further than I'd expected in such a short time.

Maybe my inner peace was thanks to the cozy jacket snugly hugging me tight. It belonged to Beau, who'd kindly shrugged it off once the chill creeped into the night air. His captivating scent wove through every fiber of the cloth. A smell that touched the deepest part of who I was. It settled the churn constantly rolling through my head.

I was proud of his friends. No one asked more of Beau than he was willing to give. Especially about me. He only explained that he had discovered he didn't want to hide after meeting me in Sea Springs and about the way his father rode in and ruined everything.

It felt good to watch him be honest with his friends and himself. The sarcasm he used with me was now gone too. Tiny bits of love began to peek through his now cracking barriers.

After a ton of conditions were issued by Beau, for example my commitment to be the DD tonight, or my promise to slow him down if anything he did looked out of control, he accepted a cold beer from Scott's case of Bud Light. The alcohol loosened him up and staved off some of the darkness that got in his way. A true beer drinker was born. He had enough to get tipsy, maybe drunk, but not to a concerning level.

"I'm out of here. I stayed longer than I planned," Katie said, abruptly standing. "I've gotta ace a finance exam tomorrow then we're diving headfirst into the wedding plans..." She beamed down at Lauren.

"It was great to see you," Beau said and rose. Even on her tiptoes, he still had to bend to accept her hug. His unsteadiness had him gripping a support beam to stay on his feet.

"Let me walk you to your car," I offered, unwinding from Beau's jacket. "The big guy over there would probably volunteer, but he may not be the best guide with the way those big feet are stumbling. We can't risk his pretty face getting scratched up before the pictures on Wednesday."

"I've got this," Beau insisted then proved my point as he tripped over his feet and had to grab the bench to stay upright. The way he beamed at me proved Beau was a happy drunk.

"Bachelor party tomorrow night," Scott called out spontaneously giving a solid whoop while lifting the beer. He'd definitely had a lot to drink.

"I promise, Scott never drinks this much. I think he's nervous," Lauren explained to me, but Scott was also a happy drunk and wrapped both arms around her, drawing her closer to his side. The can of beer in his hand sloshed onto the fleece blanket wrapped around her. His face nuzzled in her neck.

"I'm not nervous, I'm happy. I got the best girl in the world, gonna be my wife."

"I can get to my car," Katie said to me, stepping off onto the trail in the grass. "I've made the trip a hundred times."

"It's no problem." I followed, sure to make my etiquette instructor proud. I tucked my fists in Beau's coat pockets, fine to walk the entire way in silence. Probably even better that way. Who wanted to try to answer questions Beau might not like?

"It's good to see him smiling again," Katie said, once out of earshot of the others. "Are you good?"

"Sure," I said, puzzled by the odd question. "I haven't spent a lot of time in the countryside..."

"That's not what I meant," she said, slowing her steps but not stopping. "He's been through so much, and you two are very different people."

Maybe it was her approach because I certainly didn't allow anyone to trample on my and Beau's future, but I actually let her words simmer. Honestly, I never felt like Beau and I were that different—only on the surface. The minor aesthetics that didn't matter.

"We used to be more in sync than now, but I'm crazy about him. None of that's changed. I've been patient. I knew it was bad for him, but he used to be so strong willed. I thought he could handle..." I stopped dead in my tracks, my gaze colliding with Katie's. "I didn't mean it the way that might have sounded. He was always nervous about his father. When we were in Sea Springs, he didn't mind his absence..."

"It's okay. I get it," she said, lifting a hand. "We've all thought the same thing. Beau never cowed as a kid. It was easier to believe he'd become an elitist than to believe anything else. We had no idea what he was living through." She was several feet away by now, opening the gate before I could bring myself to move again.

"I didn't mean he wasn't strong enough to resist his father. I meant his father must have been severely abusive to get past Beau's own strength of will."

"It's all good. I asked more from the perspective of how different you two are. You're preppy and he's jock-country.

He's been knocking heads all his life, whether he wanted to or not. I'm not sure he understands life outside of football. People seriously talk about him being drafted into the NFL. His mom was the one who pushed his education," she said. I let the gate swing shut behind me. "Sorry for rambling."

"Not rambling," I said, my hands fisting into my pockets. Still very much mentally obsessing over what I'd almost let slip. "Can I request you not say anything about him and me until we leave Thursday morning?" Apparently, her directness encouraged my own.

"Absolutely, but the people around here live a simple life. They work, get married, have a pack of children. They're gonna see the way you two seek each other out and give those sly looks, him more than you." She pointed her finger at me then over toward the dock. "Then when you look at each other..." An expression of pure contentment sent her eyes skyward. Her hand covered her heart. "It's the sweetest thing ever."

What? *No.* "I've been doing my best to keep from appearing overly affectionate."

She giggled as if I'd said the words in jest. She was way off base. I was becoming a trained attorney after all. I knew a poker face firsthand.

A sudden slam of the gate drew our attention in that direction.

The shadow of a yeti stalked toward us. Luckily though, I didn't have to test my oath of protection to Katie. It was Beau stumbling toward our car.

"Lauren's tired," Beau stated entirely too loud. "You're drivin'. Come on. Bye, Katie."

"He's funny," she said and started around her car to the driver's seat.

I hadn't made it to the actual door with Katie, but felt like I'd done my duty, and started for my guy.

Beau beckoned. I had no choice but to follow.

I saw a nap in my future.

In the foot and a half of space I'd been allotted on the mattress, I propped up against the headboard with a coursebook in my lap. My gritty eyes felt like sandpaper from lack of any real sleep.

I faced my own challenges with Beau's reemergence into my life. Learning how to adapt to having someone with me twenty-four seven. I realized how much time I spent alone, how I'd isolated myself while waiting for Beau's return. I had a solitary existence. Chandler had only moved in with me about a year ago. That was when I began spending most of my time in my bedroom.

I hadn't adequately prepared myself for constant companionship. A flaw in my plans.

Apart from that, a drunk Beau snored like a bear. Anytime I managed to nudge him to his side, he tumbled backward, stretching out, claiming more space each time.

Another problem, Beau apparently liked to cuddle, scooping me up around him. Those heavy, stale alcohol breaths blowing down on me...really foul smelling.

Yeah, I had my own adjustment struggles to get past.

I ran my fingers through my hair out of pure frustration. I watched the alarm clock change from six fifty-nine to seven o'clock in the morning. The resulting beep was frequent and loud. Beau didn't move a muscle. I pressed snooze for the sixth time. Now choices had to be made.

In this part of the world, they'd consider Beau to be sleeping in. I personally felt like it was the butt crack of dawn. Did I wake him? He'd committed to helping Scott's family prepare the house and backyard for the wedding. He planned to spend the next thirty-six hours with Scott. Set up the venue, shop for clothes, bachelor party, final setup then the wedding.

They did extend me an invitation, but I declined. Beau didn't need the added mental anxiety of explaining me to the rest of their schoolmates. Which allowed for the nap I wanted to take, and the studying I had to do to prepare for my exam.

So, do I wake him?

As if the answer was sent from above, Beau rolled into my side, pushing one leg off the bed, the other wrapped into his body like a soft body pillow. My hip bumped against the end table.

"Beau," I said loudly. "The alarm went off." My palm ran the length of his hair, gently trying to wake him. Nothing happened.

"Wake up, Beau," I said more firmly, with a pat of my hand on his cheek. He didn't move.

"Beau!" I hollered, and used force with my hand, knocking his head away from my hip. His eyes squinted a crack, only for him to roll over again. Me and my textbook were knocked to the floor. He stretched out across the mattress as I was picking myself up.

"Get up, Beau!"

His eyes opened slightly wider than before. The confusion was real. "Why?" he croaked and moved his tongue around his mouth, searching for saliva. "Are you on the floor? Why does my mouth taste so bad?" He flipped away from me, landing face down on a pillow.

"I believe you when you say you weren't a drinker." I reached for the book, examining how it fared from the drop.

"I feel so bad. They were talkin' about swine flu yesterday..." he groaned.

"It's not swine flu. It's a hangover, and you have one," I explained patiently.

Since pajamas were a requirement in this house, I'd been in and out of the room all night, concocting the perfect hangover elixir. Well, Google and I together perfected the drink. My masterpiece sat chilling in the refrigerator, the direction I was currently heading.

My brainchild consisted of three parts blue Powerade for hydration, two raw eggs to soothe his stomach and help with a headache, ground ibuprofen for general body aches, and a decent size spoonful of instant coffee. I added a good portion of honey because I learned it fixed everything. Those last two ingredients were reported to help boost energy.

If all went well with my test case—namely Beau this morning—I planned to mass produce the drink to help make the world a better place.

Maybe I'd use dried ingredients to make the drink easier to tote around.

"Good morning," Beau's mom said, standing in front of the Keurig. "My son can snore. I had no idea."

"I think his body mass gets bigger after he drinks. He took up the entire bed," I said, reaching in for my magic potion. "I whipped up a special drink last night to help him out." I winked mischievously, keeping my potion's ingredients hush-hush for proprietary reasons.

I shook the closed bottle to help redistribute the eggs.

"I'm leaving soon. Are you going to be here today?"

"I am, I guess, but it's hard to know." After the countless mini disagreements Beau and I had on pretty much everything, she and I both knew if Beau wanted my help today, he'd get it.

I kept the bottle shaking as I entered the bedroom. Beau's eyes were open, even if he had only turned to his back. "I really think I've picked up a bug or something. If my dad felt this way every mornin', he'd have never continued drinkin'. Fuck, I feel bad."

"Here, drink this," I said, coming to the edge of the bed, giving a reassuring nod that hopefully expressed the benefit of what I held in my hands. Beau managed to lift his body, looking skeptically at the Powerade bottle.

"My stomach hurts," he said and slowly rose, pushing his back against the headboard. "I don't know if I should go today. I think I picked up somethin'. Probably at Lowes."

I'd never known anyone to hang on to the idea it wasn't a hangover for so long. And Beau wasn't teasing, which had to mean he'd stayed away from the liquor. His father must have truly been in bad shape. I took a seat and unscrewed the top. "It's a hydration drink with a few health boosting additives inside. Try it."

I took a sniff. It actually smelled pretty good. Encouraged, I passed it to him and reached for the water bottle on the nightstand. I had it ready to go. Per Google's instructions, Beau had to drink both in intervals.

Beau's skepticism became reluctance after he took a good whiff.

"No, you're smelling your own breath," I said. "It's Powerade. You know the importance of hydration. Drink it. Take a few gulps then drink the water. Scott's waiting."

Beau scrunched his face and squeezed his eyes closed, downing two long gulps. "Not too fast. You have to drink the water too."

Half a second later, his eyes popped open. He gave a solid heave.

I cringed. I hadn't anticipated such an immediate negative reaction. Beau scooted clumsily off the bed, giving a second, much louder heave.

"What's in that?" Beau's stomach gave an audible, violent sound as he heaved, and darted out of the room, running down the hall.

"Beau," his mom called.

"Move, Mom!"

With a furrowed brow of disappointment, I reached for the Powerade bottle. A longer smell of the contents had me pulling away. I got a healthy dose of the raw eggs that time. Apparently, I needed to go back in front of the drawing board if my creation was going to be the next best thing. Too bad. I wasn't throwing in the towel just yet. The drink made sense. Beau was loud in the bathroom. If the drink made that happen regularly, people wouldn't use it more than once. I'd figure it out.

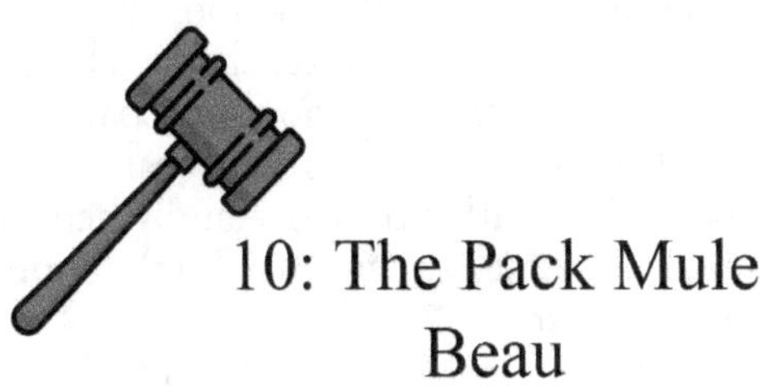

10: The Pack Mule
Beau

Wedding Night
Scott's Childhood Bedroom

I'd been eyeing Dash in the whys and the ways he used the hairdryer. I didn't have a lot of time. Scott had hogged most of the minutes in front of the mirror, making sure he looked his very best. We shared the same bathroom and bedroom to shower and dress for the big night.

Feeling too big for the small space of the bathroom, I flipped on the hairdryer and attempted to tame my unruly hair. My lack of skill and serious need for a haircut had me trying my best, pushing the hair off my face, and drying it thoroughly. It didn't take long.

I discarded the hairdryer in the sink. Thought better of it and moved it to the small edge of the vanity before staring at myself in the mirror. I ran the brush over my head, pulling my hair completely off my face. Shockingly, it stayed that way.

Scott had used hairspray liberally over his shorter new haircut. I decided I would too. I didn't want to look like a heathen in his wedding pictures.

"Clean up pretty well, don't I?" Scott asked, standing close to the window of his old bedroom. Much like I had done over the last thirty-six hours, my focus went to Scott, who was attempting to hide his nervous energy with a cocky attitude and a faux confident swagger.

Vulnerability had his brows permanently furrowed. Anxiety flushed his cheeks and neck. But he looked good in the modern cowboy garb. Decked out pretty sharp in his all-black attire consisting of a crisp black cowboy suit coat, matching vest, and a pair of brand-new dark pressed jeans. The dress shirt he wore was cinched with a timeless family heirloom: an iconic scorpion bolo tie passed down through the generations of stylish men in his ancestry.

The effort he used to perfect his hair in the mirror was about to be ruined by the dark Stetson waiting on the edge of the bed.

"Sure do," I quipped and resisted the urge to continue the competition between us by stating I look better.

His shiny new Tecovas boots were the same as mine. A dark, almost black color. He did look great. I'd worried about the cash I spent trying to find clothes to match his. I wore dark ironed jeans, about the same color as our boots, and a pressed, charcoal pearl-button, long-sleeve dress shirt. Luckily, I didn't have to wear a hat or bolo tie. I didn't like the way cowboy hats made me look, and I'd sworn off anything that needed a knot around my neck.

"Fuck, I'm nervous. What if I can't handle all this? Lauren wants to be taken care of, and I want to support my family, but what if I fail?"

Since it was a conversation we'd had over and over today, I was set to dish out some motivational pep talk, but he cut me off with a hand on his stomach. He began to pace.

"Talk about somethin' else before I hurl..."

I started to speak but he caught me instantly off guard with his next words.

"You're doin' better every day. You already seem like your old self. That's a fast improvement." He shot me a pointed look.

I just shrugged, not in the mood to chat about what was happening to me. I recognized the change inside me. I liked it. That was enough for now.

"Yeah, I'm sure you're still processin' it all in that noggin of yours. I'm glad to have you back, though. It'd suck to be doin' this without you." He abruptly jerked his head to the closed curtain window. I didn't know why. "It bugged me when you moved, then even more when you came back. Remember how you'd sprint across the roof to get outside?" His penetrating gaze came back to mine. "I have a secret I've never told you." He pointed at me. "And you're never going to throw it up in my face again."

I nodded, but there might be, to be honest, the jury was out on that promise. It might slip out again depending on what he had to say.

"I seriously have a fear of heights. I'd follow you because I couldn't let you win, but it bothered me every time."

"I win." The words were said automatically, but I didn't mean them. He acted like this was a shocking revelation. We'd known each other too well. Scott didn't have secrets from me, and I didn't have them from him—the very reason for Dash's current presence in Alabama.

As I prepared to tell him how closely I'd studied him and fought my own fears in order to keep competing, I switched tactics and fanned the flames of that spirit inside him instead. We'd both be better for it in the end. "Just so you know, when I leave here and head to Dallas, I'm gonna kick your ass financially. I was readin' that UPS drivers make serious bank..."

"Wanna bet?" Scott muttered.

My distraction worked and I held back my grin. He came at me as if we were wagering on different boxers to win the championship belt.

"The commission I earn is endless. I'll make more money than you as long as you don't use your boyfriend's coattails."

Oh man, he'd hit below the belt. "Bet."

His hand shot out to shake mine.

Something deeper ignited within me, bubbling up beyond the emotional damage I'd endured. "I'll get healthcare, holidays off, and most weekends, and still make more money than you."

A knock at the door drew both our attention. Mrs. Lee, Scott's mom, gave a time update through the closed door without waiting for us to open the door. "Five minutes. She's here." Even though I couldn't see her, I could hear the excitement in her voice.

He locked an unwavering stare on me. "Dollar for dollar. W-2's compared. We'll settle the rest once this wedding's done. Every year is a separate win." Since our hand grip continued, he shook mine aggressively and with certainty.

"Starts the beginnin' of next month," I shot out cockily. "You just made my wins so much sweeter."

The ultimate challenge. I saw the same fire building within him that flared inside me.

"Better learn to tuck your tail between your ass cheeks." Unafraid of anything now, Scott went closer to the shut bedroom door, waiting to go out.

I laughed at his unwavering confidence. And patted myself on the back for manipulating him in his quest to always be able to provide for his family. The door pushed open, bouncing off Scott's face in the swing open. I laughed at that too.

"It's showtime, babe. We're beginnin'." Mrs. Lee was oblivious to the tension Scott, and I had created inside the bedroom. And the pain he might be under from being hit in the face. She smiled sweetly at her son. "I'm proud of you, Scott. Get your hat then wait behind Beau to take your place close to the preacher." She kissed his cheek and hurried from the doorway.

The nerves were back in my friend, but they ended soon. Since the hallway had been set up to be the aisle, I went first, liking the energy building inside me.

Thoughts of Dash pulled at me like a magnet in every moment we were apart. While quiet in the hall, visions of him in his stylish suit danced around my head as the piano began to play. He'd be the best-looking guy here.

I took my place then searched for Dash. I wasn't wrong. When he grinned, I did too. What a beautiful guy, both inside and out.

As I lugged the rental chairs from the house back into the van, a couple of yawns escaped. When Mr. Lee found out I was leaving first thing in the morning, he instructed me on the different post-wedding jobs, all heavy, that needed to be done before I left. He'd effectively transformed me into one tired pack mule. I felt sure he'd find some way to justify me digging out the muck in rain gutters pretty soon.

"Hey, Beau!" Mrs. Lee called from the front porch. "They need you."

"Mama, let him finish up out here," Mr. Lee said from the cover of the garage where he watched me work.

"Quit slackin' off," she hollered at her husband. "He's done enough of your work around here. We need you, Beau. Wipe your shoes on the rug in the mudroom. Don't listen to him anymore."

Since I was on Mrs. Lee's side of the argument, I put the last rack of chairs in the truck and trudged through the garage and into the house. These expensive boots weren't living up to their price tag. If I hurried, I risked a comical slip and slide episode where I'd likely land on my ass.

"They're namin' the godparents," his mom said, standing inside the laundry room, or as she called it, a mudroom.

"Who did they pick?" I asked, scooting my boots on the inside rug to clean them.

"Well, you," his father said from directly behind me. My face instantly contorted into horror.

"What?" I burst out as if that were the dumbest idea I'd ever heard. I didn't know anything about children. "Why me?"

"Where's Beau? Everybody's waitin'," Scott hollered. Mr. Lee came in behind me, close enough to squeeze my shoulder.

"Consider it a ceremonial gesture. You won't actually be takin' my grandchildren from me," Mr. Lee said with a chuckle.

"Wait, there's more than one kid?" I asked in panic, finding myself propelling into the dining room where Scott and Lauren stood before their guests. Katie was on Lauren's side. I was shoved close to Scott.

"Finally," Scott grumbled, his frustration with me palpable. He raised his voice for his next words. "Hey. He's finally here. Focus on us again."

The house was comfortably spacious. Yet the twenty or so guests were well into their drink and catching up with each other. It took a second much louder bark by Scott to gain their attention.

"Hey! Listen up, everybody! We've got an announcement to make then you're all welcome to keep the party goin'. We have dinner waitin' on the back porch. We'll cut the cake afterward. Right?" Scott glanced down at Lauren who was tucked securely underneath his arm. She nodded with pride.

"This is our wedding day, but also a day to celebrate family," Lauren said, and put a protective hand on top of her belly. "We wanted to introduce this soon-to-be baby's godparents to our families," Lauren said, a giant grin spreading over her lips. "They're Katie and Beau, our best friends."

The guests whooped loudly and pushed forward to offer their congratulations. There I was with my hands tucked into my pockets, feeling completely overwhelmed with the way the guests bore down on me. Like a high-functioning bobble head, I nodded over and again, accepting the well-wishes. Slowly, I stepped several feet backward until my ass bumped into the dining room table where the three-tiered wedding cake and punch bowl sat waiting.

My gaze shifted above the guests' heads, an action I had repeated countless times over the course of the evening. All to catch brief glimpses of Dash. My life's joy and light had regulated himself into the shadows, close to the front door, doing his best to blend into the wood paneling. I doubted he accomplished such a lofty goal, but with as busy as Mr. Lee had me, I didn't think anyone understood that the most handsome man in the world was there to be with me.

Standing beside Dash was my mom, chatting away while they both held white plastic cups in their hands. His gaze latched onto mine. He gave the slightest lift of the cup in recognition. His dazzle was constant.

His plump lips curved into a perfect grin, growing wider with each moment I stared.

What was I doing? If I continued to allow emotional distance between Dash and myself, I was still only a puppet in the circus my father had created. True, I had a mountain of baggage to sift through. I wouldn't pretend otherwise, but look how far I'd come from dear old dad's shadow? Every fiber of my being now hinged on Dash's unwavering conviction that we belonged together. I believed that too.

My old man wasn't going to win in his efforts to keep us apart.

The strangest sensation shivered down my spine. Both my chest and cock swelled, growing hard and heavy within seconds. The sudden unrelenting desire had a laser-focused direction and purpose. I released a long, steadying breath. That attention narrowed with each step I took toward Dash.

He shot me a puzzled stare as I moved through the crowd toward him.

My shoulders rolled, doing my best to keep under control.

"What're you doing?" Dash asked. With my gaze fixed on his lips, I took the cup from his hand and passed it off to my mom. She never faltered in her assignment, making her the best wingman ever. I circled Dash's neck with my palm, drawing him toward me. I leaned in until no more than an inch of space separated our lips. My depth of love overwhelmed me. Especially since I saw it reflected back in Dash's beautiful blue eyes.

"I don't need ninety days. I want you now and forever," I whispered. My voice hoarse from the emotion spilling from my heart.

"Me too," he said more confidently.

"Don't hurt me."

"Never," Dash promised, his eyelids fluttering closed.

I pressed my lips down on his then sought entrance. He yielded, and I plunged into the kiss with a vengeance. I was home. Finally where I was meant to be. Dash's tongue matched mine, stroking, and encouraging me to let loose, like he always had. His hands caressing a burning trail around my back, pulling me flush against him. A low growl emanated, protective and fierce as I eagerly explored his sinfully sweet mouth.

Dash was always meant to be mine and I was his in return. The tangible connection we shared never wanted this kiss to end. Nothing in the world mattered more, yet I reluctantly pulled inches away. Dash's hooded brow focused only on me, his labored breaths puffing against my skin. The love of my life, my reason for everything.

"Let's get out of here," I said, gliding my hand across Dash's shoulders to steer him out of the house. Without a backward glance or even a farewell to Scott and Lauren, we made our way through the front door, I shut it soundly behind me. When completely alone, Dash spun toward me, clasping my hand to drag us into a shadowy abyss just beyond the porch lights.

"What happened in there?" he asked. I didn't stop moving until I was chest to chest with my guy.

"No more hidin'," I declared. We stepped into each other, bringing our bodies flush. My lips searched his out again. The intensity of our smoldering kiss seared away all semblance of logic and reason, silencing the negativity of my life.

Dash suddenly broke away from the lock I had on his mouth, rearing his head back in astonishment.

"You're hard." He brazenly traced the outline of his discovery before pressing his palm firmly against my shaft. The intimate touch of my dreams drew a whimper from me. I couldn't help the roll my hips gave, pushing into Dash's sculpting fingers.

Damn, my need was back with a vengeance. I cradled his face, holding him tenderly as I sought his lips again, yearning for the connection of our kiss.

"We need to leave," Dash murmured, his words spoken between the nips and swipes I gave against his mouth. "Beau, I need you, I do but in the hotel. Not here."

"Let's go," I whispered in agreement, deciding that adding a free porn show to Scott's big night might not be the best idea.

Taking his hand, he led me down the walkway, taking long, purposeful strides. With laser beam focus, I watched the way his perfect ass moved with each step.

I was the luckiest man on the planet to be spending time in that ass tonight. A tug of his hand brought him up short. "It's taking too long to get to the car. Kiss me like you mean it."

In an instant, Dash turned, bumping chests. His arms wrapped around me, gripping each ass cheek with his sinful hands, roughly bringing our cocks together. What a roller coaster of intensity. I strained against him. The craving to have him was so strong, my orgasm was already building inside my balls. Dash, the silly guy, tried to take control, thrusting his tongue into my mouth. He dove deep until the only taste I ever wanted again was his.

11: The Grip
Dash

I acknowledged, if something didn't change, Beau and I were never going to make it inside the hotel I'd chosen to be closer to the airport in the morning. The prospect of my guy fucking me where we stood might truly become a reality. Whichever way it happened, I was pretty sure I was there for, and ready to make it work.

My arms tightened around Beau's neck, holding him as close as I could as I devoured his mouth. An overwhelming feeling of possessiveness ran through me when he wrapped both arms around my waist, wanting me as badly as I wanted him. I kissed him like a randy teenager, fusing our mouths together. His erection was hard and long, pressed firmly against mine. Beau rolled his hips slightly, rubbing our cocks together. Fuck, it felt good. More amazing than any dreams I'd dared to conjure while we were apart. My mind then blipped as a peppering of stars sprinkled behind my eyelids.

Shit, that might be the need to breathe.

When he tried to break free, I didn't make it easy. I licked and nipped up his neck. He angled his head, giving me full access. His breath heaved as I worked my way up, nibbling the shell of his earlobe.

"Fuck, Dash. You're so damn sexy, but I've put on enough of a show tonight. We've gotta go to the hotel. I need you bad. So bad."

I eased off him, nodding my understanding, but I really didn't get it. Who knew I was an exhibitionist at heart? My attention was drawn to the smooth skin stretched over Beau's jawline, framing lips that promised a captivating experience.

"You have to be the strong one," Beau said. My nose trailed over the sensual path my lips had just taken. "Get us to the hotel."

"You're not going to change your mind?" I asked against his ear.

"No. Never again." He swiftly turned me by the hips to guide me down the road. "Where're we parked?"

Desire raced wantonly throughout my body. My nerve endings sizzled, humming against my skin until it all landed squarely in my cock. I ignored his question, keeping his hand in mine. "The first one's gonna come fast," I said over my shoulder to Beau.

"Same with me. Your ass is a thing of beauty."

"What you did tonight took strength. You made a grand statement," I said, giving a side eye glance to better read Beau's thoughts.

"Not that much strength," Beau murmured, watching my ass. I had forgotten how he'd do that when we were younger. "I didn't look back to see how everyone took it."

"I only had eyes for you," I said, again with the side eye. "We're gonna be fine. You'll be away from here when the gossip spreads."

"Probably not. I bet half the town knows by now," he quipped. Surprisingly, he didn't seem upset about that.

I let it be enough for now. We'd face the repercussions together. Love was in the air. I was back in the sex game. I had a lot of years to make up for. I tucked my bottom lip between my teeth as we parted ways at the car, he to the passenger side, me to the driver's side. My suit coat tossed carelessly in the back. The thrill of what was to come was almost too much to handle.

The ride to the hotel felt like an eternity. I had to navigate the road and Beau's advances at every stoplight. He was octopus worthy, growing eight hands that were all over me in the best possible way. I loved it even if our safety was in jeopardy with each mile driven.

I parked near the hotel's front doors. The grip Beau used on my hand held the perfect balance of possessiveness and desire. I sensed we'd be a couple who held hands.

A couple. We were finally where we should have been five days ago. Beau locked a hand on my forearm, keeping me from leaving the car even after I opened my door.

"Kiss me," he whispered.

"You have to let me go so we can go inside."

Beau leaned in further for a kiss, but I dodged him. My guy wanted me, but we had to get to the room. What a thrilling dilemma to be in.

"Inside. Now." I escaped his reach and left the car, taking long quick strides to the hotel's sliding glass doors. Midway there, Beau's heavy steps echoed behind me.

Once he reached me, his muscular arms roughly circled my waist, tugging me against his chest. Whoa, I was going to enjoy being manhandled in the bedroom. Goosebumps sprang to my skin. My love meter skyrocketed to untamable levels. When Beau's lips latched onto my neck, my eyes did a backflip in my head. And then I was lifted off my feet as if I weighed nothing. His thick, hard cock rammed against my slacks-covered crease.

Jesus. He'd leave a lasting mark in a spot tough to hide, but honestly, I didn't care. Over the years, I found myself envious of such a simple telltale sign that meant someone loved them.

"Quit teasing and take me inside," I insisted. Beau didn't let me go but loosened his lips and walked us toward the doors. "You can put me down," I murmured. Instead, he buried his nose in the short strands of my hair.

"It's been so long," Beau whispered huskily.

"Then put me down so we can end the drought," I urged.

He reluctantly complied. We both took hurried steps, side by side. The night staff's greeting hung in the air, going unanswered. Beau's insistent energy created a buzzing in my ears, sharpening my focus just like he had done when he first returned. Thankfully, the elevator door opened with a press of the call button. I stepped in. Beau was close behind, exuding a predator vibe.

"Our room's just around the corner."

"I like foreplay," Beau whispered.

What a happy surprise. I flashed a cheeky grin. His words were pure gold. "I do too." Perhaps all our non-bedroom adventures would be filled with kisses, caresses, and not-suitable-for-work touches in anticipation of our alone time.

He caged me in, lavishing my mouth as if his life depended on our intimacy. Since I was to be the responsible one, I focused on the dings from the call button.

The elevator doors opened. When I sprang off the wall, surprising and dislodging Beau, I was able to get us out into the hall. We had two doors to go. With my cock hard, heavy, and ready, I pulled out my wallet and started for the door. He stealthily came in behind me faster than I'd thought possible. Again, those strong arms enveloped me, drawing me backward against his chest. His deft fingers began to unbutton my dress shirt.

"How far do we have to go?" he asked huskily against my ear. The whisps of breath tickled and tingled across my heated skin.

"We're close." I kept going in the correct direction while Beau pulled my shirttails free of my slacks. I was certain there was a camera somewhere pointed down the hall as my shirt hung open.

I fumbled to fit the keycard in the door, barely getting it open when one of Beau's seeking hands went north, the other south. His fingers pinched the tight bud of my nipple while the other slid underneath the waistband of my belted slacks and underwear.

The tips of his fingers played with the head of my hard cock. It felt so damned good. He also applied expert pressure to bring my body closer to the edge. I tucked my hips into the touch, a lustful moan escaping. He had me leaking.

Despite his surprising skill, I was determined not to give in until we were locked together inside the room. With my hands on the doorframe, I forcefully pulled away, catching Beau off guard again. I stumbled several steps inside the room while he was propelled the other way.

He righted himself before the door shut in his face and barreled through, the heavy door knocking solidly against the wall. I'd made it to my suitcase for the lubricant I brought.

I kicked off my shoes to the corner, tossing a hand in the air to stop Beau from coming after me. It shockingly worked. Beau came to an abrupt halt about two feet away. "Undress, I need to get the lube," I said with more authority than I felt.

A lightbulb moment of understanding crossed Beau's brow. He tugged the shirttails free and snapped open the pearl buttons in one sure yank. I forced my eyes away to the suitcase's zipper compartment where I'd placed several packets of lube for the just in case.

I barely cracked the zipper open before my gaze darted back to Beau. Watching him undress was better than porn. When he hooked his thumb into the waistband and pushed the starchy jeans and underwear down, his gorgeous cock bounced free.

My mouth turned into a desert as I sized him up. Everything else faded as he stood there, resembling a Greek god, staring back at me like I was a prime piece of meat. Fuck, my nipples tightened harder. He had grown with age, meaning I'd have to adjust, but boy, I eagerly accepted the challenge.

Perhaps the highlight was the jeans casually chilling on the floor, covering his boots, keeping him rooted in place. I tossed the packets to the bed.

As if the mattress were a swimming pool, he dove for the bed, bouncing then jackknifing up to sit on the edge, and began working to pull a boot free.

He cocked a brow suggestively. "As soon as I get at least one of these free, it's gonna be hot."

"It is?" My guy was going to be a lot to handle in many different ways. I took the hint, undoing the buttons at my wrist before sliding my dress shirt off my shoulders. I flung the shirt over my suitcase, the belt followed, then kicked off my loafers.

I finished Beau's start on my slacks as he paused mid tug of his boot. That sexy stare riveted to my cock.

"My eyes are up here," I teased. Our gazes collided in an epic story of love, dedication, thrill, and everything else that mattered most in the world. It was a fiery, soul-stirring, intense branding moment that made the world take a backseat.

As I positioned myself directly in front of him, I pushed at the waistbands of my clothing, letting my slacks and underwear hit the floor. The hard-on that had plagued me since the first moment I spotted Beau at Parliament, jutted out, recognizing its target.

He slipped one boot off his foot and tossed it over his shoulder. It gave a bounce on the edge of the bed before it tumbled to the floor.

The weight of Beau's darkening stare on my cock was both heady and exhilarating. His unsteady, calloused hand circled my length, giving a long, sure tug that made me hiss with pleasure.

He cupped my balls with his other hand, rolling them in his palm, giving the same reverent tug there as well. My hands found their way to his broad shoulders as I closed my eyes in ecstasy. "I thought we'd be ripping each other's clothes off and fucking on the floor by now," Beau said. "This is better."

"Yeah," I whispered. On each tug, I rode the waves of bliss. Doing my best to stave off the rampant need coursing through me. Beau deserved a great experience, and I was determined to give it to him even if it killed me trying.

Which it honestly might.

My fingers found their way into his hair. The hand that had been on my balls caressed over my hip to the crease of my ass. *Motherfucker.* I gritted my teeth, stealing my spine to keep myself together.

My fortitude was tested in the most decadent of ways when my cock was enveloped into Beau's warm mouth. At the same moment, his thumb breached my most sensitive spot. Holy hell, my body responded eagerly, pumping back and forth against his thumb and into his mouth in a seductive rhythm he created. I couldn't help the small beads of pre-come building at my tip.

The way he hoovered my cock, bobbing his head back and forth, was the stuff of my dreams. "Do you taste how badly I want you?" I asked.

Beau's touch was both gentle and persuasive as he worked me open. His lips slipped over my cock, guiding me deeper and deeper into his mouth. I trembled under the assault. My gasps teased of my desperation. He was damned tender as he added a second finger, pumping and stretching my ass open.

My orgasm zinged down my spine, settling in the depths of my balls. I shook with need. My skin was so sensitive I felt the air circulating in the room. I wasn't going to last. Dammit, I tried to make this special.

In a last-ditch effort for us to hang on until we came together, I used my palms on his face to pull him off my cock. With my thumbs, I tilted his chin upward, making sure he heard me. "You need to be inside me when we come."

I leaned forward, melding our mouths together once again for a searing kiss. My tongue danced with his, loving the taste of my essence inside his mouth.

With a shove against his shoulders, I pushed him down on the mattress. I straddled him, crawling to his hips. He gave a wicked grin as he reached for the lube packets.

"How do you want me?" I murmured. Beau twisted his hips, dislodging me to the bed. "Hey!"

"Back to the mattress." Beau's voice held a commanding growl that did nothing but ramp up my excitement. He propped himself up on his elbow. I watched, both jealous and mesmerized as he tore open the packet and coated his fingers with the lube.

More than anything, I wished I were that packet in his mouth. My sexy guy appeared in total control. I obliged his demand and rolled over. My cock was so sensitive it vibrated, needing Beau's touch. I lifted my legs. My body relaxed as those skilled fingers reached for my ass once again. He pumped his digits in and out while shifting his weight to wriggle between my parted legs. "You like that, don't you?"

"So much," I murmured.

Beau shoved a pillow under my ass, aligning me to his desired angle. He was magical. His deft digits never stopped working me open. Under his persuasion, I writhed, desperate for more. His touches sank farther inside me, teasing the gland that set my body in flight. Man, this was going to be good. Somehow, I managed to pry my lids open to see my handsome guy's smirking grin. "I love the way your ass grips my fingers."

"Stop playing, Beau. I'll come," I hissed.

"Don't touch yourself," he ordered. "I'm gonna make this last as long as I can." He positioned the head of his cock at my hole, rubbing and teasing me as he squirted whatever lube was left in the packet onto his fingers and my hole. I felt my heart racing with anticipation. He didn't disappoint. Slowly and patiently he slid that fat cock inside me. Beau's features turned anguished in the most exciting way, while seating fully inside me.

"Oh fuck yeah. It's so good," I murmured, decadently stretching to accept all of him. The pure ecstasy of being with this man in this way was everything I'd ever wanted. My eyes rolled to the back of my head. I kept a death grip on my thighs, pulling them closer to my chest. My body strained as Beau filled me so good. My breaths came in short, shallow puffs.

"Oh yeah," Beau parroted, his voice raw and raspy. He finally moved, pulling out then pushing in again. The way he heaved caused my eyes to crack open into the smallest of slits. My beautiful guy was a lovely vision while making love to me. His hard body strained with every thrust he began to give. My cock bounced, drumming on my belly as Beau began to canter, picking up speed. Every muscle in my body quivered with pleasure. My breath began to pant uncontrollably.

Fuck, my only focus was to hold my orgasm as long as I could. He made it damned hard as his hips began to piston, the slap of our bodies coming together thrilled me and became the only sounds reverberating through my hazy brain. His head dropped forward, his hair falling into his face. His powerful arms caged me in as velvet steel drove relentlessly into my ass...

How did he manage to rub against my gland so decadently, coaxing me closer and closer to the edge with every thrust?

"Beau…I can barely hang on." Saying the words aloud gave me strength to end my agony. My legs wrapped around Beau's waist. The heels of my feet dug into his back, pushing his body down closer to mine. Our gazes connected and locked. Beau supported his body's weight with his elbows planted on the mattress. The stacked muscles in his arms flexed and tensed. I traced my fingers across his chest, gently teasing his nipples. "Kiss me."

He sunk lower on the bed to meet me; agony held in his face. My guy was trying to make this good for me. I thrust my tongue into his mouth in the same rhythm of his undulating hips. His taste was my brand of addiction.

The suction I had on his mouth popped free, the air turning thick and heavy with our pants coming in short bursts. My hands skimmed his body, desperately needing some sort of balance. I was completely lost to Beau. His hips turned wild, maddening, bucking in and out of me, making me crazy. Fire licked at my balls. The churning of my orgasm was no longer tamable. The breathtaking friction we created drove me to my end.

"Now, Beau, now." My body thrashed against his. No amount of willpower would stave off my release. I fisted the bedspread. My bottom lip crushed between my teeth. Sweat dampened my skin and hair.

"I love you. I do." Beau's words were both haggard and harsh. His big hand found its way between our bodies, circling my cock.

I'd respond as soon as I could think of how to form those three words. Every nerve ending in my body centered into my dick where Beau picked me up and began to stroke. Oh, there it was, our perfect harmony. That was all it took as I rode into oblivion.

Beau let out a guttural cry as his body reared back and his hips bucked feverishly into me. We came together, mine splattering on to my belly. His release had my ass clenching, coaxing every bit of come out of him. So damned good.

His body spasmed, trembling uncontrollably while he tumbled down on top of me. My muscles contracted, my toes curling under the force of his weight. I was a man in love, so much love.

We lay entwined, limbs tangled in each other's hold. As Beau's body relaxed and his cock slipped from me, I experienced a surge of energy. For the first time in a long time, my thoughts quieted and calmed. Only he and I existed in a moment of pure peace. What an enchanting journey we'd been on.

I struggled to move Beau off me. He was incredibly heavy. The more I tried, the more he circled his arms around me, keeping me in place.

"Stop wigglin' around," he said, all raw and raspy.

"I can't breathe," I responded with a surprising amount of gusto for a man currently suffocating.

Beau gave in, flopping to his back on the bed but bringing me along with him. He positioned my body over his. "Snuggle with me and give me a kiss," he whispered. His purpose filled lips pressed against my skin.

"I need a quick shower," I mumbled, running my fingers through his hair.

"No, stay here. I wanna do it again."

"Let me get cleaned up. Then I'll clean you. We'll be ready to go again," I replied and gently pulled away, mindful of where my elbows and knees might land. His attention lingered on me as I stood in front of him.

"You're ruinin' it," Beau murmured. I didn't believe it. He appreciated what he saw, but while I was buzzing with energy, Beau was the exact opposite. He was clearly ready for a nap.

"You're going to have to bottom. It feels too amazing to let you miss out," I said, very much appreciating the view before my eyes. "Come shower with me," I urged, noting the jeans-covered boot still attached to his foot.

"Okay. Someday." His words were lost to a long yawn. "You know you're perfect, right?" His heavy palm patted the mattress beside him. "Come back to bed. We'll clean up later."

I shook my head and started for the bathroom. Maybe ten seconds passed before Beau was on my heels.

"Fuck," he said. I knew those jeans were going to be a problem where they completely encased the boots. My happiness bubbled out as I turned on the shower faucet.

"I can't get out of my jeans. What the fuck?"

I couldn't contain my amusement as I darted under the spray. Everything was falling into place nicely. We were together again. I owed the universe everything.

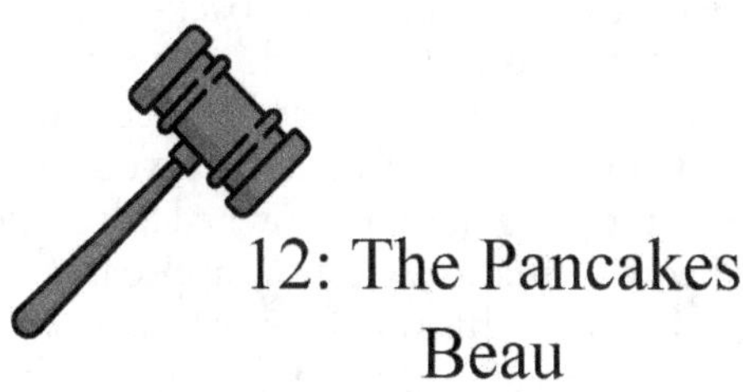

12: The Pancakes
Beau

Dallas, Texas
Thursday

"I can't drive your car," I said in such a way as to convey my utter disbelief at the mere thought of being behind the wheel of a two-hundred-thousand-dollar vehicle.

"Beau," Dash said in his classic I-can't-believe-your-stubbornness tone. "Drive me to school then return for me in about three hours. It'll give you time to drive around and become familiar with the area. Look for the companies that offer the jobs you want." Repeating it a second time did in fact make the idea sound more absurd.

Since waking this morning—in a figurative way, we never actually slept a wink last night, I now had the full scope of Dash's extravagant lifestyle—private jets, chauffeurs, expensive cars, and a badass house—I felt more confident than ever that I didn't fit in.

"Thank you, Jacob," Dash said when his side door opened.

Jacob was one of the Richmond family drivers. And there was no way I'd wait for him to open my door. I got out on my own, because I wasn't a small child, and headed for the trunk for my bags. With Dash's normal flair, no matter the rush, he spent several seconds smoothing out his clothing. I didn't remember wrinkles being such a problem for Dash before. If a possible hair went rogue, that would have to be rearranged too.

Even though we were in another typical back-and-forth, this time I stood my ground. Dash's flashy ride was way out of my league. I'd be too self-conscious and have a wreck due to my own anxiety. I needed a spacious vehicle that wouldn't break the bank to drive. Something like a pre-owned Silverado.

The trunk opened automatically on my approach. My eyes narrowed at such a feature. This was a fancy ride too.

"I got it," I said as Dash came around the trunk. The driver followed, quickening his steps.

"It's all right, Jacob. He frustratingly tends to do this," Dash explained.

Dash wore a fresh turtleneck that accentuated his long neck and covered the evidence of my desire—hickeys to be exact, and the suit jacket he wore to the wedding, but Dallas had had a significant drop in temperature. One of Dash's hands was stuck awkwardly in the jacket pocket, the other held a set of keys out to me.

I shook my head. I wasn't driving the car. "Calm down. These are for the house. You're the most maddening person alive."

As I pulled the luggage from the back of the vehicle, Jacob began a low rumble of laughter, trying his best to keep it inside. Dash tilted his chin toward the driver, a brow arched critically.

"What? Dash," Jacob said. "You know this is funny. You always get your way."

"Apparently not any longer." His no-nonsense tone and sharp words had me doing a double take. Dash nodded the driver back into the vehicle.

Jacob had driven the Richmond family for decades. Based on the conversation from the airport to Dash's place, the driver and Dash had a great relationship. He brushed off Dash's tone and went back to the driver's seat.

"You need to get to school." I hoisted the last bag, which contained almost everything I owned, from the trunk. It wasn't much. Easy enough for one trip into the house. "Are you takin' your bookbag?" I asked, surprised to find Dash had moved closer, standing inches from me by the trunk. My guy didn't care who saw him. While that was a good trait, it wasn't one I shared. Dash rubbed his hand across the curve of my ass for the world to see.

"What're you doin'?" I hissed, but it wasn't the question it might seem.

"The best part about being together is that I can do that whenever I want."

"Was there an answer about the bookbag in anything you just said?"

"You're such a challenge," he replied, staying all in my space. "I'll take the bookbag. Kiss me. I loved last night."

I leaned in for a swift, chaste kiss, something based on Dash's stern facial features, he didn't like, and I took several steps backward. "We do that inside the house." Although I sounded gruff and drawing lines all over the place, I didn't really mean it. I was in love. It made me vulnerable. I had a lot changing on me very quickly, but I didn't fear it with Dash by my side. And I was certainly going to walk him to his car to get tucked safely inside.

The ridiculous melancholy that had haunted me all morning kicked up a notch. I agreed to be in the house waiting for his return to spend another night just like last night. I figured we'd need more sleep. Dash barely closed his eyes, me, not at all, due to being lost in staring at the beautiful man currently beside the automatically closing trunk.

"Good luck today," I murmured, "Get inside your car so I can go inside."

"Mr. Beau," Amelia's cheerful voice echoed from the porch. "I'm so happy to see you."

I couldn't resist the beam I gave. She was like a warm hug on this chilly day.

"I have to go," Dash called, waving at Amelia, already halfway to his car. "Amelia, we're a couple now. He's moving in with me." He shot me a wink, tossing his bookbag in the backseat. "Come kiss me goodbye. Pretend you'll miss me. I'll miss you." He motioned for me to follow him to the driver's side. Both my body and my brain propelled me to him. They left me no choice in the matter.

"I thought I kissed you enough last night," I teased quietly. Dash stood with the car door open, waiting for me. I kissed him quickly with hints of passion. Perhaps Amelia saw us or heard the conversation, I wasn't sure.

My insecurity was shedding off me in waves.

His hand patted my chest. "That was yesterday. This is today. Last night, you set the standard of expectation." He pursed his lips tighter. I obliged and kissed him again. "We're in the honeymoon phase."

"Go to school," I said at his silliness, fixing the straps on my shoulder to keep the bags from falling forward. "Do well on your test."

"Always." The confidant, cocky expression spoke more of truth than arrogance.

"I'll be here holdin' down the fort, job-huntin'. Go so you can get home faster." I started nodding and moving away from the car toward the front door. He had the classic, old school Hollywood actor appearance and charm. Dash's indecision played out in different expressions on his adorable face. He battled whether to go or stay. I easily read him.

Amelia's soft chuckle drew me her way again. She appeared genuinely excited to see me. It felt good to be wanted. The dry winter grass crunched under my feet as I went her way.

No matter how I tried, last night stayed in the forefront of my mind. I'd be waiting for Dash to return, naked in his bed. I'd also think about bottoming. Dash's many suggestions that I needed to try kept running through my head. I'd figure it out soon enough, but not today.

The warm flush on my cheeks intensified as sling-shot images flashed inside my head. Last night, I sucked dick and swallowed like a pro, so did Dash. It felt like something we'd be doing a lot. It wasn't near as intrusive as I suspected when Dash's finger played inside my ass.

"You're back, just like he said you'd be," Amelia said, smiling brightly, moving out of the way to let me by. "Hurry inside. You look cold." She misinterpreted what was happening to me. I was hot. Steaming hot. "Dash said you like eggs and bacon—less carbs—but I made you my mother's special recipe pancakes. It's a good morning that you're back."

Stepping inside the house felt like the place I was meant to be. The feeling of belonging was so special I'd happily eat those pancakes. "My mom makes a mean pancake too. I love those things. Do I have time to put these in Dash's room?"

"Absolutely, I'll start them now."

She went one way. I went the other. I was twelve hours into happiness. It felt damn good.

In the place between awake and asleep, something tickled my nose. I did my best to ignore it, telling my brain to shut it off. Exhaustion was a bitch that owned me right now. Of course the nuisance didn't listen. The brush came again, this time across my cheek. I should turn. Whatever bothered me would be disrupted, but I couldn't make myself move. Dash was cupped against my body, and I didn't want to disturb him.

The way his heavy breaths came in slow, long intervals, I doubted he'd wake.

The flicker happened again. I opened my eyelids. The room was dark, cozy, and warm with the fans circulating the air. Realization dawned as I glanced down. Dash's silky hair against my face was the culprit. That was an easy enough problem to fix if only I had a hand to use, but both my arms were wrapped securely around Dash, who clung to them tightly.

Since I'd rather cut my arms off than move from his hold, I had a problem. Only then did I register the strong urge to go to the bathroom. The stakes changed. I drew in a deep breath, and with as little disruption as possible, I untangled from Dash's hold and scooted from the warm blankets. I instantly changed my mind about the warmth in the room. The chill went through me in an instant. The eerie sounds of wind blew like a blizzard outside. The protectively covered palm trees bent under the assault of the weather.

I moved a little faster as I went to the bathroom. If I let my thoughts go, I'd wake myself up, but that didn't seem to matter to this head of mine. I silently shut the door behind me, keeping the light off to avoid waking Dash. Since I rarely cared about other people, it was a foreign thought to worry about his comfort.

Hell, I'd never slept in bed with another person, except for Dash years ago. I honestly believed I wouldn't like to cuddle, let alone to be wrapped around someone to go to sleep. Apparently, a lot of new ideologies were headed for me.

My thoughts shifted. A wicked smile came to my face as I realized how livid my father would be with me. If he hadn't died, I'd still be under his thumb. He controlled me like the bitch I became, or better yet, the one he'd created inside me. How my mom got tangled up with him in the first place was mind-blowing. Maybe he'd preyed on her like he had me.

I finished up in the bathroom and took careful steps back to bed. Dash wasn't where I'd left him, dreaming of the world we'd now build. He was on his back, arm over his eyes. He'd turned back the blankets for my arrival.

Even though he hadn't said I love you, and I had said it a few times now, he showed me with his actions, which was so much sweeter to experience. My random thoughts came together and calmed me as I watched him for my entire route to bed. I climbed in, dragging the covers with me as Dash rolled over to face me. He opened his tired eyes.

"I tried not to wake you," I whispered.

"I don't think you did. I think I sensed you were gone," he explained. I nudged closer to his unbelievably warm and inviting body. He shifted his head, allowing room for me on the comfortable pillow we shared. "You're cold. Why're you so cold?"

"Why is it so cold in this room?" I countered. The question must have been difficult because his brow wrinkled. My feet mixed with his. The icicles woke him completely, and his eyelids popped open for him to stare at me.

"Why're your feet so cold? Did you go outside?"

"Did you turn the heater down?" I asked.

"Oh yeah," he said after a long yawn. "I wanted us together when we slept, and thought we'd get too hot. What time is it?"

"I don't know, I didn't look." My palm slid over his hair, pushing the strands off his forehead. I liked them there, made him appear human, not the male model who walked off the pages of GQ magazine.

One of my arms pushed underneath the pillow, the other wrapped around him, drawing us closer together. "I was just thinkin' about how I've never slept with anyone but you before."

"Mmm," Dash murmured and rolled me onto my back. He followed, resting his cheek into the crook of my neck, his body halfway covering mine.

"What else did you think about?" he asked, his fingertips trailing softly over my skin.

He knew me well. "I didn't like my dad."

"Me either. What else?" he asked. "Your voice relaxes me."

"How much I love you," I said, leaving the last part of my thought unsaid.

He turned his face to mine, his eyes back to being only slight slits. He grinned at me, his lips puckering. I obliged the kiss. "I love hearing it."

"I think I would too," I murmured. It took several seconds for Dash to understand before he lifted again to see me.

"I tell you that I love you. I try to show it to you all the time. Am I missing the mark?"

"No, I feel it. You just haven't said it." I tucked my arm better around him. Then lifted my hand to his head to push it back down.

"I love you, Beau. Completely in love with you. You're more special to me than I gave you credit for, and I gave you lots of credit." He pressed his lips against my chest. It did help to him to say it aloud. I didn't know relief was tied to my feelings about Dash. It seemed the opposite in fact; I was confident in us. But the verbal reinforcement helped. "Do I need to wake up and figure out what's happening to you right now?"

"No, I'm good. It was nice to hear."

"Then I'll make sure to tell you more. The word love felt inadequate for the devotion I feel for you. I'm grateful that you've allowed me back..."

"Shh," I said, letting my hand massage whatever skin I could touch. "Go to sleep. Tomorrow's coming."

Maybe for the first time ever, Dash listened, then yawned again. His soft, even snores came fast. My guy was tired. I'd put him through too much. My eyes closed too.

13: The Class Structure
Dash

One week later

"Are you sure you're doin' it right?" Beau asked seconds before I placed the raw, seasoned fajita meat on the indoor grill. Winter had finally crept its way into the DFW area. Between the cold wind and icy temperatures, outside felt like someone shook a snow globe.

With the marinated skirt steak ready to go, I hesitated with my hand above the grill. The juicy beef dripped on the hot surface below. The aromatic droplets dance over the grill. Beau had me second guessing myself. Even though I was new to grilling in general, it seemed pretty straightforward.

"What am I doing wrong? The temperature's set. The meat's been marinating all day. I have the meat thermometer out, the tongs ready..." I said, looking down at all my supplies. "The smoke's normal."

Beau looked up from slicing the bell peppers. "I don't know. I was makin' conversation. I don't cook or grill, whichever we're doin'." His silly grin and playful banter were new. The wink he gave made everything right in my world.

Instead of firing back with a witty reply, I focused on the cooking, laying the meat down onto the grill. Instantly, smoke from the sizzling beef began to fill the kitchen. I pushed the vent button on, and it sucked all the smoke from the room. Impressive. Who knew it did that so well?

"Stop trying to flirt with me and tell me about the job interview. You really think you got it?" I asked, looking at the clock. I'd read to keep the meat on one side for six minutes then flip it and do the same.

"Yeah, I got it," Beau said, his rusty knife skills making the slicing of the bell peppers and onions take much longer than necessary. "As long as my background check comes back clean, I'm good."

"You're happy with the hours and compensation?"

"Yeah, I guess. Why wouldn't I be? What do you know that I don't? Did you get me the job?" Lots of accusations in all those words.

"What?" I started. "No, I didn't get you the job. I don't know many people with blue collar employment…" The grin I tried so hard to hide wouldn't be denied. I'd just tossed the gauntlet to begin our nightly ritual. Almost anything said turned into teasing banter, complete with goofy expressions and lots of laughter. Beau was my perfect match, always up to the challenge.

"Har, har, har. You need to leave the jokes to me."

I sidled up next to Beau as his pocketknife sliced smoothly through the last piece of pepper. "In less than a week, you'll have the job you've always wanted. The universe's working in your favor." I brushed the back of my fingers over Beau's shaven cheek, a move I made over and over again, anytime he was near.

"Have you cashed the check from my mom yet?" Beau asked, a new addition to our daily routine since the check had arrived in the mail.

"No, I haven't and don't want too." I replied with the same response every time he asked. Beau reached for a hand towel, rubbing it over the knife's sharp blade. I felt the irritation wafting off him. And here we went again. I walked into him as he shifted to press his ass against the granite countertop, allowing me to maneuver between his parted thighs. The knife was forgotten, absently placed on the counter.

My nerve endings prickled, zinging across my body as the tips of his blunt fingernails trailed up then down my arms. I had to find balance with Beau if I planned to make anything more of my life. The palm of my hand rested over his heart, taking in its beat, matching mine.

Beau's answer was to manhandle me in exactly the way I craved, tugging me by the waist, drawing me snuggly against his hard cock. The pesky thing was always hungry for more. I lifted the hem of his T-shirt, teasing his hard belly with my fingers, hungry for the skin-on-skin contact.

"They'll start me out at fourteen dollars an hour. My mom sent my money to pay for the truck you bought, which is way more money that I would have spent. You cash the check then get the bills together that I'll be responsible for. You're bein' hard-headed for no reason," Beau said, all sweet and sensible and the exact opposite of what I wanted to hear.

That was a new approach to a weeklong argument in the Brooks/Richmond household. How did I tell him that he couldn't afford the utilities in this house? Fortunately, the steak needed attention, and I busied myself there, trying my best to avoid this conversation.

The steak flipped successfully. I was the new grill master. Cool.

This time Beau initiated the contact, pulling me back into the circle of his arms again. A loud thunderous crash from above had our eyes lifting to the ceiling. From the way the movers were going, I was surprised nothing had fallen through the ceiling by now. They seemed more like a demolition crew than a professional moving company. That same knocking around continued all the way down the stairwell.

Beau slipped out of my grasp, swerving toward the tinfoil to roast the vegetables on. I wasn't clueless as to the reason he left me. Seconds later, the jingling of keys landed on the kitchen island. Chandler stood in front of them.

"It's a disaster up there, but hey, the sun's setting, so I'll call it done," Chandler said with his usual flair. "Beau, it's been a blast living with you, but seriously, dude, you talk my ear off."

Beau had still never had a meaningful exchange with Chandler, but a mischievous smirk crept to Beau's lips. All Chandler caught was a side view of Beau's chin lifting in acknowledgement.

"You didn't have to be so speedy," I said and left Beau to handle the cooking. "The meat comes off in about five minutes. I'm going to walk him out."

"'Course."

Chandler, my steady friend through thick and thin, deserved more than the silent treatment, but Beau didn't see it that way in the least.

As we went for the back door, my hand found my friend's shoulder, and I gave a squeeze. "You've been my anchor for as long as I can remember," I said, my tone thick with appreciation. "Thank you for everything. You didn't have to move so fast."

"Yeah, I did," Chandler chuckled. "I'm roasted in my spot every time he puts that death glare on me. Dude's possessive of you, and I hit him the wrong way. He won't let me make it up to him."

"I get why it seems that way, but he's really a good guy," I said, feeling like the class structure between him and Chandler was more Beau's problem these days than anything to do with me. With his hand on the doorknob, I stopped Chandler, gripping his forearm. His questioning gaze met mine. How did I tell him how much his support meant to me? The quick shake of my head brought no words forward. My feelings were indescribable. "Thank you."

Chandler waved off my appreciation as if it were nothing more than a nuisance. "No need for that. I thought you were crazy like everyone else, but I figured someone's gotta look out for you." His perfectly manicured brows lifted. "And Beau came back just like you said he would. Showed us all." I continued to stare into eyes that were as familiar to me as my own. He'd been a tremendous best friend to me.

"Get over here," Chandler said, pulling me into a bear hug. "You deserve the best, but you have to ensure your happiness too. You constantly give more than you receive in everything you do."

With my eyes shut tight, I held on. An era was ending. He let go of me before I was ready and moved out of my hold. "I'll never be far," Chandler whispered. Maybe there was a tear in his eye just like mine.

"Me too," I murmured, watching him slip out the back door. The cold wind stole my breath as Chandler jogged toward the moving van parked haphazardly along the side of the house. With a cleansing inhale, I locked the door and started in the direction of my new life.

"I didn't listen but figured this might be difficult for you. You good?" Beau asked, standing like a sentry in the middle of the living room.

"Yeah." I went for my guy, wrapping my arms around him. He drew me close, both his arms circling me protectively, giving me a perfectly pressured hug. "I'd be better if you bottomed sometimes."

I lifted my gaze to watch his eyes roll. He let his arms drop from around me. "You let nothin' go. I need time. Stop buggin' me about it. So, when're you cashin' that check?"

We were cut from the same cloth. *Touche.*

14: The Splash
Beau

One month later
Dallas, Texas

"Come on!" Dash's repetitive use of those words, and deep tenor of his voice, bounced off the walls inside the bedroom. "It's lonely out here."

I barely cast a glance at the swimming pool where Dash's head bobbed in the water. He was the ultimate mood-setter. Right now, he had romance on his mind. The sparkling twinkling lights and smooth music promised a good time. The pool heater held the temperature at a warm eighty-degrees. The inside pool lights were off. One bedroom window door panel was strategically cracked open to lure me outside. Of course, the scene designed for romance beckoned me, but my mind was preoccupied.

"I can't swim for an hour after I eat," I shouted loud enough for the crazy guy in the pool to hear. I was busy planning my future. On FedEx's secure site, I dug through the two-page list of different owners who had their trucks and routes up for sale. The prices encouraged me. All I needed now was time and credit building under my belt. My goals were set. Maybe by the end of the summer...I'd be able to beat Scott's income if I owned my own truck.

"Beau, that's just an old myth. Don't worry. I'll act as your personal lifeguard. I could probably get you out of the pool, and my CPR skills are rusty, but I'm certain I remember the basics." I heard a splash of water hit the closest closed window panel.

Man, he had no patience. I peeled my gaze off Dash's laptop screen to catch a glimpse of his blond head and shoulders poking out of an innertube.

"Stop ignoring me."

What an intriguing scene. The pool and backyard had their charm, but with Dash in the mix, it was pure magic. Why was I in here when he was out there?

A mischievous sneak attack began brewing in my head.

I'd been skipping my workouts, losing some of my bulk muscle. After nine hours of heavy lifting and loads of cardio a day, I didn't want to come home and spend hours of my evening lifting and away from Dash. So I sought some pretty weighted boxes to lift at work and used his limited in-home gym equipment whenever he did. I could feel the decline in my tone, but I also wanted it to happen. I'd only ever been this buff due to my father. Which was technically another really good reason to lose the muscle.

What I hadn't lost was my inner athleticism. With a sudden burst, I leaped from my chair, whipping off my T-shirt and tossing it away as I ran. One foot landed on the flower bed mulch, the other on the Cool-Crete freezing cold concrete. With no hesitation, I dove headfirst into the pool. The warmth of the water was as perfect as Dash kept saying. Since the inside pool lights were off, it allowed me to swim along the bottom until I reached Dash's feet and tugged him under. It required some muscle power due to the innertube.

I sprang up like a rocket, the innertube did too. Dash took longer. I had my hand poised to send a wave splashing when he came up. The way he sputtered around when breaching the water made me pause and reach out a hand to help steady him.

Once I determined that he'd live and got him back to the tube, an unexpected splash of water hit me straight in the face.

Now it was my turn to cough and flail. He'd gotten it straight up my nose.

"Why did you do that?" Dash asked and whined at the same time. "Fuck, Brooks, my hair."

Of course, the hair. I rolled my eyes. He always kept it on point while I secretly preferred his natural look. His tousled locks only added to his charm. There was just something about a wet-haired Dash that got me.

"Why do you think we get along so well?" I asked, knowing anytime I brought us up, Dash lost focus on anything else. Besides, since Dash was always, *always*, on my mind, I'd been wondering about that question for the last few days.

The times of guarding my words, considering each one from every possible angle before saying them out loud was in the past. At least where Dash was concerned. He started for me until he reached my outstretched hand, allowing him to be drawn against my chest. We cozied up every time we were alone together. His body came flush against mine, his arm circling my shoulders, our faces inches apart. Love was such a beautiful connection.

"You know the answer," Dash stated. "We're a perfect match. Destined to be together."

"Hmm, I guess so," I teased, playfully poking at my guy's theories.

"You guess. How do you guess? It's clear. Couldn't be clearer," Dash shot back, not exactly calling me clueless, but his tone said it all.

I chuckled, sending the water lapping around us. "So how was your day? You were on the phone when I got home."

"Fine." His brow wrinkled as he circled back. "Why am I always the one to see we're meant to be? It's been obvious since the first day we met."

"I was messin' with you. You were fumin' about your hair, so I switched the topic," I explained. My tiptoes reached the bottom of the pool, allowing me to use both arms to wrap around him. Dash's legs circled my hips, aligning our cocks. Where he'd seemed chill with the physical distraction between us, I still struggled with the passion swirling throughout my body, all the damned time.

"You picked a subject that fires me up more?" Yep, the tone sharpened. He was going to make a great trial lawyer. In direct contrast to what was coming out of his mouth, his hold around my neck grew firmer, drawing us closer.

"So, how was your day, really?"

"It's still fine. Better when you come home. I'm not looking forward to the holidays. I watch the clock waiting for you," Dash admitted, reiterating the same complaint of every day.

"You're really uppin' the ante for a casual conversation." I waggled my brows, hoping he understood I was teasing. "Have you told your family about us?"

"No, I'm keeping us in a bubble. I asked Chandler not to say anything." His warm breath sent faint foggy clouds in my direction. I'd moved us farther into the shallow end and bent my knees until only our heads stuck out of the water. "I want a favor."

The set of his eyes begged me to understand, signaling what was about to come. Dash encouraged my versatility on the daily—several times a day. Over the last week or so, his pleas had taken on a determined edge. I wasn't certain my pleasure mattered as much as Dash's desire to feel me surrounding him. To understand the intense satisfaction of being balls deep inside the one you love.

"You want me to bottom," I answered.

Dash planted a happy smooch, both long and wet, on my lips. It reminded me of the gold stars my mom used to use when I was young. "My fella's so smart. The water will help. I have lube on the lounger. I promise to go slow." His charming, handsome, happy face was as irresistible as always.

I'd already decided to throw in the towel, surrender to the lure, but negotiating was essential in the give and take of our relationship. "If I do this, I want to contribute to the bills around here. Let me handle the utilities. And you cash my mom's check—it's my inheritance. I want to pay for my truck."

His hungry gaze locked on my lips. "Money's not an issue for us. We're covered. The truck came from an account I've been saving money in for a long time. I see myself as the provider. Let me provide."

I opened my mouth to argue, but Dash turned it into an electrifying moment when his head suddenly angled and dipped, our lips colliding. He executed the perfect dance as we battled for dominance, working us closer to the loungers. He'd managed to take us from zero to a million in two heartbeats.

We moved instinctually. The kiss left me breathless, a beautiful devastation. For him, it was a calculated move—a means to an end. My end. He guided me to the shallowest part of the pool, the lounge ledge, and guided me onto my belly. His touches were both possessive and tender.

"I'll make this good for you." His statement hung in the air, charged with anticipation. He deftly removed my swim trunks, followed by his own. The water's warm embrace added to the solid grip desire had on me. "New rule. When we're alone, we don't wear clothes."

Words escaped me as his fingers lightly traced my crease before slipping inside. Desire pulsed through every fiber of my body when his thumb began circling my hole. He applied pressure, and I surrendered to the intoxicating sensation.

I gave myself over to the feeling. My ass became the focal point of my body. Only when I opened my eyes and glanced back to look at him did I realize how much this meant to him.

I pivoted to my back and drew him into my arms, kissing him like my life depended on our intimacy. Then his thumb pushed past my barrier. The latch I had on his mouth, released. A sigh escaped. My gaze shot to Dash's, desperately needing to share this moment with him. I took all of his thumb inside me and felt the exact instant he found my gland.

Oh fuck me. I was instantly lightheaded. My balls churned. I didn't come, which was shocking. My entire body hummed, wanting in on the action of this release. I'd never felt anything like it before. The intense pressure was all encompassing, running from the tip of my toes to the top of my head.

He grinned seconds before applying pressure, rubbing back and forth over the insanely sensitive bundle of nerves. Even after all the sex we'd shared, my orgasm was ready to fucking go. "I can see it on your face. It feels amazing, doesn't it?"

I dropped my head between my shoulder blades as I huskily whispered, "Fuck yeah." They were the only intelligible words I could think to say.

The connection we shared was pure electricity, charged with something deeper, more substantial. The crisp night air wrapped around us. Dash's lips came back to mine, soft and insistent, tracing my mouth. Man, I liked when he licked me. They gave me a silent plea to let him back inside, and I did. His thumb never left my ass, relaxing me open while providing immense pleasure.

"Let's go inside and do this the right way," Dash said, barely lifting from my mouth.

His words sizzled in the air around me. Lust hung heavy. My hips rolled against Dash's hand.

"You like that, don't you?" I lost Dash's thumb, making room for a tag team of his index and middle finger, sliding in and out, scissoring my hole open.

There was an unmistakable scent of pure male surrounding me.

He rose from my hold, his free hand caressing the sensitive bud of my nipple. My body turned into a human furnace as Dash gave a solid shiver. Half his body was exposed to the cold night breeze.

"Let's go inside," I murmured, dislodging his hand.

"Good call," Dash agreed. He dunked under water, probably to warm up, then executed the perfect jump and lift from the pool. I did the same. "I'm freezing."

In the same fluid motion I used when lifting from the pool, I bent down to Dash, and tossed him over my shoulder. My guy yelped as I took a direct line into the house, flower beds be damned. Midway to the bedroom, I swiped a towel from the stack and tossed it over him.

"Beau, put me down. I can walk." Certainly, he could walk. That was never in question. I chuckled and swatted his ass with the palm of my hand. I wasn't sure I'd ever have enough of this guy. Pausing just inside the still open window panel, I swatted Dash's ass again. The towel covered his butt, denying me the satisfaction of the quick slapping sound. "Shut the panel."

"Continue spanking me like that and it'll become a frequent part of our bedroom time."

Of course, Dash was into a degree of rough play. He liked me to toss him around. I rolled my eyes. When I heard the click of the lock, I started for the bed. At the edge, I carefully flipped Dash over, landing him on the soft mattress. "Hey. The bed'll get wet..."

Damn, if my dick didn't get harder from him giving a small bounce. Dash was everything. His body was toned and fit. His hard cock bulged out, lengthy and hard.

"Fuck the bed," I murmured.

"Language!" Dash teased as I leaped on the mattress, close to him, watching him bounce again. I grasped Dash's neck and jaw, tilting his face to me. Honestly, he didn't stand much of a chance at resistance. My tongue delved inside his mouth. My ass was ready for his thumb again.

Oh man, bottoming was already hotter than my wildest dreams. The breach of my ass was both intimate and personal. It consumed me. I needed to ride this out, see how it ended.

Breaking from the kiss, I rubbed our cheeks together and inhaled deeply. Leather and spice, the room, the man. My dreams. "I want you to keep goin'. It feels good."

"I told you that you'd like it," Dash purred, pushing my shoulder until I landed on my back. Good, I wanted to watch him. His fingers crawled over my belly muscles, down my treasure trail, finally to fist my cock. One knee pushed between my legs, spreading my thighs apart.

"I like you this way. All natural," I whispered, staring at his disheveled hair and strong five o'clock shadow. "You're handsome."

"I'm unkempt," he murmured.

"You look real..." My eyes bugged out of my head as Dash bent, swallowing me whole. No test run, just taking me to the back of his throat in one sure move. Jolts of electricity ran rampant, sizzling a path straight to my balls. My love began worshiping my body as if it were made to order. His special treat.

The air hummed with sexual tension. If Dash continued, I'd certainly come in his mouth. He could give a master class in how to give a great blow job. My balls seized as I desperately tugged him off me. The pop of release was audible, vibrating through my head.

Dash drew in breath, his chest heaving. He looked like a wildcat poised to pounce on its next meal. He trailed wet, openmouthed kisses along my body, up my neck and over my jawline. He circled the shell of my ear and whispered into the path he'd just made wet. "You taste so damned good. So fucking sexy. My man. I'll never get enough." His wicked tongue lavished my ear before pushing off me again. The delight in his gaze sent my desire even higher. "It's gonna be so good. I need to get the lube."

15: The Future
Dash

I didn't expect to be this turned on, but watching Beau writhe under my touch, me the orchestrator of his immense pleasure, was fucking fantastic. See? Even the language in my head was raw and gritty. My dick pulsed with need, but I would wait until Beau was ready to take all of me. I was a man on a mission.

Clumsily, I grabbed the lubricant, having to tear my eyes away from the playground before me. In two seconds flat, I had the lube in hand when I remembered something I wanted to try. "I can't believe I'm saying this but turn over. On your knees."

"Bossy," Beau chimed, doing as I asked.

"Remember that," I commanded. The grin in my head might not have made it to my lips as butterflies took flight inside my belly. Having Beau's ass up and displayed only for me was as heady as it was a thing of beauty. I tossed the lube on the towel, my bottom lip slid between my teeth in anticipation.

Positioning myself, I reached for a cheek, kneading the flesh with one hand while the other ran along Beau's spine, ass to neck, pressing there for him to lower. The entire time, my gaze was locked on the crevice I wanted to split a part.

"You're bein' weirdly quiet," Beau said, lowering his head between his elbows.

"I know. It's strange. I'm in awe. Getting you ready turns me the fuck on. Hold tight. We're going to try something." I gripped Beau's ass cheeks and spread them wide. That pucker drew me in like a heat-seeking missile. What a tempting sight.

"Get on with it," Beau murmured, and I did. My mouth watered in anticipation of tasting all of Beau against my tongue. I greedily gave a swipe, licking across his hole. Beau's body quivered; a groan pulled from deep inside his chest.

We'd been together for over a month, every one of those days was spent loving each other's bodies in one way or another. How had I not explored eating ass? I could tell I'd spend a lot of time right here, in my future.

"Again," Beau's husky voice demanded. I was so amped up I buried my face and fucked Beau with my tongue until his body trembled under my touch.

At some point, I leaned back and circled my thumb around his opening, easily slipping inside.

"Don't stop," Beau groaned.

"Never." A satisfied grin spread over my face as I removed my thumb and kept my hold on his ass cheek. I dove inside for a second round. Beau's hips rode my tongue, pumping back and forth. He'd be good and relaxed, ready to take me balls deep. I lapped and lavished, my mouth watered at such intimacy, knowing this was all I ever wanted. I was living my dreams.

My cock had been patient, urging me to make this good, but it'd had enough. It was a selfish bastard, calling for my hand. I gave in and began stroking myself. It pulsed against my palm. I lifted and leaned in, pressing my cock against Beau's heated skin, sliding my erection between his crease.

"I'm so fucking turned on," I moaned. "You feel this? It's because of you." I bent, taking his ass cheek into my mouth, gently biting the plump fleshy globe. Goosebumps sprang up on Beau's thighs, his shuddering intake of breath caused my dick to grow even harder.

"Me too. Get on with it," Beau said, turning his head sideways. His amber eyes had taken on a darker edge, willing me to get this going. Beau grabbed his cock, stroking. I wet my finger by licking straight up the digit, and pushed it inside my guy's body, while reaching for the lube. With a snick of the cap, I drizzled the slick directly on my fingers then began driving and stretching in and out of his hole.

I'll never get enough of watching Beau's mouthwatering body joined with mine.

"I wanna see," Beau said. He didn't wait for my approval before flipping around, landing on his back. He maneuvered until I was again between his spread thighs.

"You're perfect," I whispered.

"You're more perfect," Beau said, reverently. "And you're teasin' me too much. I need to know."

Yeah, he'd know but I wanted a little bit more time to make this perfect. I pressed a kiss on his hip, mouthing the oblique there before reaching for Beau's nipples, giving the smallest pinch. He was sensitive there, and I got the expected response. He yanked me up, my body flush with his as he demanded entrance into my mouth.

Fuck, that was an enchanting move. Beau was so damned strong. I kissed him greedily, gripping his shaft, pumping to the rhythm of our kiss.

Probably the only thing that could pull me from the savory kiss was the feel of pre-come dripping from his slit. I needed that in my mouth. With my thumb, I spread his evidence of his desire over his tip.

Oh yeah, I was going to make this so special he'd want this every night. Never to willingly stray away from me again. I pushed off his chest, lowering, licking, and nipping his swollen flared head. The velvet steel teased my senses.

What a joke. This wasn't about Beau. It was all me. I struggled with my sanity anytime Beau was near. He was my brand of heroin, addictive as fuck. I craved him and sucked him down, bobbing my head on his cock for a couple of swift suctions. He'd come if I went too much further. Exactly where I wanted him—right on the edge.

"Your mouth..." Beau started, his piercing gaze on me. "Sinful." My slick fingers went back to my ultimate goal, pumping into his ass, curling to hit his prostate with every swipe. Beau issued desperate pleas, his body arching so beautifully to my touch. It was time.

I repositioned myself between his legs. He instinctively clutched his thighs, drawing them to his chest. I drizzled lube liberally on my dick then over Beau's exposed hole.

"Do it," Beau hissed, baring down. The force which he used opened his hole. He gave me entrance.

"You're gonna think of me every time you sit down tomorrow, just like I do you." I gave a single swipe of my head over the lube at his hole. Anticipation roiled in my balls. I pushed slowly inside my love, who drew me in from the inside out. Dammit, what a beautiful feeling.

My first time to top. His channel gripped and held on to me so good. My shoulders shuddered. I locked my gaze on my dick as it slowly disappeared into Beau's channel. Engulfed in searing heat, he gripped me in the most extraordinary way.

I lost myself to the vibration of Beau's body. My cock became needy and wild as Beau squeezed me into his searing tightness. Beau gave an audible gasp, drawing my attention to his straining body. His head rolled backward, his eyes clamped shut.

I froze, allowing Beau to adjust to the invasion. "You good?" I hissed, super aware of my surroundings.

Seconds passed as I took in the sound of the ceiling fan blades slowly whooshing as they turned, the hum of the bulbs lighting the room, the heater blowing air past the vents. It all defined this moment: spectacular. "You're so damned tight."

"Keep goin'," Beau whispered. He lifted his head; funny how I could feel his body movements while buried inside him. Beau's hot, sexy, encouraging gaze found mine. My trance broke. I reached for the lube, dumping a generous portion on the juncture where my dick met his ass. Beau's body relaxed into mine. He gripped his cock. My palm covered his, running the length of his shaft.

Words escaped me—they never had before—as I took in everything, just in case this was my only time here. The give and take of Beau's muscles, flexing and tensing with each of my thrusts. The delicious friction urging my dick on.

"You fill me so good," Beau moaned. The pleasure amped up with each snap and glide of my hips. We moved in unison, slowly picking up the pace. Beau's body quivered. A desperate surge of lust burned through me.

Beau brought his feet to the mattress, lifting as he pumped his hips against mine. Oh man, that was hot. I fought for control of our rhythm, becoming jerky and unrestrained. I couldn't stop my thrusts, even if I wanted to. I never wanted this to end. My guy gripped me so good. I dropped my head forward, consumed with the way Beau's body held onto me. Beau watched me. He was as much in control as I was.

The world faded. I felt Beau's heart beating with mine. We were one. I craved his pleasure as much as I did my own. My commitment to him was reaffirmed. A long life with him by my side. I wouldn't accept anything less.

"Marry me someday," I whispered roughly, surprising even me with the question.

He groaned louder. His breaths quickened. His hips slammed into me. We were perfect together. I was lost to my guy. My heart pounded against my rib cage, and my orgasm fought for release. Beau's being clamped down around me like the warmest embrace.

"Come with me, Dash," Beau said through gritted teeth. The command was all it took. I couldn't hold back. My body blew apart under the blinding pleasure of my release. I filled Beau's ass. My release wouldn't stop coming.

Whatever was left of me fell forward, barely missing the come splattered over Beau's chest. His strong arms circled around me as I floated into oblivion.

"You fell asleep," Beau murmured, lying face-to-face with me. I was still super aware of everything, this time loving the feel of the softest satin-like sheets covering both of us. My pillow was now his too. My hands were steepled together, tucked under my cheek. Every molecule of my being was now fused with his. I marveled at how love continued to grow in infinite amounts.

"I know. Weird." I had managed to clean us up before we dirtied the bedspread more, and that was about all. "I hope we stay just like this forever. I want us to be tied together in every way."

"Someday," he said quietly, contentment filling his expression.

"We should go fishing. And stone skipping. You know I practiced both while we were apart. The stone skipping is a skill I never mastered."

"You're sweet. We need to start doin' things you like," he said, fatigue edged his tone.

"We do what I like all the time, tonight for example." My brows wiggled as best they could based on my position. "Your ass sore?"

"A little. In a good way. I get why you stayed on me to try. It's different than bein' on top. It felt like my entire body was in on the orgasm."

He was right. I'm glad he liked it. I wanted us to be together in every way.

"I'm being invited out more since the mock trial," I murmured, glad to finally have some friends.

"Go, you don't have to babysit me," Beau said.

"No, I want you to come with me sometime. You might like some of them. Maybe we'd get some couple friends."

Beau looked doubtful even if he didn't say the words aloud.

"I've been thinking..."

Beau interrupted me. "When aren't you thinkin', plannin', strategizin' somethin'?"

Okay, valid point, but I didn't need to give Beau the win aloud. "We could move somewhere along the coast of Texas. I could drive into Houston to work. Maybe you start the charter service you wanted to."

Beau shook his head, his facial expression changed again. "I need time before I go back there. I heard my grandparents' house was torn down."

Oh no, I'd taken a conversational wrong turn. I didn't want him to be sad tonight. I reached for his cheek as I murmured my apology. "We could do it anywhere, I'm sure. Maybe at the cape or Coronado or Miami," I said. "I think we'd like Miami."

A yawn slipped from Beau. "Probably. It's hot there. I need some sleep; I got lost in lookin'. Can we continue this tomorrow, if you want?"

"Sure. Go to sleep. I'm going to lay here looking at you this time. Score of one to ten, did you like bottoming," I asked.

"I'll give it a nine to leave room for whatever else you have planned for us." A small grin lifted the corners of his mouth. "Do you want me to stay awake?"

"No, go to sleep. I'll probably study," I said. He gave an immediate nod and closed his eyes.

I didn't know happiness like this existed. At least I'd never seen or heard of it. I reached for his cheek again. He turned to his belly, lying flat with his face still to me. His warm body sidled up against my side. "Thank you."

"For what?" I asked.

"Everything." Sleep tugged him under. I'd have to remember to give my appreciation in the morning. I reached for a coursebook on my side's nightstand, lifting my back against the headboard. Beau's body adjusted until he was flush against my hip and leg.

Yeah, he had nothing to be thankful for. The gratitude was all mine. I loved him more and more each day that passed. Apparently love was in fact immeasurable, not quantifiable. Who knew?

I refocused on the book in my lap, needing to pay closer attention to my studies. A damned hard feat with Beau here with me. What an enchanting thought to think we'd be just this happy forever.

16: The Finger Test
Beau

Three Months Later
Late Spring

The beep of the alarm system at the front door signaled I was finally home.

"Hello," I called loudly throughout the house, taking a quick peek into Dash's gorgeous office where he never sat anymore. Something about the boundaries I gave him to study kept him out of the room. I guess he wanted me to bother him more.

"Hey, I'm in here," Dash said from the kitchen. With his review materials spread out across the table, he claimed the setting was cozy. The best spot in the house to work from. I didn't see it. But he managed to shut out the world, buckle down, and tackle the mountainous weekly reading assignments and everything else he had to do. It was so much work, all of the time.

I doubted his theory on the kitchen table's magical study powers. I didn't know why he chose possible time with me over the highly decorated office, but he did, and I happily obliged. Making sure I bothered him at least once on the hour, sometimes more if I remembered to fit it in.

Head over heels didn't begin to describe me. I cherished every moment. Last night, Dash read aloud from one of his advanced textbooks. His sharp mind challenged me to level up my comprehension, picking up the subtlety in his use of language and reason.

"How was your day?" he asked.

Our daily rhythm included him rounding the table to deliver a quick peck. There were rules there too. The kiss had to last at least six seconds, which was enough time to add a slip of tongue.

Dallas had moved into spring and was edging toward a hot summer. The temps outside, where I spent all of my day, were getting warmer. The smell of sweat on my body was turning from musky, the way Dash liked, to straight up yuck. I needed to bathe before we began our extensive greetings upon my return.

"Good. Usual." My nose guided me to the stove where my culinary guy had skill. I didn't lift the lid, careful not to disturb the magic happening there. "Smells better than decent." I cocked my head back toward Dash. "How was your day?"

"Good. Usual," he chimed in with a wink. "Any dogs today to cause you to sprint faster than them?"

Of course, I laughed. It wasn't out of the ordinary to have a dog or two chasing me through the neighborhoods. Me running from animals was definitely the only real cardio I got anymore. Well, that and sex. We were pretty vigorous in the bedroom. Both had to count as calories burned.

"I wish I was fast enough to outrun those fuckers. Their teeth hurt. A rooster came for me today. What's for dinner tonight?" My empty stomach growled.

"It's a chicken and rice dish I found online. A Gordon Ramsay recipe."

"Nice." I forced my feet to move away from the stove, grabbing a water bottle from the refrigerator. "I'm goin' for a quick rinse."

"Hold up." His tone shifted gears. Dash had a way of being direct, without seeming so. This was different. My brows shot up. We weren't big on TV, but I could sense an unwelcome series creeping into my future.

"I don't want to watch anything with a meet-cute, or fashion sewin', or bakin' in England. You can watch all that on your own."

He gave me the reaction I wanted which was a solid laugh followed by him coming to me. His charm still left my knees weak. This time was no different. I didn't think I'd ever get used to all that handsomeness heading my way. The way he walked up on me had my ass hitting the edge of the counter. He came between my parted legs, and I casually circled an arm around him, it was where they always wanted to be. All right, I'd watch anything but the meet-cute if he were in my arms.

"How about the Blair Witch Project? We can turn off the lights and snuggle together. Think scary thoughts," he suggested. A psychological horror was off my list too. It fucked with my head too much.

"Wait, do I get a vote in this, or do I have to do it no matter what?" I asked, already knowing the answer. I'd be going along no matter how he phrased whatever was about to land.

"Good point." Dash stepped away to lean his ass against the counter across from me. So he'd been buttering me up.

"My parents are coming to town..."

Oh hell no. He should've approached this differently. Let me get cleaned up, maybe have a beer. I enjoyed the cold bitter flavor, and I liked being clean even more. My ass pushed off the counter on its own accord.

"Dash, no," I began, lifting the uniform shirt over my head. "It's only been around four months. I won't know how to act around them. Why don't you just tell them? You know how to handle it."

"Be yourself. They'll see why I love you. The first time, we'll roll in, meet and greet my parents. Then the following day we'll have lunch at the club where my brothers and sisters and their families will be. You'll remember Joy..."

"Club, like country club?" I interrupted. "No, I can't do that. I'm not comfortable meetin' your parents yet." The path to the laundry room was on my way to the bedroom. I tossed my shirt on the dryer and kicked off my work boots. Dash padded after me, altering my normal way of undressing in here before my shower. I couldn't get trapped in this room with him all in my face, trying to change my mind. My altered course had me undressing further as I started down the hall to the bedroom.

"I can't just say hello and leave. That seems rude." *Fuck*, I'd dreaded this meeting since I first realized I was going to have to meet his family at some point. I'd naively hoped he'd handle them. Dash viewed situations how he wanted them to be, not actuality.

How on freaking earth was I supposed to dine at a fancy club? Remembering which fork to use was a serious problem for me. No matter how I tried, from one etiquette training session to another, I couldn't retain any of it. It seemed overly complicated for no reason.

"They won't have time for us. They'll be swamped with engagements. Half an hour, max," Dash said, trailing behind me. Clad in my knee-high socks and underwear, I paced the bedroom before going inside the bathroom. I attempted to shut the door in his face, but he bounced it back on me.

"When?" I finally said, dropping down on my ass on the closed commode.

"Next weekend," he answered calmly, like that wasn't only seven days away.

"So you'll be done with school? Because you have a lot ridin' on right now." I desperately tried to make the misfiring cylinders in my head find a real way out this mess. To distract from the panic building inside me, I finished undressing. My socks came off first, tossing them toward the door where I left my shorts and undershirt—they'd make it to the washing machine soon and dropped my underwear where I stood, those were toe tossed toward the rest of my clothes.

I need space and time. A concept Dash didn't believe in, but I needed to think properly. There was no scenario where I saw his family happy with me in the picture. I went to the shower, flipping it on. As the water cascaded down, my mind raced.

"Give me fifteen minutes," Dash countered, standing next to me. "I can tell them alone, but I'd rather you be there."

"I don't have anything to wear," I said lamely.

"That's not true, but I'll get you something new, or you can wear a pair of jeans. However you present is fine." A caring, caressing palm ran the length of my bicep. The touch was probably meant to be positive and encouraging. Instead, I felt the invisible shackles clamping shut around my wrists and ankles.

Blue jeans? Right. The release of my pent-up sigh said it all.

"I'll get you something that's comfortable but appropriate. Not a problem."

A myriad of new concerns arose. No one shopped like Dash shopped. He enjoyed browsing everything, trying on most of what he saw, spending more money than I'd make in a lifetime. Now I'd be the one trying on the clothes? Going from store to store...

I loved him. I did. I loved spending time with him. Except when shopping.

Without finger-testing the temperature, I stepped under the spray. Thankfully, the water temperature was perfect.

I scrubbed my hands down my face. I didn't want to lose Dash. My gut told me nothing good could come from surprising his parents with me. When I started to speak those words, his warm, strong palms pressed against my back, massaging my sore muscles.

I glanced back to see him naked behind me. My grin was instant. My God, I was the luckiest guy in the world. Tingles raced across my nerve endings, like they always did when Dash was around. He doted on me, putting my needs first in every way. The press of his lips kissed my left shoulder. Then his thumbs dug into those muscles, loosening their tight hold.

"I didn't mean to upset you. I'll go alone. I liked the idea of us being a united front. Also, I might want to gently rub it in their faces that you came back to me." His lips touched my right shoulder. "My father worked to get you away from your father. We just didn't have contacts in Mobile, but he tried to help you. When you do meet him, you'll like him. He's easy to be around. I promise." His thumbs went to work on the muscles on that side of my back. "If you decide to go, we'll be fast. I want them to see you and meet you. See why I put my life on hold for you."

Warm water cascaded over my head and down my body, soothing me through the entire run. My shields lowered. I let his words sink in as my muscles relaxed. We both understood I'd cave eventually. I'd straighten out my thoughts. Maybe not until we were driving up to the house, but I'd get there.

Dash never did anything fairly. He kept up the persistent massage, winding his way to my belly, caressing down my stomach muscles. Of course, I was hard as stone. When wasn't I? Dash had had me in every way, over and again, and still wanted me in bed and out.

My real fear in facing his family was the same fear I lived with daily. If I stayed true to myself, embraced who I was and who I was always meant to be, I wouldn't fit in the world of the Richmonds.

I pressed my forehead to the tile as he reached around, clasping my hard-on with both hands. "At least you're happy to see me."

"I'm always amped up when you're around. You know that," I said, grumbling and closing my eyes, feeling every tug of his fist. The small nipping kisses trailed to my ass. His right hand left my cock, my body tightened. I loved when he licked my ass.

So, when I turned and took his forearm, drawing him up against me, it came as a surprise to both of us. "Save it for later. I'll go meet them. I'm not sure about the club, but I'll do my best."

"Thank you," Dash murmured happily and pressed his lips to mine. I shifted my head away from his offer. I wasn't finished.

"Promise me, when you see how badly I don't fit in, you'll let me down easy."

Dash's face morphed through multiple expressions. I pressed my fingers against his lips to keep his words on the inside.

"Just promise me."

I slightly lifted my hand off his mouth by a marginal degree. "Are you saying because you might not—" My hand pressed down again, stopping him from speaking.

"Promise me." I brought my other hand to the back of his head, keeping him locked there.

"Well, I don't know how to do that with your hands actively keeping me quiet," Dash mumbled against the firm press of my finger. "But yes, I promise not to let you leave me because you're uncomfortable." Frustrated with being silenced, he tugged my forearm away, dislodging my hold. "I went to your world and tried my best to fit in. I wasn't always comfortable, but I tried. Can you please try for me?"

The underhanded, dirty, con man got me good with that reply. He wasn't wrong. And no, his efforts only made me want him more.

"Yeah, I can." I nudged him under the spray and snatched the soap from the shelf.

Now, what was my plan to get through it all? If I stayed cool, remained quiet, and followed Dash's lead, maybe I'd unravel the mystery of rich people...

Nah, I'd humiliate Dash. My nervous energy struck double time fast, sending me into super negative mode.

The demon of insecurity began running loops inside my head. The push I gave to the soap bottle dumped way more out than I wanted. Maybe it was a sign. Of what? I didn't know. I had bigger problems. I ran my hands over my body, washing away the grime of the day. Maybe it'd rinse the layers of me off with it, remove all the country hick so I'd present better to be worthy of Dash.

"Hey, come here," Dash called from the kitchen, where he was no doubt preparing something delicious for us, probably ice cream. I love that stuff. "Amelia's not thrilled that you're taking over her duties." I couldn't help but roll my eyes.

"It's not right for her to do all the dirty work," I said, giving my perpetual response as I planned to tackle my laundry after

I finished sweeping the foyer. My work boots always left a trail of the outside when I came in.

"But that's her exact job," Dash laughed, stepping around the pile of dirt I'd created, with a bowl of ice cream in hand. He took a bite from the one bowl, two spoons and two scoops. "She's asked me to put a lock on the laundry room door to keep you out. Your vibe's messing up her flow."

I glanced his way while drawing the dirt into a tight circle. All I'd ever done was my laundry. How did that mess with her flow? I vacuumed and swept what I left behind...

"You're overthinking it." The spoon entered my peripheral vision, laden with a tempting scoop of ice cream. "I may have embellished a bit. She wants to take care of you like she takes care of me. Now, come join me on the sofa. It's my attempt to begin using other rooms in this house rather than the two we stick to. Dig into this with me. I put extra hot fudge, so the ice cream is beginning to melt."

He sashayed closer, reeling me in with his unmitigated charm. I took the bait and leaned in for a bite. His pucker came next. Ice cream was on his lips, and the tip of his tongue slipped inside my mouth. Dash was a goofball, offering me a bite to then steal it. Another spoonful followed. This time, he let me have it all to myself.

I grabbed the dustpan, ushering the small amount of dirt I found inside, and started toward the trash can. If I didn't do it now, there was zero way he'd allow me to finish. Everything Dash did had a romantic edge. Floor sweeping was likely to ruin the mood he was creating. "Go sit down. I'll dump this and be there."

"I just received an email that Dedman accepted me into their accelerated program, allowing me to graduate a semester early. I then called Haynes, Baker, Smart, and Reed. They seemed happy that I can begin work on January 6th," Dash explained, following me until we ended on the sofa facing the backyard. The bite he scooped went into his mouth as I dropped down beside him.

"Exactly what you wanted. Good for you," I chirped. I took the second spoon and scooped up a mouthful of ice cream, savoring it when it hit my tongue.

"I also heard today from admissions," he added, his expressive face turning neutral, lawyer mode worthy. And here we go again. What had Dash cooked up now? "You have a place at SMU. They're offering scholarships to help fund you."

Right, I wasn't letting that fib slip past. "Don't lie to me over things I know about. You're payin'."

"No." Dash shook his head innocently. "I'm not lying. They wanted you to play football, but I said you were out." Whatever expression I had on my face caused Dash to laugh. "I told them that I thought your goals had changed and you wouldn't be attending college there."

That was a very good answer. If I needed college, I'd do some night classes or online, I heard that was becoming a thing. My appetite returned as suddenly as I'd lost it. I scooped up a big bite. Dash enjoyed nibbling at his food, savoring the experience. Me? I hunkered down into the meal. My current goal, I wanted the hot fudge that had slipped to the bottom. Whip cream and a cherry came with it.

"How'd you fit all that in your mouth?" Dash asked. "Do you have brain freeze?"

Oh, I definitely experienced brain freeze, but tried my hardest to hide the sharp, piercing pain from my face. Through the effort, I absentmindedly dropped the spoon in the bowl then reached for the remote.

"My schoolmates have planned an end-of-semester party at a nearby swim bar. Wanna go?" Dash swiveled his whole body my way, excitement dancing in his eyes.

So *yeah* another uncomfortable setting for me. "When is it?"

"After lunch with my family. A group of us rented the club for the day and night. Families in the day, adults at night." Adult meant he'd have me wearing something skimpy. The few times we'd gone dancing, as the night progressed, my clothes began to fall off. Depending on the situation—no that wasn't right. Depending on nothing, Dash put maximum effort into everything he did.

I could feel his penetrating stare straight at my profile. Another bite teased at my lips. Of course, I accepted it, but it landed in my stomach differently this time. “I paid my portion to keep the club private and said we’d be there. It’s a pool club environment. I believe I said that. We’ll have a buffet, swimming, dancing, and drinks. It’s the kind of place I feel like we’d enjoy.”

We did have a great time out in the world together, but they weren’t in places I could embarrass him. We danced, got tipsy, and taxied home. It didn’t matter that he had a sophisticated take on everything, while I was more redneck in my approach to life. This one was going to matter. "Dash."

“Beau,” he mimicked. Yup, I was way past tired of that.

Why were we doing all these things at once? I had new clothes, I was cutting my hair tomorrow night, getting a barber shop shave...

My guy didn’t get life. I scrubbed a palm down my face. Why didn’t he adore our cozy cocoon like I did? He needed to handle all this on his own. I’d wait here for his return and listen to everything he had to say about it. “You go and have a good time—”

Dash interrupted before I had the word *go* out of my mouth. “You fit in my world easily. Everybody loves you.”

“Stop lying. None of your friends know me. I’ve never met them.” Absently, my palm reached for my heart, rubbing there. My guy was trying to give me a heart attack.

Dash erupted into laughter before I finished again. "You're a legend! Everyone's heard about the epic moment you whisked me out of that bar like a hero in a fairy tale."

My eyes did a full-on spin inside their sockets at the ridiculousness of a bunch of competitive law students getting lost in make-believe romantic notions. I aimed the remote at the TV, tapping the power button. With a raised eyebrow, I said, "Not the way it happened."

“You’d never convince anyone of that.” Dash waved away my reality check. “We aren’t what you think. There’s lots of people like you and me there," he said, his palm coasting over my hair. "Change of subject. You were talking about the new haircut you scheduled. I found something you might like. It's long, you wouldn't cut much off the top, and the sides fade. I think it'll frame your face really well, and this front part can be tied back. It's a cool look."

I let him shift gears, because ultimately, I was going to the swim party, just like going to meet his family. "Do you have a picture?"

"Loads. Let me get my laptop." In a single fluid move, he lifted off the sofa, bowl in hand. My mind went distracted as I scrolled through the television guide, lost to the thoughts in my head. Too much was happening too quickly. Anxiety quickened my heart rate. I hadn't settled into any of this. Something didn't feel right.

The crash and burn felt inevitable, and I couldn't find a way to stop it. As I clicked the channel button, I stared at the enormous screen. The patter of Dash's feet became louder as he made his way back to me. I let go of a steadying breath, a technique I'd learned for when anxiety became palpable.

We'd be okay. I trusted Dash, and he trusted me. If he thought I could handle it, I'd do my best to figure it out.

17: The Old Me
Dash

Thank goodness the day was finally here. Beau's extreme apprehension was contagious. The unease of the moment caused me to grip the steering wheel tighter than normal and chat endlessly about nothing. As I took the turn onto my parents' secluded road, I attempted to view my world through Beau's perspective. It was difficult. These surroundings were etched into my being as a place that held comfort and belonging. This was my home.

I slowed the ride on the massive tree-lined road, leading to the house, allowing Beau to absorb the beauty of the scenery. With the sunroof open, a gentle breeze wafted inside. Nature happened around us as the birds chirped and a leaf or two blew in the car. The sun filtered over us through the canopy of branches above.

"What kind of oak trees are these?" Beau asked, his sunglass-covered gaze shifting to look through the sunroof.

My handsome guy was clad in the new clothes we'd bought him. Far different than the tattered jeans and T-shirts he normally wore. His hair was meticulously styled in a cut that did in fact accentuate his strong jaw and chin. His lips appeared plumper and somehow more inviting. The time it took for Beau to follow the stylist's instructions to gain the perfect natural sweep off his forehead was wholly endearing. He'd mastered the art of hair products in only a few short days. Put it all with his deeply tanned skin and my guy was a thing of beauty. He belonged in my world. We'd do well here.

"I believe it's a variety of different oaks. It's the longest tree-lined driveway in Texas. They've deemed it an official road. Richmond Drive," I explained, maintaining the slower speed. In the distance, two ornate gates opened slowly. Just beyond the gates was a flower-edged circle drive with a grand waterfall fountain in the center. All of it had been designed as a backdrop to showcase my parents' stately home.

"Dash, you actually grew up here?" I couldn't see his face as it was turned away from me, but I heard a sense of awe in his voice.

"I did," I replied, nodding, and steered the car around the curve to park in front of the house. "It's been a while since I've been here, but it still feels like home."

"How big is it?" Beau asked, turning my way. I slipped the gearshift in place, taking in the slight furrow of his brow. I lifted his Ray-Bans to see the uneasiness in his expression. "Let's make a pact: I'll stay quiet. You handle the conversation. If they ask me a question that requires more than a yes or no, you answer for me. Got it?"

"I do." I put the sunglasses back in place and reached for the door handle.

"Do I call them ma'am and sir?" Beau asked, his voice was a pitch higher. He was freaking himself out.

"Whatever's comfortable to you," I answered and pushed open the door.

"We're in and out of here. No dillydallying. We have a reason, we give it, then we're done. Over time, we'll gradually begin to get to know one another," Beau declared as I hopped out of the car. His hesitancy was adorable. The fact I'd gotten him this far was a positive. Although we weren't to the goal line yet. He had to leave the vehicle and walk up the steps to see for himself that everything was like I promised. I'd tease him about this for eternity.

I shut my door. Beau still didn't voluntarily open his. Hmm. It was up to me to get him out. I circled the vehicle, reached for his door handle, and pulled it wide open. Without waiting, I began a slow gait up the steps to the front porch. Beau lagged behind, taking in the house as I pushed the front door open.

"Dasham, dear. You're not to use the front entrance. We've discussed this at length. Why're you always such a test?"

I couldn't help my smile at her reprimand. It had been years since I'd seen her last. I'm glad our relationship hadn't changed: me always being myself no matter the situation, her being frustrated with my actions. But her appearance had changed. Her face didn't have a single wrinkle.

She was pretty. More relaxed in long linen pants and a colorful top. Her hair was swept back neatly, fastened with a matching tie. What was more surprising, though, was that she opted for flat sandals. I'd never seen her in anything other than a traditional skirt suit and high heels.

"Mom," I said happily, leaving the door ajar for Beau and heading toward her. "You're glowing today. I like the new look."

Her surprised expression slowly turned endearing. "Son, this is my usual look these days," she explained, her hands gently smoothing down the front of her pants.

"I've never seen you look like this before. I prefer you this way," I explained, leaning in to give her a spontaneous hug. I missed her.

"Dasham," she said quickly, her hands going to my chest, blocking my affection. "We don't purposefully wrinkle our clothing."

The reprimand made me chuckle. While her attire might have changed, certain habits never would. "Where's Dad?"

"He's in the den. We've been expecting you," she said as if I weren't right on time.

But no matter her words, I'd guess she truly appreciated the compliment. Her hand floated around my back, guiding us toward my father. Glancing back, I noticed Beau's entry. He shut the door behind him. With a practiced move that appeared effortless, he swept his hair back in place. He was undeniably handsome. Pride rushed over me. I couldn't wait to share him with my family, and nodded for him to follow.

"Father." I beamed, genuinely happy to see him. It had been years. I took strides across the large room, a space where he and I had had many long conversations. I felt a rush of emotion, realizing how much I had missed him. A set of open blueprints held his concentration.

As I approached, he switched gears, removing his readers to give me all his attention. His arms opened wide. I was pulled into a warm, fatherly embrace. He gave the best bear hugs.

"You're looking sharp, son. I heard about your success at the mock trials. It made your siblings green with envy."

I smiled and leaned back. He held on, apparently unwilling to let me go. He always had a way of brightening my mood and upping my self-esteem.

"I have someone I'd like you to meet," I said. My mother had meandered close by, now leaning against the table my father worked from.

"You've finally rid yourself of the silliness?" she asked. Her words were sharp even if the delivery came with a smile.

"Margot," my father scolded my mother, but added his own judgmental thoughts. "We never have to utter another word of that nonsense again. We'll be able to spend more time with you."

My stomach knotted, but I put it aside to dissect later. "Well, father, mother, I didn't rid myself of anything." I beamed happy, full of pride, my smile spreading wide. "My guy came back to me. Meet..." I turned, sweeping my arm out to...no one. I scanned the entire room. Beau wasn't there.

Perhaps a sudden bout of anxiety got the best of him, and he'd hightailed it out of there. That worry had me retracing my steps in order to find him.

At the door of the den, I turned and bumped straight into Beau. "What're you doing?" I whispered.

"Y'all were havin' a moment. I gave you space," Beau answered quietly.

"Come on." I reached out a hand to hold Beau's, guiding us back into the room. "This is Beau. He came back, just as I knew he would. Beau, this is my mom, Margot, and my father, Jack."

I couldn't have been more pleased. My family was complete. Beau rooted in his spot a step or two behind me. He didn't budge when I tugged him forward, making me look back at him. I spotted the nervousness in his expression, but there was something more there as well.

I tilted back toward my mother and father, trying to see what he saw.

"Jack, you said you took care of this." I couldn't make sense of the words as my mother stared at Beau, reaching for the armrest of the closest chair to sit. My father looked business angry. The stern face he gave to his enemies.

"I believed I did." His entire focus was also on Beau. "Boy, where's your father?"

"His father died." In that second, everything became clear. Time froze. The blood seeped from my face, my body tensed, and my thoughts turned harsh.

My mother lowered her head into her hand. My father's mouth was moving while he reached for the landline telephone. While I couldn't hear all of his angry outburst, I did catch phrases like "*contracts in place*" and "*money transferred*" and "*that degenerate bastard.*" As those watchwords filtered through my brain, my anger increased. Reality zipped back into place.

"Are you implying you're responsible for keeping us apart?" The words were absurd, barely out of my mouth before I rejected them. These were my parents. They witnessed my pain firsthand. They'd promised to help me.

"Son, you can't be serious," my mother said, tossing out a careless hand as if I were being ridiculous. "You've always tested us at every turn."

With my father still on the call, he pointed a finger at me. "We will not have our family name tainted with trash. It's past time you grew up and stopped flaunting your irresponsibility and ludicrous world views in our faces."

"What did you do?" I asked again, putting the rest of this bizarre discussion on hold. Beau was my only concern.

"Grow up, Dasham. Your father did what he had to do, and the boy's father accepted. It was supposed to be over with." My mother answered for my father as if she were saying the most reasonable things.

A glance at my father showed his cheeks red with anger. Then he slammed the phone down on the receiver.

"You listen to me closely, Dasham," my father said harshly, his index finger pointing at me. "If this relationship continues, ours will not." I took his words like the blow of an unexpected right hook. My entire body numbed. I was stunned.

"All this time, you were ultimately responsible for my unhappiness, not Beau's father. Do you know what that man did to him?" Pain washed over me in waves.

"What I should have done to you, I'm certain," my father replied flippantly.

"I always said you were too lenient with him," my mother added, apparently seconding my father's view of abuse as an entirely appropriate choice. "You were always pushing him to pursue his dreams."

"He's a homosexual, Margot. A liability. We can't have him in the family business, no matter how smart he is," my father explained, stating his reasoning even further. "He had to learn a trade."

Again, I put a pin in his words, shoving them aside to deal with later. Beau. How did he fare through all the bombshell reveal? I glanced back, but he wasn't there. *Shit*. Nothing mattered more than the apology I needed to give him, then begging him to stay with me.

Everything important inside me demanded I make this right. I couldn't lose him now. I started out of the den. My father's booming voice followed me. "You keep this up, and you're no longer a part of this family. You'll be cut off and removed from everything. We won't tolerate you or your foolishness for another second."

Once I didn't see Beau anywhere, I began to jog through the foyer then the front doors. Beau wasn't anywhere to be seen.

"Beau," I called loudly, panic setting in.

A groundskeeper working on the flower beds pointed me in the direction of the long drive before my father came out of the house.

"You're making your decision, Dasham."

My jog turned into a run toward my car, in full agreement with whatever decision he made because he was no longer in my life until he made this right for Beau.

"I'll never willingly leave him, but you certainly may have destroyed my chances." Before dropping into the driver's side seat, I turned toward the porch, looking him straight in the eyes where he stood close to the front door. "He was nervous about coming here today. He didn't believe he'd fit in. You disgustingly proved him right. I'm utterly disappointed in you."

My father lost his shit, face reddening, drawing in a breath to continue his ranting and raving. I had no time to waste on his pointless words. As I plopped down into the driver's seat, the unexpected turn of events brought tears to my eyes. A young Beau had been right about everything. He'd never wavered in his belief even when I'd argued on behalf of my family. I'd foolishly believed my father was always on my side and, therefore, on Beau's. Those rose-colored glasses had been firmly in place. What a silly boy I'd been.

I peeled out around the circle, letting the car's rev show my irritation. Racing down the driveway, I prayed I'd find Beau. Dread of what was to come coiled in my gut. My love. How did this end?

18: The Run
Beau

The scorching sun didn't faze me. I spent most of my days outside in the elements. What caused me problems right then were the stupid Italian loafers on my feet. Dash assured me they were worth the buy, being made by hand from a region that produced the softest leather. But they weren't faring well during my run.

I'd begun running because I didn't know what else to do. Facing Dash's parents brought all my fears to life and then a whole lot more. My mind went into overdrive, my anxiety reached alarming heights. As I left the house, waiting outside for...well, I didn't know what, the open road of the long driveway called to me. Then a sudden urge to channel my inner Forrest Gump took over. From the second I left the porch, I sprinted in an effort to outpace my demons.

My speed and stamina hadn't suffered much over the many months since I left playing football. I'd stripped off my dress shirt about a mile back. My undershirt now hung untucked as I pushed through the pain in my feet. At least I'd never have to wear these shoes again.

Sweat trickled down my face. I lost track of the time and direction, fixing my gaze on the road below me. Over the years, I'd wondered how my father had found the photos of

Dash and me at the Fourth of July fireworks celebration in Sea Springs.

It had never occurred to me that the information had come from Dash's father. How had I not considered that? In hindsight, it was so obvious. That man, Dash's father, had willingly destroyed my grandparents, both financially and physically, without a second thought. My paw died as a result of his actions, and my nana followed him a few years later. My mother had gone through living hell. I had too. All for daring to fall in love with Dash.

The money my crappy old man had in savings made more sense now.

Perhaps the guilt of my father's actions led him to the increased amounts of alcohol he'd consumed. My head shook. It didn't matter whether it bothered him or not, he chose the money over my well-being. He still chose to make my life hell.

With each passing of my loafers on pavement, I questioned what was so wrong with me that led Mr. Richmond to completely destroy me? Did he find satisfaction in the life he'd set up for me? Or did he give me no thought at all?

Ultimately, I had held myself accountable for everything that happened. When we moved to Sea Springs, I'd taken too many risks despite knowing the reality I lived under.

I grew to hate myself. I'd contemplated suicide many times, only not to act due to the pain it'd cause my mom.

Step after step, I ran tirelessly through the roads. Time and location faded while I pushed my body in a way I hadn't done for six long months.

What did I do next? The sudden and complete anguish at the idea of losing Dash was unbearable. My breathing turned erratic, disrupting the rhythm of my pace. My feet began to slow until I came to a stop. My hands went to my knees and I bent over, my head hanging low. As I closed my eyes, I found it took effort to avoid passing out due to hyperventilation.

I *loved*Dash. I loved our lives together, and I knew he loved me in return. I believed in his belief that we were always meant to be together. But the idea of him losing everything... Dash had no understanding of what that truly meant. What a life of poverty looked like. I did though.

Reality slingshotted back in place. Of course, he had to stick with his family. Dash had never had to survive on repeated Kraft Mac & Cheese dinners because there was no money for anything else.

Acar door shut behind me. I hadn't heard the approach. From between my legs, I saw an upside-down Dash walking up behind me. Maybe I had sweated too much, causing dehydration to create hallucinations, or perhaps I'd run too far, my muscles were revolting, including my brain, but as I rose, my equilibrium shifted. I had to take a woozy balancing step backward. I lifted my undershirt's short sleeve to swipe at the sweat on my brow and in my eyes.

Dash approached with his hands in his expensive slack's pockets as he took his spot between me and the bustling road. We'd apparently caused a stir on the street. The vehicles slowing for a peek of us as they passed by.

The serious direct stare he and I shared had an ominous undertone.

"I'm sorry," Dash began. The pain in his eyes and voice destroyed any remnants left of my heart. I understood the meaning of the apology and nodded, turning my face away. The tears refused to be held at a distance any longer. I needed to brave up, be a man. Dash didn't need any more burdens weighing him down.

"It's all right. You need to do what's best for..." I couldn't finish the words. I tore my T-shirt over my head, swiping the already wet material down my face.

My tears fell freely. One hand fisted the shirt as I dropped them to my knees again, my head followed.

"Beau." I watched as his shoes came into my view, and his slacks lifted off his ankles. Seconds later, he squatted, placing a reassuring hand on my back. The tone he used, warm and gentle, did calm me. "My apology's for my naivety. I unintentionally caused you pain and hurt your entire family. If you'll give mean other chance, I promise to spend my life making amends."

Listening was damned difficult with the way self-pity had a hold on me. Yet his words eventually bounced around my head long enough that I made sense of them. I squatted, balancing on the balls of my feet as I met his gaze. There was no denying the tears in my swollen eyes. I was surprised to find his in the same condition.

"You can't stay with me. I'm sure he'll cut you off. I have to go. You don't know the reality of life without money." Though I nearly choked on the bitter words, they had to be said.

Dash responded by extending his hand between us. It took a moment for me to understand he wanted me to hold it. Then another few seconds longer to get that he was rising, intertwining our fingers together.

"Let's discuss this on the way home. I have cold bottles of water in the car for you. You weren't easy to locate. There was a guy selling them on the side of the road who had seen you run like a bullet in this direction." Though the guy holding my hand and speaking to me resembled Dash and shared his thoughtfulness, his tone conveyed a blend of sorrow, uncertainty, and frustration that Dash had never used with me before.

I followed because I had no other option. I was destined to always go wherever he led. The cool burst of air conditioning along with the cold leather seats, drew me in like a kid in a candy store. I reached for one of the two bottles, draining it in a few long gulps.

"Both bottles are for you," Dash offered and reached for my hand again. He carefully pulled back into traffic, never once releasing me to navigate the streets. We covered many miles in silence.

I wanted to say something to ease his burden, to lighten the load he'd just been handed, but the words felt inadequate. Instead, I gripped his hand tighter. I'd be his life preserver for however long he needed me.

We'd come within a few miles of home before any more was said.

"You were right about everything in Sea Springs. I should've trusted your gut. I honestly had no idea they were capable of such a heinous act." Dash raised a hand off the steering wheel, motioning his disgust. He shook his head before reaching to pull his sunglasses off. A tear trickled down his cheek. "I believed him when he claimed he'd tried to protect your grandparents and tried to intervene in your case. I accepted his inability to change the judge's decision."

"It's not your fault," I said, not liking where this was headed. "You can't take the blame. We're past that point—"

"It's only my fault," Dash interrupted sternly. "You were right all those years ago. Had we stayed hidden, had I not mentioned you to my father, had I read his responses properly..."

"Hidin' is no way to live," I said the truth that I'd discovered after returning to Dash. "We couldn't have lasted that way. Let's just be straightforward." The words clogged my throat, refusing to be said until I forced them out. "I'll take off tonight. I need you to promise to cash the check so I can take the truck."

"Please don't leave," Dash said. His voice was small and pleading. I didn't like to hear him that way.

"Your parents were serious, Dash," I said, turning toward him. This was no time to be hardheaded. He had to see the reason. "You have no idea what it's like to live without..."

"That's not true. I managed my life without you," Dash said.

"Not the same thing."

"We won't be without. I own my home. I have money in the bank. When I graduate, I will have a job. We might have to watch our spending, but we're not destitute. And I have you."

His explanation sat between us, resonating with previous conversations about the future. He'd just described the life he had always wanted.

"How can I be the one that separates you from your family?" I asked, covering all the bases as hope began to trickle in.

"You're not. You're the best person I've ever known. If they don't want to be in our life, that's their choice," Dash said as he left the highway and came to the red light closest to his house.

He drew my hand between his. His gaze directly on me, imploring me to listen. "I'll never be able to forgive what they did to you. If they hurt me, that's one thing, but hurting you is unforgiveable. Never you. Please don't leave me. Let me have the chance to make this right. I'm truly sorry." His fresh tears were my complete undoing. I leaned across the console, drawing our hands toward my lips. I kissed him there then rose to place another one on his lips. My devotion to Dash was forever. Fear was certainly there. No, I didn't see the vision of our future, but I'd help him like his presence helped me through my life.

The streetlight turned green, forcing Dash to let one hand go. My grip was stronger than ever. "You have nothin' to make up for, Dash, but I want you to agree to always be honest with me. If there comes a time that I need to go, I'll leave. Just tell me."

Dash nodded, but his words were different then the agreement he'd given. "That'll never happen. Not ever."

He turned the car into the driveway and pushed the button to open the garage door. "We have the money I'm makin' too," I said, no longer willing to let my money gather in a savings account untouched.

Dash grinned and nodded, his chin hitting his chest. "We might need that. Maybe you can get me health insurance too?"

"I don't know, but I can ask. It finally feels like we're becoming partners." I nodded my affirmation. Better because I hadn't lost him yet. We stared out the front window as he pulled into the empty garage. He put the in park and he cut the engine.

"I don't like seeing you cry," he said, quietly, with his eyes still forward.

"I don't like seein' you cry either. I certainly don't like what happened to you today," I said, glad to be in the safe harbor of this home again. I couldn't help but feel as if Dash still had a long way to go before this ended, but I wouldn't walk away on my own. I was never going to be able to voluntarily leave him. "All of this happened because we were drawn to each other."

"Hmm," Dash hummed, and finally glanced at me. "Very true."

The garage door began to close, a timed deal that always happened just this way. He reached for the door handle, pushing it open, and finally let go of our hold. I watched him go to the car's hood, waiting there for me to join him. "You sure can run. You were at least seven miles in the wrong direction before I found you."

A weighted faint smile lifted the corners of my mouth—barely. "The shoes are ruined." I gestured to where the leather had detached from the sole.

"Probably not designed to run like you did," he said teasingly. His arm encircled me as we walked together to the door. "Beau, listen to me. You have to listen to me this time. I love you more than the life they tried to give me. Please don't leave me unless you can't get past what happened under my watch." He pushed the door open. The air conditioning poured out as I faced him straight on.

"Then you hear me. You've done nothin' more than love me. What's happened is on them and my shitty old man, not either one of us. It's hard to learn that my father put a financial price tag on my happiness."

Mylove gathered me in his arms, burying his face in the crook of my neck. "I'm sorry for your life. Not because I caused it, only that you suffered."

I gently pushed away from the embrace. We had to move on. Find our way into the future. We couldn't do that with all the negativity of the day following us inside our home. "You're on a budget now. We can't be air conditionin' the entire neighborhood."

He chuckled, likely never hearing such a remark before. A lot of new things were coming his way. We'd have tonight and maybe the rest of the weekend before his father played his next hand, whatever that scheduled I followed Dash inside, rolling my shoulders, readying for a fight I didn't understand.

The End

I hope you enjoyed the first installment of the Gravity series.
The second book, Fusion, is scheduled for release, 12/27/24.
Click the link for more details: https://amzn.to/3TqL3Zk
The third book, Force will release early 2025.
Signup for my release day emails at www.kindlealexander.com.
Please email me your thoughts about the series at kindle@kindlealexander.com. I'd love to know the good, the bad, and the ugly… (Not really the ugly, you can leave that out.) Did you suspect the ending? Did I surprise you? Let me know.
Last, reviews and ranking truly help and I'd be thankful for yours.

Note From The Author

Thank you for reading Friction. For more information on future works visit kindlealexander.com and click the new release newsletter option, or friend me on all the major social networking sites.

Reviews and rankings help so much. Please consider doing so here.

Other Books by Kindle Alexander

If you enjoyed Friction then you won't want to miss KindleAlexander's bestselling novels:

Breakaway
Reservations
It's Complicated
Painted On My Heart
The Current BetweenUs (with Bonus Material)
Closet Confession
Secret
Texas Pride
Full Disclosure
Double Full
Full Domain
Always
Forever
Havoc
Order
Chaos
Justice

A Wilder Inc. Story

Secret
Breakaway
Level Up
Reading Order Secret, Breakaway, Level Up

A Reservations Nightclub Story
Reservations Book 1
It's Complicated Book 2
Reading Order of all the characters mentioned in A Reservation Nightclub Story Series
Secret, Painted On My Heart, Reservations, It's Complicated

Always & ForeverDuet
Always
Forever

Nice Guys Novels
Double Full
Full Disclosure
Full Domain

Tattoos and Ties
Havoc
Order
Chaos
Justice
Tattoos & Tinsel available 11/11/24

Layne Family Duet
The Current Between Us
Painted On My Heart

Reading order of all the character mentioned in Tattoos and Ties
Up In Arms, Painted On My Heart, The Nice Guys Novels, Havoc, Order, Chaos, Justice

Gravity

Friction
Fusion
Force

www.ingramcontent.com/pod-product-compliance
Lightning Source LLC
Chambersburg PA
CBHW070648180626
46817CB00006B/2278